CHILDGRAVE

KEN GREENHALL was born in Detroit in 1928, the son of immigrants from England. He graduated from high school at age 15, worked at a record store for a time, and was drafted into the military, serving in Germany. He earned his degree from Wayne State University and moved to New York, where he worked as an editor of reference books, first on the staff of the *Encyclopedia Americana* and later for the *New Columbia Encyclopedia*. Greenhall had a longtime interest in the supernatural and took leave from his job to write his first novel, *Elizabeth* (1976), a tale of witchcraft published under his mother's maiden name, Jessica Hamilton. Several more novels followed, including *Hell Hound* (1977), which was published abroad as *Baxter* and adapted for a critically acclaimed 1989 French film under that title. Greenhall died in 2014.

By Ken Greenhall

Elizabeth (1976)*
Hell Hound (1977)*
Childgrave (1982)*
The Companion (1988)
Deathchain (1991)
Lenoir (1998)

* Available from Valancourt Books

Ken Greenhall

CHILDGRAVE

VALANCOURT BOOKS

Childgrave by Ken Greenhall
First published by Pocket Books as a paperback original in 1982
This edition first published 2017

Published by Valancourt Books, Richmond, Virginia
http: / / www.valancourtbooks.com

ISBN 978-1-943910-86-1 (hardcover)
ISBN 978-1-943910-87-8 (trade paperback)
Also available as an electronic book.

All Valancourt Books publications are printed on acid free paper that meets all ANSI standards for archival quality paper.

Cover by Henry Petrides
Set in Dante MT

Preface

There was a time when my life was like yours. I ate veal occasionally and avoided people who had a serious interest in God. I smiled at clients during the day, disappearing beneath the black velvet hood from time to time to steal their souls.

"Watch the birdie."

I actually said that to them. It astonished them all: perturbed executives, goose-eyed professional beauties, ascetic rock singers, worldly clerics.

"Think about what interests you most." After I said that, there was usually a puzzled look. I waited for it to subside. "Don't move. Thank you."

I would smile again and shake hands, my grip carefully gauged to respond with slightly less pressure than offered. For the feminine, a hint of caress.

At night, my daughter would sit on my lap, her toes like pale beans.

My name is Jonathan Brewster. I am thirty-six years old, and I have always been devoted to moderation and the inexplicable. I am reassured by the Bermuda Triangle, and I admire the person who refuses the second drink. I read only the beginning of mystery novels, delighting in descriptions of oddly deceased victims discovered in locked rooms. When the detective says "Aha," I stop reading.

One of the personal faults I'm most aware of is that I'm never sure which things should be taken seriously—the result, I think, of being raised by parents who took all things seriously. My spirit of moderation tells me that my parents were wrong, but to honor their memory, my policy has been: when in doubt, take things seriously; but always look around to see who's giggling.

As I have mentioned, I used to steal people's souls. That is, I was a portrait photographer. My materials were as simple as I could make them: no lens, no shutter, no film. Only a box (black, of course) with a pinhole in it; exposures directly on paper. The methods were simple enough to have been called primitive. Perhaps that is why I believed fully in the primitive notion that a person's soul may be captured when the person's image is captured. My belief was no more complicated than that. No esthetics were involved, and I didn't distinguish among the souls I captured. I merely believed I practiced a form of magic.

What I'm saying may sound silly to you, but think for a moment. Think of the photographs you are carefully saving: the fading images pasted on the pages of albums or buried at the bottom of a drawer. Dad at the cottage, 1947; Rose Ann, graduation, 1960. Or perhaps, in the closet, the face of a nameless person: the first one to have touched your body in a certain way. Why do you keep those bits of paper? Why do you feel a vague fear or excitement when you look at them? They are more than a reminder of the past. Dad, Rose Ann, the person who touched you, they still live in those images. Run your finger over the paper. Touch the tiny features. Now tell me there is no magic involved. Perhaps you are still not convinced. But I assure you it is true . . . true in ways I never imagined when my life was like yours.

In any case, my clients seemed to recognize something uncommon in my portraits of them. I made their souls captive, and they paid me ransom for the return of the enchanted images. My clients had the increasingly rare opportunity of taking part in an act of sorcery, and I made a living.

Don't be alarmed. I realize that people don't enjoy reading about how other people make a living, and I won't speak to you of the mysteries of depth-of-field or of direct-positive printing. But I have other mysteries to tell you about—the mystery of love, for example. I've been in love twice, and regardless of what you've heard elsewhere about the experience, I'm not sure I recommend it. Love leads to immoderate acts and to the illusion of perfect understanding.

And yet I knew those things before I met Sara Coleridge. It's possible that you know what Sara looks like. There was a summer when some pictures I took of her were published in gossipy magazines and in an overpriced book devoted to the questionable theory that photography is an art. Sara was not identified in those pictures; she was part of an odd but insignificant mystery.

But there is the possibility that—if someone were to become indiscreet—you might see her again someday. You might see her calm beauty projected behind a newscaster's shoulder. You would be puzzled by the contrast between that beauty and the terrifying things being said about her. Or perhaps you might see her in one of the newsmagazines. She would be smiling in monochrome above the legend, "A taste for the unthinkable." The magazines, eager to please, like to pretend that some things are unthinkable.

You're probably like that, too. And I suppose that's the way to be. Forget you've heard of Cronus. Buy an automatic door for your garage. And if one night as the door closes behind you, your daughter (bound like an abductor's victim in her safety harness) says, "I had a scary dream last night," release the straps and answer, "I'll let you put gravy on your ice cream tonight." It's that simple. That's how it was for me before I loved Sara Coleridge; before I stood at the door to her apartment and found that she had vanished; before she led me to the darkness and mysteries of Childgrave and faced me with my impossible decision.

Chapter 1

I'm a person who hesitates before opening a letter; someone whose stomach tightens when the telephone rings. I always expect accusations, announcements of misfortune, the voices of the Furies. Sometimes my fears are justified, although it's not always immediately apparent. It was through a phone call that I met Sara.

"Jonathan? We're going to the opera tonight."

It was my agent, Harry Bordeaux, who is not afraid of telephones and who has my total admiration. He knows precisely when something should be taken seriously.

"Why are we going to the opera, Harry?"

"A lady wants to have her picture taken. A singing lady ... Mediterranean sort. She's flirting with obesity, and I think she also flirted with me."

I photographed two kinds of people: clients and subjects. I supplied the subjects, and no fees were involved. Harry supplied the clients. He also determined their fees, according to a complicated formula involving their income, degree of celebrity, and eagerness to be photographed. He always gave me a chance to veto his arrangements.

"You'll be able to get a good look at her. It's a concert performance. No heavy makeup, and she'll spend a lot of time just sitting."

"What's the opera?"

"*Orfeo* by Gluck. And don't pout." Harry knew I didn't care much about music written later than the tenth century. And he knew I considered opera to be just about the most foolhardy of human activities. He tried to console me. "You'll enjoy it. A man going through hell because of a woman. Realism."

I wondered whether Harry was making a personal reference, and if so, whether he was referring to my life or to his own. He knew that I had gone through a hellish period as a result of my marriage, but he wouldn't have been inconsiderate enough to refer to that. And I doubted whether he could have been referring to anything in his own experience. As far as I knew, no woman had played any kind of significant role in his life since childhood —if then. In whatever tours he had made of Hades—or of Paradise—gender had been incidental.

Harry apparently realized he was on treacherous ground. "No one will demand that you enjoy yourself, Jonathan. Think of it as a business trip. But the evening won't be without its pleasures. Meet me at the Lincoln Center White Rose about seven. I'll tell you what life is like."

Unlike most resourceful people, Harry was always trying to explain life. His explanations, like everyone else's, were inadequate.

"Tell me about it now," I said.

"Life is like eating a bowl of mixed nuts. You're noshing happily along, not conscious of making any choices, and suddenly there's nothing left but filberts. Filberts, Jonathan. Filberts and broken things you can't identify. No more cashews. Not even any peanuts. Right?"

"Right, Harry. See you at seven." I didn't see any reason to tell Harry that I always made a point of eating the filberts first. After all, he answered telephones eagerly, and he made my life comfortable. Before I met Harry, my life was dominated by objects; the kind that are displayed in mail-order catalogs. I was paid to photograph the objects with fidelity—which meant I made them look better than they actually looked. Make people want to buy them, I was told. I decided to make them all look like food. It wasn't easy, especially with blue objects, but I was successful. There may even have been an element of art in what I did. Art seemed important to me then, and I decided that art was simply metaphor . . . creating an object that made you think of something else. I began to confuse light bulbs with onions.

I think I was insane at that time. I found comfort in reminding myself that derangement was the natural condition of the artist. Harry Bordeaux saved me from art. I had done a series of portraits in my spare time, out of an artless impulse. Harry saw one of the portraits in a show at a Madison Avenue gallery. He knew immediately that the portrait wasn't art. He also knew that certain wealthy persons were bored with art and were looking for distinctive ways to spend their money.

He telephoned me. "It's not art," he said. "What is it?"

"It's magic."

"Mahvelous," he said.

He's gay, I thought. But I was wrong about that. He later explained to me, with some disinterest, that he was merely a sissy. At forty, he still had not experienced pubescence, and he lived in fear that it would suddenly confront him. In the meantime, he retained that remarkable energy and power of concentration that so many of us have as eleven-year-olds and that most of us lose when the sex glands begin to make their terrifying demands. I envied Harry. He regarded his sex-absorbed compatriots the way the benevolent nonsmoker regards smokers: with occasional irritation and frequent incomprehension, but without feelings of superiority. Harry is a heavy smoker.

He brought a series of wealthy, emaciated women to my studio, usually at five or six in the morning. I settled them in front of my camera while Harry prattled with them about the parties they had just left.

"Her husband's in packaging. You'd think she would have learned something."

"The one displaying her titties, you mean. It wasn't wise, was it?"

"Hardly. Much ado . . ."

I watched the client's face and adjusted the skylight shutters while waiting for what Harry called postpartying depression to set in. When the client had given up caring whether she was onstage, Harry would get up and wait in the adjoining room. I would explain the necessity for a long exposure time and would stress the need for patience. I would put the headrest in place and talk about souls, and I would disappear beneath the black velvet hood. The hood was Harry's idea. It wasn't technically necessary, because I didn't use a view camera. I saw nothing when I was under the hood. It was simply part of a ritual—a ritual that became important. With the hood in place, I became invisible. My subjects became totally aware of the silent black box. I waited until their natural fear subsided. It was obviously the first time some of them had relaxed in months.

Several of my subjects at this time had fallen asleep while posing, which led to the portraits known as the Morpheus Series, referred to by Harry as the death masks. Splendid young ladies from trendy magazines began to interview me; the Morpheus Series became a book; Harry raised our fees, and I moved to an enormous loft studio in a fashionably inconvenient neighborhood.

My career was entirely in Harry's steady, if often perspiring, hands. Our fees continued to increase, and we became more particular about the commissions we accepted. I bought glove-leather shoes, cut my own hair, and walked the streets of Manhattan for two and a half hours each day.

Apart from my work, I lived as I chose. That is, I modestly and patiently prepared for disaster. It arrived quickly, disguised as one of the splendid young women. She married me, gave me a daughter, and involved me—and perhaps herself—unpleasantly with God. She also died.

After that, in my grief and innocence, I assumed I would have no further dealings with God and only the one, inevitable subsequent dealing with death. It was a spectacularly faulty assumption. I worked hard, tried to satisfy my daughter's unpredictable needs, and occasionally joined Harry in his bright, dangerous world.

The night of the opera, I met Harry near the concert hall at a comfortable bar that he was probably in the process of corrupting. The bar was one of the few remnants of the old West Sixties —the neighborhood of slums and would-be slums that developers had pulverized and trucked away to make room for Lincoln Center for the Performing Arts and the vast penal-colony-style apartment buildings of the Lincoln Towers complex. Most of the old neighborhood bars had been razed or had been converted into restaurants that displayed more ingenuity in choosing names than in preparing food. But the White Rose had survived, shabby and plain, serving corned beef sandwiches and cheap drinks to off-duty cab drivers, pensioned biddies, and machine operators who were not certain what their machines produced.

"Harry," I said, "you ought to be ashamed of yourself."

"I am, Jonathan, I am. Most of my traits are shameful. Which one do you have in mind?"

"Are you trying to put the blight on the White Rose?"

"Which blight?"

"Are you going to make it fashionable?"

"Why would I do that?"

"You can't help it, Harry. You're a carrier."

"Maybe. But, after all, it's my profession." Harry was blushing. It significantly improved his complexion, which normally had the quality of a long-unwashed, rain-splattered window. In the summer, when even he couldn't avoid being exposed to an hour or two of sunlight occasionally, he developed an imposing crop of freckles.

"I never come here with frivolous people, Jonathan—only with proletarian types like you. Customers aren't going to be upset by your army-surplus wardrobe."

"L. L. Bean. And my shoes are expensive."

"They're not looking at your feet. They're watching the hockey game—and in black-and-white."

"It's basketball, Harry."

"Whatever. But I see your point." Harry removed the flower (could it have been a hollyhock?) from his velvet lapel. "Is that better?" He dropped the blossom in his empty glass.

"You could rumple your hair," I said. Harry had recently begun greasing his hair and parting it in the middle in tribute to someone—possibly T. S. Eliot, but more likely Edmund Lowe.

"You go too far," he said.

"One of us does."

"Not I, Jonathan." He was serious. "I go just far enough. Again, it's my business."

I never argued with Harry about his business. I knew he lived in a treacherous, tangled world—the world of fashion, essentially. Aside from me, he handled a couple of painters. They were competent and quirky, like hundreds of other artists in New York. Harry made their paintings acceptable to curators and irresistible to collectors. Art had become a world in which no one was sure what the standards were. Harry had standards, although he never defined them. He let the critics try to do that, and most of them obliged him, grateful to have been shown what to define.

"Speaking of business," I said, "does the singing lady we're seeing tonight really want me to take her picture?" After the death of my wife, Harry sometimes misled me about such things. He wanted to get me out into the world.

"Oh, yes. It's important to her. She's Sicilian and knows about evil eyes and such things." Harry put the back of his hand to his forehead and switched to his falsetto voice, which was never far from the surface. "*La maledizione*," he shrieked. He ignored the pained glances of several patrons. "She thinks someone has put a curse on her torso, and from the looks of it, I'd say there's a strong possibility that she's right. She thinks you might be able to relieve the affliction."

"Therapeutic photography?"

"Yes. We charge extra for that," Harry said. He was looking at me carefully. I realized that—as was often the case—he was more serious than he seemed. I rolled my eyes, wondering what new phase he was leading me into.

If loud is good, my would-be client—Arianella Stradellini—was a good singer; if accuracy of pitch is good, her status was arguable. Harry and I sat in the third row and did more watching than listening. Stradellini was not what I had expected to see. She was young—in her late twenties, probably—but with the type of presence and dignity usually associated with maturity. There was a striking darkness about both her voice and her appearance, and the frantic applause and yelping that the audience produced following her arias seemed more justifiable than usual.

Nevertheless, my attention soon began to wander. Gluck's music is not complex as music goes, but even the simplest music confuses me. I studied piano once, attracted by the symmetry of the keyboard: the neat groups of black keys on the white field. Eventually I was told that the black key that supposedly produces both G sharp and A flat actually produced neither tone, but a tone similar to each of them. At first I was intrigued. G sharp and A flat were in reality—and inexplicably—not the same note. To avoid the inexplicable, the tempered scale was introduced, and since then, all music has been based on an acoustical lie. Bach; Mozart, and Beethoven were all liars. I was upset for weeks. I am still upset. The other odd thing that happened to music was the decision to allow two different melodies to be played at the same time. People shouldn't complain about the chaos of modern music. It was inevitable.

I was growing restless. The contralto who sang the role of Orfeo had stood up, her large face apparently trying to express some strong but unidentifiable emotion. There was a pause while the conductor waited for her to maneuver into position.

I whispered to Harry: "What happens next?"

He answered, without bothering to whisper: "Orpheus is about to enter hell—and so are we all, I suspect."

The contralto's hearing was more acute than her singing had led one to suspect. She was glaring at Harry. The conductor had his baton hand raised, and he was looking to his left. He was looking at Sara Coleridge.

Sara was seated at a large golden harp, the curve of which rested against her left shoulder. Her arms were extended around the instrument as if in embrace, and her legs were parted slightly to receive the soundboard. I had never seen anyone or anything more attractive.

The conductor lowered his arm, and Sara began to play the music that represents the sound of Orfeo's lyre. I watched Sara avidly through the rest of the performance, never glancing away from her and possibly never even blinking. As I watched Sara I knew that my standards of beauty and excitement were being changed. I had no doubt that in the last few minutes my life had been influenced in a fundamental way, but there was no way I could have known how far-reaching that influence would become. I thought I was having a profound but simple experience —perhaps the kind that Albert Einstein had the first time he saw an equation.

I tried to figure out why Sara was so attractive to me. She was beautiful—but I saw dozens of beautiful women every day, and I sometimes spent hours photographing them. I never had any difficulty turning away from any of them. But I would not have turned away from Sara even if someone had announced that the auditorium was on fire. For one thing, I wouldn't have heard the announcement—just as I no longer heard the music.

Sara's beauty was the kind that results from balance and symmetry. Nothing about her appearance was spectacular—no violet eyes or regally high cheekbones. Her hair was the feature that most people would have looked at first. It was unevenly cropped and the color of the gilding on her harp, like a cap of bright feathers.

It wasn't Sara's hair that had captivated me, though. And I certainly wasn't impressed by her apparent mastery of the harp—an instrument that had always seemed to me slightly ridiculous. What I found so overwhelming in Sara was simply her presence: that total impression that people instantly and so mysteriously create; that revelation of personality. I knew that Sara was the kind of person who would often be amused but would seldom smile. She would not seek people out, but could be a devoted friend. She was intelligent, but she mistrusted her mind. All my impressions of her, however, were overridden by a sense of her strong calmness—a calmness that grew out of some central mystery. I was somehow certain that Sara had a type of knowledge that few other people possessed. I had always believed that there were a few people who knew remarkable things—people who had a kind of knowledge that never shows up in textbooks or even in scriptures. According to my theory, these people were never rich or famous; it might even be that there was nothing they could do particularly well. The only reason you might think they were anything but ordinary was that they looked as though someone had just told them an incredibly pleasing secret.

I hadn't had much of a chance to prove my theory before I met Sara. But I could tell as soon as I saw her that she knew some important secrets. I decided that I wanted to share some of her secrets—if not her life. I was gratified to see that she wore no rings.

Sara seemed to wear no makeup, either. There were things that were more important to her than her appearance. One of those things was obviously music. I wondered whether another of those things was a man. I wanted to be that man.

During the intermission I found Sara's name in the program's list of orchestra members. I don't remember much else that Harry said to me that evening. I think he assumed I was ill. He mentioned acute contraltoitis. He put me in a cab, and, oddly enough, I didn't resist. It didn't occur to me to go backstage or to wait for Sara at the artists' entrance.

When I got home, Nanny Joy was sitting up as always, sipping Southern Comfort and listening to music. Sixty and pensive, she loved and nurtured my daughter, Joanne. The three of us made a home of sorts in the vastness of my studio.

After the death of my wife I had interviewed dozens of women, looking for someone who could comfort Joanne and who wasn't contemptuous of life. It seemed to be an impossible task. Applicants assured me of their inexhaustible virtues. They smiled, unfolded references, touched my arm, demonstrated their French, and terrified me and Joanne.

I decided to wait for a sign.

Nanny Joy had come unannounced. The agency had not sent her; she had heard of the job through an acquaintance.

She had little to tell me about herself: her name was Joy Ory, she had been born in Louisiana and raised in Harlem.

"From what I heard about the job, I thought I might be the right one for it," she had said. Her voice was quiet but husky and dramatic. She made the statement sound like lyrics from a song.

I didn't know what to ask her. For no particular reason I said, "Are you a patient woman?"

"I've learned to be." Her answer was casual. Then she looked at me carefully and added: "If you're serious, I could show you."

I hadn't been serious, but now I was intrigued. "I'm serious," I said.

Joy stood up, turned her thin body away from me, and kicked off her shoes. I wondered if she had once been a dancer. She made a quick, confusing movement, bending over and then straightening up. She was holding a pair of panty hose, which she draped over a chair. Then she turned and walked to where I was sitting. She raised the right side of her skirt, revealing a slack-muscled thigh that at one time must have been admirable. Her brown skin was light enough so that the tattooed inscription stood out clearly: I CAN WAIT. Then I realized that the tattoo had been altered at some time. A letter had been unskillfully removed. The wording had originally been I CAN'T WAIT.

A sign had been given, and with Joanne's unhesitating approval, Joy Ory became Nanny Joy. There had been no regrets. Nanny Joy had never heard of Dr. Spock, but she had borne a daughter of her own, who "got away from me while I was letting the good times roll." The good times apparently stopped rolling fairly quickly, and Joy stopped trying to live up to her name. She claimed she had lived for a time with Billie Holiday, "trading sadness." I wasn't sure I believed the part about Billie Holiday. Lately, a lot of people were claiming to have known Billie—people who weren't available when she needed a marker for her grave. But whether Nanny Joy had known the singer or not, she knew the music and the sadness. But now she was bringing happiness to me and to Joanne in an inexplicable way.

Joanne had learned to sing "Miss Brown to You" and was developing a quiet dignity that I never could have given her.

When I got home from the opera that night, I went to sit with Nanny Joy. She was listening to her favorite music, a tape she had made of all the slow-tempo blues recordings that Charlie Parker had ever made. It sounded to me like a monument to suffering, and it made me uneasy.

Whenever I was home, Nanny Joy usually kept to the bedroom and sitting room I had had built for her in a corner of the studio. She listened to music and she telephoned friends. I never saw her read anything except the books we got for Joanne, and she said she didn't want a television set. On the evenings I was away she would sit out in the main apartment and play the stereo set I had there, which was bigger than the one in her room.

I sat down next to her. "You want to listen to your angel music?" she asked. She meant the few recordings of Gregorian chant and plainsong that I would play occasionally.

"No," I said.

"Good. That music's bad for you."

"Why is that?"

"Because angels never get laid."

I could see what she meant. Most plainsong had been composed and performed by people with no sex lives, and it couldn't be called passionate music.

"We don't get laid very often either, Nan," I reminded her.

She allowed herself one of her rare smiles. "Yeah, *that's* the truth," she said. "But damned if I'm going to give up *remembering* those times."

She got up to turn off the Charlie Parker tape.

"That's all right," I said. "Let's listen for a while." Nan sat down gratefully and began to sip her drink, glancing at me occasionally.

Had I stopped remembering? Probably. I almost never thought of my wife, but there were good reasons for that. What was more important was that I had stopped thinking of everything that had happened before her death. I had lost some skills of emotion. Now there were occasional seductions in the studio: scufflings, maulings, or displays when they were invited or allowed. But that seemed like part of my work. A little bonus. Thank you, ma'am.

When the music stopped, Nanny Joy asked: "Something strange happen to you tonight, Mr. B.?"

"Does it show?"

"Oh, yes, it shows. Something to do with a woman?"

"I looked at a woman. Just looked."

"You think you might want to take another look?"

"I definitely think I might. But maybe I shouldn't. In the opera I saw tonight, the hero lost his wife because he got impatient and looked at her when he wasn't supposed to. But nobody has warned *me* not to look."

"Maybe the opera was a warning."

"It's an old opera and a very old story. Lots of men have had the warning."

"Lots of men have lost their wives."

Nanny Joy wasn't being tactful, but she was being accurate. I went to bed.

I have always gone gratefully to my bed, my eyeballs eager to do their little dance. Yet there have been surprising, sleepless nights. The night I first saw Sara Coleridge was one of them. I was cursed with thought, and, unexpectedly, the thought concerned Barbara, my bizarrely departed wife.

Barbara was a connoisseur of glamour. Articulate and observant, she came to New York from a midwestern suburb, determined to make a living by telling certain thoughtless people how they should look. The city welcomed her. She was soon on the underpaid staff of a smug magazine, waiting each day for the happy hour to begin so she could sit muzzily in the currently approved bar, certain that people sensed she was ingenious enough to be wearing the kind of panties Jean Harlow had worn.

I'm being unkind, of course, and probably inaccurate. Most likely, she was what I imagined her to be when she first came to my studio to interview me: as handsome as a dik-dik and totally deserving of love.

I set siege to her consciousness, listening with approval as she praised the cleverness of people I had thought of as cloddish and pea-brained. I nourished her romantic energy with anecdotes I had once found offensive.

I learned to play backgammon and told her what my sign was (Leo), and I blushed gratefully when she announced we were compatible. I photographed her, explaining how I captured souls and hoped desperately to capture hers.

I demonstrated my modest virility, but only after I was asked, and honoring the old-fashioned convention that ladies should come first.

But to be truthful, I had no notion of what Barbara expected —of me or of the world. She often said she loved me, but in the same tone that she said she loved feathered boas. We both knew I was not what she needed. We decided to get married.

It was during the marriage ceremony that Barbara discovered what she needed: God and the Reverend Elliott Mason, although maybe not in that order.

Barbara had assured me that frivolous ceremonies had been fully discredited. No sunrise on the mountainside, no Kahlil Gibran for us. A fan-vaulted chapel and the Book of Common Prayer were required, even though neither of us had been inside a church since squirmy childhood.

Pastor Mason, who performed the ceremony, was the handsomest white-haired man I had ever seen, and he dealt in presence. Barbara thought it was God's presence, but I suspect it might be something closer to stage presence. In any case, after we were pronounced man and wife, Barbara kissed first me and then Elliott Mason. Elliott got the better of the two exchanges, and I had thought of walking up the aisle by myself and leaving them at the altar in their spiritual embrace.

Barbara announced that she had become a Christian, which was as incomprehensible to me as if she had said she had become Chinese. She became a member of the pastor's flock, as the saying has it. I suspect the saying was particularly appropriate in this case. She began taking private instruction with Mason—learning about the Christian mystics, she said. I would find her at bedtime weeping over St. John of the Cross. I did some weeping myself.

But I was not contemptuous. The change in Barbara was too profound for me to be nasty about—or to allow me any hope for change. But despite my tolerance, I saw no reason to thank God for the development, and I sure as hell saw no reason to thank Elliott Mason.

Shortly after Joanne was born, the Reverend Mason's car was found crushed against the support of a highway overpass. In the car was the dead body of my wife and the mangled but breathing body of Elliott Mason. When the pastor regained the use of his arm, he wrote me a letter. I weighed the letter in my hand and held the envelope to the light: a succinct letter, a single page, most likely. I supposed it was an explanation. I tore it in half but then put the two pieces in the bottom of a drawer on the improbable chance that someday explanations would appeal to me.

Such was my introduction to the mysterious ways of the Lord. I decided I would continue to seek my mysteries elsewhere.

Nice memories to have available for sleepless nights. And the night I first saw Sara Coleridge was entirely sleepless; it was a night lived not in the present but in the grotesqueries of my past and in hopes for the future. Two of my hopes were that Sara was not married and that she was not a churchgoer.

Chapter 2

At seven-thirty each morning, my daughter Joanne would enter my bedroom, recklessly offering me a mug of orange juice and taking me into her surprising world. She was four and a half years old, and the quiet orderliness and charm she had shown in the previous year were being interrupted more and more often by sinister smiles and messy selfishness. Her first words to me were usually: "*You* must be . . ." "*You* must be the baby. *I'm* the mommy." Her eyes narrowed, and the smile appeared.

I resisted. "Don't we say good morning first? Kissy-kissy?"

She ignored me. "Baby has been naughty. Baby knows she mustn't be hostile, doesn't she?"

The "hostile" must have originated with Ms. Abraham at the nursery school. Nanny Joy and I didn't talk that way. Enrolling Joanne in nursery school had probably been a mistake. Ms. Abraham's thoughts were obviously about theories of education rather than about children, and she thought of Joanne merely as a footnote in a college of education thesis. But I thought Joanne should spend some time around other children, and the nursery school was the only practical way to arrange that. It was a swift crowd, apparently. Arnold showed Joanne what he called his wee-wee, and Kimberley electrified everyone in the sandbox by putting a little sand on her thumbnail, raising it to her tiny nostril, and announcing that she was "getting off a snort."

"Daddy. You're not playing with me." Joanne had managed the difficult task of furrowing her porcelain-smooth brow.

"Daddies can't be babies." I reached out and lifted Joanne onto the bed. I kissed her brow and then opened the drawer of the bedside table, where I kept a supply of candy. I pulled out the UN Jelly Babies (white, black, yellow, red). "Here are some babies."

Joanne took the candies hesitantly. She was still not pleased. "This baby is you," she said, selecting a white one. "I'm going to eat your face . . . and your toes . . . and your heart."

She ate the candy ferociously, and I tried not to be disturbed. I said, "Oh, don't chomp me up. Oh, it tickles." But I wasn't tickled. I thought of one of the gruesome nursery rhymes she loved to recite:

My mother has killed me,
My father is eating me,
My brothers and sisters sit under the table
Picking my bones,
And they bury them under the cold marble stones.

It was a traditional rhyme, so apparently it was something that many children had liked. But I didn't like it, and I wished I had never bought the book that we found it in.

Joanne picked out a black candy. "This is Nanny Joy, and I'm eating her arms."

I decided it was time to end the game. "Anything goes," I shouted and carried Joanne toward the Anything Goes Room. The room, which I designed, had plastic-covered walls and a tile floor with a drain in the center. It was equipped with paints, crayons, clay, plastic blocks and dolls, and a sink. It was waterproof, paintproof, and indestructible. Joanne had never been very fond of it, but I had spent many happy hours there, finger-painting on the walls and singing.

As I carried Joanne out of the bedroom she whispered in my ear: "Can you get me another mommy?" She had never asked me anything like that before. If she had asked the question a week before, I would have felt like a character in a soap opera and would have changed the subject. I stopped and held her close. "Funny you should ask," I said.

The telephone company had no listing for a Sara Coleridge. My instincts were being confirmed. Sara was a person I could understand; she had the good sense and strength of character to live without a telephone. Of course, it was also possible that she was an uncompromising recluse. Whatever her reason for being unlisted, I was relieved, because if I had her number, I would have had to call her, and I had no idea what to say to her.

I decided to call the musicians' union next, and they were a little more informative. They listed Sara Coleridge, harpist, as living on West Seventieth Street, which was within walking distance of Lincoln Center. I had found Joanne a mommy; or almost found her one. What next? Would I write to her? Lurk in her lobby?

I spent the rest of the morning thinking about the situation. I developed and rejected dozens of approaches. I decided that Sara Coleridge was probably the kind of young woman who, if a stranger who looked like me approached her on whatever pretext, would not be favorably impressed. I'm not bad-looking, but I've never had the sort of appearance that inspires confidence in strangers. It's my hair, I think: curly and a strange shade of red.

I needed advice. As usual, I decided to consult Harry Bordeaux. Not that Harry had ever gotten a girl, but he had spent a lot of time being an objective observer of other people's attempts to get and be gotten. Since my problem didn't exactly fit the category of business, I asked Harry to come to my place for dinner. He agreed, but only on the condition that I let him do the cooking.

Harry and I differ profoundly in our attitudes toward food. My view is that eating is a waste of time; the biggest waste of time. A universal joke. Here we all are, many of us planting, livestocking, fishing, harvesting, processing, grocering; and all of us dining, snacking, banqueting, brunching, picnicking—not just every day, but two or three times every day. And let's not overlook the tedious suspense of cooking or the most boring of all activities: dishwashing. A joke. I could see having a nice dinner once in a while on special occasions, but mostly I say it's spinach. The word I detest among all words is "gourmet."

Harry, like a lot of people who are not much interested in sex, is seriously interested in food. And being in his peak earning years, he's a gourmet. Since Nanny Joy's views on food are similar to mine, our menus are pretty much decided by Joanne's capricious appetite. And Harry, rather than risk being subjected to canned lima beans and potato chips, stops off at purveyors of bizarre foodstuffs before joining us for dinner.

That night he enthusiastically and efficiently produced snails, creamed sweetbreads with broccoli, and apricot tarts. Nanny Joy and Joanne joined us. Joanne, of course, refused to eat the snails and left the table while we disposed of the rubbery little creatures. I sympathized with her and was reminded that people will eat anything—including one another. We're not just omnivores; we're psycho-vores.

When the main course was served, Joanne gave it another try, but when she discovered that sweetbreads are neither sweet nor bread, she lost interest again and began to play with her snail shells. The apricot tart pleased her, however, and she went off to bed reasonably happy. After my contribution to the meal—some not too effective dishwashing—I joined Harry and Nanny Joy to explain my problem. Nan and Harry get along well together. Harry liked Nan because she had been to rent parties and for a number of other reasons, but mostly he was in awe of her because she had aged well. Harry was still hoping, despite evidence to the contrary, that his golden years were going to be his most attractive years.

When I joined them, Harry was saying: "Physically, I wrote off my first forty years. I knew from infancy that I had some unimposing decades to get through. From the time I was twelve, my body was like a pear with four pieces of string attached. I'm beginning the transition now. I plan to be gaunt but natty; white hair, thicker than it is now; a few amusing creases." Harry looked over at me as I sat downs "What does your photographer's eye think, Jonathan? Am I gaining a certain distinction of figure?"

"Not yet, Harry. I'm afraid you've got a few more years of boyishness ahead."

Harry flared his nostrils at me and then turned to Nanny Joy. "I want you to tell me your secret, Nan. Why do you look so good?"

"I did my living early," Nan said. "By the time I was sixteen, my body felt sixty, so now that I *am* sixty, my body hasn't all that much reason to change . . . and then are a lot of good things I don't bother much with now. I don't eat a hell of a lot of snails."

Nan was telling Harry more than he wanted to know, and I thought I'd spare them both a little embarrassment. "Why don't you ask me the secret of *my* unchanging youthfulness, Harry?"

"Because I don't have to ask you. You're obviously in love, and lovers always confuse feelings with appearances."

I thought for a moment of denying that I was in love, just to watch Harry's self-congratulatory smile disappear. But I suppose he deserved his little triumph. "What makes you think I'm in love?" I asked.

"Nothing else could explain your behavior at the opera the other night. I just hope it isn't the contralto who undid you."

I turned to Nanny Joy for reassurance. "Do you think I'm in love?"

"I *know* you're in love, Mr. B. I've been waiting for you to ask me if you could borrow some Billie Holiday records."

"Okay. I have an announcement to make. I'm in love."

Harry and Nan looked at me expectantly. Harry said, "Yes. You're in love . . . but?"

"But I need some advice about how to let the young lady know what everyone else seems to know." I explained the situation while my audience tried to hide their condescending smiles behind glasses of cognac.

After I had explained my dilemma, both Nan and Harry rose to the occasion and made suggestions. I wasn't quite sure how serious either suggestion was.

Nan looked solemn enough. "I think you ought to send Joanne to the lady's house. Have her say, 'My daddy's in love with you, but I think the two of us ought to get to know each other first, because if we don't get along, there's going to be P-O-B-T.'"

P-O-B-T was Nan's abbreviation for Plenty of Big Trouble—a concept that Joanne was especially familiar with.

"Nan's probably right," Harry said. "You have to think of more than just you and Ms. Coleridge."

"I suppose so," I said, "but it works the other way, too. If things don't work out between me and Sara, there won't be any need to involve Joanne."

"Your daughter's already involved," Nanny Joy said. "She told me this morning that you're going to get her a new mommy, and she wishes you'd let her do the choosing. She thinks she would probably choose Peter Rabbit."

I wondered why no one was smiling. "There, you see," I said.

It occurred to me that nobody really wanted me to fall in love. I've never heard of someone giving a falling-in-love party. But in my case, I guess it was premature anyway. You can't give a falling-in-love party for one person. Although maybe that's what I had arranged for myself.

"Well, if you think Ms. Coleridge wouldn't measure up to Peter Rabbit," Harry said, "I've got another suggestion. I'll call her agent and say you're doing a series of portraits of musicians and that you'd like to include Sara in the series."

Harry's idea appealed to me in general, but the details would have to be worked out. "How do you know she has an agent?" I asked.

"Everyone has an agent," Harry said. "Especially harpists. They're ethereal people." Harry was warming to his task. With a few exceptions, Harry didn't have friends or acquaintances. Instead, he had "contacts," and he was proud of the number and variety of those contacts. One of the important occasions of his life was the day he found he could no longer fit new cards into the wheel index on his desk and had to order the next larger size.

Nanny Joy, whose experiences with interested men had probably tended to be direct, looked skeptical about our plans. "What if the lady doesn't want to have her picture taken?"

"That's the least of our problems," Harry said. "Everyone wants to be photographed. I'm certain there's been an increase in the number of bank robberies since they began installing those movie cameras. The first time I saw one of those lenses staring down at me, I immediately straightened my ascot and began composing a stickup note."

I think Harry was almost right. And even the few people who don't want to be photographed have a difficult time refusing a photographer's request. It's like turning down an offer of immortality. One of the earth's truly exclusive groups is the one made up of people who have never been photographed.

In any case, it seemed like a safe bet that Sara Coleridge would agree to whatever arrangements Harry wanted to make. I gave him her address, the party ended, and I settled back to wait for news from Harry.

The wait was short, but the news was troublesome. When Harry called me the next afternoon, he was as close to losing his composure as I had ever heard him.

"Am I your friend?" he asked.

"My friend and mentor," I assured him.

"Good. That's good. I want to do some mentoring. Forget about Sara Coleridge. I know another young lady . . . a tympanist. She even has a telephone."

"I don't like lady drummers, Harry. What happened?"

"I was put on hold, that's what happened."

For a person like me, being put on hold is a commonplace event, a part of the give-and-take of telephone life. But for a person like Harry, the push of the hold button is like the sting of a glove against his cheek. I wondered whether he wanted me to act as his second. "Did Sara do that to you?" I asked.

"No, of course not. It was her piranha of an agent—a Ms. Lee Ferris—who not only sullies a noble profession, but who says Sara Coleridge is not available to practitioners of a third-rate art. Ms. Ferris knows your work, by the way. She said, 'Oh, yes. He's the one who does the oversized passport photos.' "

"She said all that without provocation?"

"Jonathan . . . you malign me. You know I've spent my life learning not to provoke people. What you forget is that, unlike you, most people are suspicious of other people's enthusiasms."

I thanked him for his help and hung up. I lapsed into a state of patient discouragement, and I thought of what Harry had said about my willingness to share other people's enthusiasms. He was right. I like things secondhand; things filtered through other people's personalities. For example, although I have never read a novel by Dickens, I probably know his works as well as some experts do, simply because I once had a friend who was a Dickens enthusiast. I willingly spent hours listening to my friend's retellings and interpretations. I learned plots. I could speculate about the significance of characters with monosyllabic surnames: Scrooge, Drood, Heep. But when I tried to read *The Pickwick Papers*, I found it vastly complicated. I soon found myself taking my pulse, which is what I do in response to overwhelming boredom. What I enjoyed, I decided, was not Dickens but my friend's enthusiasm for Dickens.

Perhaps the reason I was being hesitant about approaching Sara Coleridge was that she was the object of my own, rather than someone else's, enthusiasm; she was an unaccustomed responsibility. And although I understand the need for responsibility, I think it is definitely an area in which moderation is called for. An unrestrained sense of responsibility can too easily lead to sanctity or indigestion.

For the next few days I devoted myself to making a living. Harry completed arrangements for a sitting with the soprano Arianella Stradellini, and he warned me that she would bring not only her curse but a few props as well. She arrived promptly for her appointment, accompanied by two muscular young men who carried a chaise longue and by an unmuscular old man who carried a large black book, a large candelabrum, and a small handbell. The young men left after positioning the chaise and the candelabrum in front of the camera. The signorina, after lighting the candles, unwrapped and discarded her silk wraparound dress. Then, wearing only high-heeled shoes, she subsided immodestly onto the chaise. The old man opened his book and began to read aloud in Latin, pausing occasionally to tinkle the handbell. The soprano looked at me sternly and said, "Please to begin."

I remember having thought that I should be amused, outraged, or titillated by the situation, but something about the signorina's manner kept me serious and businesslike. Leaving the matter of poses up to my subject, I worked quickly, taking a dozen pictures. She had me add a thirteenth for luck, and then she promptly rewrapped herself in her dress. She walked slowly round the studio, moving her hands over her breasts, ribs, and belly. Eventually she smiled and said, "*Bene*. You have done most well. The evil is vanished from me now." She extended her right arm and sang a startlingly high pianissimo tone. "Yes," she said. "It is good. Burn them."

"Burn what?"

"The photographs. All of them."

"You don't want to see them?"

"No one must see them, *caro mio*. The evil is in them now; it must not be let to escape." Her arm was still raised. She walked toward me and took my right hand in hers. She looked at my palm. "I have a favor for you. I shall give you a message." She ran a long scarlet fingernail across my palm, sending a series of intriguing ripples along various paths of my nervous system. Most of the paths seemed loinward bound. At about the time I began to wonder whether message-seeking had become dalliance, the signorina asked, "You are seeking someone?"

"Yes."

She looked at me undramatically but seriously. "It is better you do not seek," she said. She kissed the palm of my hand. "Burn the photographs and do not seek. I am trusting you." She turned to the old man and said something in Italian. He gathered up his book and bell, and he went to her side. She smiled at me again and gestured at the candelabrum and the chaise. "These are yours," she said. She and the man went to the door. As I let them out, she said, "*Addio*. Do not seek."

I closed the door, went back to the studio, and began to disobey her various instructions. First I carried the morning's exposures into the darkroom and prepared to develop them. As I worked I wondered whether I attracted more than my share of bizarre people. Maybe not. Stradellini wasn't noted for being bizarre; she was a respected singer who made people weep and cheer. Yet she believed people could cast spells and that I could uncast them. She could read palms.

What should I think of all that? I suppose I really didn't make much distinction between the natural and the supernatural. My falling in love with Sara Coleridge was no more easily understood than Stradellini's bewitchment or Harry's devotion to snails and garlic. It was helpful to be able to explain certain kinds of magic, such as the interactions of photochemicals and light. But the interactions of human beings with the personalities and objects around them might just as well go unexplained.

As I immersed the first sheet of exposed paper in the developing fluid I began to feel an emotion that was different from the usual suspense of wondering what kind of image was about to be revealed. It took me a few moments to realize that what I felt was guilt; the anticipation of seeing what I had been forbidden to see. I remembered the Orpheus legend and wondered whether I should follow Stradellini's instructions and burn the pictures without developing them. But she hadn't said I should not develop them; just that I should burn them. I could burn them after looking at them.

I hurried the development, not taking my usual care to control the tonal range of the prints. As the first image appeared my emotions became stronger but less complicated; they changed to simple sexual excitement. When I had been photographing the soprano, I had been too distracted by the strangeness of the situation to notice what an oddly attractive body she had. For even though she could honestly be called fat, her flesh was smooth and firm; no washboard ridges or aspic jiggles. And though her dimensions were operatic, they were reasonably proportioned. A thick but undeniable waist intervened between the buoyant excess of her breasts and the ballast of her hips. But most important, she projected a sense of mobility that kept her from qualifying for obesity. It seems to me it is not fatness as such that makes obese people unattractive, but their clumsiness . . . the promise of confusing, feeble actions.

Stradellini was right when she said the pictures were evil. At least, they were evil in the sense that they had the quality of classic dirty pictures. That probably wasn't the kind of evil she had in mind; but it was good enough for me. I decided to burn only twelve of the photographs. I preserved the most decorous of the poses, telling myself flippantly that it would be irresponsible to destroy every trace of what was certainly my first example of nude portraiture and what might have been history's first example of photo-exorcism. But under the surface of my flippancy, there was a more serious concern—one that I wasn't eager to examine.

That day probably marked a turning point of some kind in my life. I still tended to whistle in the darkness, but I began to realize that there was more darkness in most people's lives than was generally admitted. And I began to accommodate myself to the darkness.

I wasn't sure whether I was grateful to the signorina for helping bring about my change in attitude, but I was definitely indebted to her for adding to my sparse collection of furniture. (Like most honest photographers, I was in a constant state of gratitude toward my subjects anyway, knowing that they and the camera did most of my work for me.) I was less than appreciative, however, of the palmistry demonstration I had received from the singer. I concluded that the warning "Do not seek" either meant nothing at all or merely confirmed my belief that the best way to become part of Sara Coleridge's life was to be patient rather than to pursue. I couldn't consider the possibility that I was being warned away from her.

My gratitude toward Stradellini became really profound, however, about three days after she posed for me. She sent me a note to let me know that her voice was continuing to improve and that by the following week, when she was going to record *Orfeo*, she would probably be well on her way to becoming opera's *primissima donna*. She invited me to the recording sessions and enclosed two guest passes. I dropped the passes in a wastebasket and resumed what had become my dominant activity: building elaborate reveries and fantasies around the imperfect image I had of Sara Coleridge.

It wasn't until several hours after I had thrown the tickets away that I realized it was more than likely that Sara would be in the orchestra at the recording session. I ran to the wastebasket, knelt before it, and began to sort through its contents.

The tickets weren't revealing themselves, so I dumped the contents of the wastebasket onto the floor. Then I heard a small, familiar voice behind me: "Oh, my goodness." It was Joanne. I turned immediately to look at her, wondering which of her moods might be on display. I think I was afraid of my daughter in those days, just on the general grounds of the unpredictability and intensity of her emotions. And I recalled that I had said some unfriendly things to her the previous day about her newly acquired habit of dumping out and then abandoning the contents of wastebaskets. I was relieved to see that she was looking at me indulgently. The indulgence was excessive, of course, involving sighs and akimbo arms. "Oh, goodness," she continued, "what a mess." She waited for me to react. I merely smiled and wondered where she had found the enormous hat she was wearing.

She suppressed her own smile and said, "What a fuckin' mess, Daddy." She knew she was using a forbidden word, but she also knew that it was a word she had heard from me the day before. She was reprimanding me.

"I like your hat," I said, accepting the reprimand. And the hat really was attractive. It was a broad-brimmed, plum-colored felt hat that had belonged to her mother.

Joanne squinted seductively and embraced me. "I like it when you stand on your knees in the mess," she whispered.

By that time I was overcome with emotions that were too strong and diverse to sort out immediately, but they obviously had a lot to do with love, past, present, and future. It occurred to me that what I feared in Joanne wasn't the intensity of her own emotions but her ability to stir up emotions in me.

"I'm searching for treasure," I said. "Help me find it, Joanne, and I'll give you something unusual." I described the tickets and moved aside as she began an enthusiastic search through the trash. As I watched I remembered Nanny Joy's suggestion that it might be better to have Joanne meet Sara before I did. If Joanne were to come to the recording session with me, she might—without too much urging—strike up a conversation with the pretty lady who played the harp. There would probably be some sort of obscure immorality involved in creating such a situation, but I wasn't going to worry about it.

Joanne found the tickets quickly, which was fortunate, because her attention span in those days didn't allow her to do things that didn't have quick and obvious results.

"What do I get?" Joanne asked as she handed me the tickets.

"Would you like to watch a lady sing into a microphone and make a record?"

Joanne's eyes opened all the way. "Billie Holiday?"

"No."

Her eyelids relaxed. "I would rather have another birthday, if you don't mind."

"A birthday party?"

"No. A birthday."

"But I can't give you that. No one can give you that. You just have to wait."

She took her hat off. "Wait till when?"

"Until next November—the second day of November."

"When is that?"

"After the summer. When the cold weather comes back."

Surprisingly, Joanne began to refill the wastebasket as she considered the inflexibility of time. "I have to wait? That's all?"

"That's all."

"Then I need a toad and some nail polish."

"Do you want to go to the recording studio?"

"Is it near a nice store?"

"I think so."

"I could go, then," she said, standing and putting her hat back on. "Now I have to see Nanny Joy." She threw me a kiss. "Good-bye, Daddy."

"Good-bye, Joanne."

I put the tickets in my pocket, wondering where I would be able to buy a toad.

Chapter 3

When Joanne and I entered the recording studio a few days later, my excitement was verging on panic. On the way uptown I had made two detours to visit men's rooms before I realized that what I was dealing with wasn't a full bladder but its psychic equivalent. My daughter tried to calm me. The studio was in midtown, just east of Fifth Avenue, and whenever Joanne was in that area, she underwent a mysterious change of personality. She liked to stroll through what she called the nice stores—Bergdorf's or Saks'—exchanging knowing glances with slender, fiftyish ladies. Although I was grateful for the signs of potential maturity, I hoped Joanne wasn't recognizing her destiny among the haughty shoppers.

But the trace of haughtiness helped us as we entered the control room of the studio. We were admitted between takes, and the producer glared at Joanne and seemed about to deliver a few words of warning or banishment to me, when he recognized Joanne as the tiny matron she had temporarily become. He nodded and turned his attention to the musicians on the other side of the glass partition.

The control room was fairly crowded with other visitors, but we found two empty chairs and settled down to listen. I was afraid to look into the studio; afraid that Sara would not be there.

The producer turned the pages of his score and spoke into a microphone: "Once more, maestro?"

The conductor's voice replied, godlike and amplified, through a pair of enormous speakers. "Once more. Measure 236."

"Whenever you're ready," the producer said. Then he switched off his microphone and spoke quietly to his engineer, who sat before a terrifyingly large, ominous panel of switches and dials. "The contralto is a disaster." The engineer nodded and reached out tentatively to turn a dial, as if making a move in a game of chess. "Stradellini should sing both parts." The engineer nodded again, reaching across the panel but withdrawing his hand before touching anything.

Through the speakers came the sound of coughs, murmuring voices, and instruments being tuned. I couldn't hear a harp, and I was still afraid to look. The conductor's baton rapped, and he announced that he was ready. The producer switched on the tape reels and announced Take Six of *Orfeo*, Act Three, *Che fiero momento*.

The music began, filling the control room with the odd kind of facsimile sound that recording equipment creates. The producer was doing what I used to do in my catalog photography—making something seem better than it was. Stradellini did indeed sound better than she had at the concert, but that wasn't all the result of the engineer's skill. For one thing, her pitch control was greatly improved, and that can't be faked.

I listened nervously to the music—or through the music—trying to pick out the sound of the harp. But I couldn't find it. I tried again and again, and finally I looked tentatively and excitedly into the studio. The harp stood impressively at the rear of the orchestra, isolated by three movable partitions. The chair that stood behind it was empty. I said something impolite. Joanne looked up at me disapprovingly and put her forefinger to her lips. My disappointment was strong enough that soon my jaw began to hurt, and I realized that I had been clenching my teeth. But I was also relieved, because once again I had been spared the meeting with Sara, and its possibilities for the faux pas or the unpleasant revelation.

I looked at the harp again and the empty chair behind it. Then I realized that there were other empty chairs scattered through the orchestra, including three rows of seats at the rear for the temporarily unneeded chorus. Of course! For a recording session, players or singers who weren't needed for a particular movement wouldn't have to stay in their chairs as they would during a performance in an opera house or a concert hall. In fact, they would probably be required to get out of the way to avoid the chance of their knocking over a music stand or making some other inadvertent noise and spoiling a take. But I didn't see any spare performers in the corners of the studio. The only non-participants were in the control room.

I treated myself to another "Of course!" and looked at the man sitting to my right. He seemed to be dozing, although he might have been doing some intense listening. But on the floor at the side of his chair rested the intricate golden plumbing of a French horn. I looked to my left. Sitting next to Joanne and trying to read a music score in the semidarkness was Sara Coleridge.

I fought off an urge to head for the men's room. Then I did some serious swallowing and teeth-clenching. I no longer heard any music, and I thought for a moment that the producer had interrupted the performance. But I glanced into the studio and saw that violinists were bowing and Orfeo was lamenting. I had merely gone temporarily deaf, having diverted all my sensory energies to the difficult assignment of allowing me to stare at Sara without turning to face her. During the next few minutes, by making unreasonable demands on my peripheral vision and by engaging in an orgy of sidelong glances, I got a fairly good idea of what Sara Coleridge looked like. Her eyes, pale-lashed and chestnut, were inquisitive but not inviting. It was hard to tell where her cheekbones were, and her skin was not well cared-for. Her cloche of pale hair had probably not been combed but only rumpled by her slender, strong fingers. Her body, which was concealed by a voluminous, somber blouse and a full-length skirt, had an angularity that was relieved only by the curve of her full, low-placed breasts. She looked to me exactly the way a woman should look.

As I sneaked my little snapshot-glances at Sara I was reminded of the basic problem a portrait photographer has to deal with: a person's appearance isn't revealed through a single brief impression but through a spectrum of gesture and subtly altering expressions. Sara's appearance didn't assert itself, but, as I had been so aware the first time I saw her, her presence was prodigious. Joanne, who had particular reason to be curious about women in the young-mother age group, was doing her own share of sidelong glancing. The glances eventually turned into a frank stare. And then my daughter did what I wanted to do but could never have done: she reached out and put her hand on Sara's. Sara turned her head slowly and smiled, first at Joanne and then at me.

I returned the smile apologetically and nervously, and I reached over and removed Joanne's hand from Sara's. Still smiling gently, Sara turned her eyes back to her score.

I leaned over to Joanne and whispered, "Don't bother the lady. It's not polite to touch strangers."

"She makes me feel good," Joanne said, too loudly.

It was my turn to put my finger to my lips. I took one more long, direct look at Sara, who was still vaguely smiling, and I began to relax for the first time that day. I stopped thinking about stratagems; soon I stopped thinking altogether and listened to the music. Stradellini was nearing the end of an aria. I tried to ignore the orchestra and to hear only the voice, which combined a childlike clarity with adult power. The vocal line of the music was not complicated; probably not very different from the sort of simple melody that was sung at the time the story of Orpheus first began to circulate. That was a long time ago, and people were still interested. Music and love.

I began to feel more comfortable about my feelings for the unknown woman who was sitting so near me. I was simply in love: a commonplace event that people have been writing and singing about for centuries. I suppose nonlovers tend to think that love occurs—or should occur—only in books or on stages, where its excesses can be shaped and controlled. Maybe everybody loves a lover, but not everybody wants to be one. But once you become one, you might as well try to enjoy it. I listened to the final notes of the music, and I began to cry.

At the end of the take, there were a few moments of silence; something I suspected didn't happen very often in such circumstances. Finally, the producer said, "I liked it . . . a lot. Is there anyone who didn't like it?" After more silence, he said, "We'll play it back for you and then break for lunch. The chorus and full orchestra will be here at two o'clock, and we'll start with the big parts."

The playback was piped only into the studio, not into the control room, and for a few moments I looked through the glass at what might have been a scene from a psychiatric ward or a crowded subway car: a diverse collection of people ignoring one another, staring at nothing, and seriously considering something apparent only to themselves. In the control room, people were finding out whether they could still talk; one of them was Joanne, who was saying to Sara, "I'm four and a half. How old are you?"

Sara glanced at me and then looked down at Joanne. "How old do you think I am?"

Joanne said, "Oh, phew," and rocked back and forth on her chair a few times. She was obviously intimidated by the question, but she wasn't defeated. "I think," she said, "you are either nineteen or forty-one."

Sara was smiling, but Joanne seemed dangerously close to saying something that might embarrass or bore her new acquaintance—a privilege I thought should be mine. So, fighting off a severe attack of adolescence, I looked into Sara's eyes and spoke: "She means well. Her name is Joanne Brewster." Sara continued to smile noncommittally, but she didn't jump at the chance to introduce herself. She looked away.

"My daddy takes pictures," Joanne said.

Sara looked at me again, this time with full attention. "Brewster," she said. "You're the man who wanted to photograph me. You called my agent."

Guiltily, and probably unconvincingly, I tried to produce an expression of dawning recognition. "Of course . . . you're the harpist."

"Sara Coleridge. I hope my agent wasn't rude. She tends to be a little brusque."

"She was rude to my agent. He said she was a piranha, but he said it with true admiration, I think."

Sara began to put her score into a briefcase, and her attention once again drifted away. She didn't seem unfriendly, but she seemed more comfortable attending to something within herself than to the things around her. I couldn't let her get away that easily.

"You haven't changed your mind about posing for me?" I asked.

She glanced at me and stood up. "No."

No explanations and, fortunately, no irritation. Just disinterest. I had failed to make an impression, and it would have been immoderate and probably counterproductive to push things any further. I looked down at my daughter, hoping she would have something arresting and immoderately interesting to say to the nice lady. But Joanne had picked that moment to have one of her rare attacks of introspection.

Sara had gathered up her belongings and was looking for a way out. My mission had been a failure. Sara only had to move past us and she would be out of our lives. "Nice to have met you," she said and started to squeeze in front of Joanne. But Joanne still had a slightly puzzled expression and was oblivious to what was happening around her. She was forming a little roadblock. Sara leaned over and said, "Pardon me, dear." When Joanne still didn't move, Sara looked to me for help.

I took my daughter by the shoulders, grateful to her for keeping Sara from leaving but wondering what was troubling her. "Sweetie," I said, "let the lady past."

Joanne looked up at me as if I just awakened her. "I have a new girlfriend," she said. Which was more than I had. "She's in the snow and her name is Colnee."

"That's nice. Now let the lady past."

But Sara no longer seemed so eager to leave. She sat down again and took Joanne's hand. "Where is your friend now?" she asked, with surprising seriousness.

"On my lap," Joanne said. "I have to make her warm."

My fears were confirmed. I was hoping Joanne's new friend was someone she had met at nursery school, but I knew there was a good chance that she had come up with another invisible companion. Joanne had spent a distressingly large part of her third year muttering at and attending to an invisible animal friend. And even though I had been assured that imaginary friends were not the cause for alarm in four-year-olds that they were in forty-year-olds, the situation disturbed me. And besides, the first unseen companion was a capybara—a creature we had seen in the Central Park Zoo. Capybaras are the world's largest rodents and are astoundingly dim-witted and unattractive; not ideal companions for young ladies. It was somewhat reassuring that Joanne's new friend seemed at least to be a human. But I thought maybe it was time Joanne began to choose her friends from the world of the visible.

For the moment, however, the development had its advantages. Sara had regained some interest in us; or in Joanne, at least. I stood looking down at them and listening to their strange little conversation, afraid to interrupt and hoping they were in the process of forming a lifelong friendship.

Sara's voice was high-pitched, but it was agile and not nasal. It didn't sound like a voice that got used too often, but Sara was using it eagerly now. "Does Colnee talk to you, Joanne?"

"No. Colnee's a baby. But I can hear what she thinks."

"What does she think?"

"She thinks about the angel."

"Which angel is that?"

Joanne hesitated. She was looking down into her lap, where I assumed her new friend was still sitting. Then she looked up at Sara. "Would you like to be Colnee's friend, too?"

Sara glanced at me before answering. "Maybe it would be better for your mother to be Colnee's friend."

I bestowed an enormous imaginary embrace on Joanne and Colnee. The Most Important Fact could now be tactfully revealed to Sara. And after a suspenseful pause, Joanne spoke the magic words: "I don't have a mommy."

As long as imaginary events seemed to be in order, I conjured up a sumptuous fanfare. Joanne looked up at me as though she had heard the trumpets, and then she continued to say the right thing: "Colnee is hungry, Daddy."

"Well, let's get her something to eat." I thought it was time I took over the script. I looked at Sara and added in what I hoped was a casually appealing tone, "Since you're Colnee's friend, too, Miss Coleridge, maybe you'd like to join us." I followed the speech with a quick, silent entreaty to whatever powers watched over recording studios: *Please let her say yes*.

Joanne came to my rescue again and said, "Please come, Miss Coleridge."

And Sara said yes. Or, more exactly, she said, "All right, Mr. . . ."

"Brewster. Jonathan Brewster." It was just like being in a movie. I called for another fanfare: French horns this time, instead of trumpets. And I began the exciting, mysterious, and difficult process of finding out what kind of person Sara Coleridge was.

The first thing I found out was not encouraging. When I asked her where she would like to have lunch, she said it didn't matter much, but that she didn't eat meat except on special occasions. Our lunch obviously didn't fit into her category of special occasions, although it headed the list on mine. Sara reassured me somewhat by announcing that she found most health-food and vegetarian restaurants depressing. She wasn't a vegetarian, she said; she just didn't like to eat meat. When I pressed her, she admitted that she didn't much like to eat anything. My delight increased.

We headed off toward a delicatessen on Sixth Avenue, where Sara could order one of their dairy specialties, and Joanne could make one of her usual exotic choices. As we walked to the restaurant I began to lose some of the gratitude I felt toward Joanne's new invisible friend for making the lunch possible. Joanne insisted on cradling Colnee in her arms, which drew some puzzled glances and condescending smiles from passersby. At least the old capybara had gone about unobtrusively at the heel. My daughter and I would have to have a conference later.

The restaurant was crowded and decidedly unromantic; an advantage, I thought, since I didn't want to seem to be in search of romance. But I felt better than I had in years. Just the fact that there were three of us instead of two would have been gratifying; that Sara was the third person made my pleasure almost unbearable. I was not only in love, but I was part of a loving family. I suddenly realized that that was something I had never before been part of.

It wasn't exactly a relaxing occasion, though. I directed a lot of my energy toward keeping my hands from trembling and trying to prevent my consonants from bunching up. There wasn't much energy left for being charming. I sat facing a mirrored wall, and I found myself sneaking glances at my reflection, regretting my poorly matched features and wondering for the first time since my teens which was my good side.

Sara ordered noodles and cheese, I asked for corned beef on rye, and we waited to see what would capture Joanne's fancy. After a consultation with the waiter, she placed two orders: for herself, a cherry blintz, a dill pickle, and plain soda water; and for Colnee, a glass of tomato juice and a slice of rare roast beef.

Sara was calmly attentive, but she volunteered no information about herself. I asked her a few questions about her background, but she tended to answer with questions of her own. Soon she knew a fair amount about me, but I got the idea she wasn't especially pleased by what she had learned.

My daughter, who seemed to have found a complete rapport with Sara, had no need for conversation. While we were waiting for coffee to arrive, Joanne leaned across the table and put her hand on Sara's, and the child and the woman smiled at each other. Tears filled my eyes, and I pushed my chair back and stood up, impelled by several strong emotions. Two of the emotions were jealousy and resentment over the rapport that I wasn't being invited to share. But I also had the feeling that there was something unwholesome in that rapport—something that shouldn't be encouraged.

Sara looked up at me in surprise, and she moved her hand from Joanne's to mine. I sat down, and all feelings of unease vanished. Sara's touch seemed to work as a kind of transfusion, filling me with a consciousness of something I had never felt before. I couldn't define what was flowing between us, but it was certainly nothing unwholesome. It had to do with virtue and pleasure.

My jack-in-the-box performance had drawn some attention from people at surrounding tables. Sara didn't seem to mind the puzzled glances, but I thought I owed her an apology. "I don't know why I did that," I said.

"It's not important," Sara answered.

"I think it *is* important. I think you're making me—and my daughter—have feelings we've never had before."

Sara took her hand away from mine. "I'm not making anyone do anything," she said. "You're overrating me. I'm an ordinary person who isn't courageous enough to refuse random invitations to lunch."

"You're not enjoying yourself?"

"That's not the point . . ." Sara made a little sound that might have been the beginning of "Jonathan." Whatever she had been about to say, she decided it was better left unsaid. "The point is," she continued, "you're making it sound as though I'm trying to have some kind of malicious influence on you."

"No. I don't believe that. It's just that I haven't figured out *what* you are."

"I'm a musician who has to get back to a recording studio now."

Sara stood up. Joanne followed suit, after putting her uneaten pickle into her purse. Before we left the table, I glanced at Sara and saw for the first time the expression of peculiar animation that I would see on her face many times in the future—an expression of fleeting, private passion. She was staring at the untouched meal that Joanne had ordered for Colnee: the glass of thick red liquid and the thin slice of almost raw meat that partially concealed a faint smear of blood on the white plate. As she looked at the plate Sara's lips were moving slightly, as if in prayer. I turned away from her briefly, feeling that I was intruding on some sort of private act, and when I looked back again, her usual expression of calm, cheerful detachment had returned. I wondered whether I had imagined the strange moment and whether the concept of sorcery was as much out of the question as it had seemed a few moments earlier.

Joanne and I parted with Sara in the corridor outside the recording studio. My emotions were not simple. In a way, I felt more relaxed than I had since meeting Sara; the strain of wondering how to behave had subsided. But the panic was growing in me quickly as I realized I might never again have the opportunity of behaving in any way with her.

As we parted, Sara ran her fingers through her hair, tilting her head, and seeming a bit tense. I was pleased for an instant, thinking she might be displeased at having to leave me and Joanne. But then she said, "I have to start tuning up. I'm in the next take." Her tension was stage fright. "Harpists spend a good part of their lives tuning up," she said. She smiled at me.

I felt encouraged for the first time. The part about tuning up was the only thing she had said that had been not quite necessary; the only time she had told me something I had not asked. Lovers feed on crumbs. I was about to ask whether we might see her again, when disaster struck. The elevator doors opened, and Arianella Stradellini emerged, scattering energy and vowels. She detached herself from her companions and engulfed me in a more than casual embrace.

"My magician," she said.

When I disentangled myself, Sara was gone. The signorina escorted me into the control room, explaining that she was not involved in the scene they were recording next. Since I was her guest, I couldn't ignore her, and I sat trying to smile as she alternately enthused and railed over the complexities of her life. Whenever possible I looked through the glass into the studio, where Sara was applying a tuning wrench of some sort to the pins at the top of her harp, plucking strings, and listening with absolute concentration. The speakers in the control room were turned off, and Sara's actions were a pantomime to me. The lack of sound emphasized the intensity of her movements. She had as much vitality as the soprano who sat next to me chattering, gesturing, and reaching out often to touch me. But Sara was more careful about what she touched.

The director returned to the control room and asked for silence. The musicians and singers—including a chorus—now went through some trial takes while microphones and sound balances were adjusted. And eventually they began to record the scene in which I had first noticed Sara at the concert: Orfeo entering the Underworld. Everyone in the studio was tense with the peculiar mass concentration that takes place when music is being well performed. The harp part in the scene didn't seem especially complicated to me, but it was the foundation on which the other parts were based. The restraint and detachment that Sara had shown earlier had vanished. Her eyes were focused on her music, glancing occasionally at the conductor or the strings of her harp, but she seemed to be seeing something else. Her lips parted occasionally and just perceptibly, as though she were whispering in a language she didn't know well. The sound in the control room became almost painfully loud as the contralto and the full chorus and orchestra joined in a crescendo. The sound of the harp could no longer be distinguished from the sound of the other instruments. Again, Sara seemed engaged in a pantomime. Her face had taken on the unsettling expression I had seen briefly in the restaurant as she looked at the blood-smeared plate.

Gradually I turned my attention away from the activities in the recording studio and began to think about the importance that Sara had suddenly assumed in my life. Now that I had spoken to her and had been close to her, I was more certain than ever that she had something I needed to complete my life. Yet there was also something forbidding about her, and I suspected that if I were ever to share her life, it would turn out to be a life made up of something more than simple pleasures. But I told myself that maybe that's what I needed.

Then I remembered that it wasn't only my own feelings and needs that I had to consider. I turned to look at Joanne. She was cradling her invisible friend Colnee in her arms, and I can't say I welcomed that development. There was something distasteful about the intensity that Joanne was showing in playing her new game. She had been taken away from me, into another world.

But as I watched her she turned to me and smiled; it was a smile that was more mature than any I had seen her use before. She was learning things in her new world, and apparently one of the things she was learning about was pleasure.

Joanne hadn't learned a lot about endurance, though, because in another five minutes she was asleep. I stayed in the studio until the end of the next take. I gathered that the performance had begun to deteriorate. None of the performers looked pleased. Sara had begun to chew her lower lip, and she seemed to be unhappy not with herself but with someone else in the orchestra.

As I carried Joanne from the studio I took a farewell look at Sara—who had obviously forgotten us entirely. The recording director had begun talking to the performers about overtime. The studio had definitely turned into some sort of battleground. Sara Coleridge seemed to be enjoying the battle now, and I sensed for the first time the unusual strength of her will. I wasn't sure that my will was as strong as hers, but I knew I had a good supply of patience and stubbornness. I didn't know whether my attraction to Sara would lead me to something good, but I suspected it would at least be stimulating.

Chapter 4

I had no appointments the next day, so I spent a lot of my time thinking about Sara. "Thinking" might not be the right term, because it wasn't exactly a rational process I was indulging in. I wasn't analyzing her personality or cataloging her virtues; in fact, much of the time I was simply being vaguely but pleasantly aware of her existence.

I suppose one of the ways you know you're in love—maybe the only way—is that the person you love commands all unused parts of your consciousness at all times. In any case, during the next few days, if I wasn't asking my mind to devote itself to reading a light meter or making conversation, it automatically asked me to remember Sara. The things I remembered were powerful but unclear. Did she have a slight squint, or was I recalling something about the light in the recording studio or the restaurant? Was there an unevenness about her lower front teeth? Or did she even show her lower teeth when she smiled? She had become a collection of obsessive, pleasant mysteries, and what had become important to me was that I should get to see her again—not so much to solve the mysteries as to assure myself that I hadn't imagined them. One mystery I did have to solve, though, was how I was going to get to spend some more time with Sara. While I was considering the matter, Harry Bordeaux paid me a surprise visit. He said he had just dropped by to leave a present for Joanne. That was improbable for two reasons: first, Harry was always working during business hours; and second, although he was reasonably fond of my daughter, she was still a member of a part of human society he couldn't take very seriously—the very young. I don't know whether he tended to ignore children because they seldom needed agents or because they reminded him of some traits he unfortunately still shared with them.

Joanne joined us, and we watched as she unwrapped a large box that turned out to be filled with tiny objects: furnishings for the dollhouse I had given her the previous Christmas. She embraced Uncle Harry elaborately and then ran off to inspect and install the furniture. I noticed that Uncle Harry didn't display his usual nervous smile during the embrace. He even came up with a reasonably convincing representation of pleasure and gratitude.

"The past is cute," Harry said.

I raised my eyebrows, waiting for him to explain.

"Those little things. They're all colonial style. Bed warmers, candlesticks, wooden buckets, cradles. Cute. Little modern things aren't so cute. There's something depressing about tiny vacuum cleaners . . . TV sets with quarter-inch screens. It's the distance of time, I guess. When you look back three hundred years, you don't want things to look big and real. You know why no one likes reconstructed colonial villages? They're too big. Gross. You expect some smelly, hard-eyed Puritan to appear and lead you away to the stocks."

"Or the gallows."

"Right," Harry said. "A two-inch gibbet is no threat. Come to think of it, a two-inch anything is no threat." He was smiling foolishly, and I wondered if his entendre had been double. If so, he was truly having an out-of-character day. Harry's rules of sexual neutrality usually dictated that he was never the one to bring sex into a conversation, and certainly not facetiously. I let it pass, though. His smile faded quickly, and he asked, "How's the romance proceeding?" The question seemed more than casual. In fact, it seemed earnest enough to have been the purpose of his visit. I filled him in quickly on the events at the recording session. But he didn't seem as interested in events as he was in emotions. "That's how it looked," he said. "But how did it feel, Jonathan? How *does* it feel?"

I wondered for a moment whether I should really try to explain to Harry how I had been feeling since my discovery of Sara. But that would have meant getting more serious than Harry liked anyone to get. And besides, I wasn't sure I could have explained my feelings anyway. I settled for the almost-serious: "You know, Harry. The classic inexplicable: I freeze, I burn . . . you're the cream in my coffee . . . let me count the ways . . . *sempre tua*."

"Oh." Harry sounded disappointed.

"It's like someone said about jazz. If you have to ask what it is, no one can explain it to you. But why *do* you ask?"

"Curiosity, Jonathan. Just curiosity."

I began to wonder about Harry. Love was a subject that he was usually even less curious about than he was about sex. As I considered Harry's behavior, a strange possibility occurred to me: Could someone have moved—even a fraction of an inch—the rock under which Harry's tender passions had been hibernating for forty years? It would have been madness to ask him such a thing, but I kept the possibility in mind.

"So what's new at the office?" I asked.

"I reminded the piranha that there are also sharks in the pond."

The old Harry had returned. It took me a moment to remember who the piranha was: Sara's agent, who had done Harry the indignity of putting him on hold.

"How did you remind her, Harry?"

"As follows: 'Ms. Ferris? Mr. Vladimir Horowitz on the line. Please hold.' Then I put my hand over the mouthpiece and sat back and listened. Seven minutes she waited. Seven! I had given her five maximum."

"Wasn't that a little petty?"

"You think so? After all, I was defending your honor. She had called you a passport photographer."

I wasn't going to argue about whose honor had been at stake. But just as I was about to change the subject, I realized that Harry hadn't finished his story. "There's more?" I asked.

"She was undone. Completely undone, Jonathan." Another pause. What came next was the difficult part, I assumed. I encouraged him: "And then?"

"Then . . . the piranha . . ."

"Yes?" Harry was suppressing either rage or a giggle. "The . . . ninny . . . invaded my office."

"How did she locate you?"

"A good ear, she said. After my prank, she concentrated on my voice—she supposedly never forgets voices—and remembered my previous call about Sara Coleridge. Looked me up in the phone book, found that my office was three blocks from hers, and decided that a confrontation was called for. Swept past my receptionist—who thought we had all been time-machined into a scene from a Rosalind Russell movie—and called me a piss-tonsiled jabbernowl."

"Were any blows struck?"

"God forbid. She's a large person, Jonathan. Definitely peasant stock; probably Slavic. Very large and not well controlled."

"You definitely provoked her, though."

"Perhaps."

"Did you apologize?"

"Let's say I pacified her." Harry managed to look sheepish, which I hadn't suspected he was capable of. Then he said, almost guiltily, "We had lunch together." Harry feeling guilty about having taken someone to lunch was like a psychiatrist apologizing for invading a patient's privacy. Then Harry added the clincher: "She knows about wines and sauces." There could be no doubt. Harry was in love.

That was about all I was prepared to hear on the subject of Harry's emotions. He was my anchor, and it looked as though he had turned to cork. Fervently hoping that I might be misinterpreting his signals, I tried reminding him that he had a living to make. "I thought you might have a new assignment for me."

Harry kept his eyes on the cigarette he was stubbing out. "It might be interesting," he said, "if you did one of her."

"Her who?"

"Lee. Lee Ferris."

"The Slavic piranha? Does she need a passport?"

Harry looked offended. "Well," he said, "just a thought." He glanced at his wristwatch, stood up, and announced that he had an appointment at a nearby gallery—the Ballroom—that specialized in exhibiting things that were globular or circular. "Can you take round pictures?" he asked.

"Sure."

"Of round things?"

"I don't do *things* anymore. But find me a round person."

Harry's melancholic expression faded, and a more familiar glint of amused avarice appeared in his eyes. He shrugged his shoulders a few times, probably trying to get his fisherman's-knit blazer to settle around his thick waist. But the shrugs might have been an attempt to shake off an emotional burden. If so, I hoped he would succeed.

After Harry left, I considered the possibility that he had merely been playing some kind of psychological game with me; trying to show me how ridiculous my pursuit of Sara Coleridge seemed to him. If that's what he had in mind, he was partly successful. I decided not to try to see Sara again right away. I took a subway ride and looked at fellow passengers, vaguely hoping I would encounter a round one.

That evening was long and unpleasant. I spent most of the time thinking about Sara Coleridge, and I began to understand a little more about the change of attitude that had begun to overtake me. The change was subtle and seemed at first to be simple boredom or loneliness. I tried watching television, and when that failed me (which it often did), I went to the darkroom to do some work. But even that failed to distract me (which it almost never did).

I went to Joanne's bedroom and stood watching her as she slept. She had pushed aside her covers, and her white nightgown was illuminated oddly by the dim night light that glowed near her bed. Soon I seemed to be in a sort of trance that I thought at first might have been self-hypnosis resulting from the semidarkness and my concentration. The skin on my arms and on the back of my neck began to prickle. Tears filled my eyes, and Joanne seemed to have become a pale, formless mass suspended a few inches above the bed. I began to tremble, and I was swept with an emotion that combined a pleasing sense of discovery with an unpleasant, sharp fear.

Although my feelings were strong, they were vague. I thought that there must be some quality I lacked that kept my emotions from becoming specific—that kept me from seeing some remarkable presence that was in the room with me and Joanne. I thought the missing quality might be innocence. If I had been as innocent as Joanne, I was certain I would have at that moment been having a vision of some kind. Maybe I would have found a spectral acquaintance along the lines of Joanne's invisible friend Colnee. But I really didn't need one of those. I needed Sara, my new visible but elusive friend.

I would leave the visions to the innocent—to my daughter and perhaps to Sara Coleridge, or even to my camera. I could share their vision and whatever came with it.

But I wasn't in a position to share anything with Sara. I decided to forget about trying to develop some elaborate, indirect way of getting to know her. I got out some stationery and began to compose a letter. The first version consisted of six pages of confused entreaties, apologies, and wanderings. I had to be more concise. I tried again. Two hours and several versions later, I had settled on the following:

> Sara Coleridge:
>
> I seem to have fallen inexplicably in love with you. Please let me know where and when I can see you to discuss the matter.

But I still wasn't satisfied with my efforts. I had become obsessed with the need to be succinct. I went to the telephone and told the operator I wanted to send a telegram. I sent the following message to Sara's address:

I LOVE YOU. PLEASE ADVISE.

Then I went to bed, where I lay awake most of the night, thinking I had made a major blunder. As soon as I sent the message, I began to fear that Sara would find it ridiculous or offensive. I thought of trying to have the telegram canceled, but what then? I had told the truth, and according to some systems of thought, that's the right thing to do. Before I went to sleep, I spent some time thinking about right and wrong, but it was a subject that had always confused me—and one that I knew relatively little about at the time. There was no way of knowing then that the telegram would eventually give me a chance to find out a lot more about the subject.

When my daughter woke me up the next morning, I had a difficult time paying attention to her. My stomach was churning, and at first I couldn't remember the cause.

Joanne threw a small blanket on my bed and asked, quite seriously, "Do you love me, Daddy?"

Love. Of course. Please advise. The previous evening's efforts came limping into my memory, and there was no time to answer Joanne. Please advise.

"You're horrid, Daddy." Joanne was trying to remove one of my fingers. "And you have a very short attention span."

"You know I love you, Joanne."

"All the time?"

"All the time."

"And do you love Colnee?"

"I can't see Colnee."

Joanne picked up her blanket, rolled it into a baby-sized lump. Then she took it in her arms and looked at me calmly. "Do you love God?"

God was something I had decided Joanne should not take too seriously. Piety had not done her mother much good, and agnosticism had not done me much harm.

"Who's been telling you about God?" I asked.

"Colnee."

"I'm serious, sweetie. What about Ms. Abraham at school? Does she believe in God?"

"Ms. Abraham believes in silence. We have silent prayers."

"Does anyone but Colnee talk to you about God?"

"No."

"How does Colnee know about God if she's a baby?"

"She's *with* God."

"Which god, Joanne? There are lots of gods."

Joanne, who usually liked to argue, merely smiled. "Only one for us, Daddy," she said, a little patronizingly.

Before I could react, Nanny Joy called us for breakfast. The table was set for four. I was about to ask Joy if someone was joining us, when I noticed that the fourth setting consisted of a glass of tomato juice and a plate containing a small slice of meat—a sight that was to become unpleasantly familiar to me during the next few weeks.

I looked at Nanny Joy, who looked indulgently toward the ceiling. Then I looked at Joanne, who seemed altogether too happy. I liked her to be happy, but not at the expense of her sanity.

"Colnee is joining us, is she?" I asked.

Joanne nodded vigorously. She was stirring her cereal, which she couldn't seem to bring herself to eat. I didn't blame her for that, since it consisted of glasslike pellets in several pastel colors. She never missed an opportunity to try a new cereal, provided that someone assured her it didn't have the word "natural" on the box.

We all tinkered with our food for a while, and gradually I became aware of a faint but undeniable aroma. "Does anyone else smell garlic?" I asked.

"It's Colnee's pastrami," Nanny Joy said.

"God's little girl likes pastrami?"

Joanne, looking less happy, said, "Colnee likes veal best. But we didn't have any."

"I'll get some today," Nanny Joy said.

"Wouldn't a little crisp bacon be acceptable?" I asked.

Joanne shook her head. "It shouldn't be cooked."

I shuddered at the prospect of having to start my mornings in the presence of a piece of raw veal. Then the telephone rang. My misery increased.

Nanny Joy went to the wall phone. She said, "Yes?" and then held the phone out in my direction. "A lady."

The lady said, "This is Sara Coleridge."

I held my breath. I wasn't sure that she was going to say something I wanted to hear, so I concentrated on the sound of her voice, which was more distinctive than it had seemed when I spoke to her in person. It was like some form of musical instrument, I thought; an instrument that in the sixteenth century would have been made of carved and inlaid wood; one that isn't made anymore because there is a more efficient version made of brass.

"Mr. Brewster? Are you there?"

I managed a faint "Yes," which had a definite brassy quality.

"Did you send me a frivolous telegram?"

"It wasn't frivolous. It was honest."

"Honest or dishonest, I think it has to be considered f-frivolous."

Maybe I just imagined the hint of a stammer. I hadn't noticed anything like it the day we had lunch. A lover enjoys discovering flaws in his beloved: it proves that his love is deterred by nothing. But Sara was obviously out to deter. "You asked me to advise you," she said.

"Yes."

"I advise you not to try to involve me in your life."

"It's the thing I want most," I said, surprising myself with my certainty. Joanne and Joy, who were listening intently, exchanged smiling glances over the empty orange-juice glasses.

Sara said, "You're not really serious about this, are you?"

"I'm a really serious person," I said. I thought of Nanny Joy's tattooed thigh. Maybe I wasn't such a serious person, after all.

"Perhaps you're considered serious in Manhattan, Mr. Brewster, but there are places where you'd very definitely be thought of as frivolous." She didn't stammer this time. Perhaps she was less upset now. But I didn't know what to say to take advantage of the possible change in mood. Joanne and Nanny Joy were waiting eagerly for my next words—perhaps more eagerly than Sara.

But I never did manage a reply. Sara said, in a calm, reasonable tone: "If you really have an interest in me—if you want to please me—the best thing you can do is to leave me alone."

What could I say? If she had been angry or sarcastic, I'm sure something would have occurred to me; vehemence is an invitation of sorts. But reasonable disinterest doesn't lead to chattiness. I stared at the finger holes on the telephone dial. Eventually Sara said, "Thank you," and the line went dead.

My first reaction to that was to glare at Joanne and Joy—who promptly cleared the table and went away. They wisely concluded that I didn't require any comments or questions about the phone call. My second reaction was to try to figure out exactly what my little discussion with Sara had signified. There hadn't been many words in the conversation, and the only thing that seemed to tell me anything beyond the obvious fact that Sara didn't want to be my friend was her statement about frivolity. What seemed odd to me was that she hadn't just said that there were people who would consider me frivolous, but rather that there were "places" where I would be thought of as frivolous. It sounded as though her lack of interest in me wasn't as much a personal reaction as it was the result of a community code.

Now that I thought about it, I realized that Sara had a vaguely foreign look about her. It was nothing obvious or dramatic, but if I had seen her strolling on Fifth Avenue near Rockefeller Center, I would have thought she was a European tourist. It wasn't just that she didn't look like a New Yorker—she didn't look exactly like an American. I hadn't detected an accent of any kind in her speech, though, so maybe her foreignness was just a matter of what she believed and not of where she had lived.

Was she right in accusing me of frivolity? Probably. But I had always thought that my tendency to shy away from seriousness was mostly a way of protecting myself from a stronger than average inclination to gloominess. As I had demonstrated to myself the previous night, I was never far from lapsing into serious, inexplicable states of mind. Didn't Sara Coleridge realize that flippancy was one of the fundamental strategies for survival in a city like New York? And hadn't it occurred to her that I might change my strategies if she asked me to?

Before I could do any more speculating, Joanne came back into the kitchen to check on the state of my temper. Like most people her age, she looked appealing rather than weak when she was feeling apprehensive. It occurred to me that I hadn't photographed her for a while and that I hadn't been spending enough time with her. "Would anyone like to stay home from school today?" I asked, a little too energetically.

Joanne pretended not to hear me. She was probably wondering what price she would have to pay for a day away from Ms. Abraham. On most days, few prices would have seemed exorbitant to her. But she suddenly showed a definite flare for camel-trading. Or, in this case, toad-trading.

"You never got me a toad," she said.

"That's right. Or any nail polish. We can take some pictures and then go shopping."

"Maybe we can take pictures second."

"That's allowable, sweetie."

Nanny Joy had rejoined us and was starting to wash dishes. "Don't let Harry find out about it," she said.

"About what?"

"The toad. Harry probably has some country French recipe that calls for toad feet."

I looked at Joanne to see how she was taking Joy's speculations. But apparently she wasn't listening. "Doesn't the lady like us?" she asked.

"What lady is that?"

"On the phone. The Colnee lady."

"Oh. Yes. She likes us."

"What will she do?"

"Do?"

"Will she live here?"

"No, sweetie." I smiled my best Pagliacci smile. "No, she's very busy."

Joanne and I showed a lot of poorly directed determination that day. First we visited one of those unsettling stores that lurk around corners all over Manhattan—the kind of place that has so much of some commodity that only an immoderate, or possibly unbalanced, person could feel comfortable about it. The store Joanne and I went to trafficked mostly in tiny, garish fish, but it also featured a little sideshow of reptiles and amphibians.

We strolled along half a mile or so of aisles lined with glowing, gurgling tanks, which were filled with fish that looked as if they had been designed by someone who does the decor for disco parlors. It was a relief when we got to the comparatively drab goldfish. Actually, if I had seen some gray fish I might have been tempted to buy a few. As pets go, fish have a few things to be said for them. They aren't pushy; they don't even want a direct share of your oxygen. They don't subject you, the way a dog does, to silly attempts at being a person. A fish knows a lot about minding its own watery business.

Joanne wasn't much interested in the fish. She was looking for something that likes to gulp a little air once in a while. I led her to a grimy, out-of-the-way tank that bore the inscription Toad Hall. I read the inscription to Joanne, and she began to show signs of profound pleasure: wide-eyed silence. I didn't see anything that pleased me at all. I suspected that what my daughter liked was not the truly unattractive creatures that were in the tank but their name. "Toad" is admittedly a pleasing word, and Joanne often confused names with the things they identified.

She would probably end up marrying a murderer named Arch-angelo.

As I had expected, the toads did not exactly have a winning appearance. I think you really have to care about warts to get along with toads. The selection wasn't large: one large pair (olive with off-rust warts), and half a dozen grayish specimens, each about an inch long.

Joanne seemed pleased. "Don't you think they're nice, Daddy?"

"No, Joanne."

"I think they're nice. The little ones are nicest. Do you think they're the littlest ones in the world?"

"I hope so."

"What will they eat?" Joanne wanted to know.

I thought I'd rather not know. I hunted up a salesperson—a young woman whose T-shirt proclaimed I'm Keen on Things Piscine—and let Joanne complete the transaction. As I wandered away I heard the word "mealworm" mentioned a couple of times, together with something about "moving food." I paced the aisles and frowned at fish until Joanne found me and presented me with a bill.

"I got two little toads so that Colnee could have one too—and some worms for them to eat—and a house." She could see I wasn't sharing her enthusiasm.

"Would you like to hear a joke?" she asked.

"Why not?" I said, preparing myself for puzzlement rather than amusement.

Joanne was already suppressing giggles. "Why did the toad cross the road?"

"I don't know. Why did the toad cross the road?"

"Because it was a piece of cake." The giggles could no longer be suppressed.

"*What* was a piece of cake?"

"Oh, Daddy. I told you." More giggles.

"You said 'it' was a piece of cake. 'It' could have meant either the road or the toad."

"The road or the toad," Joanne echoed. The giggles turned to guffaws.

"Also, 'a piece of cake' could have meant either that the road or the toad was literally a piece of cake or just that the road was easy to cross."

"You don't understand, Daddy."

"I know. That's why I'm asking questions—so that I *can* understand."

"But it's not funny if you understand."

She was right. I had been guilty of analysis—an activity that is self-destructive in someone who has made a career of being mystified. Only love could have produced such a lapse. I decided to stop loving Sara Coleridge. It should be possible; after all, I had quit smoking. On the other hand, I still loved cigarettes—or the memory of cigarettes. But I had given them up. I would give up Sara.

Joanne collected her toads, and we went home to the studio.

Chapter 5

After settling the toads into their new home, my daughter put on her big hat and, in a remarkable display of cooperation, struck a series of inventive poses in front of the camera. I realized for the first time that Joanne would almost certainly turn out to be a beautiful woman. She had always been attractive, but it was the attractiveness of extreme youth. It's almost impossible not to be alluring when you're less than five years old. But Joanne's features were becoming more definite now. She looked like her mother: gray eyes, pale skin, hair an almost Oriental black, a narrow nose and lips. About all you could say about her body so far was that it was slender—my contribution to the genetic grab bag. At least, I hoped it was mine.

As Joanne posed she showed no signs of being aware of me, and although she spoke occasionally, her mutterings weren't directed at me. She seemed to be playing with her new friend Colnee, and though Joanne's actions would probably have looked eccentric to someone who didn't know about the invisible guest, there was an exciting intensity about her performance. I was delighted. I had often tried to photograph her before, but she had always been restless or distracted, and the results had been disappointing. Now, however, I was getting what I was sure would be a distinctive series of shots. But there was something about her manner that disturbed me—something forbidding and cold. And then I noticed that she seemed literally cold. She began to hunch her shoulders and cross her arms across her body. Soon she was shivering, even though the studio was unusually warm. Late-spring sunshine washed over the skylight, and I was perspiring.

"Are you all right, sweetie?" I asked.

Joanne looked at me in surprise, as though she had forgotten I was there. "I'm cold," she said. I went to her and took her hands. It was like taking eggs from the refrigerator. Joanne seemed to be surrounded by an envelope of January air. I picked her up and held her against my body. She put her face against my ear. Her hat fell off as she said, "Take the man's picture."

"Which man?"

"The man with the black suit."

Now I began to think she might really be ill. "Where is the man?"

"He's here, holding Colnee."

"Maybe you'd like to take a nap, Joanne. You can get under the blanket."

"Take the man's picture."

I put Joanne down. She was staring at the chair that my clients posed in. Her expression was a blend of fascination and either apprehension or sadness. She was still shivering slightly, although she didn't seem to be aware of her body. "He's waiting," she said.

I loaded the camera and shot a series of exposures.

I sat down, and Joanne climbed up on my lap. "He's gone now. I can go to sleep."

"Do you know the man's name?" I asked.

"He's Colnee's father."

"Is he a nice man?"

Joanne said what sounded like "chilegray," and then she fell asleep. Her hands, which had been gripping my arm, began to relax. I could feel their warmth through my shirt sleeve. I carried her to her bedroom. She seemed heavier than usual, and her arms and legs hung as though their bones had melted. I put her on the bed and covered her with a blanket.

As I left the bedroom I walked past the glass tank that held Joanne's toads. One of the little charmers was using a long, agile tongue to collect some "moving food." It was not the kind of performance I needed to see at that moment. What I needed was some simple pleasure. The simplest pleasure in Manhattan—at least during the daylight hours—is to take a walk. So I walked.

When I got home, Joanne was awake, looking healthy and acting sophisticated. She was having a before-dinner drink (apple juice on the rocks) with Nanny Joy (warm pink gin). I joined them (lots of refrigerated bourbon).

"Do you feel all right?" I asked Joanne.

"Yes, Jonathan." (Joanne and I were on a first-name basis when she was undergoing attacks of chic.) "Joy and I are talking about who I could marry. I don't think I could marry anyone."

"Why?"

"'Cause."

"'Cause why?" I could be sophisticated too.

"Well, Billy Travis hits me, for one thing."

"What about the man in the black suit?"

"Don't be silly."

"Why is that silly?"

"He's dead."

Nanny Joy looked at us both wearily. She sipped her drink and then said to Joanne, "Why don't you see how the toads are doing, sweetie? Then wash your hands and we'll have some berrycake."

Joanne said, "Excuse me, please," and then abandoned her sophistication. She ran from the table, shouting, "Toads."

"Who's the man in the black suit?" Joy asked.

"Somebody Joanne imagined today. I took his picture."

"Did the camera see him?"

"I don't know. I haven't done any developing yet."

Joy reached out and put her hand on mine. "Don't worry," she said. "Kids are weird. But they change. It's the weird grown-ups you have to worry about. They *don't* change." She took her hand away, and it occurred to me that we had almost never touched. I was also aware that Joy was still an attractive woman. Hands-off was a wise policy.

"Do you believe there are such things as ghosts?" I asked.

"Oh, sure. But they don't matter."

"You really believe there are ghosts?"

"You have to believe in something that people never give up on. Did you ever hear of any people, anywhere, anytime, that didn't have theories about ghosts?"

"I guess not."

"Of course not. They're one of the Big Subjects—like love. People keep seeing them."

"But they don't matter?"

"Ghosts don't matter. All they can do is scare you a little. But love matters. It can do a lot of things."

Nobody had to tell me that. In fact, nobody had to tell anyone I knew—with the possible, but now doubtful, exception of Harry Bordeaux.

Nanny Joy and I stopped talking. I finished my drink and poured another as I wondered what to do. Everything I could think of involved love or ghosts. I decided to stay in the kitchen and watch Joy make dinner. She was an informally inventive cook. Her meals usually consisted of one impressive item surrounded by unimpressive afterthoughts. The impressive item this night was berrycake, a spectacularly original, chewy cake buried under strawberries or raspberries and thick cream. The afterthought was fried eggs and Spam. Until Joy became part of our household, I thought Spam was something comedians talked about. Now I had grown fond of it and the other little loaves of mysterious meat that frequently appeared on our table. I think one of the things Joy liked about these meats was the process of getting them out of their metal jackets: engaging the slotted key and producing the unstable, springlike roll of metal as the rubbery jelly oozed out in its wake.

There wasn't much conversation at dinner. The berrycake featured raspberries, which gave Joanne a problem—the same sort of problem she had with watermelon: she liked the flavor but not the seeds. We philosophized about that. Then Joy cleared the table and headed for her records while Joanne took Colnee by the hand and withdrew to toadland.

I went to the darkroom and got ready to develop the portraits I had done of Joanne. My less morbid instincts took over as I prepared the chemicals and began to unload the film holders (paper holders, actually). Maybe some photographers have a reasonably good idea of what their prints are going to look like, but I never knew what to expect. I was always surprised—often unpleasantly.

That night I had the biggest surprise ever. I submerged the first sheet in the developer and began to feel the inevitable symptoms of anxiety and suspense. The image began to form on the paper. I watched with absolute concentration, as I always did. Because I timed my exposures so casually, there was usually a fair amount of variation in the tonal range of the prints, and I seldom left them submerged until the developing process had been completed. I had learned to pull the print out of the tray and stop its development in an instant, at some point before the image spoiled itself by becoming complete. As a result, some critics said my pictures were distortions. My theory was that all photographs are distortions, and that a photographer's style was merely a reflection of his or her taste in the area of unreality.

Unreality took on a new meaning for me that night, however. It was evident from the moment I submerged the first sheet of paper that something abnormal was about to take place. For the first minute or so, no image appeared at all. I decided that I had probably forgotten to expose that particular sheet—something that happens fairly often as a result of my informal procedures. I had stepped on the pedal that opened the top of my trash container, and I was about to discard the print, when I noticed that minuscule, random traces of gray had begun to appear on the surface of the paper. For the next five minutes or so I watched as the grayness gradually took on a recognizable pattern. When I was sure that the image had reached its final form, I put the print in the fixing bath and then examined it closely.

In the center of the picture was the faint but unmistakable figure of a man. His head was lowered, and he was standing, as if on uneven ground, against a featureless white background. He was wearing a dark, strangely styled costume, and he was obscured by a curtain of tiny white flecks and streaks. It was as though he were lost in a blizzard. His clothes were from another era—the seventeenth or eighteenth century. There was another interesting element in the picture: the man was holding something in his right hand. It seemed to be a knife.

I didn't take time to think about what I had seen, but quickly developed the rest of the pictures. The first exposures in the series were normal in all respects, and a couple of them captured Joanne's qualities in a way that satisfied me completely. But about halfway through the sequence, the images began to show signs of distortion. White specks appeared on the surface of some of the prints, and although I kept telling myself that there was merely some defect in my camera or in the processing chemicals, I finally had to face up to the fact that my daughter was not the only person I had photographed that afternoon. In several of the shots, Joanne was holding an infant on her lap—an infant whose image looked fairly substantial in some instances but in others had the kind of translucent appearance that results when two exposures are superimposed. Another word that describes the effect is "ghostly."

I left the prints to wash and went out into the comparatively real world of my apartment. Nanny Joy and Joanne were listening to records; a man who didn't put enunciation high on his list of priorities wanted everyone to know that he felt depressed enough to drink muddy water and sleep in a hollow log. Actually, his ideas sounded pretty sensible to me, since I had just noticed that Joanne was holding on her lap a blanket-shrouded doll that she hadn't paid any attention to in recent months. She was smiling at it compassionately—an expression that didn't suit someone of her age. I yearned to see her project a little rage or shy cuteness.

"Bedtime," I said. I thought that would bring on some pouts and frowns—maybe even a discreet tantrum. But Joanne stood up obediently, kissed Nanny Joy and me, and headed for her room. I joined her at prayer time. Prayer was a ritual that neither Joy nor I had ever recommended to Joanne, but it had still become important to her for some reason. The part I enjoyed was the ingenuity she showed in her requests for blessings.

That night, the litany went as follows: "God bless Mommy, who died." (A conventional beginning.) "God bless Daddy's camera." (A first!) Joanne looked at me. "Is that okay?"

"Is what okay?"

"To bless something besides people?"

"I think so. Sure, why not?"

"I just wanted to know."

Joanne closed her eyes again and considered the matter for a moment.

"God bless Leo."

"Who's Leo?"

"Ms. Abraham says she's a Leo. And that's why she's a teacher."

"Oh, *that's* why."

"God bless TV."

TV, like prayer, was something Joanne had got interested in

without my encouragement. At least she had the good taste to prefer the commercials to the programs.

"God bless Daddy and Nanny Joy."

The list was short that night. She always ended that way—saving, as I liked to think, the best for the last. But there was no "Amen," and she was still on her knees. "God bless the lady."

"Which lady?"

"The one we had lunch with."

"Why bless her?"

"She brought me Colnee."

"Oh?" All the lady had brought me was misery.

"And God bless Colnee and keep her warm."

Yes, be sure to do that.

"And God bless Chilegray. Amen."

There it was again.

"Who's Chilegray?"

Joanne jumped into bed and said, "Goodnight, Daddy."

"Daddy asked you who Chilegray is."

She smiled. "It's not a who. It's where Colnee lives."

Oh, well. I kissed my daughter's still-smiling lips.

"Kiss the nose," she said. I complied. And then, on request, I kissed her ears and her chin. Joanne might be going crazy, but she was doing it in an affectionate way.

I went to the kitchen and poured myself a drink. On the note pad we used for making grocery lists, I wrote the word "Chilegray," and put the note in my wallet. I felt I had to talk to a worldly person; so, after steeling myself with the drink, I telephoned Harry Bordeaux. Harry never answered his phones directly. At home a machine answered, and in his office a secretary answered. Judging from the number of secretaries who had left Harry's employ during the time I had known him, I suspected he tended to treat them in the same way he treated his answering machine.

But at least he didn't use the machine as an excuse for indulging in whimsy. A lot of people—probably out of embarrassment—try to be witty in the greetings they record for the machine. Harry had too much respect for telephones to do anything like that. I dialed his number.

"Harry Bordeaux's residence. Please leave your message when you hear the signal."

When the signal sounded, I left a message asking Harry to call me. Then I went to the darkroom to take the prints out of the washing tank and to run them through the dryer. I was hoping that what I had seen earlier was some kind of aberration and that I would find an ordinary set of portraits. Nothing had changed, though. That is, the prints hadn't changed; but since my shock had worn off to some extent, I was able to see them more objectively. They were striking photographs. Probably anyone who looked casually at some of the stranger prints would assume that I had made them by superimposing separate exposures. But when you looked at them carefully it became apparent that there was an inevitability about the way the images were related to one another. You knew that what you were seeing could not represent reality, but you also knew that it could not represent the manipulations of a fanciful photographer.

For one thing, the infant that Joanne was holding in the picture —I might as well call her Colnee—did not look like your ordinary baby. She had a look of affliction that no photographer could have come across except in doing the illustrations for a book on child abuse. And the man who appeared in the last picture in the series did not look as if he had ever heard of T-shirts or Perrier.

I took the prints to my bedroom and spread them out on the floor. I lay down on the bed, with my head over the edge of the mattress, facing the prints. I stared at the little exhibition, and I wondered what to think about it.

The phone rang. It was Harry.

"You're conscientious, Harry."

"I always return your calls, Jonathan. I know you don't make them idly. And I thought you might have some circular pictures for me to vend."

"Not circular—spectral."

"Spectral? Indeed!" I had given Harry pause. The pause was filled with distant sounds of clicking tableware and loud voices. He seemed to be in a restaurant in which people did more drinking than eating. I wondered whether I had nonplussed Harry, but, as I was well aware, he was not exactly nonplussable. His pause was brief. "That's the third time this week that I've heard the word 'spectral.' The other two people who used it are part of a restless group that has concluded that there must be more to life than roller skating. Séances are enjoying a bit of a vogue. People chat quite a bit about ectoplasm. Do your new efforts exhibit any ectoplasm?"

"I'm not sure. Just ghosts, I think."

"Are they real ghosts, Jonathan?"

"Are any ghosts real?"

"I mean, did you fabricate them?"

"All I did was let light into the box. If any fabricating was done, the camera did it."

"How many prints do you have?"

"About six that are any good."

"Will you be having more?"

"I'm not sure. It's a complicated situation."

"Then you're talking complications and not business."

"I guess so, Harry." I was beginning to whine.

"Do you want me to stop by tonight?"

"It's up to you. I'm not doing anything but working up some self-pity."

"You need to meet some new and stimulating people, Jonathan."

"Did you have anyone in mind?"

"I'm with Lee Ferris at the moment. We've been sharing a ghastly gastronomic experience. I can see the pastry cart from here, and it seems to be displaying the winning entries in a stomach-upset competition. They've even resorted to chocolate cake. We could cut things short here and adjourn to your place for dessert."

"I think there are some raspberries here."

"We'll bring something to go with them."

"Wait a minute, Harry. I'm not sure Lee Ferris and I would get along. I don't like big, aggressive people who hate my photographs."

"Nonsense, Jonathan. She loves your work."

"She said something about passport pictures."

"No, no. You know I exaggerate sometimes."

"She invaded your office."

"That was business, dear boy."

"You know I don't like to be dear-boyed, Harry."

"I won't allow you to be truculent, Jonathan. You need company."

"Why don't you come alone?"

"Impossible. You'll love Lee."

"I gather that's your department. I don't have anything to say to her."

"You could ask her to tell you about Sara Coleridge."

He had me. "See you shortly," I said and hung up. I still wasn't pleased about meeting Lee Ferris. I didn't mind meeting strangers as long as I was free to allow them to remain strangers, but no-option friendships made me uncomfortable. Harry usually understood that, so I could only assume that Big Lee still had control of his emotional immunity systems. But maybe he just wanted my opinion of her and not necessarily my approval.

Harry showed up with comestibles. There was nothing surprising about that, but Lee Ferris was definitely a surprise. Harry had said she was large and Slavic, and I had expected to see someone who might win a bronze medal in one of the more obscure Olympic events. Instead, she turned out to be invitingly unathletic. I would have cast her as a hostess in a posh European restaurant. She wasn't exactly petite—perhaps an inch taller than Harry, and she was a trace over the weight that would have been ideal for her—but there was nothing at all Amazonian about her. She was a blonde, but seemed more Scandinavian than Slavic to me. Her strength seemed to be in her speech, which was back-of-the-throat, side-of-the-mouth, and undiplomatic. Nevertheless, the effect was defensive rather than aggressive. I think she was dressed unfashionably, but I'm never sure about those things. Maybe the quality that Harry originally found terrifying about her was that she projected a powerful, unrelenting aura of sexuality.

Harry was doing a lot of fluttering. He made the introduction and then wandered off to the kitchen with the parcels he had brought. Lee and I sat down. She crossed her legs, allowing her moderately long skirt to slide above her knees. And she was displaying a somewhat immoderate stretch of well-formed thigh. I might have written that off as accidental, except that she was wearing old-fashioned, garter-secured stockings that ended just above her knees. Thus, the thigh she was displaying was bare. No accident.

Gentleman—or coward—that I was, I kept my eyes on her eyes and put my peripheral vision in charge of the rest of her anatomy. I wondered how Harry was dealing with such problems.

Lee glanced around the shadowy stretches of the studio. "You've got an oasis here, Jonathan . . . an oasis. God, it's soothing to be in a place that hasn't been savaged by some parasitic asshole of a failed painter trying to establish some nauseating visual theme that will get some color supplement to add to the boredom of everyone's Sunday by reproducing pictures that are only looked at by other twits that want to have pictures of their places published. And you get sweaty hands trying not to think about what garbage it all is, and the color comes off on your fingers. And I really need an oasis today after dealing with that camel of a piano player who just *had* to have his own Bösendorfer shipped to some suburb of Detroit for one recital that's sure to be ill attended. Their Steinway wouldn't do—as if he or anyone else interested in hearing him could tell a Steinway from shoe polish. A real oasis, Jonathan. We had to skirt (forgive me) obese transvestites on our way to this restaurant that was a culinary equivalent of a massage parlor, where they served us meat—not fish, but meat—that had sand in it. Probably camel meat. God, Jonathan, I was ready for an oasis. Do you like crêpes?"

"Do I like who?"

"Crêpes. Little pancakes."

"Oh. Oh, sure." She made the word sound like "krepps," and I thought maybe that was the piano player she had mentioned. She meant the things that I thought of as "crapes"—rubbery disks rolled into tubes and filled with leftovers.

"Babes wants me to concoct a few."

I supposed "Babes" was Harry; a Harry I hadn't known before.

"And I suppose I have to do *something* for him."

Lee recrossed her legs. She had been revealing the left thigh, and now she displayed an even more generous portion of the right, which was decorated with a pink pressure mark. I thought the momentary silence was meant to give me a chance to talk, but it was apparently just for looking.

Lee forged ahead. "I have phenomenal good fortune in the kitchen. I can do no wrong there, although God knows I can call up disaster almost anywhere else. Just put me in contact with a musical instrument and you'll wish you were deaf. But I can cook. Irony is too much with us, I think. That's what they'll find when they finally crack the genetic code—the force that controls all is irony."

Lee seemed to have stopped talking. I gave her a few seconds so that I could be sure, and I wondered whether what slowed her up was a real regret over not being able to be a musician. I took the part of the host and tried to console her. "Who's to say that music is more important than food? After all, you can live without music."

"That's just the dreary point. Escoffier—are you ready for some wisdom?—was trying to give somebody a beautiful time, but J. S. Bach was making time itself beautiful. I know that sounds like a failed attempt at profundity, but I really do think about old Bach on his deathbed, dictating a chorale, and it just doesn't seem to matter a hell of a lot whether the sauce needs a pinch more chervil. Well, I couldn't harmonize a hymn tune for shit, but you'll never fool me about chervil. Also, he had about twenty children—Bach—and Ferris is bringing a new meaning to the word 'barren.' I don't suppose Escoffier had any children. But you do, don't you, Jonathan?"

Harry had reentered the room. He walked over to her, pulled her skirt down over her knees, and said, "Escoffier had two children." He took Lee's hands and urged her to her feet. "Now, dearest girl, go and imitate Escoffier—in his kitchen, rather than bedroom, persona—while Jonathan and I discuss some business."

Lee smiled at me and headed for the kitchen.

"What do you think of her?" Harry asked.

"Chatty . . . and sexy. Not the ogre you described at all."

"You're only seeing her more restrained side. In the office, she's a wolverine. A master of agentry. She doesn't have my cunning, but she excels me in ruthlessness."

"It sounds as though you're ready to form a partnership of some kind."

"More of that anon. Let's look at pictures."

I got the prints for Harry and sat back as he looked at them. His air of giddiness vanished quickly. He went through them three times. Then he said, "These are pictures of ghosts, Jonathan."

"That's what I told you."

"But we don't believe that ghosts exist, do we?"

"I don't."

"Then explain yourself," Harry said.

I told him about the portrait session with Joanne, and about her invisible friend Colnee.

"You don't take good enough care of your daughter, Jonathan. I think there's some parental neglect here."

"What the hell do you mean, Harry? What the hell do you know about parenthood?"

"You're being truculent again, dear boy. All I mean is that well-bred children don't attract ghosts."

We glared at each other. At least, I glared. Harry looked injured. I wondered what had happened to the basically pleasant accommodation I had made to life.

Lee came in and broke the grim silence for a moment: "I thought you two were friends." No one answered her. She went over to Harry and took the photographs from him. "May I?" she asked. No answer. She looked through the prints slowly and then said, "These are beautiful."

"Are they?" I asked.

"Of course they are," Lee said.

"Of course they are," Harry said.

"Well, why didn't someone mention it before?"

Harry smiled. "Didn't I mention it? They're stunning. We'll need some more, of course. But I'll leave that up to you. I'll set up a show right away. And we'll do a book. No text. No text at all, because these are obviously inexplicable. What should we call them? 'Spectral' is what I think you said, Jonathan. What about 'The Specter and the Child'?"

"Is it your child?" Lee asked.

"Yes . . . Joanne."

Lee looked at me with what might have been envy. Then her expression turned panicky. "Oh, my God," she said, "the *framboises*."

"The what?" I said.

"The raspberries," Harry said.

We rushed to the kitchen, and Lee and Harry headed for the stove and ministered to the raspberries. The table was set for four. Coffee was warming over a little votive candle, and Lee had found the cognac Harry had brought on his last visit. I gathered that the berries were under control. Harry said, "I thought maybe Joy might want to join us." I went to get her, and we all sat down to the crêpes, which were wrapped around raspberries and doused with warm raspberry sauce and cold whipped cream.

Nanny Joy and Lee seemed to like each other, and they did most of the talking during the meal. Lee thought Duke Ellington was undoubtedly the most important American composer. Joy had known a booking agent who had handled Ellington, and she kept Lee fascinated with a description of the complications of one-night stands and cross-country bookings. When it was time for cognac, Harry tapped a spoon on his glass.

"An announcement of unparalleled importance," he said. "Miss Ferris and I are to be married."

There was a silence that was longer than it should have been. Everyone looked a little embarrassed.

I raised my glass and said; "To the happy couple." It wasn't a very original—or a very appropriate—thing to say. For the first time since she arrived, Lee Ferris was subdued. And Harry was now wearing an expression of simple fear. My own reactions were fairly complicated. Basically, I was feeling shock and disbelief. Marriage seemed unthinkable for Harry. But I was also conscious of another unpleasant emotion, which might have been jealousy. Why should Harry be allowed to have his version of a soulmate, when Sara Coleridge was ignoring me? It had been a bad day. What had become of my *bon vivant* nature? I made a valiant effort to look delighted. I asked, "When's the big day?"

Harry seemed grateful for my smile. "Oh, we haven't gotten to any of the dreary practicalities yet. In the summer, perhaps, when business dwindles a bit."

Lee was smiling again. She reached over and put her hand on Harry's. He started and looked down at his hand as though Lee had poured some *framboise* juice over it.

Then Lee looked up at me with what seemed to be surprise and adoration. "Hello, dear," she said. Then I realized she was looking past my shoulder.

I turned, and Joanne was standing a few feet away, clutching a blanket around her shoulders. "I was cold," she said. She ran to me, and I picked her up and put her on my lap. She looked sleepily around the table. She said hello to Uncle Harry.

"Say hello to Miss Ferris, Joanne."

"Hello, Miss Ferris." It was a warmly delivered greeting. Joanne knew an admiring gaze when she saw one.

"Uncle Harry and Miss Ferris are going to get married."

Joanne gave the standard response to that announcement: silence and a puzzled stare.

I decided a little prompting was in order. "Isn't that nice?"

Joanne didn't answer right away. Finally, she said, "I couldn't marry Uncle Harry anyway, could I?"

"No, sweetie," I said.

"Then it's all right. I'll go to bed again now."

Nanny Joy got up and took Joanne in her arms. "I'll tuck her in," she said. "And maybe I'll stay with her for a while. Nice to have met you, Lee. Congratulations to both of you." She winked at Harry. "You devil," she said.

After a flurry of goodnights, Joy started for the bedroom with Joanne. When they were a few feet away, I heard Joanne say, "There was blood on their plates, like in my dream." I hoped the dream was just the result of too much berrycake.

Lee said, with a tone that seemed more than merely polite, "Joanne is stunning. You're not as lucky as Bach, but you're lucky."

"I know," I said. And then I realized she was right. I began to feel better than I had all day. My eyes developed a little preweep prickling.

Lee said, "I suddenly and definitely have had enough consciousness for one day."

Harry stood up. "Maybe I'll talk a little more business with Jonathan, Lee. I'll put you in a cab."

Put her in a cab? This is the lover talking? "Never mind, Harry," I said. "I can see you in the office tomorrow."

"I'm pretty well booked up, I'm afraid. And I think we should move quickly on this new series."

Lee didn't seem upset by the arrangement. I said goodnight to her. At the door, I gave her a chaste embrace and directed my lips toward her cheek. She intercepted my mouth with hers and presented me with a moist, not exactly chaste kiss. I wondered what sort of performance she gave with people she loved, or at least had known for more than a couple of hours.

When Harry returned, I said, "What the hell kind of thing is that—letting your lover wander the streets alone?"

"She's not my lover, Jonathan. She's my fiancée."

"What does that mean?"

Harry had recaptured some of his boulevardier self-confidence—although not all of it. "It means," he said, "that I've been avoiding intimate encounters with my intended."

"It seems to me that that might take a little effort."

"Constant vigilance. The lady has a passionate nature."

"And you don't?"

"Not as yet, Jonathan. Actually, that's what I wanted to consult you about."

"You want some passion lessons?"

"One might put it that way."

"One *did* put it that way. But one is afraid one can't help you."

"It's simply a matter of reviewing a few basic techniques."

"So buy a book. There are lots of them now—with pictures."

"You know I'm particular about pictures, Jonathan."

"Some of them have drawings. Picasso did some."

"Too many, I'm sure. He did too many of everything. Not at all good for the market."

"Look, Harry, it's out of the question. Why don't you just put yourself in Lee's hands—so to speak—and tell her you're a virgin? She'll love it. She's obviously a take-charge person in that department, anyway."

"But I want her to respect me. Do women respect virgins?"

"Everyone respects a virgin, Harry. At least, they respect the opportunity to remove someone from that category. Take my word, she'll love it. And besides, if the first time is a fiasco, which it usually is, you'll have an excuse."

Harry considered my advice. I felt uncomfortable. I suppose I should have been scratching my head and chuckling, but I was not amused. I have never been interested in anyone else's sex life except in the few instances in which I wanted to become a permanent part of it.

Harry began to perk up. "You're right," he said. "Of course. You're right. I'd like to use your phone." He dialed. "This is Harrykins, little one. . . ."

(Little one?)

". . . My business with Jonathan isn't taking as long as I expected. When you get home . . ."

He was talking to her answering machine.

". . . why don't you get comfortable and open a bottle of something out of the ordinary? I'll be there soon." Harry's eyes were glinting as if he were about to complete a big sale. I guess he was. He straightened his mustard-yellow cravat, shook hands with me, and went off into the night.

I went into my bedroom. I took my shoes off and then decided I wasn't up to taking anything else off. I collapsed onto the bed, realizing that I hadn't found time to talk to Lee Ferris about Sara Coleridge. It hadn't been my night for advancing my romantic impulses.

Harry, however, did pretty well for himself in that department. Sometime before dawn, my telephone rang. I struggled with the instrument for a while, getting the receiver to my ear in time to hear Harry's voice saying: "You were right. Absolutely right. It went off smashingly."

"As long as it went off."

Harry paused to sort out entendres. "Oh. Yes. Very good. Twice, as a matter of fact."

"I'm glad for you, Harry."

And this was the man I had admired—the captain of commerce, the shuck-buddy of the chic.

"It's not going to be an imposition at all, I'd say. *Au contraire.*"

"Oh, go to bed, Harry."

Harry wasn't listening. "And you'll never guess what she told me."

"I won't even try."

"She told me I'm well hung, Jonathan."

"She *told* you that? Didn't you *know* that?"

"Well, no. I hadn't given it much thought."

I replaced the receiver. I'd leave Harry to his thoughts, whatever they were. Not that I wished him ill. *Au contraire.*

Chapter 6

The next thing I was conscious of was Joanne's voice reminding me that I had been sleeping with my clothes on.

"Why didn't you take them off, Daddy?"

"They said they didn't want to leave me. They're very fond of me."

"I'm very fond of you, too, Daddy. And I don't want to leave you. Maybe I shouldn't go to school today."

"What would Ms. Abraham say?"

"Something only other teachers understand."

I took my daughter in my arms and wondered why I thought I needed any other ladies in my life.

"I could let you take some more pictures," Joanne said.

"Not today, sweetie."

I lifted Joanne up to my shoulders and horsied her to where Harry and I had left the portraits I had taken yesterday. I spread the prints out on the floor and put Joanne down among them. She picked them up one by one, handling them as if they were newborn kittens. She was respectful, pleased, and completely absorbed. Then she began to cry softly.

I asked, "Do the pictures make you unhappy?"

Joanne shook her head.

"Do you know who those people are?"

"Colnee and her daddy."

"Do you see Colnee and her daddy outside the pictures?"

"When I want to."

"Only when you want to?"

Another nod.

"They don't frighten you?"

"No."

"Do you know why you see them?"

Joanne jumped up and headed for her bedroom. "I have to go to school now," she said. And in the distance I heard her reciting that nursery rhyme, which no one should have to hear before breakfast—if ever:

My mother has killed me,
My father is eating me,
My brothers and sisters sit under the table
Picking my bones,
And they bury them under the cold marble stones.

Who the hell ever made such a thing up? It didn't even get around to rhyming until the end.

As I ate breakfast I thought of Joanne's tears and the photographs I had taken of her. Was she telling the truth when she said that she wasn't frightened by her visions of Colnee and Colnee's father? I decided that her emotions were really beside the point. The important thing for me was to figure out a way of getting rid of the visions. It was one thing for Joanne to have imaginary friends, but it was something else for her to have ghostly friends.

How would I go about getting rid of her visitors? Every approach I could think of—such as exorcism—seemed ridiculous, and I began to do what I had done throughout my life when I was faced with a serious problem of any kind: I tried to turn it into a joke. But as I looked once more at the photographs, I had to admit to myself that whatever they were, they were definitely not funny.

Next, my speculations led—as all my speculations did sooner or later—to Sara Coleridge. What was her connection to Colnee and the spectral portraits? Before long, I had forgotten about Joanne and the supernatural, and I was immersed in worshipful recollection of Sara.

And then the phone rang. I was sure it was Sara, calling to apologize for having been so abrupt the last time we talked. I picked up the receiver slowly, and a muscle under my right eye began to twitch. The twitch stopped when the caller spoke.

"Lee Ferris, Jonathan." She was using her business voice—the one with no trace of randy smile in it. "I wanted to thank you for your hospitality."

I remembered Harry's small-hours call. She had a lot more than hospitality to thank me for. "It was a pleasure," I said.

"And an item of business. I was just talking to Sara Coleridge. She changed her mind about letting you do her portrait. Don't bother to ask me (a) why she changed her mind, (b) why she didn't call you herself, (c) why she wants to do it for free, or (d) why she wants to drop in at your studio this afternoon at three. All I can tell you is she's a harpist. They're just below oboists on the instability charts. Can you see her today?"

Lee paused just long enough to let me squeak out an enthusiastic "Yes."

"I'll tell her it's okay. Busy day here. Thanks again."

After she hung up, I decided I'd better start trying to make myself irresistible. I headed for the shower. I'm of the school that showers first and shaves after, and when I got around to looking into the steam-fogged mirror, still thinking only of Sara, I discovered there was a definite blush under my stubble. I decided that what was embarrassing me was that I hadn't bothered to put a robe on or even to tie a towel around my midriff. The combination of my bareness and thoughts of Sara made me realize that the possibility of her seeing me without my full quota of clothes was unacceptable. For although I found Sara attractive in every way, I had never had any overtly sexual thoughts about her; and I didn't want to have any—at least not immediately.

After my shower, I faced the challenge of figuring out how to stay sane until midafternoon. Business was always a steadying influence on me. So I went into my studio and got the camera ready. I wanted to be sure that it would be in good working order for Sara's visit, and I also wanted to be sure that some unlikely defect in my equipment wasn't responsible for the peculiar results of yesterday's session with Joanne. Although I wasn't admitting it to myself, I also wanted to find out whether the specters had taken up permanent residence in the studio or the camera.

I set everything up in my standard arrangement: a medium-value backdrop; diffused illumination from the skylight, boosted on one side by a reflector panel. My subject was the chair I usually seat my clients in—a heavy, low-backed oak affair that I assume had been made for or by a photographer in the nineteenth century. It had an unobtrusive leather headrest at the back, attached to an adjustable vertical steel rod. The headrest was not only necessary to keep my subjects from moving during the long exposures I usually made, but it was also largely responsible for the odd quality of apprehensive dignity that many of my pictures had. The people who posed for me usually looked on the headrest as a little ally, but they were also reminded somewhat of a dentist's chair, which accounted for varying degrees of apprehension that I captured. But, basically, the device added a sense of formality to the procedure. Photography had become too cozy and familiar an activity to most people. Sometime I would like to try a really long exposure—say, three hours—to let the subject know that a significant, mysterious event is taking place; an event as important as the painting of a portrait.

In any case, I was fond of the chair, and I took as much care in photographing it that morning as I would have taken if it had been a person. I altered the intensity of the light several times and changed the position of the reflector for each shot so that no two exposures would be identical. I wasn't aware of any spectral bystanders as I worked.

When I got the prints developed, everything about them was as it should have been. There were no phantom images, and nothing was inexplicable except what is always inexplicable about photographs. The chair and its setting had undergone the usual subtle transformation. You probably know the kind of transformation I mean if you've ever taken a snapshot of a room you've lived in for years. When you see the picture, you notice things you've never noticed before. You're aware for the first time that a lampshade is the wrong size or that a bookcase is tilting. I'm not sure why that happens, but I think it's because when you see a photograph, you're not part of the space you're looking at. Something like that. I didn't know whether I felt better or not. I had apparently proved that the camera and the studio weren't haunted, but maybe that just meant that my daughter Joanne *was* haunted. I decided not to think about that problem for the rest of the day.

But I had to find something else to think about. My anxiety over Sara's impending visit was becoming unmanageable. My stomach was undergoing the back-to-school syndrome, and I began to prowl the apartment. When I found myself in front of a bookcase, taking books that were arranged by subject and rearranging them according to their height, I decided it was time to leave the apartment for an hour or two.

I went outside and began to wander. The only thoughts I could summon up were depressing little speculations about the disasters that might develop during Sara Coleridge's visit. I was definitely in need of some diversion, so I fell back on my old habit of borrowing someone else's enthusiasms. I remembered Lee Ferris's apparent devotion to the music of Bach. Had Bach written any music for the harp? Not likely. But I knew how to find out. I took a cab to a record shop in the West Forties. It was one of the few shops in the city—if not the only one—that still had booths in which you could listen to records before buying them. It was also one of the few places that required you to pay the full list price for records. But since Al, the owner, also gave you the benefit of his impressive knowledge of music and the recording industry, I figured the extra expense was justified.

Al started to tell me about the latest releases of medieval music. When I told him I was interested in something later, he asked me whether I had fallen in love. I thought his question was a little presumptuous, but since it was also appropriate, I 'fessed up. Al said that thirty years of experience had convinced him that when a person shows an abrupt change of musical taste, the reason for the change—in ninety-six out of a hundred cases—is that the person has fallen in love with someone whose musical preferences differ from his or her own. Al thought that all good music was an expression of love, and that the best music expressed a love either of God or of music itself. In Bach's case, it was an expression of both.

But apparently neither Bach nor any other important composer had much of a love for the harp. Al picked me out a few things that harpists had transcribed from Bach's music, and he also gave me an orchestral recording of Bach's *The Art of the Fugue*, an unfinished work. The recording ended with the deathbed chorale setting that Lee had mentioned.

I bought everything Al had picked out for me, and I went

home and did some listening. As much as I wanted to like the harp music, the harp sounded to me like a piano that had been involved in a really serious accident. *The Art of the Fugue* was entirely too complex for my ears and brain, and it sounded as if it had been inspired by a love not of music but of simultaneity. I think portrait photographers aren't interested in simultaneous events. They like to deal with one thing at a time. Maybe that's one of the things that bothered me about my spectral pictures: they seemed to involve not only an overlapping of images but an overlapping of time.

The only music that pleased me on the records I brought home was the chorale setting. It was a relatively simple harmonization of a Lutheran hymn, and it had none of the unbearable virtuosity of the fugues I had been listening to. It was like a perfect little apology, and I listened to it several times, until I had memorized the melody. When the doorbell rang at three o'clock, I was in a relaxed, almost devout mood that helped me fight off the panic that I began to feel when I heard the announcement over the intercom system: "It's Sara Coleridge."

I went into the hallway and waited at the elevator door. The memory of the Bach chorale began to disintegrate under the sound of whines and clanks that issued from the ancient, but supposedly safe, freight elevator that had been designed originally to haul printers' supplies. Then the door opened, and there was Sara, looking enigmatic but not displeased.

I led her into the apartment, and we sat down. Neither of us spoke for a few moments. Joanne hadn't returned from school yet, and Nanny Joy was off on a shopping trip. I was uncomfortably conscious that I was alone with Sara. She was sitting in the chair that Lee Ferris had sat in the night before. But now I had no torrents of words or tantalizing expanses of bare limb to defend myself against. Sara was wearing a dark-gray pants suit and a white turtle-neck sweater. Only her strong, slender hands and calm, apparently cosmetic-free face were uncovered. She looked about the room, glancing at me occasionally and smiling almost imperceptibly.

Sara apparently thought that I should speak first. And I finally did. "Well . . ." Then I ran out of small talk.

Sara's smile broadened. "Lee Ferris said you had some unusual pictures of your daughter."

"Lee Ferris told me you had agreed to let me take some pictures of you."

"Will you show me the pictures of your daughter?"

"I will if you'll pose for me."

Sara hesitated. "There's a distinction to be made, I think."

"What's that?"

"I'll let you take my picture, but I won't pose for you."

"I'm not sure I understand," I said.

"It's simple. I'll sit for you, but I won't take direction."

"That's no problem. I never give direction."

Sara seemed more assertive than she had the first time I talked to her. I knew there were more questions or conditions on the way. She said, "And I don't understand the purpose of this. You said you were doing a series of portraits of musicians, I think."

I'd forgotten about that desperate bit of deception.

"Yes, I said that. But it was a desperate bit of deception. I just wanted to get to know you."

"Then you don't want to take my picture?"

"Yes, I do. I honestly do."

"I don't understand the obligations. Does anyone pay anyone? And who keeps the pictures?"

Why hadn't I been thinking of these things instead of listening to Bach? What should I tell her? I decided to take a chance on the truth. "I hadn't really thought about anything except having a chance to see you again. I'll make any arrangement you want, except that I'd like to keep one of the pictures."

Sara was no longer smiling. I felt like an inept gladiator in ancient Rome, waiting for the emperor to give the thumbs-down sign. Surprisingly, the thumb went up. "Why don't we forget about any payment," Sara said, "and each get a set of prints?"

"I don't make multiple prints. There's only one of each."

"Then we'll divide them between us."

"Perfect," I said.

"And as a bonus, I get to see the pictures of your daughter."

"And I get to know you better."

"You get to try, Mr. Brewster. But as I told you once before, you're foolish if you do."

"Then why did you come to see me, Sara?"

"I didn't come to see *you*, Jonathan."

Maybe not, but now I was Jonathan.

I got out the spectral portraits and gave them to Sara. I sat across the room and watched as she examined them. I would have enjoyed watching Sara under any circumstances, but there was a particular intensity to my pleasure in looking at her as she looked at the pictures. She seemed to be undergoing some strong emotions, but I couldn't identify them. She was looking through the pictures for the second time, looking at each one for about ten seconds before going on to the next. She was chewing delicately on her lower lip, and her toes seemed to be flexing inside her scuffed, expensive shoes. I gave up trying to guess her thoughts and began to concentrate on her appearance. I had just figured out that she was long-waisted, when she put the pictures aside and said, "How do you account for these?"

"I don't account for them," I said. "Joanne has some friends that only she and the camera can see."

"Do her friends talk to her?"

"The baby does, I think. The baby's name is Colnee, and it—she—seems to be interested in food. You'll have to ask Joanne for the details. She should be home . . ."

Sara had lowered her head and covered her eyes with her hand. Her cheeks looked a shade or two paler than they had when she arrived.

"Are you all right, Sara?"

She managed a constricted little nod. And then a tear appeared on one of those white cheeks. I had no idea what I should do. Tears call for comfort, as my daughter had given me plenty of opportunity to learn over the last four and a half years. And out of mindless habit I started across the room to take Sara into my arms. But after a couple of steps I realized that she might not recognize that my motives were paternal (if that's what they were). So I just stood in the middle of the room, trying to think of the right thing to say. Nothing very appropriate sprang to mind.

And then one of life's great rewards was presented to me. Sara stood up and moved quickly into my arms. For a moment she kept her hands over her eyes, and then she put her head against my chest and embraced me. There was nothing timid about the embrace. It was fierce, as a matter of fact—and ferocity was something I hadn't expected. But I had only a few milliseconds for such speculation before my mind collapsed under a pleasureful sensory overload. My sinuses eased their tyranny enough to let me examine a complex aroma, one element of which was definitely shampoo and another of which might have been harp strings. I saw that Sara's hair, which seemed ambiguously blond from a distance, was a complex blend of auburns and flaxes. I examined a flushed ear, which was almost rimless. As the result of some odd maneuver, my tongue encountered her cheek for a moment and was rewarded with a trace of the mineral pungency of tears. Sara's body felt unexpectedly strong, and my sly senses concluded with much excitement, and a little embarrassment, that she was probably braless. All this was punctuated by her rhythmic sobbing.

My sense of time was badly dislocated. We stood there quite a while, I think—long enough for some moralizing corner of my brain to conclude that an act of consolation had become a less noble kind of act. But however long we must have stood there, some corner of my brain kept asking for more time.

But time ran out, or, rather, Nanny Joy walked in. She gave us a tolerant but hardly joyous glance and made a detour toward the kitchen. I was annoyed, but I wasn't sure whether it was because Joy had discovered us or because she didn't look as if she wanted to give us her blessing. Sara's back had been to the door, and I don't think she knew that anyone had come in. But she probably realized that I had regained some of my powers of reason—and that I was therefore becoming dangerous. She drew away from me and came up with a question that's as good a spellbreaker as any: "May I use your bathroom?" I gathered we were to pretend there had been no magic interlude. I gave her the directions she needed, and she said, in a disturbingly calm voice, "I'll be ready for picture-taking in a minute or two."

Business as usual. I went to the studio and got things ready. My brain and my knees seemed to have turned to porridge, but I was feeling extraordinarily pleased.

When Sara came into the studio, she seemed to have regained her usual look of unassertive self-assurance, but there was a dullness to her eyes that I hadn't noticed before. I hoped the dullness was a reflection of her own pleasure. She went immediately to the posing chair and sat down. I usually adjusted the headrest for my subjects, but I thought Sara might misinterpret my motives if I went over to her and took her head in my hands. Besides, I had promised not to direct her.

Sara adjusted the headrest herself. "Are you ready?" she asked.

"Whenever you are."

"How many shots do you want to take?"

"I usually do a dozen."

"Fine," she said. "I'll tell you when."

Sara closed her eyes, frowning slightly, as though she were trying to add a couple of four-digit figures. When she opened her eyes a few seconds later, the dullness had gone from her expression. She seemed not to be conscious of me or the camera, but she was obviously giving her attention to something that interested and gratified her. I thought maybe she was thinking of some music. Her look of pleasure intensified, and I was beginning to wonder whether she had forgotten about me, when she said, "Now." I made the exposure.

We repeated the process eleven times. I felt a little as if I were working with a professional model who was going through her repertoire of poses. There were a couple of important differences, though. Most models are able to call up only three or four expressions, and those expressions are vapid and strained. Sara seemed to be taking part in, or observing, some kind of drama—not a drama made up of scenes worked out neatly by a playwright, but one consisting of unexpected events involving friends.

Sara's performance astounded me, and I began to realize how little I knew about her personality. I had thought of her as a person who didn't believe in casual displays of emotion. At first I was annoyed to see how easily and convincingly she put on her little show, but soon I began to admire the performance.

After I had taken the last picture, Sara's look of asceticism and self-containment returned. She smiled calmly and asked, "Was it all right?"

"More than all right. I'm eager to get them processed."

"How long will it take?"

"I'll do it tonight. They'll be ready in the morning."

"Do you mind if I stop by tomorrow to look at them?"

"You could see them tonight, if you'd like. You could stay here until they're ready." I stopped short of suggesting that she accompany me into the darkroom.

"I can't do that, I'm afraid. I have some friends coming in to play chamber music."

I tried to keep my distress from showing. Sara stood up. "I have to leave now, Jonathan."

I wanted at least a few more minutes with her. How could I let this enigmatic person leave me? "My daughter, Joanne, will be here any minute. She'll be upset if she doesn't get to see you."

"I'm sorry, I really have to leave. Tell Joanne I'll see her some other time."

"Why don't we make a date now?"

"Not now. We can talk about it tomorrow. What time should I be here to see the pictures?"

"Any time you want, Sara."

"Ten?"

"Fine."

Sara got her bag. I watched fondly as she walked through the room. She held her body straight—too straight, perhaps—and there was a slight stiffness in her movements.

At the door, she simply said, "Thank you." Then she brushed her fingertips across the back of my hand and walked away. I closed the door and went to a window where I would be able to see her leave the building. As I looked out Joanne's school bus was pulling up at the curb. As Joanne left the bus Sara came out of the building. They looked at each other for a moment. Although I couldn't see their faces well enough to be sure, their expressions seemed to indicate pleasure more than surprise. Sara squatted down and rested her hands lightly on Joanne's shoulders. The two of them began an earnest conversation that went on for about five minutes. Sara appeared to do most of the talking. Finally, they kissed each other, and Joanne ran into the building. Before Sara walked away, she stood for a few seconds staring solemnly at the doorway.

When I let Joanne into the apartment, she didn't—as I had expected—start immediately to tell me about her encounter with Sara. Instead, we said our hellos, and I lifted her onto my shoulder. "Did anything good happen today?" I asked.

"Ms. Abraham got hit by a ball."

"That's not good, Joanne."

"Then why did it make everybody laugh?"

I didn't want to get into a discussion of moral issues. "Did anything else happen?"

"Billy Crotters said my teeth will all fall out."

"That's right. But you'll get new ones."

"But I like the ones I've got."

"You'll like the new ones better. They'll make you look like the ladies on the front of magazines."

"Will I have to take my clothes off?"

"Not those magazines. I mean the ones with ladies' faces. The ladies with the nice shiny teeth."

"My teeth have to eat a cookie now, I think."

I put my secretive daughter down, and she ran off toward the kitchen. Why hadn't she told me about having met Sara? The thought of Sara reminded me that twelve moments of her life were lying in the studio, waiting to become visible. I collected the exposures and went into the darkroom, ready to see Sara in a new way—ready to look at her with the kind of intensity that people can accept in person only from someone whose love they return.

The photographs gave me a new view of Sara, all right. But it wasn't exactly comforting. In each of the portraits, Sara was surrounded by the same kind of ghostly images that had appeared in the portraits I had done of Joanne. Baby Colnee was there and so was the man in the black suit. But there were also two other translucent figures in some of the prints: a middle-aged woman and what seemed to be an American Indian.

The time I spent in the darkroom was not relaxing or enjoyable. When I saw the first portrait, I was furious. What the hell was going on? Wouldn't I ever be able to take normal pictures again? I had set out to do a visual celebration of the woman I loved, and instead I got some kind of paper hallucinations. Actually, Sara looked stunning in the photographs. But although I tried to convince myself it wasn't true, there could be no doubt that she had been aware of the spectral figures that showed up in the prints. In every case, she was looking at or reacting to one of the other figures.

Since I had tried out the camera and proved that it didn't photograph ghosts when it was alone with me, I could only conclude that Sara and Joanne were the ones who attracted the unnatural visitors. I remembered that Joanne first began to see her friend Colnee on the day that we met Sara. I really didn't care if Sara was haunted, or whatever; that only made her seem more interesting. But I didn't want my daughter to be burdened with more than her share of unreality. From the beginning, Sara had been more interested in Joanne than in me. Was I rumpling my daughter's psyche just so that I could satisfy a romantic impulse?

I would have put the whole thing down to some kind of dementia on my part, but that wouldn't explain away the evidence of the photographs. And as I examined the photographs my professional pride, such as it is, began to assert itself. I had twelve more arresting exhibits for the show Harry was setting up. Or, actually, only six, since I had promised to give half the portraits to Sara. And they were, without exception, well worth looking at—and buying.

Sara not only looked stunning in the photographs; she displayed an unusual type of vitality, which probably grew out of the contrast between her warmth and the cold deadness of the spectral figures that surrounded her. She no longer looked like a musician or like a member of any other profession that devoted itself to an abstract subject. She had also changed physically: she looked undernourished, and the flesh of her cheeks seemed to have tightened up. I was beginning to understand that the young woman I had fallen in love with was no less complicated than anyone else.

I looked at the portraits once more, and my nervous system began to close down in protest against what I had subjected it to that day. It was time for a little moderation. I left the prints to wash, and I took a tour of the apartment. Joanne was watching some fluorescent puppets on television, and Nanny Joy was sequestered in her room.

I went to my bedroom and stretched out on the bed. I stared at the ceiling, where afterimages from Sara's portraits began to appear to me. I was surprised that they didn't seem frightening or repulsive. In a way, they comforted me, and after a few minutes I achieved the moderate person's ideal state: dreamless sleep.

When I reentered the world, it was with Joanne's help. She was snorting and whooshing in my ear and reminding me that I make complicated, disgusting sounds when I sleep—a fact that various females, beginning with my mother, had pointed out to me at various times. For a few years I refused to believe that something I enjoyed as much as sleep could lead me to do anything grotesque. But the testimony to the contrary was unanimous, so I accepted it as the truth.

"I don't like you when you sleep, Daddy."

"Why not?"

"You make funny noises and you look funny and you don't talk to me."

Having someone wake me up and criticize me was not my idea of a good time, and I was about to say something to that effect, when I got a better look at Joanne. She was wearing only panties and ankle socks, and she was as beautiful and unselfconscious as a melon. A child's body is handsome in a way an adult's can never be. For one thing, most of us can look at an immature body without getting our hormones stirred up. And a child's flesh doesn't usually display too many reminders of the ills that it is heir to.

Nothing immoderate in the way of smells and hair. A hint of rib, a tightness to the tummy.

I embraced my daughter, who then asked, "Will you miss me when I die, Daddy?"

Oh, fine. Spreading cheer. I didn't want to show my dismay, so I said, "Is that something you're planning to do soon?"

"Will you miss me, Daddy?"

"I won't have to. I made a pact. You don't have to die."

"Somebody has to die."

"Not you, sweetie."

"It's all right if you miss me."

"We'll discuss that when you have a few stretch marks."

"Yes."

"Aren't you going to ask me what stretch marks are?"

"No. I think you're being silly."

I let my jaw fall slack, and I did some noisy throat-breathing. Joanne giggled, but I was wondering what the hell was going on in her mind.

I spent as conventional an evening as I could manage. I dried Sara's portraits and forced myself to forget about them and her. I asked Nanny Joy if I could deprive her of the stupefying pleasure of washing the dishes. I concentrated on the multicolored strings that made up the dishmop. I counted the chips (23), cracks (12), and different patterns (5) in the dishes.

After indulging myself with a couple of giveaway-show reruns on the telly and taking my pulse a few times, I sat down with Nanny Joy.

"Does Joanne know what death means?" I asked her.

"Does anyone?"

"I'm serious. She was talking about it today."

"Joanne doesn't know what next week means, Mr. B. Time is hard to get the hang of. And I don't think you really know about death unless you know something about time."

"Then why does she talk about dying?"

"All kids talk about it. It's in all the stories."

"Why the hell is that? I've never understood why it's in the stories."

"Probably just because it makes a good ending."

"A good ending is everybody living happily ever after."

"Nobody lives ever after. Especially not the wicked witch."

"But you don't think Joanne's turning strange or anything?"

"Lord, no. I wouldn't let that happen."

"You like her a lot, don't you?"

"I love her, Jonathan. And I'm grateful that you gave me the chance for that. I'd forgotten what it was like."

"Does she love us?"

"Oh, sure. But when you're that age you tend to love everybody or nobody. She goes for everybody."

"But we're special."

"Of course we're special."

"You're special, Joy." I kissed her on the cheek and started for bed.

As I left the room Joy said, "Nothing bad is going to happen to Joanne. I'll see to that."

Soon I was staring at my bedroom ceiling again, watching pale, now-familiar shapes. For a moment I wondered whether I had fallen into Joanne's habit of attracting invisible friends. But the forms I was seeing were not my own creations; they were the creations—or maybe "discoveries" was a better term—of Sara and Joanne. Were the discoveries good or bad? I didn't have to worry about that, because Nanny Joy had just told me she wouldn't let anything bad happen to Joanne. Before I closed my eyes it occurred to me that Joy and I might not have the same definition of good. That could cause us problems, I supposed.

At quarter to ten the next morning, I began peeking out the window into the street. At two minutes after ten, Sara Coleridge turned the corner. She was walking quickly, and I took that as a sign that she was eager to see me. Of course, it also could have meant that she wanted either to see her portraits or to get out of the light spring rain that had begun to fall.

I had made coffee and had left it warming in the living room next to two cups (carefully chosen to match) and the portraits of Sara. We sat down and I poured the coffee while Sara looked through the portraits. There were no tears this time—a development I didn't welcome, because it meant that there would be no occasion for a consoling embrace. Sara divided the prints into two equal stacks. She picked up one stack and said, "I'd like to have these, if I may." The portraits were on their way into her handbag before I could say anything. Sara sipped her coffee absentmindedly, and I waited for her to tell me what she thought of the portraits.

"This is good coffee," she said.

"Harry Bordeaux bought it—my agent. He likes good food. He'd also like me to exhibit your portraits. Do you have any objection?"

"No. But I suppose *my* agent might."

"Lee Ferris? She and Harry are thinking of getting married. They can split his commission."

Sara looked interested. "Someone is in love with Lee Ferris?"

"Does that surprise you?"

"Yes. Quite a bit."

"Why?"

"She's not the type."

"I didn't know there was a type."

"Yes. I think there is."

"What is the type?"

"I'm the type."

I couldn't argue with that. But I wasn't pleased to hear it. It seemed to mean that I had competitors. And it didn't sound exactly modest, although I decided not to say so. But I didn't have to, because Sara said, "That might sound immodest, but I don't mean it that way. It's just that people do fall in love with me—often enough so that I've had to think about why they do it."

I began to get the feeling I was being warned off. "So why do they do it?"

"Some people like mysteries. They think I have a mysterious personality. But they're wrong. I don't have any personality at all. Hadn't you noticed that?"

"No. Of course not."

"Then tell me what kind of personality I have."

I hesitated.

"You see?" Sara said.

"I don't know you well, that's all."

"There's nothing to know, Jonathan. If I were to continue to see you, I would begin to take on your qualities. I'm a chameleon that way. When I'm with Lee Ferris, I turn aggressive and my sentences get long. There's really nothing much to me—certainly nothing mysterious."

"Your portraits are a little mysterious."

"That has nothing to do with my personality."

"What *does* it have to do with, Sara?"

Sara weighed a few words. Then she made the worst possible announcement: "I think I'd better go now."

A little too vehemently, I said, "But you can't do that." Sara raised her eyebrows slightly. "All right," I continued, "you *can* do that. But it would be irresponsible."

"Do I have a responsibility to you?"

"Not to me, but to Joanne. You've given her your hallucinations or whatever they are. I've got photographic evidence of it."

"That won't last. I'll go away and everything will return to normal."

I drank a little cold coffee. Sara put her cold, wet shoes on. We stood up and walked to the door.

Despair and anger were competing for my attention, and I was wondering which one would win the battle. Sara looked as if she had only pity to contend with. She said, "I've caused a disturbance in your life. I'm sorry."

"It's one of the better disturbances I've come across. But I'd like to know at least one thing. I saw you talking to Joanne when you left yesterday. Will you tell me what you talked about?"

"She did most of the talking. She was telling me that her toads died."

"Her *toads* died? She didn't tell me that."

"She was afraid you'd think it was her fault."

"She was talking about death yesterday. I guess it was the toads that put it in her mind."

"And you thought maybe I had put it in her mind?"

"I suppose so."

"What makes you think I would do something like that?"

"I don't know. You're an unusual person."

"A mysterious person, you mean."

"Yes. I love you."

Sara smiled. "Good-bye, Jonathan." She tried to open the door but couldn't deal with the three locks that adorned it. She stood aside, apparently expecting me to help her. I held my ground and tried to think of something to say that might keep her from leaving. I didn't have much luck. "Were you born in this country?" I asked.

Sara gave me an unkind glance. She moved back to the door and began to turn various knobs and to pull on the door handle.

Sara continued to struggle with the locks. What she needed to know was that the top and bottom bolts had to be turned to the right, and the middle one to the left. I sidled over to see how angry she was. She had begun to smile again. "I wasn't born in Manhattan, if that's what you mean. Most Americans think of Manhattan as a foreign country, and I suppose it shows." She stood aside again. "Open the door, please. And don't expect me to answer any more questions." The smile was gone, but she still didn't look angry.

I took a chance: "Are you romantically involved with anyone?"

"No."

"You don't like men?"

"I don't like *silly* men—or women."

"I'm a serious person."

"You told me that once, but I haven't any evidence of it."

"Hold still," I said. I put my head close to Sara's interesting ear and began to hum the melody of Bach's last composition.

Sara drew away. "You're not musical and you're not amusing, Jonathan."

"I wasn't trying to be amusing. Wasn't Bach a serious person?"

"He was more than that. He was devout."

Then something occurred to me for the first time: Sara was a religious person. That would account for the ascetic undercurrent in her personality—or, as she would have it, her nonpersonality. It was natural that I would have trouble recognizing devoutness, because I had never before known anyone who could convince me that they had that quality. I reached over and unbolted the locks. Sara pulled the door open and went out without saying anything.

I didn't bother to close the door, and I didn't bother to find a chair. I sat down cross-legged on the floor. My eyes began to sting, so I closed them. I felt like some kind of Eastern holy man who had discovered the secret of life only to have it slip his mind. I thought I might as well have a mantra. I began a rhythmic chant of "Damn . . . damn . . . damn . . ."

After a few moments, I thought I heard a woman's voice tentatively speak my name. I stopped muttering and opened my eyes. Sara was standing in the doorway. "I forgot my raincoat," she said.

It seemed best not to try to explain my activities. I devoted myself to some serious blushing instead. Sara walked over to me and put her hand on my head. I responded by pressing my cheek against her thigh. Instead of drawing away as I expected her to, Sara held my head tightly to her body. "Do I really mean that much to you?" she asked. Her voice was distant, and I thought I could feel its faint vibrations in the warm flesh that lay beneath her thin wool skirt. I put my arms around her legs and hugged. In the process, I caught her in back of her knees and unintentionally threw her off balance. She made a little squeak of distress and then, not too gracefully, joined me on the floor. I was glad to see that she was smiling as she scuttled about on her hands and knees and settled into something resembling the lotus position and faced me across the rug.

"You're not hurt?" I asked her.

"No. But you are. There's blood at the left corner of your mouth." Now that she mentioned it, I realized that the left side of my face was a little painful. Sara's knee had probably hit me there when she fell. She leaned forward and touched the corner of my mouth with her finger. Then she held the finger up so that I could see that a bead of blood clung to it. I reached toward the back pocket of my trousers to get my handkerchief. But then Sara did something that stopped my hand in midair. She touched her fingertip to her tongue and tasted the blood. I had no idea how to react. Was she trying to be amusing, or disgusting, or—in an unsettling way—erotic? Since she was staring distractedly over my shoulder, I supposed it was none of those things. Whatever her little gesture meant, it was not for my benefit.

I got out my handkerchief and said, "A little vampirism in the family?"

Sara stopped looking at the wall and started looking at me; first at my eyes and then at my mouth. She smiled and said, "It's nothing that simple." Then she crawled forward, extended her tongue slightly, ran it up my chin, and gently kissed the corner of my mouth. I put my hands around her upper arms, but she moved backward and pulled out of my grip. I was excited and confused and a little embarrassed. I was less certain than ever of what kind of person Sara might be, but I was as determined as ever to find out more about her.

"Why can't we just have dinner together once in a while?" I asked.

"If we could do that, I wouldn't have any objection at all. But you're looking for more than a dinner companion, Jonathan. You want someone who has a history you can become part of and who can be a mother to Joanne. I won't give you those things."

"I won't ask for those things. We'll just have dinner."

"We would have to talk. Unfortunately, people always have to talk."

"We'll talk about music; about why G sharp and A flat aren't the same note. You can tell me about the harp."

Sara looked at me skeptically, but I thought she might be relenting a little. I continued to press whatever advantage I might have gained. I was holding my handkerchief against the side of my mouth, and though I lost a little in enunciation, I picked up quite a bit in poignancy. "I could do some portraits of you and Joanne together."

That suggestion seemed neither to gain me any points nor lose me any. I decided that the next plea would be the last. There had to be something that she would find irresistible. It was obvious that she had been able to resist what she had seen and heard of me so far. So, if Sara was not interested in my mind or my body, what was left to tempt her with? Should I offer to sell her my soul?

With an agility that I could never match, Sara uncrossed her legs and moved into a squatting position that could only signal the approach of another good-bye. I had to play my last card.

"You could tell me about God," I said.

The card turned out to be a high one. Sara gave me a nice warm steady stare. "Beware of people who want to tell you about God," she said. "The best way to find out about God is to listen to God."

It would have been helpful if someone had given my late wife that warning. "You're warning me to beware of you?" I asked.

"You should be careful of all strangers, Jonathan."

"I *thought* that might be your policy."

"But I'm not going to tell you about God."

I tried to look disappointed, but I didn't get the feeling I was being successful. I thought I'd better resort to honesty. "Actually," I said, "I wasn't so eager to hear about God."

"I know. But it was clever of you to think of Him. I'll have dinner with you."

"When?" I asked.

"Whenever I'm free."

"Tonight?"

"Yes."

I felt like dancing—an impulse I had had maybe twice before in my life. I scrambled to my knees and, with no motive but joy, put my arms around Sara. In the process, I pulled her forward so that she was also on her knees. Sara didn't seem to be having any uncontrollable impulses. She kept her arms in front of her, with her hands on her thighs. For a few seconds, she was patient with me, and maybe even compliant. But then she put her hands on my arms and slightly levered herself away from me. I stood and took Sara's hands and helped her up. Her hands, like mine, were strong, warm, and slightly damp. But, unlike mine, hers were limber—which she proved by maneuvering them quickly out of my grasp.

"Where would you like to eat?"

"That doesn't matter. That is, the food doesn't matter. Somewhere quiet, though."

"I only know of one quiet restaurant. It's quiet because the food is bad and expensive."

"That sounds nice."

"Will I have to do all the talking?"

"I can talk."

"But you won't talk about your personal history, or marriage, or God."

"There are other things."

"G sharp and A flat?"

"We'll do better than that, Jonathan. We'll do all right."

We arranged to meet at her apartment. I got Sara's raincoat —a garment I was indebted to—and went with her down to the street entrance. The rain had stopped. As we stood saying our farewell Sara moved just imperceptibly in my direction. I took the movement to be an invitation, so I kissed her cheek. It was a timid effort, but enough contact was involved to give me a twinge that reminded me I had had a little accident with my mouth. I had left a little trace of that reminder on Sara's cheek. "You've got blood on your face," I said.

Sara Coleridge smiled and walked away.

Chapter 7

Sara lived in a big old apartment building that had been designed —appropriately enough—to accommodate artists and musicians. Essentially, that meant that it had large rooms and thick walls—two qualities that construction companies hadn't been bothering much with in Manhattan since the late thirties, which is when Sara's apartment house had most likely been built. I was surprised for a couple of reasons when I saw the building. First, I wondered how Sara could afford to live in such a place; and second, I didn't expect that the landlord would let professional musicians or painters stay there, no matter how large their income. Such places were usually occupied by people who sold art rather than by those who made it.

I had another surprise when the doorman turned out to be polite and cheerful. He announced me on the intercom and sent me up to apartment 3-C. On the way up, I speculated on how Sara's place would be decorated. I thought Middle-Period Spartan would be most likely. I arrived at 3-C and found that its door was fitted with a brass knocker in the shape of what seemed to be an infant's head. I knocked. When the door opened I decided that I must have got the apartment number wrong, because standing in the doorway was a tall young woman of decidedly Oriental heritage.

She looked inquisitively at me and said, "Jonathan?"

I nodded.

"I'm Pamela Kim, Sara's roommate. Come in."

The surprises continued. For one thing, I'm unsophisticated enough to receive a little shock when I meet someone with Oriental features who sounds as though she had been born in Ohio. But even if there had been nothing distinctive about Pamela, I would have been startled just to find that Sara had a roommate. My apparently inaccurate lover's instinct had told me that Sara was a solitary person. I was relieved to find I had been wrong.

I was also wrong about the matter of apartment decor. Pamela escorted me through a short hallway that was decorated with Oriental scroll paintings. Most of them were atmospheric landscapes in delicate colors, but their restrained effect was offset by the fact that there were dozens of them. The hallway led into an enormous room that looked something like an exhibition area at a textile designers' convention. Floral-patterned draperies were hung on all four walls, making it impossible to tell where the windows might be. The room contained six chairs and two sofas, all upholstered in contrasting floral fabrics. Hanging from the high ceiling was a sort of segmented dragon kite, which was not made of paper but of intricately printed fabric. My eyes had a lot of difficulty deciding where to settle until they spotted, in a corner of the room, a low platform on which rested a cello, a straight-backed wooden chair, and a music stand.

As Pamela led me through the room I wondered how Sara could live there amid such clashing colors and shapes, and still retain her calm manner. After only a minute or so, I was already beginning to twitch a bit. And Pamela, although she wasn't very talkative, was moving a little more quickly than most people do. As we entered the room, she had picked up a lighted cigarette from an ashtray and was puffing eagerly on it. We went to a door at the far side of the room, and Pamela knocked on it and called out, a little more loudly than seemed necessary, "Jonathan's here, Sara." Then Pamela turned quickly and put her hand on my arm. "Nice to meet you," she said. Her gaze still seemed frankly inquisitive, and although there didn't seem to be any hostility involved, she didn't exactly overwhelm me with friendliness. But before I had time to speculate any further about Miss Kim, the door opened, and Sara invited me into another world—one that I understood much better. Sara's part of the apartment was unadorned. Nothing at all hung on the white walls, and the room was dominated by an enormous golden harp. After a moment I became aware of another, smaller, harp, together with a sofa and two chairs upholstered in natural linen. Middle-Period Spartan style, I would have said.

Sara seemed a little more pleased to see me than Pamela had been.

"You have a roommate," I said. And I realized that I was a little jealous of Pamela. I had probably stared at her more inquisitively and belligerently than she had at me.

"Pamela was born in Korea," Sara said. "She's restless, but she's a good cellist."

"Have you known her long?"

"No. Actually, I don't know much about her except what I've just told you. I've also noticed that she doesn't like to sleep alone. But we have separate bedrooms, and the way the apartment is set up, I don't see much of her visitors."

"She has an odd sense of interior decoration."

"All that fabric? That's mostly to control the room's acoustics. Pamela thinks printed fabrics absorb sound differently from plain fabrics. And she might be right. She has incredibly sensitive ears."

"You don't worry as much about acoustics?"

"In my own way, I do. But the harp is different from the cello. I like a lot of reverberation in the room."

"And not as much visual distraction?"

"I don't like to use too many senses at one time. I like concerts more than opera; books more than television."

I tried to figure out what this might mean in terms of my friendship with Sara: eyes closed while we chatted? Touching in the dark would seem to be allowable esthetically, but there might be objections to it on other grounds. Actually, I was not eager to get into a sexually provocative situation with Sara. I'm too easily provoked in that area. There are very few women—regardless of their age, character, or physique—who wouldn't arouse me under the right conditions; and, like many people, I tend to confuse sex with love. I remember that as an adolescent I seriously thought love was the emotion I felt on the few occasions when I had seen a girl or a woman in her underwear (seeing a naked lady created more complicated feelings—which might be classified as either love or as mere dirtiness). And although my feelings about such matters had changed since early adolescence, I still believed that a relationship was on much firmer ground when its participants remained fully (and modestly) clothed for a reasonable period.

In any case, I was relieved when Sara didn't offer to show me her bedroom. We left immediately for the restaurant. When we opened the door that connected Sara's studio with Pamela's, the sound of some extremely complicated but rich-sounding cello music engulfed us. Pamela was installed on her little dais. A cigarette dangled from the corner of her mouth, and her legs were straddling the body of the cello immodestly. Her skirt was raised, and if I had been twenty years younger, I would have fallen in love with her.

But, being an emotionally mature individual, I proceeded instead to take Sara to a restaurant and tell her what a splendid person I was. The restaurant was called The Book of the Dead, and it seemed to be run by a family of ill-tempered, dull-palated, money-crazy Tibetans. The dining room wasn't crowded. We both ordered what turned out to be unsymmetrical noodles garnished with something I assumed was curds and whey. Whatever it was, it gave me a new understanding of the concept of sourness. But I wasn't offended; I was unassailably happy. The best thing about the restaurant was its lighting, which was in the best film-noir style. Sara sat in rich shadow, with a tiny highlight haloing the back of her head. She kept her eyes on me. I thought at first she might simply be trying to avoid looking at her plate, but it was obvious after a few minutes that she was looking on me with interest and kindness. She wasn't exactly returning my loving gaze, but I didn't require that.

As I had every reason to expect, Sara didn't have much to say. But, less predictably, she turned out to be a challenging listener. She made me say the best kinds of things I was capable of saying. She never seemed to miss a nuance, but she never let me feel that what I said was quite good enough. In fact, goodness was very much on my mind. I didn't only feel good; I wanted to *be* good. That gave me a big problem, though, because I had no idea of how to go about being good; it was a topic that didn't come up very often in most of my conversations.

As we talked and ate, Sara rested her hand in the center of the small table, and I occasionally reached out and stroked her fingers. She always responded with a moderate, tolerant smile. The reaction seemed just right to me: neither a fierce returning grasp nor a flinching withdrawal.

"You're just right," I said.

"Not everyone thinks so," she said.

"That's why you should encourage my attentions."

"But you might be wrong about me, Jonathan."

"That doesn't matter. Love is probably more often than not a mistaken opinion. As long as the opinion doesn't change, there's no problem."

"But there can be big problems if the opinion changes."

"Mine won't change."

"You don't have much to base your opinion on, do you?"

"I have my senses and your presence. It all seems just right."

Sara's color seemed to have deepened a little. "Your senses can mislead you. You used to think G sharp and A flat were the same note. If you'd ever tuned a harp, you would have known that that was just an illusion. The senses thrive on illusions."

"What's wrong with an illusion that permits Bach to write *The Well-Tempered Clavier?*"

"Not much, I suppose. But some illusions lead to less admirable things; things such as meaningless death."

"I thought all death was meaningless."

Sara said, quite seriously, "Oh, no."

If any other woman I knew at that time had made a serious remark to me about death, I probably would have said something flippant and accused her of bad taste. But there was something about Sara's manner that made death seem like an acceptable, or even a pleasant, subject. But even though the topic didn't seem unpleasant, it was something I had never thought enough about to be able to discuss intelligently. Illusion seemed like a safer topic.

"What about visual illusions?" I said. "Or apparitions?"

"What about them?"

"The portraits: you and Joanne and your visitors. What is that all about?"

"There aren't any apparitions involved, Jonathan. It has to do with the past."

I couldn't resist making another reference to the risky topic. "Does it have to do with death?"

Sara stared at me for a moment. She started to say something and then apparently changed her mind. She probably sensed that I was a little apprehensive, and she must have thought it was best not to answer.

Whatever her reasoning, I noticed she didn't answer with a simple no. I assumed that meant the answer would have been a complicated yes.

I suppose I had begun to look worried. Sara smiled, then lightly and briefly squeezed my hand. In a heavy whisper, she said, "Not to worry, sweet."

The internal fanfares I had heard at our first meeting returned, only now they were accompanied by artillery. Me worry?

I had no worries for the next couple of weeks. Sara and I shared a fair amount of exotic cuisine and did a lot of devil-may-care hand-touching. I sat in the comfortable red plush of Carnegie Hall and watched as she took part (a small part) in a performance of Mahler's *Kindertotenlieder*. It was an unsettling experience for me, and I didn't listen very carefully. For one thing, I wasn't eager to hear a lady sing about the death of children. But more important, I was constantly undergoing little attacks of jealousy. Sara was in a world that excluded me. As the orchestra members straggled onto the stage before the performance a gawky young man carrying a ridiculous bassoon stopped to say something to Sara. She nodded earnestly at him. And during the performance there were tears in her eyes (I had brought binoculars). Obviously, she was not giving any thought to her sweet new friend Jonathan.

Finally I had to stop watching Sara. I looked at some of the other people on the crowded stage. The soloist, whose voice didn't seem low enough for her part, was looking apprehensive. The conductor's shoulders were slumping a bit. I spotted Pamela Kim in the cello section, and I got the impression that she needed a cigarette. My depression was mounting, so I lowered my binoculars and read the text of the songs. I hoped the German words the would-be mezzo was singing had more grace than the English translation that appeared on the program. But maybe graceful words aren't appropriate to a description of children being dragged out to die in a storm. My depression was complete as the last song ended. The children were at rest and were being "watched over by God's hand." I was left with an image of a large blue-eyed hand reaching down out of the clouds.

Sara had asked me not to meet her after the concert. I did as I was asked, and after I got home, rain began rattling across the skylight. I remembered the song about the children and the storm, and I had to look into Joanne's bedroom. She was sleeping quietly.

I felt a little shameful pleasure the next day, when a newspaper critic couldn't find much virtue in the previous night's performance of the Mahler. He thought youthful, part-time orchestras ought to be a little less ambitious in selecting their programs. When Sara and I met for dinner that night, we didn't mention the concert. I felt as though we were having our first fight—which confused and worried me.

Another thing that worried me was that Harry Bordeaux wasn't having any success in arranging an exhibit of my spectral portraits. For one thing, there were not enough of them. But more important, Bill Freedman, the owner of the gallery in which my previous shows had been held, was not too happy with the portraits. He said he didn't think a display of trick shots would do my career any good. The big virtue of my work, he said, had always been its simplicity and honesty, and he was sure that in producing the spectral series I had used multiple exposures or multiple printing.

Harry and I assured Bill that no trickery was involved, but he wasn't convinced. Harry and I suggested to Bill that we schedule another session with Joanne or Sara—or with both of them—and that he could watch the whole procedure, including the processing. But Bill was skeptical. Even if we were to convince him, he thought, that wouldn't do anything to convince anyone who didn't attend the session.

Then it occurred to me that Bill, who was a photographer himself, could take some shots of me as I photographed Joanne or Sara. If all went as it should, Bill would have some prints that showed me as well as the images I was photographing. Then he could display his evidence of my simplicity as part of the show. Bill agreed to that arrangement, and the next Saturday morning, he, Sara, and Harry came to my studio.

Harry was the first to arrive. He was wearing what seemed

to be a velour jump suit. But in line with the new dignity he had acquired since becoming engaged to Lee Ferris, the suit was charcoal-gray rather than the chartreuse I would have expected to see a few weeks earlier. Harry had never been one to be daunted by the responsibilities of life, but he was looking especially dauntless this morning. I asked him how his romance was going. He put a hand on my shoulder and looked around the room to be sure we were alone. "It's more than a romance, Jonathan," he said. "It's a veritable opera. And I need your advice."

"You're the man of the world, Harry."

"But you're a father," Harry said.

"I hope you're not going to tell me what I think you're going to tell me."

"Yes. Isn't it incredible? Lee is, as they say, with child."

"She doesn't take precautions about such things?"

"Never had to. She tried through three marriages to get into a maternal way. Finally just gave it up, and hasn't seen any need for precautions since then. Until she encountered my particular type of virility, she seemed to be immune."

"So, what kind of advice do you need from me?"

"Essentially, Jonathan, I want to know whether you think I would be an adequate parent. I mean, I would be willing to dine out less often, and if necessary I would change my tailor. But would that be enough?"

"There are all kinds of parents, Harry. I think the important thing is that you should really want the child. What does Lee think?"

"She's enthusiastic. But she's thirty-nine, Jonathan. We'd be taking a chance."

"You already took your chance. Anyway, no chances, no winners."

"And no losers."

"No anything, Harry. No chances, no anything."

"I wasn't in search of inspirational messages, Jonathan. I just wanted to know if you think I'm parental timber."

"A veritable oak."

"We have to decide soon, Jonathan. It's a more solemn sort of decision than I generally have to make."

"No, it isn't. Just think of yourself as taking on a new client."

Harry looked offended for a moment, but soon he was smiling. "A new client," he said. "Of course. What are most of my clients except children?" He wrapped me in a velour embrace, and I wondered if I was doing the right thing in encouraging him. When I had wriggled out of his hug, Harry surveyed me in a fatherly fashion and said, "I think Sara Coleridge is doing you a lot of good, dear boy."

"That's possible. But we're not as close as you and Lee."

"No marriage plans yet?"

"No, Harry. Not even any children on the way. And speaking of marriage plans, what are yours?"

Harry looked perturbed. "We had planned something simple. But now we might arrange something sordid. The Municipal Building on a Saturday. I have trouble imagining what that would be like."

"I've been through it as an observer. It's not bad. Five minutes standing in front of a hearty failed actor. The waiting isn't so good, though. Sitting on wooden benches with a lot of other people who are either poor planners or just plain poor. Nervous whispering. Not much eye contact going on. But it'll be a change for you, Harry."

Harry adopted his solemn look, which had never been very convincing. "I really have changed," he said. "Everyone has commented on it. Someone called me a nice person yesterday. Nice! Do you think it will hurt me professionally?"

Before I could tell Harry that he would never be *that* nice, we were interrupted by Joanne, who was approaching at the gallop and who was apparently in some kind of distress. She was calling for her daddy, but her tone indicated she was looking for help and not for combat. I squatted to give her a better target, and she ran into my arms.

"I still can't learn to tie my shoelaces right," she said. To offer conclusive proof, she handed me a shoe whose laces looked as if they had been attacked by a drunken boy scout.

"Never mind, sweetie. Just keep trying. You'll catch on all at once." I started to unravel the enormous knot she had put in the lace, but I realized it would take a few minutes' work to get the job done. "Maybe you could wear some other shoes today," I suggested.

"No, I don't think so. These are my picture-taking shoes."

My thigh muscles were starting to feel the strain, so I shifted around slightly and sat on the floor. I immediately thought of Sara. That seemed like a good thing to do, so I began a little reverie and started to pick at the knot. I said to Joanne, "You haven't said hello to Uncle Harry. Maybe he'll tell you a story while I fix your shoe."

Harry had been watching the proceedings with extreme interest. I wouldn't have been surprised if he had started taking notes. Joanne said hello to the father-to-be, and he picked her up and carried her toward the sofa, saying, "I had the most incredible phone call yesterday, dear girl." Joanne looked at me in panic as they moved away. I began to test my patience and the strength of my fingernails on the shoelace, feeling a little guilty that I preferred thinking about Sara to being with my daughter. I wondered whether I was beginning to neglect Joanne.

As I worked, the doorbell rang, and soon Nanny Joy was escorting Sara into the apartment. Sara took note of my cross-legged position and said, "Are you sure you don't have some Native American blood in your family, Jonathan?"

Joanne had left Harry and had run over to cling to Sara's leg (an understandable impulse). Joanne said, "What's Native American blood, Daddy?"

"Native Americans are what people used to call American Indians, sweetie. And blood doesn't really mean blood, but just what your parents or your parents' parents were like."

Joanne said matter-of-factly, "I see the Indian sometimes, Miss Coleridge."

I looked at Sara, who seemed to be blushing a little bit. Before we could investigate Joanne's remark, the doorbell rang again, and Harry, who had joined our little group, said, "That must be Bill Freedman." Harry was right. I stood up, still clawing at the shoelace, as Nanny Joy brought our new guest in. Joy was looking definitely pleased—probably because Bill Freedman had one of his impressive arms around her waist. Bill had been on the wrestling team in college, and I don't imagine he lost many matches. He was also handsome and black, with a few touches of gray in his modest Afro. I hoped another romance wasn't in the offing, although I didn't think there was much chance of that. Joy and Bill were both wary people; especially Bill, who I'm sure had learned some caution in performing the unlikely feat of becoming a success in the white world of Madison Avenue galleries. Also, Joy still thought of Harlem as home, but Bill thought of it as an unpleasant joke that preceded college and career.

I made introductions and handed Joanne her shoe, with its still-knotted lace. She gave me a disrespectful glance and squeezed her foot into the shoe. We all adjourned to the studio, where Joanne and Sara posed together for a couple of dozen portraits. It didn't take more than half an hour, and it was one of the more dramatic interludes of my life. Joanne and Sara were both wearing dark, unadorned, long-skirted dresses. Since they hadn't spoken to each other before the session, I could only assume the similarity of costume was a coincidence. They performed like a well-rehearsed team, and there was an obvious affection between them.

The spectators were absolutely silent, and the only sounds were an occasional exchange of whispers between Joanne and Sara, punctuated by the whine and click of Bill Freedman's self-processing camera as he stood off in a corner photographing the whole scene. Before I made my first exposure, he brought me over a little print that showed Joanne and Sara, who were almost obscured by the grayish images of several of their ghostly friends. Apparently there was going to be a spectral crowd to deal with.

Joanne and Sara seemed to be having a good time. They both looked more beautiful than I had ever seen them look before. They struck pose after pose in a solemnly dignified but unselfconscious style. Sara was seated on the chaise longue, with Joanne seated sometimes next to her and sometimes on her lap. I had a definite sense from the way they arranged themselves that they were not alone. I had moved the camera back from the usual position so that there would be room in the picture area for five or six people. Bill came over every once in a while with another of his prints. It was obvious the visiting subjects were—possibly with some coaching from Sara—trying not to clutter up the composition too much. There seemed to be three adults and an infant, and they would sometimes appear all together and sometimes one at a time. At one point, both Sara and Joanne moved out of the picture area, and I got a shot of what seemed to be just the empty setting, but I was hoping it would turn out to be a group study of the visitors. For the last six exposures I moved the camera in closer to get some larger and more detailed—if partial—images. When the last shot was taken, I kissed Joanne and Sara and sent them off with everyone but Bill to start a little brunch party. Bill and I examined his prints more carefully. He had made twenty exposures, all from far enough back to include me and the camera as well as my subjects. He had been working without flash so as not to interfere with the natural lighting of my exposures, and his hand-held shots were sometimes a little blurred from the movement of his camera. That, combined with the small size of the images, made it difficult to distinguish much detail. But even so, it was obvious that I was going to have some spectacular pictures.

We went quickly through the prints, and Bill said, "You've got yourself a show, Jonathan. I have no idea what the hell it's all about or whether people are going to want to buy any of it, but it'll get talked about. And those pictures have to be seen. But we're going to have some problems."

"What kind of problems?"

"The critics, for one thing. They're not going to know what to say."

"They'll think of something. They like mysteries."

"They like to create mysteries. You know what most of them like now—the commonplace. Their game is to explain why something really isn't the commonplace thing it obviously is. Give them something truly mysterious, and they'll call it banal. Or they'll just ignore it."

"Does it matter what they do?"

"Of course it matters."

"Nobody reads them but other critics."

"That's why it matters. Critics are your most intelligent, perceptive audience."

"But you said they're just playing a game."

"Certainly. But it's an enduring game. Critics are what make art seem immortal. Actually, though, it's not art that's immortal. Criticism is immortal. Praxiteles."

"Praxiteles?"

"The greatest of the ancient Greek sculptors. Everyone agrees, even though there's only one statue left that he might have made. But the critics of his time spread the word. J. S. Bach."

"J. S. Bach?"

"He didn't attract the critics in his time. He was considered a good rural organist until some critics in the nineteenth century decided he was a genius. Now he's immortal—at least, as long as there are critics."

"I think you're spreading a little manure, Bill. But in any case, it doesn't affect me. I'm not an artist. I'm a witch doctor."

"You're an artist if the critics say you are. In fact, that's the only way you can be one. Photography is the best example of all. It wasn't an art at all until a few years ago when a few art critics started taking it seriously. I used to sell paintings. I didn't dare try to do a photography show until I could come up with a catalog that contained an approving essay by somebody who was supposed to know about art."

"So get a witch doctor to do my catalog."

Bill was silent for a moment. And then he grabbed my arm and said, "Very clever, Jonathan. I think I'll do that."

"Get a witch doctor?"

"Sort of. One of these doctors of psychology who do psychical research."

"I don't think so, Bill."

"Why not?"

"I don't want to be researched. Or, actually, I don't want my daughter and Sara Coleridge to be researched."

"You aren't curious about all this?"

"Not much. It's just one of the mysteries."

"But what if your daughter is going to mess her life up with this business? She might be in some kind of danger, you know."

"There's no danger."

"You're sure of that?"

"I've been assured by the best of sources."

"Sara Coleridge?"

"Right."

"I get the feeling you're not too objective about her. You don't have any doubt she's the best of sources?"

"She's the best of everything."

Bill shook his head in mild despair. "Jonathan," he said. "Nobody's the best of everything. Most of us want to believe that about someone once in a while. I've believed it myself a couple of times. But take my word, nobody's the best of everything." I gave Bill my less-cynical-than-thou smile. "Okay," he said, "I gather there's nothing I can do to convince you of my sincerity."

"I don't question your sincerity, Bill; just your luck." Actually, Bill was noted for his luck in most areas—particularly the area of romance. But I knew that he had betrayed a couple of good ladies who had thought he was the best of everything. And though I understood that that was his right, I think I resented his cavalier treatment of people whose capacity for belief was stronger than his. Maybe it had something to do with his training as a wrestler—not being able to resist capitalizing on an advantage. I was glad Harry was the one who transacted our business with Bill. And, remembering our business, I went up and sat on the chaise longue and had Bill take a picture of me with his camera. We watched in uncordial silence as the print went through its magical development. But it revealed nothing magical; just ordinary Jonathan, made irritable by love and belief.

When we rejoined the others, it was obvious that the party was becoming meaningful. Lee Ferris had arrived, and affections and vodka were being dispensed lavishly. I sat down next to Sara and took Joanne on my lap, and I began to feel very good indeed. Lee was regaling an appreciative Harry with a complicated story about her attempts to buy some pignola nuts from a transvestite clerk in a health-food store. Bill and Nanny Joy were reminiscing about the more bracing days they had spent during their separate but similar childhoods in Harlem. No one was talking about the picture-taking, but I think part of the festive atmosphere grew out of a realization that something extraordinary had just been recorded.

Joanne, Sara, and I formed the calm center of the group. My daughter was almost purring in my lap. She was playing games with her spectral friend Colnee, murmuring pleasantly, and pausing once in a while to look up at me or to reach out and touch Sara. I had expected Sara to rush off to a rehearsal after the portrait session, but she settled in and sipped vodka and tomato juice with me—looking certainly more beautiful and perhaps more sensual than usual. Joanne soon fell asleep, and Sara and I lapsed into an adolescent state, holding hands and gazing at each other. The conversation drifted over us. Everyone seemed to be talking about God:

"... and he said, 'God damn, baby, I think I kicked my habit. No fixes in three days. I just been layin' up here sippin' from this case of Scotch' ..."

"... and I think even in that tacky-chic sort of emporium I had a God-given right not only to expect the word 'affinity' to be understood, but to be spared the evidence of someone's sexual confusions ..."

"... That's what started it, I think. I knew that Lady Day had never seen a sailboat in the moonlight, and that she would never see one. And, God help me, I wanted to see one ..."

"... He said, 'I am not *hiding* my pignolas, darling. I simply don't *have* any, thank God' ..."

"... Like Miss Holiday said, 'God bless the child that's got his own' ..."

The words were not exactly devout, but I was struck by the fact that everyone was finding it hard to talk without making some kind of reference to the Ultimate. I certainly was feeling the ultimate in something. It wasn't long before everyone stopped talking. There we were: three pleasure-sodden, hand-holding couples and a sleeping child. No one wanted to break the silence or to leave, and it occurred to me that the Quaker custom of silent meetings might be one of the great ideas of the Western world.

After a while, I was sure we had set a record for nontalking in a New York social gathering, and I glanced at my watch so that I would have an idea of how long we would actually keep it up. After four and a half minutes, Harry and Lee stood up, waved, and quickly let themselves out. Less than a minute later, Bill

Freedman leaned over to Joy and kissed her lightly on the forehead. Then he got up, showed me that he was taking along his pictures of the portrait session, and left. Nanny Joy gave me an affectionate glance and retired to her room.

Sara and I put Joanne to bed.

Then we went to my bedroom and, in quiet astonishment, put ourselves to bed.

I suppose that from the moment I first glanced at Sara, some unkempt gnome in the recesses of my personality had been winking, nudging, and trying to get obscene calls through to my central nervous system. But although Sara's physical attractiveness had never slipped my mind, I hadn't allowed myself to think that we might someday share a bed.

And, in a sense, "share a bed" is a fairly accurate description of what we did that day. It was easily the strangest, most chaste, and most rewarding sexual experience I had ever had. I don't know whether the odd, silent gathering and farewells that had led up to the encounter had anything to do with our behavior, but when Sara and I entered the bedroom, we moved like people sent on an urgent errand by a hypnotist. We didn't speak, and we didn't touch. Grateful, and awed, I watched as Sara unbuttoned her dark dress, parting the material to reveal her pale body. I was dazzled, as though I had been in a windowless dungeon and someone had slowly opened the door to reveal the sand of a Mediterranean beach on a cloudless June day. Sara was looking into my eyes with an expression of puzzled pleasure. She kicked off her shoes, let her dress drop to the floor, turned her back to me, and removed her white cotton bra and panties. Then she turned again to face me. There were tears in her eyes, and she was breathing rapidly and shallowly. The muscles of her belly were quivering.

If Sara had been a stranger, I would certainly have thought of her body as being remarkably handsome, although I'm not sure I would have been wildly aroused by the sight. But she was not a stranger, she was my love. Her beauty was miraculous, and her carnality was perfectly transmitted. I felt as though I were undergoing a metamorphosis and were becoming a different kind of being—one that had a new and superior way of seeing and feeling. I shed my clothes like a chrysalis. My body was tense and trembling, and for a moment I thought that rather than being reborn, I might be dying. I went to the bed, not necessarily as an invitation to Sara to join me but because my legs would no longer support me. I lay on the bed, watching Sara. She had turned her head in my direction, but she had not moved toward me. I pushed my body toward the head of the bed, sitting up slightly and resting my shoulders against the wall.

Then Sara walked toward the bed. She sat down on the mattress, facing me in a cross-legged position, her back straight, and her hands on her knees. I changed my position to match hers, sitting forward, spreading my knees, and crossing my legs under me. We sat as we had sat on the floor that recent morning. My strength began to return, reinforcing my excitement. Sara's eyes were still wet with tears. She was moving her gaze slowly over my body, stopping occasionally to glance into my eyes. Her expression surprised me; it wasn't exactly bold or lascivious, but it had an odd appreciative sureness.

I watched a tear move quickly down Sara's cheek and drop upon her right breast. The tear rested for a moment on the slightly concave slope of the breast. Sara was breathing more slowly now, but much more deeply, and her chest was rising and falling in an uneven rhythm. Both breasts were tear-dampened and glittering, and her nipples were like tiny dark mollusk shells on a wet beach.

Sara was crying uncontrollably now, and some tears had made their way past the full lower curve of her breasts and onto her belly, lodging in a few small horizontal creases. The creases vanished as she suddenly arched her back and contracted the muscles of her lower body. She relaxed for a moment, and then she laughed, and the contractions began again. There was almost no fat on her body to conceal the elaborate patterns made by the tightening muscles. Sara removed her hands from her knees and leaned back, putting her arms straight out behind her for support. She closed her eyes and began to make a sound I thought was a moan. But I soon realized that she was humming a melody that sounded vaguely familiar.

I had been so absorbed in watching Sara's body that for a time I had become unconscious of my own. But now, as I watched Sara abandoning herself to the spasms that were still sweeping over her, I realized that I was on the verge of my own spasm. I leaned back in the same position as Sara, trying to control my body. Sara's humming was louder now, and I recognized the melody: it was the hymn that Bach had based his last composition on—the melody I had memorized recently. Rather than distracting me as I had hoped, the sound of the melody increased my excitement and made me lose the last bit of control I had over my body. I began to hum the melody in unison with Sara. She opened her eyes and gasped. A surge of terrifying pleasure rose in me, extinguishing all my senses.

When my vision returned, Sara was still sitting across from me, but she was relaxed and smiling. She glanced down at her right thigh, where a few drops of semen were resting—the pearly outposts of a sodden, broken trail that led to my own thigh. I was back in the real world again. Sara and I exchanged smiles of what were for me—and, I hoped, for her—gratitude and love.

And then I reached for the bedside tissues. In five minutes we were dressed, and Sara had left the apartment. We still had not spoken.

Chapter 8

A man who believes in moderation doesn't expect to avoid feelings of guilt after the dungeon door opens and the chrysalis is shed. And he isn't surprised when the Furies arrive to tear off his wings and escort him back into the darkness. My regrets began as soon as Sara left the apartment. I went back to my bedroom and looked at the bedspread. I ran my fingers across the dark, circular stain that marked the place where Sara had sat. The stain was cold and vaguely sticky, and I didn't see it as a reminder of pleasure, but as something more like the evidence of a crime. I wondered whether it would fade as it dried and whether I could conceal it from Nanny Joy.

And then I heard Joy calling me. I threw a lap robe over the bed and went to find her. She was standing outside Joanne's bedroom, looking less at peace with the world than usual.

"Joanne's a little under the weather," she said.

I started to reply and found that I was clenching my teeth. Joy wasn't one to worry much about illness. She had probably had enough experience in that area to give her some confidence about the body's ability to take care of itself. But I didn't share that confidence. I had always been awed by how complex the body was and how versatile it was at finding ways to misfunction. I tried not to let Joy see my concern. "Tummy upset? She's had a lot of excitement today."

"She's got a funny chill."

"With fever?"

"No. If that was it, we could give her some aspirin. But her temperature's sort of low. I don't know what to do about that."

"How low is it?"

"About ninety-seven."

"About?"

"Well, almost ninety-seven. More like ninety-six and a half."

"Maybe the thermometer's not working right."

"I tried it out on myself. It was okay."

"I'll talk to her," I said. "It doesn't sound very serious." I hoped I sounded more convincing to Joy than I did to myself. Joanne had always had remarkably good health—which I thought probably resulted from her lack of curiosity about her body. Her teacher, Ms. Abraham, told me that my daughter was less interested in the "palpable" than most youngsters. Not that Joanne was any better than most at dealing with "conceptualization," I was told, but she supposedly had an unusual interest in "relationships and the spiritual." Since I didn't place much trust in Ms. Abraham or words like "conceptualization," I hadn't paid much attention to the pronouncement—but I had to admit that one of the things I admired about Joanne was that she didn't often want to be pampered.

When I got to her bedroom, she wasn't exactly pampering herself—but she certainly was trying to warm herself. She was staring out from under an enormous mound of blankets, coats, and stuffed toy animals. Her face was pale, and she seemed to be shivering, but she managed to look fairly cheerful. I sat on the edge of the bed and touched her brow. My hand withdrew involuntarily, and I began to feel a little frightened. Her forehead wasn't cold in the way it would have been if she had come into the house after playing in the snow on a January day. Instead, her chill seemed to come from somewhere inside her body.

I wondered whether I should take her to a doctor. The problem with that was that I didn't know of any doctors. There was a pediatrician who had given Joanne checkups a couple of times, but he didn't have office hours on Saturdays—and, like virtually every other doctor in the city, he didn't make house calls.

Joanne was stirring, and her eyes were open. I asked: "Don't you feel good, sweetie?"

"I feel good, Daddy. It's only the cold."

"I'm not cold. Nanny Joy's not cold. It's a nice warm spring day."

"The people are cold. They're always cold."

"What people?"

"The people in the pictures."

"Those people aren't real, Joanne. You shouldn't think about them so much. They might make you sick."

"No. They're very, very good, Daddy. They wouldn't be bad to me."

"How do you know that?"

"Sara told me."

"Sara Coleridge?"

Joanne nodded, smiled, and shivered. What the hell was I supposed to do? I wanted her to be happy, but I didn't want her to be crazy. Why couldn't life be simple and sensible? Sara was bringing a new kind of pleasure to me and Joanne, but maybe the price was too high. Even if the doctor had been available, I would have hesitated to take Joanne to him because I was afraid of what he might say about her fantasies.

I put my hand on Joanne's forehead again and tried not to make the association that is easiest to make when dealing with the presence of a cold body. "Is there anything I can do for you, sweetie?"

"You could tell me a story, Daddy."

"Are you sure you feel well enough for that?" I meant that Joanne would need a fair amount of strength to go through our usual storytelling routine, because she always ended up doing all the work. I don't have a lot of imagination—which is as it should be for a photographer—but Joanne had a lot even for an almost-five-year-old. My stories consisted of a gray warp of questions around which Joanne would weave oddly colored narratives.

"What should my story be about?"

"About Colnee and her mommy and daddy."

"And what should they be doing?"

"They should be lost in the snow. There should be snow all around, and they should have no food."

"Where is the Indian?"

"He shouldn't be there yet."

"And what happens?"

"Colnee should get sick, and the snow on her face should stop melting. And her daddy should cry." Joanne paused, and her head began to move from side to side. "And the angel . . ."

"You didn't say anything about an angel."

". . . and the angel . . . sayeth . . ."

"*Sayeth?*"

"... and the angel sayeth... except ye."

Joanne's head stopped moving, and she closed her eyes. The tension I had felt in her body disappeared. I wondered whether she had fainted. I would have wondered something much more disturbing, except that some warmth seemed to be returning to her forehead. And I realized that the dampness I felt beneath my hand was being produced by Joanne's skin and not mine. I reached beneath the blankets with my free hand and found her wrist. Her pulse seemed fast, but it was even and strong. I moved my hand to her chest, which was warm under her slightly sweat-dampened pajama top. I removed everything from the top of the bed except one blanket. Joanne was sleeping soundly. I kissed her parted lips and left the bedroom.

I had had enough strong emotions in enough bedrooms for one day. I headed for the kitchen, because Nanny Joy would probably be there and because it's a room that inspires moderation in me. I would have stopped by the kitchen in any case, because it was sending out the aroma of fried onions—which is the only thing besides shoe polish that I would go out of my way to sniff. I arrived as Joy was adding chopped green peppers to the skillet in which the onions were frying. "You're destroying its purity," I said.

"That's my specialty. How's Joanne?"

"She's all right, I think. She's warm now, and asleep."

"I was worried."

"You would have been more than that if you had heard what she was saying before she fell asleep."

"Talking like someone out of the Bible?"

"You know about that? And about angels and Indians?" I got a fork and maneuvered a few onions out of the skillet, trying to look unconcerned.

"I heard some of that, too."

I nibbled the onions and looked at Joy's back as she cooked. I wondered if she was going to express an opinion, but she just kept puttering.

"It's been a strange day," I said.

"We've had a few of those lately."

"Since I fell in love with Sara."

Joy turned to face me. "It'll work out, Jonathan."

"But what about Joanne?"

"It'll work out."

Good, handsome Joy. I appreciated her efforts to console me, but I couldn't think of any reasons why I should share her optimism. But it was time I stopped thinking about Sara and Joanne. I asked Joy what she thought of Bill Freedman.

"He's nobody I would trust."

"You seemed to like him."

"I spent quite a few years seeming to like men I didn't trust, Jonathan. Bill was like old times."

"He's always been good to me."

"He's been good to himself. You've made money for him. You can count on him to get a good price for your stuff, but don't ever get to where you have to ask him to put up bail for you."

I wished that my opinions of people could have been as certain as Joy's. I wasn't sure how accurate her opinions were, but that didn't seem to be too important. Life is just easier to get through on a day-by-day basis if you form quick, definite opinions about people. I know a little more about good and bad now than I did then, but I still have trouble fitting people into those categories. It's easier than it used to be for me to decide whom I like and dislike, but as Mae West said in another connection, goodness has nothing to do with it.

Nanny Joy was a case in point. There was never a time when I wasn't fond of her, although the time came when our ideas about right and wrong didn't exactly coincide.

But on that spring Saturday, when I was awash in portraits, partying, sex, and illness, Joy was my gyroscope. She kept me stable enough so that I could get myself into the darkroom and spend a few quiet hours getting some meticulously finished prints of what the camera had seen that morning. The cast of characters had become familiar to me: the vague images of the two men, the woman, and the infant; the more substantial and —in this sequence—intensely dramatic and attractive figures of Joanne and Sara. The photographs were not only singular and disturbing, but remarkably beautiful. It was hard to tell what was going on in the pictures, but there was a quality of violent and dangerous action in them that I had never before seen in anything done in a studio.

My pictures usually had a domestic quality. My subjects were sometimes devoted to debauchery, but I soothed them with a little Vermeerish light, and they took on the personalities of seventeenth-century Dutch embroiderers and harpsichord students. But there was nothing domestic about the spectral portraits. And it wasn't just the presence of the exotic, see-through figures. The whole quality of the light in the photographs was forbidding; it wasn't diffused spring sunshine but the harsh, snow-reflected light of January in a northern latitude.

And there was a new element in four of the photographs—an element that seemed at first like a formless, nearly transparent overlay. It was as if the wing of a dragonfly had been held in front of the camera. The thought of wings stayed with me as I examined the four peculiar prints, and as I stood back from them the apparently formless overlays took on a barely discernible pattern: the pattern of wings. But they weren't at all like the wings of an insect, or quite like the wings of a bird. They were the elaborate kind of wings that Flemish Renaissance painters attached to angels in scenes of the Annunciation or the Nativity.

Joanne, in her chilly delirium, had talked about an angel. So now the cast of spectral characters was complete. The thing that was nowhere near complete was an explanation of their significance. But I wasn't feeling up to searching for significance. I had run out of energy and curiosity.

I left the darkroom and went into the kitchen, where the aroma of onions and green peppers had been joined by a lot of other, less bold aromas. There was a large pot on the stove. I spent a couple of minutes examining the contents of the pot and stirring a thick soup. I couldn't identify all the items that came burbling to the surface, but there were definitely signs of sausage, chicken, okra, speckled beans, turnip, and tomatoes. As I put the lid back on the pot Joy came into the kitchen. She was wearing an outfit she often featured when she went out on Saturday nights. It was an ensemble that really upset me. If you didn't look closely, it seemed to be what a poor lady would wear to a church meeting: navy-blue, basket-weave, inverted-pot hat (with decorative veil);

a satin floral-print dress with a lot of lavender in it (mid-calf hemline, and button-up front, with matching cloth-covered buttons); medium-heeled navy-and-white shoes. What was upsetting was that the dress was translucent, and if you looked carefully you could see that Joy was wearing skimpy lemon-yellow lingerie that wasn't exactly right for church meetings. I knew it wasn't my business, but I truly wanted to know where Joy went when she wore that outfit. Her usual clothes were the sort of things casual young women wore—mostly jeans and sweaters or shirts.

"Going out?" I asked.

"Yes. . . . Joanne's awake, but she doesn't feel like getting up. I think she's okay, though."

"I'll take care of her."

"Did the pictures come out all right?"

"Better than all right. I think there's an angel in some of them —I mean, aside from Joanne and Sara."

"That's better than a devil."

I was encouraged by Joy's thought, until I had a thought of my own: "Satan's an angel—a fallen angel," I said.

Joy, as usual, had an answer: "Satan wouldn't want his picture taken. He'd be like the murderers being brought into police headquarters. He'd have a newspaper over his face."

Instead of answering, I frowned.

"You worry too damn much, Mr. B. Most people would be pleased to have a visit from an angel. Why don't you spend the rest of the day fooling around and smiling? That's what I'm going to do. I'll be back about midnight."

Joy turned to go. She hadn't exactly consoled me. There's nothing that puts me in a bad mood faster than having someone *tell* me that I'm in a bad mood. As Joy reached the kitchen door she dropped her gloves (white; I forgot to mention this finishing touch of her ensemble). As she leaned over to pick them up, her yellow bikini-type panties showed distinctly through her dress. Fooling around and smiling, indeed.

Then I began to feel guilty. Why should I begrudge Joy her pleasures? Probably it was because I was uncertain about my own pleasures. I didn't know when I'd see Sara again. Why didn't she have a telephone? Why didn't she call me?

I began to realize how much my life had changed. If I was hoping the phone would ring, I wasn't the Jonathan Brewster I had been before. And why wasn't I in Joanne's bedroom giving her whatever comfort I could? The answer was simple enough, I supposed. Sara had become more important to me than my daughter. I was a little frightened by that thought, and I left the kitchen and headed for Joanne's room. But before I got there, it occurred to me that I should drop a note to Sara. I went to my own room and scribbled out a few not too coherent words of love and gratitude, addressed the envelope, and quickly left the apartment. I ran to the mailbox at the corner of the street. According to the schedule on the box, the letter wouldn't be collected until the next morning. I knew that collections were made more often at mailboxes at busier intersections, and I suspected that if I went a few blocks more to Houston Street, I would find a box that would get the letter to the post office that same night.

I began to walk quickly toward Houston Street, and then I remembered that Joanne was alone and I hadn't told her I was going out. If she needed me and found I wasn't there, she might panic. I had never left her alone before. I went back to the mailbox I had just left and started to put the letter in. But then I hesitated. Mail delivery was getting to be erratic. I wanted Sara to know that I was thinking of her, and an extra five minutes of my time now might make a day's difference in the delivery of the letter. I pulled my hand back and began to jog toward Houston Street, wondering what had become of my well-practiced patience.

I found the mailbox I was looking for within two minutes, and I was back in the apartment in another ten minutes. As I jogged home I began to imagine disasters that might have taken place while I was away. I saw Joanne in the kitchen, accidentally spilling scalding soup over herself or setting her clothes on fire. I saw her wandering through the apartment, or even going out into the street, calling for me.

My jog became a sprint, and my body began to protest the unaccustomed strain. My conscience was protesting even more strongly. Was I going to sacrifice my daughter's safety because of my love for Sara? I had thought there was no need to make such a choice; that I could love them equally. But maybe it wasn't that simple. Maybe this was just the first of many such choices I would have to make. Dilemmas, unlike mysteries, didn't appeal to me.

When I got to my building, I didn't have much strength left. The elevator car was up on the sixth floor, and I didn't want to wait for it to come down. I started to run up the stairs, but before I got to the first landing, I had slowed to a walk. There was no moisture in my mouth, but there was a lot of it on my forehead. The lights on the stairway seemed to have dimmed. I was strongly aware of being in my midthirties, and I wondered whether I would ever see my late thirties.

I was doubly relieved when I got to the door of my apartment: first, because it meant the end of my climb; and second, because I didn't see any smoke seeping out around the frame. Inside the apartment there was a silence that at first reassured me and then alarmed me; was it a lifeless silence? But there turned out to be life in Joanne's room, although it was not exactly boisterous life.

As she so often did when she was apparently sleeping soundly, Joanne opened her eyes when I entered the room. "Was I asleep?" she asked me.

"I think so, sweetie." I knelt beside the bed and took Joanne in my arms, along with the bedclothes.

She didn't seem overjoyed. "You're all sweaty, Daddy."

"Am I sweaty, sweetie?" Joanne offered a feeble giggle in exchange for my feeble attempt at wit. "I'm sweaty because I love you so much."

Joanne pulled free of the covers and put her arms around my neck. "I love you, Daddy. But now I'm hungry."

"You stay right here, and we'll get full in the tummy and have a nice time." I went into the kitchen and loaded a tray with bread and bowls of soup, and we had dinner in bed.

After dinner I suggested we adjourn to the Anything Goes Room, but neither of us had the energy or inclination for strenuous silliness. We lay on the bed and talked about baby animals for a while and then tried to get some idea of how long it would be before we would have another Christmas. Joanne finally decided that there was no reasonable way to tell. Numbers—whether number of days or months or seasons—didn't really mean anything when applied to yearnings and emotions. I understood her perfectly. It might be two or three days until I could see Sara again, but it was my needs and not the calendar that decided what that wait would feel like.

Joanne finally came up with the idea that maybe we could sleep long enough so that when we woke up it would be Christmas. We gave it a try, but I only made it until about midnight, when I got up and took the dishes into the kitchen and rinsed them. Then I took a large glass of whiskey into the bathroom, filled the tub with uncomfortably warm water, and sipped and soaked until the water was tepid and I was ready to try the Christmas marathon again.

The next day—Sunday—was comfortably routine for Nanny Joy and Joanne. But the routine wasn't so comfortable for me. I thought of Sara continuously, but in a less abstract, more disturbing way than I ever had before. What I mean, I suppose, is that I thought a lot about her body, and several times I found myself exhibiting definite signs of excitement. If it hadn't been for that physical excitement, I would have gone to Sara's apartment. But as my needs become more understandable, I became more careful about trying to fulfill them. I spent the day mounting my spectral portraits and getting them packed up for delivery to Harry, so that he could start showing them to wealthy and influential people. I wondered what an objective, sensible person would think of them—and whether that kind of person would want to buy any of them. That really wasn't my business, though; it was Harry's business. He would find more than enough of the particular—or unparticular—kind of people who would find life more significant with one or two ghostly portraits on the wall. I wasn't overjoyed with the thought that because of my selfish ambitions a lot of strangers would be living with images of Sara and Joanne, and for a while I thought of canceling the whole project. But I decided that it would also be selfish to hoard the pictures for myself. In the end, as usual, the kind of selfishness that pays the rent won out, and the next morning I delivered the photographs to Harry Bordeaux.

Harry was pleased. He usually looked through collections of

prints pretty quickly, taking a telephone call or two in the process. But after looking at a couple of the spectral portraits, he told his secretary to hold his calls, and he looked through the rest of the series attentively.

"Rich and famous," he said.

"Who?"

"You, Jonathan. That's what you've just become—rich and famous. There is no person on this earth who wouldn't take some pleasure in looking at these pictures. Two beautiful subjects and some striking ghosts." Harry fingered his ascot. "And, Jonathan, do I detect an angel? An angel?"

"That's how it looks to me."

"Rich and famous. God, I knew my good years were upon me. Amour, paternity, and now a heavenly being to represent. My Pommard goblet runneth over."

"So, what are your plans?"

"Audacious. Simply audacious, Jonathan."

Harry's secretary came in and said a Dr. Kammerman or something of the sort was in the waiting room.

I asked Harry if he was ill.

"Just a surfeit of joy," he said, and stood up and went to the door with me. "Now that I'm about to become a father, you won't misinterpret this, I trust, Jonathan." And Harry kissed me on the cheek. "You go and seek your own pleasures now, dear boy. I'll be in touch."

The only person in the waiting room was a no-longer-young man who seemed to be trying to relive the 1960s. It wasn't just his ponytail hairdo and elaborately informal clothes that made him seem like a throwback; it was his expression of uncompromising earnestness, which recalled the burning of draft cards, university offices, and flags.

I hurried gratefully into the duller Manhattan of the 1980s. I walked home, making plans to visit Sara's apartment that night. A few minutes after I got to the apartment, the phone rang. For perhaps the first time since Nanny Joy had been with me, I picked up the receiver before she did. I was certain I would hear Sara's voice.

"Jon Brewster?"

It wasn't Sara's voice. It was an earnest male voice. I wanted to hang up, but, instead, I said, "Yes."

"My name is Richard Kammerman. We almost met at Harry Bordeaux's office this morning."

"Yes. You're the doctor who makes office calls."

"It's not M.D., it's Ph.D.—psychology. But listen, Jon, Harry showed me the spectral portraits, and they really wigged me out."

Among the things that irritate me are Ph.D.'s who use outdated slang and people who call me by my first name before they've met me. I decided I didn't have anything to say to Dr. Kammerman. But, as I suspected, he had a few more depressing remarks to make.

"Bill Freedman wants me to do a little essay on the portraits for the catalog he's going to pass out at your show."

"Are you a photography critic?"

"No, Jon. My thing is psychical research."

"I'm afraid your thing doesn't interest me very much, Mr. Kammerman. I told Bill I don't want essays about the show—especially your kind."

"This is dynamite stuff, Jon. Absolutely the best spectral photographs ever—and I've seen them all. They're too good, man. Nobody's going to believe them unless somebody like me certifies them. I just want to talk to you and your daughter and the woman in the pictures."

"That's out of the question. Why don't you just go back to your laboratory and do some telepathy?"

"You're skeptical, Jon. I understand that; I deal with that all the time."

"I'm not skeptical about people who do things; I'm skeptical about people who explain things. I'm going to talk to Harry Bordeaux now and have him call you off."

I broke the connection and started to dial Harry. Then I noticed my hand was trembling. Why was I so upset? Why was I afraid of Kammerman? He was obnoxious, but no more so than a lot of other people I had managed to deal with in a calm and rational way. Obviously, I wasn't as upset by Kammerman himself as by the actions he was likely to take. I didn't want him talking to Joanne and Sara—but was I trying to keep *him* from finding out certain things, or was I trying to keep *myself* from finding them out? Was it a case of what you don't know won't hurt you?

I realized that a delicate balance was developing in my life. Sara and Joanne and I were making one another happy, and if that meant we had to close our eyes to certain things, so be it.

I called Harry and told him to get Kammerman to leave us alone. Harry warned me that I was cutting down on my chances of becoming rich and famous, but I told him I was willing to make that sacrifice.

It wasn't until Joanne got home from school that I realized I had made a big mistake in my handling of Kammerman. Joanne was looking a little glum, and I asked her what the trouble was.

"They're all gone," she said.

"What's all gone?"

"Colnee and the other people. They went away."

At first that sounded like good news to me. Joanne had become so devoted to her invisible friends that she had begun to neglect the real world. I didn't want her to spend the rest of her life in bed, shivering and muttering.

"That's all right, sweetie," I said. "You've still got a lot of friends. You've got me, and Nanny, and everybody at school, and Miss Coleridge."

And then I made the disturbing connection. Did we still have Sara? It was Sara who had brought Colnee. Maybe it was Sara who had taken her away. I turned Joanne over to Nanny Joy, and I went out and got into a cab and headed for Sara's apartment.

Pamela Kim let me in. She looked a little flustered.

"Is Sara here?" I asked.

Pamela shook her head.

"Do you know where she is?"

"She went away, Jonathan."

"Where did she go?"

"I don't know. She packed her things and left. All she said was that she was going home."

"Where is that?"

"No idea. She never talked about that kind of thing."

I pushed Pamela out of the way and went into Sara's part of the apartment. Her room looked pretty much the same as it had the first time I saw it. But it was so sparsely furnished that it would have been hard to tell if anyone was living there or not. The harp was still there, though; a large, gilded presence that dominated the room.

Pamela had come into the room behind me. I said to her, "Sara will have to send for her harp, won't she?"

"No. She rented it. That's what made me think there was something strange about her. A good musician gets very attached to her instrument. Playing a rented instrument is like sleeping with someone you picked up in a bar. Good musicians are usually too moral about their playing to do that."

Under other circumstances I might have been interested in what Pamela was saying, but at that time it just irritated me. Then I noticed that Pamela was holding a letter at her side. She raised her hand slowly, and I saw that the envelope had my name written on it. I took the letter and tore it open. Pamela left the room. I sat down and read the following words:

Beloved Jonathan:

I had a visit this morning from a Mr. (Dr.) Kammerman. He asked me a lot of questions—questions I didn't answer—and it made me realize that my fondness for you and Joanne has caused me to make some major mistakes. It was a mistake for me to let you think we might be able to form any kind of permanent friendship. We don't belong to the same world. For a time I thought I could live safely in—or at least on the edges of—your world, but the dangers and complexities are too great. If I had let our friendship develop, I would eventually have asked you to make a sacrifice—a series of sacrifices, some of them beyond what you could imagine. I would have asked you to give up your congenial, comfortable way of life.

You are probably sweet enough (and frivolous enough) that you would have made the necessary sacrifices. But I don't think you ever would have understood why they were necessary or what they signified.

I hope you (or Mr. Kammerman) won't try to find me. I plead with you not to try.

Kiss Joanne for me.

Good-bye,
Sara

I read the words twice, flinching and feeling as if someone were hitting me across the chest with a length of rubber hose. I put the letter in my pocket and let myself weep for a couple of minutes. Then I felt like destroying something, or someone —preferably creepy, meddling Dr. Kammerman. I wasn't feeling well disposed toward Harry Bordeaux or Bill Freedman, either. But I decided the first thing to do was to find Sara, regardless of the instructions in her letter.

I searched the room, frantically but thoroughly. The closet was empty except for a pair of shabby, low-heeled brown shoes. They had been made in Italy and sold in Manhattan; no clue to where else Sara might have lived. The drawers in her bureau held only a pair of white cotton gloves, strangely worn at the fingertips. Had she sometimes practiced her harp while wearing gloves? I was on my hands and knees, looking for something Sara might have dropped in packing, when Pamela came back into the room. I stood up, apparently looking a little dangerous, because Pamela backed away from me. "You really don't have any idea where Sara is?" I asked.

"No. I swear."

"Were you here when Dr. Kammerman showed up this morning?"

"Yes. What an asshole *he* was."

That seemed like a fair appraisal. "Did you hear what they talked about?"

"Most of it. He didn't come in. I answered the door. He didn't look like a doctor to me, so I kept the chain on the door and called Sara. She talked to him at the door—just for a couple of minutes. He said he wanted to interview her about some portraits. She said no, and she went and started to pack. She made me take some money and kissed me and left. She was crying."

Pamela's eyes were puffy. She was holding a cigarette that had burned down to the filter. She was obviously almost as upset as I was. I wrote my name and phone number on a slip of paper and asked her to let me know if she heard anything from Sara or found out where she might be.

I left, carrying Sara's shoes, gloves, and letter, and went to the nearest telephone booth and called Lee Ferris. Her secretary put me right through.

"Jonathan?" Lee said. "What in the hell did you do to Sara Coleridge, and where has she gone?"

"All I did was fall in love with her. And I was hoping you would know where she's gone—or at least where she comes from."

"Not a clue, Jonathan. All I know is that she's a remarkably good and—until now—reliable free-lance harpist."

"I gather you talked to her today. What did she say?"

"Good-bye is what she said. *Ciao*. She's canceling all her commitments and adding a little tarnish to my glowing reputation. An agent has to be trustworthy, Jonathan. It's known that my clients are prone to a bit of temperament, but they *show up* and they play the notes right. It's those ludicrous pictures of yours, I suppose. Did you ever experience anything as outlandish as that gathering at your place on Saturday? It was like a mawkish séance, for God's sake. Or did you put some Valiums in the vodka? No. Nothing that naive. Well, forget her, Jonathan. But, of course, you love her, don't you? Do things really have to become so Byzantine? It's enough to make one regret one's pregnancy. If it weren't for J. S. Bach, I think I'd make an appointment at the neighborhood abortion clinic. Don't think I'm not sympathetic, but take my advice: Photograph some cab drivers and spend some time with Joanne. Take her out of that training camp for neurotics and apprentice her to a stonecutter or something. Forbid her to engage in paperwork or art . . ."

Or to talk on the telephone, I thought as I replaced the receiver. Lee obviously wasn't concerned about my problems. She was worried about being pregnant. It wasn't too late for her to have a doctor relieve her of the dangers and responsibilities of motherhood, and I thought maybe that would be the best thing for all concerned. Lee and Harry were not going to be devoted parents. Lee, despite the advice she had just given me, would want the child to learn to conduct the *St. Matthew Passion*. Harry would want to be not the child's father but his or her agent.

Which reminded me that I had a few words to say to Harry. I picked up the phone again and dialed his number. His secretary said he was in the middle of a call to Europe, so I took a cab home and tried him again. He had his defense prepared by then.

"I've heard all about it," he said. "I've sent Kammerman back to academe. We won't have any essay in the catalog, my friend. We'll do it your way."

"Let's not do it at all, Harry."

"Oh, come now. Rich and famous. Don't you want that?"

"I want Sara Coleridge, and you messed that up, Harry. You didn't keep faith with me."

"Sara will be back. Or we'll find her. Look, Jonathan, I miscalculated. I admit that. But I've got a lot on my mind. Lee and I are getting married next Saturday. Do you roller-skate?"

"Do I *what?*"

"Roller-skate. We're thinking of having the reception at a roller-disco rink."

Harry's attempt at flippancy just increased my anger and misery. He made me realize there was no room for mournful emotions in his life. He was in love with Lee, but his love was nothing like mine for Sara. If Lee should vanish, Harry would feel distress, but he probably wouldn't miss a day at the office. And Harry's attitude was probably healthier than mine. People like Harry kept the social and economic kettle boiling. He also had kept my temper boiling that day, and I thought it would be better for what was left of our friendship if I steered clear of him for a while. I said, "Let's talk about it later in the week, Harry."

Harry thought that was a good plan. But before he hung up, he invited me to the wedding. "Don't dress," he said. "And bring skates if you have them."

For the rest of the week I spent my time either brooding or doing a little clumsy, unsuccessful detective work. I had dinner with Pamela Kim and tried to get her to recall something that might give me some idea of where Sara might have gone. But Pamela was no help. She had been immeasurably more interested in her cello than in Sara.

She did give me the names of a few other musicians Sara had worked with, and I talked to all of them. Without exception, they were more concerned with things like the idiosyncrasies of instruments and conductors than they were with Sara's disappearance. After that I couldn't think of much reason to leave the apartment. I began to organize my days around the delivery of the mail and the ringing of the telephone and the doorbell.

I did go to Harry and Lee's wedding, and I found it uninspiring. I suppose my lack of enthusiasm was partly a result of my anger at Harry's having sent Dr. Kammerman after Sara—a move that I was still convinced had frightened her away.

To enjoy a wedding ceremony in the shabby, bureaucratic atmosphere of New York City's Municipal Building, you probably have to be either the bride or the groom. Furthermore, you have to be so deeply in love that you have eyes only for your lover. Since I was only an onlooker whose beloved was not to be seen, I was aware primarily of the ceremony's tackiness and lack of dignity.

A number of Harry's and Lee's friends and acquaintances had taken the suggestion that they bring roller skates. As I had expected, it was a wildly varied crowd made up of people who seemed more interested in their own pleasures than in honoring the bride and groom. The ceremony was brief, and as soon as it was over, I went over to offer congratulations and to beg off attending the reception. My lack of goodwill faded a little when Harry and Lee turned to face me. For an instant they looked young, innocent, and devoted to each other. When I wished them well, I meant it more than I had expected to. I asked them what their honeymoon plans were and found that they were going to spend the weekend at the Plaza Hotel. There was not time for anything more elaborate, they said. As a sort of wedding present, I told Harry to go ahead with the showing of the spectral portraits. I kissed Lee, who responded with some passion, but with a pensiveness that I thought was merely the happy-sad attitude that is traditional for such occasions.

I went home and spent the rest of the weekend trying to add some happiness to my sadness, but not doing so well with it. Then, on Tuesday, I got a surprising call from Harry. It was surprising first because it didn't come through his secretary, and second because I didn't hear the usual hectic background noises. At first, I wasn't even sure it *was* Harry. There was no *joie de vivre* in his voice—or any kind of *vivre* at all. He sounded like an ordinary human being who had been given one too many reminders that the light at the end of the tunnel might be accompanied by a lot of heat.

"Jonathan?"

"You guessed it, Harry." No response. "It sounds like a quiet day at the office."

"I'm home, Jon." I knew then that there was real trouble. He never called me Jon, and he never stayed home during office hours.

"Trouble?"

"You've been suffering lately, haven't you, Jon?"

"'Acquainted with grief.' I believe that's the phrase."

"You know about loss."

"Does this have something to do with Lee?"

"In a way. She had an abortion, Jon. This morning."

"This morning? A couple of days after getting married?"

"She made the appointment sometime last week."

"Why? And why now?"

"It's complicated, Jon. For one thing, she's a little older than I thought. Forty-five. The rest, I'm not sure I understand. She wanted to marry me first, to show me that she loved me and that she wasn't just marrying me because of the baby."

I wasn't sure I followed the logic of that. "She could have married you after she had it done."

"Yes. But maybe she thought I wouldn't have wanted to marry her then."

"Would you have?"

"I don't know. Not that I don't love her. But it's the abortion. Doesn't that make it something like marrying a murderer?"

"I don't think so, Harry. You didn't marry the doctor."

"I hope you're not trying to be witty, Jonathan."

Our switch in roles was confusing me. I wasn't used to being less serious than Harry. "Sorry, Harry. I don't know what I'm trying to do. I don't know what I think about abortion."

"I just keep thinking my child has been killed for no good reason."

"I guess so. But it's not that simple. Lee must have had some reason other than her own safety."

"Yes. But she can't make me understand it. She says things about stonemasons and Bach."

I remembered that Lee had said that kind of thing to me—and had also mentioned abortion—on the day Sara disappeared. I asked Harry if Lee had said anything about Joanne and the portraits.

"Yes. I think that suddenly the whole supernatural business started to outrage her. It's as if she didn't want to have children if they could attract ghosts. But it wasn't ghosts per se—they just represented the quirks that we're heir to, I think."

"Why didn't she talk to us about it—to Sara or Joanne, or even to me? Quirks aren't all bad. Joanne was a lot happier when she had her quirks, I think."

"The specters are gone?"

"So Joanne says. They disappeared along with Sara."

"Then there won't be any more spectral portraits?"

"No, Harry. Even if I could get some, I wouldn't want to."

"Then the ones we have are even more valuable than we thought."

I was glad that Harry's business sense hadn't completely deserted him in his troubles. I was sure he was planning to raise the price tags on the prints. Maybe that's why we pay so much attention to business; it takes our minds off loss and quirks. At any rate, it seemed to work that way with Harry. He paused, and then—his voice edging up a little closer to its usual alto range—he said, "You're a balm and a tonic, Jonathan." (I was no longer Jon.) "You're a sage and a gent. I'm going to take your advice."

"Anytime, Harry." I wasn't sure what advice he supposed I had given him. "Give my best to Lee," I said. But Harry had already broken the connection. I imagined him heading for his office and searching his wheel of phone numbers for the one that would make us both rich, and me famous.

As it turned out, that's exactly what happened. Three weeks later, four of the Spectral Portraits (now made official with initial capitals) appeared in a magazine that was usually described as influential and was ordinarily devoted to a style of writing that combined indifference with hysteria. However, the magazine's editors printed the portraits without any text except (in small type in the lower-right corner of the two-page spread): Photographs by Jonathan Brewster.

From the day the pictures were published, my life began to seem like one of those sequences in a 1930s B movie that shows days being mysteriously torn off a calendar while confusing, superimposed images fade and cross-fade in the foreground. The sound track seemed to consist entirely of the amplified ringing of a telephone.

The Spectral Portraits became that summer's international fad—the silly-time topic that substituting reporters and interviewers settled on to fill in the time until the vacationing deep thinkers returned to the job. There were two big questions that were asked about the pictures: whether they were fake, and who the people were (substantial and otherwise) who appeared in them. Harry and I refused to answer the questions (those we could have answered). I refused as a matter of principle (the principle of the sacredness of the inexplicable), and Harry refused on the grounds of sales strategy. Inquisitive and inquisitorial people began to follow me around, whining in my ears and stinging my eyes with electronic flashes. Joanne became the princess of the preschoolers, and I was about to take her out of school, when Ms. Abraham sent a message to me telling me that Joanne's celebrity was upsetting the school's routine. Since Joanne was enjoying the attention, I indulged in a little simple spite and decided to let her stay in the place a few more weeks until they adjourned for the season.

The opening of the show in Bill Freedman's gallery was a little decadent for my tastes, but Harry and Bill were delighted with the proceedings. At one point I saw them consulting a laconic young man who looked as if he had spent his youth in the vicinity of the Persian Gulf (Saudi Arabia, as it turned out), and when their little conference ended and the young man headed for the exit, Harry and Bill spent what must have been a full five minutes giggling and shaking hands with each other. I didn't begrudge them their ecstasies, but for my part, I wasn't feeling too jolly.

Actually, in the days preceding the opening, I had been in a relatively good mood. I had spent less time than usual brooding about Sara's disappearance, and I had even begun to take occasional pleasure in the thought that I had become a celebrity. But as I circulated in the crowd during the opening I became afflicted by another motion-picture effect—the sort of thing in which you see a noisy, crowded room that becomes illogically deserted for a few seconds and then returns to normal. In the little periods when the gallery seemed deserted, I was aware only of the portraits—or, actually, of Sara's image in the portraits. I wanted her to be there with me. Sometime during the evening, I realized that I had not kept one of the portraits for myself. At that point in the imaginary movie, the room seemed deserted for a longer time, and the camera panned slowly along the walls of the gallery, showing the portraits in close-up: Sara with left eyebrow raised slightly; Sara on the verge of a smile; Sara looking with satisfaction at Joanne; Sara with lascivious sidelong glance, partially obscured by the angel's wing.

When the crowd flashed back into the room, I pushed my way through them and went to the lascivious portrait. I took it down from the wall, put it under my arm, and started to leave the gallery. A Pinkerton man at the other side of the room began to shout and make his way toward me. Harry, who had been watching me, stopped the guard and said a few words to him, then gave me an odd, grave salute. I left, hailed a taxi, and headed home, grateful for the relative quiet and darkness, and daubing at my wet eyes with the cuffs of my shirt.

Joanne was still awake when I got to the apartment. She and Nanny Joy, both wearing flowered pajamas, were dancing to a brisk-tempoed number by a freespirited jazz band of the 1930s —Fletcher Henderson or Jimmy Lunceford, I supposed. Joy had her eyes closed, trucking or lindying, and Joanne was mimicking the dance, having one kind of good time and probably trying to imagine another, more grown-up kind. I watched them for a few minutes and thought of joining in, but decided against it.

I went into the kitchen and made some coffee. I propped Sara's portrait up against a food-processing machine that I don't think had ever been used—one of my dead-end enthusiasms. I sipped coffee and stared at the photograph. Would my enthusiasm for Sara ever vanish entirely? It didn't seem likely that it would—no more likely than it was that I would ever see her again. I had made a few more attempts to play Philip Marlowe. I had talked to her landlord, to some people at the musicians' union, and to a few more of her acquaintances, but no one seemed to know anything about her background. I had thought of hiring a real private investigator, but out of some kind of fear I didn't fully understand, I decided against it. I would be patient instead.

As I sat brooding, my daughter came jitterbugging into the kitchen. She was singing "Miss Brown to You," and my gloom couldn't stand up to that. When Joanne's little performance was finished, she climbed onto my lap and let her body go limp. I asked her whether she was tired.

"Oh, yes," she said. "I'm so tired I want to crawl inside you and go to sleep, Daddy. Would you like that?"

"I don't think so," I said. "I'm going to close my mouth so you don't crawl inside when I'm not looking." I closed my mouth.

"I could crawl inside somewhere else."

I kept my mouth closed.

"You know where I could crawl in?" Joanne asked.

I shook my head.

"I could crawl inside your penis."

My mouth dropped open. After I regained control of it, I said, "Who's been talking to you about penises?"

"Ms. Abraham. She told us about putting penises into vaginas and having babies."

"Oh, *did* she now?"

"Did she tell a fib?"

I calmed down a bit. I supposed I was being an old grouch. "No," I said. "She wasn't telling a fib." But fib or no fib, it seemed to me that Ms. Abraham could have found other things to talk about. "What else is happening at school?" I asked Joanne.

"Nobody likes me because I see ghosts."

"But you don't see ghosts anymore, do you?"

"No."

"I thought everyone liked your ghosts."

"Not now. Except the man."

"Which man?"

"The man who asks me about Miss Coleridge. Can I have some Chinese noodles, please?"

Joanne liked chow mein noodles—the wide, flat kind. I got some out of the cupboard and waited for her to go through her little ritual of putting them into her mouth one at a time and sucking them until they were soggy—something I found hard to understand, since for me their only attraction was their crispness. But I was more concerned with the inquisitive man—a reporter, I supposed—than I was with the noodles. I asked Joanne what she had told the man about Sara.

"That she's a nice lady and she plays the harp and she knows about Colnee and she is going to be my new mother." Joanne put a noodle into her mouth and let it marinate for a few seconds, but then she began to gag, and she spit it out.

"Are you all right?" I asked. "Did it go down the wrong way?"

Joanne shook her head. "It tastes wrong."

I took her in my arms. "What do you mean, it tastes wrong?"

"It looks right, but it tastes wrong."

I tried one, and it tasted the way chow mein noodles always taste. Then I remembered Nanny Joy mentioning the day before that Joanne hadn't been eating enough lately. I raised the sleeves of Joanne's pajama jacket and looked at her arms. She had never been what you would call a pudgy child, but I was sure that her arms were thinner than usual. "You're just tired, sweetie," I said. It didn't do me much good to see my daughter wasting away or to hear about obnoxious reporters following her around. And I decided that maybe it was time for us to get out of town for a while. I put Joanne to bed and telephoned Harry. I knew he would still be at the gallery, but I thought I would leave a message with his answering machine and see if he knew of a place where Joanne and I could spend the summer.

But Lee answered the phone. Neither she nor Harry had been willing to give up their own apartments, and they now lived alternately in the two places, according to some sort of schedule I didn't understand. Since having her abortion, Lee seemed to be as gabby and energetic as ever, but once in a while you would find her staring at the floor, looking as though her tongue had just discovered a hole in one of her teeth.

"Lee? Is Harry there?"

"Of course not, Jonathan. This is the transcendent evening of his life, or of his business life, anyway—I think I furnished him with something avocationally comparable once. But I couldn't compete tonight. Harry had no idea I was in the vicinity, so I departed it—the vicinity, that is. As you did, I noticed. And here we are. Are we the losers, Jonathan?"

"We have each other, Lee."

"And you have Joanne."

I ignored the hint of remorse that had shown up in Lee's voice. "That's why I'm calling," I said. "Joanne's getting a little more attention than I think is good for her. And I'm feeling besieged myself. I thought maybe we should get away for a while. But I don't know much about getaways."

"Nantucket," Lee said.

"Is that on Long Island?"

"Not exactly, dear. But it does have islandlike qualities. It's in the Atlantic, about thirty miles off the coast of Massachusetts—it's a base for a preppy crowd that is looking for quaintness. But, fortunately for you, I'm one of that crowd. I own a cottage there. Clapboards and roses—if my renters haven't absconded with them—so why don't you use it? Send me a picture. I haven't seen it in years—not since I stopped confusing charm with happiness—and I haven't rented it this year. Stay for the summer if you like. Maybe Harry and I will come out for a weekend. I'll send you the key if you're interested."

"I'm interested."

"Excellent. Take some sound equipment. Listen to some music. It's the best thing in the world, Jonathan." Lee paused for about a second, which for her was a dramatic interval. When she continued, the remorseful tone was back. "God, I envy you," she said. "You've got the time and the temperament to make something truly hellish out of your lost love. You're a fortunate man."

I didn't know how much mockery Lee intended—probably none at all. "I'm fortunate to have generous friends, anyway," I said. "Thanks for the cottage and the advice, Lee."

"I've hardly begun with advice, dear. But I have some contracts to look over, and someone at the gallery forced a capsule on me that seems to have been some sort of a downer. I'm unraveling, I'm afraid."

"Get some sleep, Lee, and tell Harry I'll call him at the office tomorrow. And thanks again."

Lee hadn't quite finished unraveling, though. "You must keep in mind, Jonathan, that we don't live by photography and music alone. See if you can't arrange to do a bit of screwing in the dunes. Chastity is bad for the prostate. Night-night."

Joanne and I left for Nantucket two days later. Lee's cottage was basically sound, but it needed some repairs. So, for the first couple of weeks I devoted myself to carpentry. While I was at it I built a new camera and tried my luck at photographing the scrubby landscape of the island. My luck wasn't good. I didn't even *try* to photograph the sea—which was too featureless and relentless for me to be comfortable with. I could hear the surf at night, and I decided that I didn't like things that don't sleep or go dormant once in a while.

But Harry sent me a few clients, and I photographed them outdoors under a canopy I built to diffuse the light. By using a couple of reflectors I soon got lighting that pretty well matched the conditions in my studio. The only difference was that the backgrounds were a little more exotic than in my indoor shots. But I soon managed to get the effect of painted backdrops, and I began to like the work I was doing.

My subjects were mostly summer visitors—some of them people I had photographed before in the city. I was interested in how they seemed less distinctive in their informal clothes, which allowed them to reveal more body but less sense of purpose. I soon began to encourage them to wear the most formal outfit they had available. One young lady didn't care much about the suggestion and insisted on wearing nothing at all. She also invited me to spend some time with her on the dunes by moonlight. I remembered Lee's suggestion that I seek out some female companionship, but I also remembered my love for Sara Coleridge. I decided I would be faithful to Sara—on the theory, I think, that my faithfulness might increase the chances that Sara would change her mind and return to me.

Joanne thought the sea was about as nice as anything else she had seen. She made some friends among the children of neighbors, and she spent most of the day away from me. At dusk she would return to me exhausted and, I was relieved to find, hungry enough to eat even my cooking. She was intrigued by the outdoor grill at the cottage, and she insisted on having broiled meat almost every night. But it was hardly worth the trouble to build a fire, because she also insisted on having the meat extremely rare. In fact, when we had ground beef, she would nibble little chunks of it raw while we were waiting for the charcoal to heat up. And when we had steaks, she would only let me cook them enough to take the chill off them. When the steak was on her plate, I would cut it into bite-sized chunks for her and try not to watch as she took pieces of bread and soaked up the blood that covered the bottom of the plate. It was an unpleasant sight, but she ate heartily and gained back the weight she had lost in the city.

I suppose it occurred to me at some point that Joanne's interest in red meat had actually begun while she was seeing her friend Colnee and while we were both seeing Sara. But I didn't read any significance into that, and if I *had* found it significant, I'm sure it would have seemed simple and innocent. I don't know if I was a better person than I am now, but there is no doubt that I was a more innocent person.

Although I didn't take Lee's advice about sexual matters, I followed her suggestion about listening to music. I bought a little audio cassette player and a few tapes. I used headphones instead of a loudspeaker with it, and most nights after Joanne was asleep, I turned out the lights and put on the headphones. Nantucket and the surf disappeared, and I committed myself to the world of music—or, actually, to the world of Orfeo and Euridice, since what I listened to every night was Gluck's opera. I had to hear at least the part where Orfeo is mourning the death of his love and thinking about killing himself. Then the moment I waited for—when Amor enters and announces that it was only a test of Orfeo's love. Euridice is brought back to life, and the good times roll. Of course, I realized that in the original myth, as in most real-life situations, there wasn't any resurrection and reunion. But I put my money on Gluck. I kept the sound volume turned down so that if Amor should knock on the door of the cabin with some good tidings, I wouldn't miss them. There was no knock.

Just in case Amor hadn't heard about my change of address, I telephoned Nanny Joy and Harry Bordeaux once a week. No one had any news of Sara. Joy was lonely and Harry was busy.

Toward the end of August, Harry and Lee visited me for a weekend, primarily so that Harry could show me the proofs of the book that was being published of the Spectral Portraits. Since there was no text in the book, it was simply a matter of approving the reproduction of the portraits. I approved almost totally. The publisher was using a new kind of coated stock, and the presses were being monitored by a computer that had a keen eye for tonal balance. My only reservation concerned the hundred-dollar price tag they planned to put on the unlimited-edition book. There was a time when I was lucky to get a hundred dollars for each of my edition-of-one prints. Then Harry told me that one of the original Spectral Portraits (or SPs, as they were now called) had fetched fifty thousand dollars. It was the result of a combination of genius (his and mine) and inflation, Harry said. He advised me to buy some real estate.

While Harry and I were conducting our business, Lee spent her time with Joanne. In fact, Lee spent her time with Joanne regardless of what her husband and I were doing. When the ladies decided to have steak *tartare* for dinner, Harry rebelled and insisted that we go to a seafood restaurant. Things got a bit nasty and complicated, and Harry and I ended up going to the restaurant alone, leaving Lee and Joanne at the cottage table with their banquet of raw ground beef, egg yolks, and onion. The real problem, though, had been created by the garnish of canned anchovies, for which Lee had made a special trip to town. Harry said that civilized people don't eat things that are preserved in metal. And he also wanted to know what kind of wine could conceivably accompany such a dish. I said that everything that was involved in that particular meal made me a little queasy. So Harry and I went to a restaurant and ate some kind of fish I had never heard of before and drank nonsparkling champagne. Harry confided in me that he and Lee were no longer living together. But judging from the sounds that emerged from their bedroom in the cottage that night, they either worked out a reconciliation or weren't as estranged as Harry wanted me to think.

The rest of the weekend—and the rest of the summer—was uneventful and doleful. I went gratefully back to Manhattan in September, but my gratitude didn't take the expected form. What I would have expected was that, being a confirmed city person, I would have been gratified just to get away from rusticity. But what I found was that I was simply thankful for the busyness of the city, which would keep my mind off Sara's disappearance. Surprisingly, the attractions of the city no longer seemed irresistible to me, and I realized that it would be possible for me to live happily away from the city if conditions were right—which meant if Sara were living with me.

But, all other factors aside, I had to leave the island of Nantucket—as the whalers had to leave it in the nineteenth century—to meet the demand of commerce. Sooner or later you've got to get back on board the *Pequod* or the crosstown bus and wait for the beast to surface and spout.

My beast surfaced timidly enough. It happened in the middle of November, during the first snowfall of the season, after I had bought a new wallet.

Chapter 9

I haven't owned many wallets in my lifetime. I've made every one last as long as I respectably could, and I've parted sadly with each discard, eyeing the replacement suspiciously, knowing it was not going to be as satisfactory as the one that preceded it. Throwing away an old wallet is like throwing away part of your body—a valuable part. Worn smooth by your own touch, matching the curve of your hip, it is the receptacle through which has passed a good part of your fortune, and which has contained names and mementos of people who have been important to you. How can anyone part easily with an object like that—or part with it at all? But the time comes when you find your pocket full of leather shreds and loose currency and credit cards, and you admit that it's time to shop around to find a replacement; something as much like the expired wallet as possible. Which is what I had done that day.

I got home and began the sad process of digging out the contents of the old wallet: dog-eared snapshots, mutilated postage stamps, forgotten reminders, meaningless phone numbers, eccentric shopping lists, and cryptic notes. I sat before a wastebasket, tossing bits of the past away, when I found tucked away in the corner of a pocket a slip with the word "Chilegray" scribbled on it. I flipped the note into the basket and began to dig around in the wallet again. And then my hand stiffened. Chilegray. What was that? I retrieved the slip and stared at the word, trying to remember when and why I had written it down.

Then I remembered: Joanne had said the word when she was in her Colnee phase. She said Chilegray was where Colnee lived. And if Colnee lived there, maybe Sara lived there too. I felt like Jonathan Brewster for the first time since Sara had disappeared. All I had to do was find out where Chilegray was. I put my new wallet in my pocket, grabbed my coat, ran down the stairs, got into a cab, and headed for the reference room of the main library.

Somewhere near Thirty-fourth Street, the cab driver asked me if I'd mind not whistling. I hadn't realized it before, but I was whistling the little orchestral figure from the scene in *Orfeo* in which Amor announces that Euridice is going to be brought back to life. I was feeling good enough that I wasn't even upset by the fastidious cab driver, who had decorated the taxi with badly lettered signs prohibiting everything except paying the fare and tipping. I paid the fare, but I didn't tip. I left the cab amid a stream of abuse, and the driver actually got out and started to follow me up the library steps, shouting for his tip. But I was moving too fast for him, and he gave up quickly. I guess he realized that there's no use trying to keep up with someone who's received a call from Amor.

My plan was to go through the index of the biggest U.S. atlas I could find. If that didn't help me, I would ask a reference librarian for advice. By the time I got into the library I was so excited that I had to stop off in the rest room. The main branch of the New York Public Library has always awed me anyway. It seems like the closest thing the city has to a temple. The cathedrals, the universities, even the stock exchange, seem a few notches below the library in importance, when all the motives and benefits are taken into account.

There were lots of atlases available. I picked out the biggest one and turned to the index. I knew things were going well when the book opened automatically to the page that listed the CH's. But despite the good omen, it took me a few seconds before I could bring myself to start reading the page. I wanted to put my hands over my eyes and slowly separate my fingers just enough to get a glimpse of the words. But I got my courage up and did things the adult way.

There was no Chilegray on the list.

I looked through the names a dozen times, thinking maybe I had forgotten how to alphabetize. But there was no Chilegray. Then it occurred to me that as good as Joanne was at enunciating, she still needed a few more years of practice before she could handle all the sounds in TV-commentator fashion. She tended especially to neglect the consonants. I looked at the list again, and there—I was certain—was the name I had been searching for: Childgrave.

Childgrave, New York; estimated population, 250. I turned to the map. Childgrave was a little more than a hundred miles north of New York City. I closed the atlas and kissed it. Then I went to a public telephone and talked to various long-distance operators, who assured me that there was no telephone service to Childgrave, New York. I wasn't discouraged by that news; in fact, it only made me more certain that I was on the right track. Sara hadn't thought of telephone service as a necessity when she was living in Manhattan, so it was only logical that she might have been raised in a place that didn't have telephones. The only thing that disturbed me was that I didn't think there was a community of any size in the United States that was without phone service. The more I thought of it, the stranger it seemed. You'd think that at least the mayor or the chief of police or the doctor would have a telephone. However you looked at it, you had to conclude that Childgrave wasn't your ordinary all-American village.

As I left the library I got out my new wallet and removed twenty dollars, which I dropped into a donations box in the lobby; a little offering at the temple. Outside, the snow was falling more heavily. I stood in the storm for a couple of minutes, letting it add to my exhilaration. Then I went to another telephone and called my apartment. I told Nanny Joy I had to go out of town on business and that it was possible I'd be away overnight.

I walked to a car-rental agency. I thought I would be able to make it to Childgrave in only a couple of hours, even taking into account the snow and my cautious, inexperienced driving.

As I drove north into the Catskills the freshly fallen snow, which was patchy as I left the city, became deeper and unbroken. Before I reached the approach to Childgrave, I drove for miles without seeing a person or even anything a person could live in or drive around in. When you're in the city, there's almost always someone around; maybe someone objectionable or threatening, but at least a person and not a rock. When I finally sighted the village, it was in heavy shadow. It lay in a remarkably small, steep-walled valley. Sunlight was still reflecting off the surrounding peaks, but a few lights were already visible in the houses of the town. I reduced my speed as I approached a hand-lettered roadside sign. The top lines read:

CHILDGRAVE
Founded 1636

At the bottom of the sign was an inscription that I had to stop the car to be able to read:

We did come unto this
incorrupted Wilderness
that we might live as
Sainctes under a Covenant
with Christ Jesus

I switched off the ignition and wondered if I should try to find a motel to spend the night in. I told myself it would be easier to get my information in the morning. But I was trying to deceive myself. What I should have told myself was that I was frightened. The darkness seemed to be increasing faster than it ever did in the city. I kept glancing at the sign. For the first time, I let myself think about the town's name. Death and children had become two of the big themes in my life in recent months, and I was glad I hadn't brought Joanne along on my trip. It would be wisest, I thought, never to bring her here, no matter what I might find.

Then I realized I was not alone. There was a crunching of snow somewhere nearby. An animal? Were there bears up here?

The car was suddenly filled with light, and I looked up into the beam of a powerful flashlight. There was still enough daylight for me to see that the flashlight was held by a short, overweight man wearing what I took to be a police officer's uniform. Whatever he was, he was armed. He switched off the flashlight, opened the door of my car, and eased himself into the seat beside me.

"Rudd," he said. "Delbert Rudd. Chief of police down there in Childgrave."

I sat and watched him grin. It wasn't what I'd have called a welcoming smile. And who the hell had given him permission to enter my car? I didn't think it would be wise to say what I wanted to say, so I didn't say anything. It was quiet; the ringing type of silence you never experience in the city. I was grateful for the occasional click of cooling metal beneath the car hood.

"I'm interested in fundamentals," the chief said. "I'm interested in food, God, and unlawful acts." He unzipped his jacket and chuckled. His shirt, tight across his belly, gapped open, revealing a patch of shiny, hairless flesh. He produced a battered metal lunch box and settled it in the folds of his lap. "I come up here every night about dusk to have my dinner. From New York City, are you?"

"Yes. My name is Jonathan Brewster." Suddenly I wanted to please him. "Is it that obvious? That I'm from New York, that is?"

"Just a lucky guess, Mr. Brewster." Chief Rudd patted his lunch box, making a series of drumlike little thuds. "This lunch pail belonged to my father. So you could say I'm also interested in tradition. The people realize that. It's one of the reasons they trust me, Mr. Brewster. Some of those lights you see coming on down in the village are kitchen lamps. The people are stocking their ovens, handling cold meat, and reading recipes that were written out by parents and grandparents. So the people share my interest in food and tradition. And even though they pretend not to, they share my interest in unlawful acts." The chief opened the lunch pail and removed the foil wrapping from a pale, skinless chicken breast. "Care to join me?"

The only thing I wanted was to have him get out of my car. I was frightened, not so much by his appearance as by his words. I thought people in small towns were supposed to be either friendly or taciturn. "Thanks," I said, "but I had dinner a few miles back." That wasn't true, but it seemed simpler to say that than to explain that I had suddenly lost my appetite.

Rudd nodded, still staring down at the village. "Not many laws get broken in Childgrave," he said. "But that doesn't mean that some of the people don't have unwise impulses. People can get frightened by some of the impulses they have. I understand that. That's why they made me their chief. They feel better knowing I'm here to look after them. That's not to say they're my friends, though. I can see the fear behind their smiles. They know I'm aware who went in or out of the wrong door; who's walking too fast."

He lifted up the piece of chicken and closed his eyes. "I thank thee, Lord, for nourishing me both physically and spiritually. And

I thank thee for revealing your desires to this community." The chief opened his eyes and looked at me with what might have been amusement. "Grace," he said. "Grace is what makes our town different from most others, Mr. Brewster. Strangers don't always understand that."

Oh, *don't* they? I thought. Oh, *don't* they? I was furious, but at the same time my fear was growing. If he had put handcuffs on me and searched my car, or if he had hinted that a cash contribution would keep me out of jail, I would have been less disturbed. To be pushed around or coerced by a cop is within the realm of possibility. You can deal with it. To have him talk about grace is against the rules and therefore terrifying. In any case, by that time it was obvious that I wasn't expected to say anything. I let him go on.

"There's not a stranger enters Childgrave that I don't know about in five minutes. I like to have a little chat with them like this, Mr. Brewster. I like to let them see how the leather of my holster is worn and shiny after twelve years, and I let them notice that my patrol car is painted black instead of the baby-blue you see in some places. I like them to know that this is a town of grace and law." He turned to me and smiled. "And I give them a chance to tell me how long they're planning to stay and for what purpose."

He took a bite of the chicken breast. That was my cue, I supposed. I wished there had been time to rehearse my lines as the chief had obviously rehearsed his over the years. I had the feeling that I would have to be careful in what I said. But I didn't want to seem hesitant. I plunged in.

"My business is simple, Chief, and I think you're just the one who can help me." The chief continued to chew, looking down at the village. I went on: "I'm looking for a young woman named Sara Coleridge. I understand she lives here."

Rudd swallowed. "She lived here once, but she left about a year ago. A year and three days ago."

"I thought maybe she'd come back recently."

"No."

There was obviously no reason to ask him whether he was certain. "Would you know whether she's expected back?"

"I'd say not, Mr. Brewster. I'd say definitely not. But you might want to talk to Sara's mother about that."

"Then she has relatives living in Childgrave?"

"Her mother. Her husband."

The chief turned to look at me. I guess he wanted to watch the color drain from my face. I wondered whether my vocal cords were still operating. "She has a husband?" I asked, in what came out as a stage whisper.

"Ex-husband. I forget that sometimes. We don't have much divorce in Childgrave, Mr. Brewster."

I was very tired of Childgrave's chief of police. There was no reason I had to put up with his moralizing. I wasn't trying to do anything illegal. I just wanted to drive into an ordinary village in New York State and get some ordinary information.

"Maybe you could give me the address of Sara's mother," I said. "I'd like to talk to her."

Rudd looked displeased. "Evelyn Coleridge will be going to a meeting tonight. The historical society. Maybe it would be better for you to come back tomorrow, Mr. Brewster. Yes, I think that might be better altogether."

It was totally dark now; a darkness that was the equivalent of the silence; more intense than anything I was used to. Rudd had finished eating and was taking noisy gulps from a thermos jug. The smell of coffee filled the car, and immediately I felt more confident. Coffee was something from my world. Rudd didn't exist on night air; he drank coffee, not blood. I switched on the interior lights. "That wouldn't be very convenient for me, chief," I said. "I have to be back in the city tomorrow. So I think I'll just have a word with Mrs. Coleridge before her meeting."

Rudd looked at me blankly for a moment and then smiled. "I'll show you where the house is," he said cheerfully. "Why don't you follow me down?" He got out of the car and walked away. A couple of minutes later, headlights appeared behind some low trees, and the chief's black car pulled out onto the road. I followed it down into the darkness.

Sara's mother lived in the center of the town in a frame house which, from the little I could see of it, was in need of repairs.

Chief Rudd came with me to the door and rapped several times on a tarnished brass knocker. No lights were visible in the house. The chief rapped again and then spoke for the first time since we had driven into town. "Like to see brass shine, myself," he said, running his fingers over the knocker, which seemed to represent the head of a cherub or a young child. Rudd made it sound as though Mrs. Coleridge's failure to polish brass were some kind of felony. I said nothing, but I had a little moment of pleasure as I remembered that there had been a knocker similar to it on the door of Sara's apartment in the city. The chief rapped once more. "She might be out visiting," he said.

It seemed obvious that there was no one in the house. And it also seemed obvious that the chief was not surprised. I wondered whether this was even Mrs. Coleridge's house. "I couldn't telephone her tomorrow, could I?"

"No telephones in Childgrave, Mr. Brewster. Is your astrological sign Leo, by any chance?"

I didn't answer the question. I didn't want to give him the satisfaction of knowing he had guessed right. "I think what I'll do," I said, "is wait in my car for a while. If Mrs. Coleridge doesn't get back, I'll write her a note and leave it for her."

The chief hesitated, obviously trying to think of a way to keep me in his sight or get me out of town. "You could always leave a message with me," he said. "My office is up at the head of the street in the Meeting Hall."

"Thanks. I may do that. You've been a big help, Chief Rudd. I hope I'll see you again."

"I think you might, Mr. Brewster. Yes, I think so."

I went to my car, almost breaking into a sprint, eager to shut myself away from grace and the law. They make you tell lies. I sat shivering and wondering whether I had only imagined Delbert Rudd. Perhaps a defect in my car was producing fumes. I could be having carbon monoxide hallucinations. I wanted a slender, solicitous woman to appear and offer me shelter and the kind of pie crust you can't buy in Manhattan. I wanted Sara to dance before me like a courting falcon.

Instead, the black patrol car reappeared and pulled up across the street from me. A woman got out of the back door and walked toward my car. I lowered the window and heard her say, "Mr. Brewster? I am Mrs. Coleridge."

"Yes." I wouldn't have been sure about the relationship. The woman was wearing a long, hooded black coat. Shadows hid her face. But she stood unnaturally straight and pronounced my name oddly; both things that Sara did.

"You are looking for my daughter, Sara?" she asked, her voice faint in the cold night. "She is, I regret to say, not here."

"Not in Childgrave?"

"Precisely. I had a note from her. She said she was to be traveling in Europe. She would let me know later exactly where she planned to stay. She was vague." Mrs. Coleridge looked back at Chief Rudd. I wondered whether there was fear in that glance, but when she turned back to me she was smiling slightly, as if in perfect collusion with the chief. "Forgive me if I cannot talk to you any longer," she said. "I am late for an appointment."

I reached into my pocket and found one of my business cards. I held it out to her. "When you find out where Sara is, perhaps you can let me know," I said.

She stepped toward me, her boots squeaking in the packed snow. Her eyes were on the card, not on me. "Yes," she said. "I regret I am unable to be of more help." She reentered the patrol car and drove off with Rudd. I suppose when you tell lies you can expect people to respond with lies. There was no choice but to leave town.

The main street—Golightly Street—ran only about four blocks. I drove slowly along the street past the old two-story buildings: solemn, awkwardly designed residences. I didn't see the church that I thought every small town had on its main street and that I would have expected in a community of saints. At the end of the road was the Meeting Hall, its lighted windows supplying the only feeling of life I had sensed in any of the buildings. Then there was only the night before me. My headlights picked out a heavy iron gate directly ahead, and beyond the gate I could make out what seemed to be the tallest structure in Childgrave: a mausoleum surmounted by an enormous stone angel. In its setting, the building had a more impressive scale—and certainly more dignity—than Manhattan's World Trade Center towers. I drove up to the gates, and my headlights revealed an inscription carved across the facade of the mausoleum: THE FOUNDER'S CHILD. I got out of the car and tried to open the gate, but it was firmly locked. There couldn't be much doubt that this was the child's grave that the town was named for. But that didn't tell me much. I wanted to know what remarkable thing the child must have done to have been commemorated in such a way.

I stood staring at the angel and listening to the occasional sounds coming from behind me in the town: a barking dog, the muffled clink of dishes. And then I became aware of a noise ahead of me: a faint, sibilant sound. It could have been someone dragging his or her feet through the snow. I looked intently ahead. Surrounding the mausoleum were neat rows of small, white-marble tombstones, barely distinguishable against the snow. Then, where the glow of my headlights blended into the night, I saw a quickly moving figure. It was a man dressed in black. He wore a short cape, knee breeches, and a high-crowned, wide-brimmed hat. It was the costume that one of the ghostly figures wore in my Spectral Portraits.

As I got back into the car, wondering whether I had really seen the figure, light appeared behind me, and a car pulled up, braking hard and scattering snow. It was a patrol car—not baby-blue—and in it sat my new friend Delbert Rudd. We lowered windows.

"Looking for the way out of town, were you?" the chief asked. He didn't wait for an answer. "Only one road out: the same one that comes in. If you turn either left or right, you'll circle back to the main street."

I circled back and drove out of town toward the highway.

Before I reached the highway, I pulled the car into a narrow side lane and parked. I didn't have any plans at that point, but I needed time to think about what had happened. It had stopped snowing, and it seemed to be warming up. A couple of inches of wet snow lay on the ground and on the branches of the pines that grew heavily in the area. With the car lights out, I thought maybe I had gone blind. Melting snow thudded onto the roof and hood of the car occasionally. I sat there, not so much thinking of what I had experienced in Childgrave as letting images flash through my mind.

It was a measure of how much I wanted to be with Sara again that I decided not to go right back to Manhattan. I was confused and frightened, but I wasn't going to give up. I knew there was no point in driving back to Childgrave, because Chief Rudd would undoubtedly be watching for my car to return. That meant I would have to walk back to the village. Sure. Down an unfamiliar, snow-covered hillside in the dark. Canvas shoes. No flashlight. A man with a handgun watching for me. Only an idiot would try it.

The idiot got out of the car and started to walk.

Obviously, if I wanted to keep from getting lost or breaking a few important bones, I had to stay close to the road. I was aware of the pines that loomed above me. Their snow-covered branches were slightly lighter than the sky, which made navigation possible, if not pleasant or simple. I stumbled along with my arms stretched out in front of my face. When I got free of the lane and onto the road to Childgrave, things got slightly easier. The snow on the road reflected enough light from the moonless sky to give me a sense of location. My biggest problem was that I kept stepping into holes or tripping over stones and branches. After twisting both ankles, I worked up a little audacity and moved out into the road, following the tracks that my tires had made earlier.

I started to make decent progress, and if my feet hadn't been so cold and wet, I would have felt like a clever boy scout earning a merit badge in night-hiking. Then the road curved sharply and began to rise. I was getting close to the crest of the hill, where nosy, devout Rudd would probably be lurking, making sure I wasn't walking too fast. I moved back to the side of the road, where I promptly tripped and fell over a rock, scraping my hand as I went down. I lay there for a moment, pitying myself and listening for signs of Rudd. Just as I started to push myself to my feet, a brilliant light flashed on in the area to my right. I dropped back into the snow. In the glare, I could see now that there were two lights—headlights. Then there was the sound of an engine being started, and Chief Rudd's car moved slowly out of a thicket. It was making straight for me. He's going to squash my head, I thought. I would give him another five seconds, and then I was going to run for the pine forest.

At the count of four, the lights moved away from me. The

chief was turning onto the road, in the direction of Childgrave. I realized that I had been holding my breath and that I was gripping snow in each of my clenched fists. I relaxed for a moment and then stood up and watched the lights of the police car recede down the road to Childgrave. My eyes gradually adjusted to the darkness again, and I set out walking in the tracks that the chief's car had conveniently left for me. I moved off the road again when I got close to the first house on the edge of the village. I navigated awkwardly but accurately by the lights of the houses and I got to what I hoped was Mrs. Coleridge's house without encountering any more automobiles or any strolling citizens. When I got to the door of the house, I was fairly certain I had the right place, because the cherubic (unpolished) knocker was where I expected it to be. On the other hand, the houses on the street looked pretty much alike, and maybe that type of door knocker was a town motif. There were lights on in the house, both downstairs and upstairs. I thought I had better take a peek through a window before I announced myself.

I scuttled around to the side of the house and slowly raised my head to the corner of a window. The room on the other side of the glass was a shadowy, deserted dining room, lit only indirectly by the lights from an adjoining room. I crouched again and crept around to the other side of the house; icy water dripped on me from the eaves. The next window I tried was more strongly lighted, although far from bright. It was also heavily curtained, but that made me feel a little safer and less likely to be seen by anyone inside. I was looking into a starkly decorated—or under-decorated—sitting room. And, appropriately, there was someone sitting in the room: Evelyn Coleridge. Seen through the diffusing material of the curtain, she looked younger and more attractive than she had when I saw her earlier. She also resembled Sara more closely than I had thought.

Evelyn was sitting in profile to me. I couldn't decide what she was doing. She seemed just to be staring at the bare wall. It occurred to me that she might be listening to music, but I would have heard any reasonably loud sound in the house. The excitement I had been feeling about my spy work began to turn to embarrassment. Also, now that I had stopped moving around,

I began to realize how cold my body was. There was a fire burning in the large fireplace that dominated the room, and I found myself becoming more interested in that than in anything else.

Whatever Evelyn Coleridge was thinking about, it occupied all her attention. If I hadn't been so miserable—I had begun to shiver—I would have felt guilty about interrupting her. Before I went to knock at the door, I took another look at the room. It was as stark as Sara's apartment had been in New York, but something more than my desperate condition made it seem inviting. And then I realized that the room was lighted not, as I had thought, by electric fixtures in the shape of candles but by actual candles. The yellowish light softened the effect of the bare walls and angular furniture. My shivering had become uncontrollable, and my neck was jerking strongly enough that I was afraid my head would bang against the window. As I started toward the front door Mrs. Coleridge stopped whatever she was doing and stood up. I heard the faint sound of a woman's voice coming from somewhere in the house. I hesitated.

Mrs. Coleridge walked out of the room and went to stand at the foot of the stairs and spoke a couple of times. Her voice was louder than the other one I had heard, but it wasn't clear enough for me to hear anything she said. If I had been even reasonably comfortable, I would have waited before revealing my presence, but I was almost hysterical with the cold. I ran quickly to the front of the house. I paused long enough to be sure there was no one on the street, and then I went to the door and tapped as lightly as I could with the door knocker.

Sara's mother opened the door immediately. She didn't seem to like what she saw, and for a moment she moved involuntarily to push the door closed. I tried to speak, but all I could manage was a little chattering of my teeth. Mrs. Coleridge opened the door wider. "Mr. Brewster," she said.

I took it as a good sign that she remembered my name, but I still couldn't talk.

"You had better come in," Mrs. Coleridge said.

I didn't hesitate. The hallway wasn't much warmer than the porch I had been standing on, but I was grateful just to have the snow out from under my feet. Mrs. Coleridge leaned out of the doorway and glanced up and down the street before she closed the door. "Come with me," she said and led me into the sitting room. I headed for the fireplace. Mrs. Coleridge watched me with what seemed to be a combination of fear and sympathy. The sympathy won out. She brought a chair to the edge of the fireplace. I sat down and put my feet practically into the flames. My feet had become the center of my universe. I was particularly interested in the fact that even though they were about to become torches, there was no sensation of warmth in them.

"Maybe you should take your shoes off," Mrs. Coleridge said.

I managed to articulate a reasonable facsimile of "If you don't mind." I leaned to untie my laces, only to find that there wasn't much more sensation in my fingers than there was in my toes. The laces were wet and caked with snow, and I couldn't make much headway.

"I had better help," Mrs. Coleridge said. She knelt in front of me and, more clear-minded than I was, simply yanked the shoes off without bothering to untie them. She took my socks off and began to rub my feet with her hands. It could have been a scene out of the Bible. My gratitude certainly had a biblical quality. Evelyn Coleridge seemed like a saint.

She was wearing a full-length black wool robe, and her hair, which was close to my face as I leaned forward, was almost totally white, although there were traces of the varied pale tints that I remembered from Sara's hair. Mrs. Coleridge must have been about fifty, but her face didn't have any lines that I could make out in the light of the fire. Her hands had the same graceful strength as Sara's. I wondered if Evelyn also played the harp.

A little sensation had begun to show up in my feet, and along with it came a new wave of embarrassment. "I think I'll be all right now," I said. "Why don't I take over?"

Evelyn leaned back and smiled at me. It seemed like a friendly smile. "Let me make you something hot to drink," she said. But when she left the room, I thought I heard her footsteps going up the stairway.

If I had been warm and dry, I probably would have done some peeking around corners or into drawers. But my curiosity wasn't as strong as my discomfort. I had stopped shaking, and sensation had returned to my body, but that just made me aware of a collection of aches and pains, and especially of my wet clothes. I hadn't exactly dressed for the kind of activity I'd just been involved in.

I heard Mrs. Coleridge on the stairway again, and in a moment she was back in the sitting room with me. She was holding a collection of somber but invitingly dry clothes.

"These belonged to my husband," she said. "Maybe you would like to put them on—if you have no objection to wearing someone else's clothing."

"I don't mind," I said. "Thank you."

"I shall make the tea. Have you eaten?"

"Not too recently."

"I can fix something. When you have changed, you might want to come into the kitchen, where it is warmer."

Evelyn left the room again, and I quickly got out of my sodden Manhattan garments, which I had mistakenly thought of as being practical simply because they weren't especially fashionable. As I changed I noticed that, despite everything, old Jonathan's sexual instinct hadn't been completely deflated. For a moment, he knew he was naked and (presumably) alone in a house with a reasonably attractive woman. I wasn't proud of myself at that moment, but I didn't take responsibility for the impulse. It was merely my job to suppress it.

It was easily suppressed, particularly when I got a look at the clothes Sara's mother had brought me. Everything looked homemade: black trousers of a heavy, hand-finished fabric; a grayish denim shirt; a bulky, loosely knitted black sweater; gray cotton underwear; gray woolen socks; and black shoes. I wondered whether Mr. Coleridge had spent some time in prison. All the clothes were a little too small, but not small enough to cause me any discomfort.

I went into the hallway. I noticed again that the temperature there was on the cool side, and I decided that the house was not centrally heated. The kitchen was tropically warm, thanks to a magnificent cast-iron stove that apparently operated on wood or coal. Oil embargoes weren't going to have much effect on the Coleridge household. It also occurred to me that I hadn't seen many—if any—automobiles (except the chief's) in my ramblings around Childgrave.

Mrs. Coleridge was at the sink, and I was glad to see that the kitchen was equipped with faucets rather than a hand pump. I was glad, because I was about to ask if there was a toilet I could make use of, and I didn't want to have to deal with an outhouse. Evelyn directed me down the hall, and when I returned to the kitchen, an odd but satisfying meal was waiting for me.

"I suppose you are not a vegetarian," Evelyn said.

"No," I said, a little apologetically.

"I do not keep meat in the house. Do not feel obliged to eat anything that is distasteful to you in my little offering."

I liked it all: corn muffins with honey, a vegetable salad with oil and vinegar, fresh pears, and tea with lemon. As I ate, we talked.

Mrs. Coleridge began with a reasonable question: "Did your car break down, Mr. Brewster?"

"Call me Jonathan, please. No, I just wanted to talk to you alone before I went back to the city, and I thought I'd have a better chance of getting past Chief Rudd if I walked. He doesn't seem to care much for outsiders."

"That is true of most of us in Childgrave, Mr. Brewster. Mr. Rudd speaks for us all."

So I was still Mr. Brewster, and I was not as welcome as I had thought. "I'm sorry to intrude," I said. "It's just that I'm in love with Sara, and I wanted you to know about it, and . . . Well, I'm not sure what I wanted, except to see Sara again."

"Does Sara love *you*, Mr. Brewster?"

"I thought she did—or that she was beginning to. I thought maybe she had told you about me before she left for Europe."

"No, she did not."

"Then she was here recently?"

"Just for a few days."

So Chief Rudd had been lying to me. His interest in God didn't extend to truthfulness. I wondered how truthful Mrs. Coleridge was being. And I wondered who was upstairs in the house. "You don't have an address for Sara now?" I asked.

Mrs. Coleridge produced a few wrinkles in the smooth brow

I had admired before. "I answered that question for you before, Mr. Brewster."

I wasn't going over too well with the lady I hoped would become my mother-in-law. "Yes, I'm sorry," I said. "It's just that I drove down here expecting to see Sara. I felt better than I had felt in months. I didn't expect to get run out of town and to have to impose on you this way." As had become my custom since meeting Sara, my eyes began to mist up. "You've been very kind to me, Mrs. Coleridge," I said.

"Call me Evelyn, please. And tell me about yourself—and Sara."

I told her. I didn't do any more lying, but within that considerable limitation, I did everything I could to make myself sound like the perfect son-in-law. Evelyn seemed especially interested in what I had to say about Joanne and the Spectral Portraits. After I had made my presentation, we moved back into the sitting room. Evelyn put a log on the fire, showing a surprising amount of strength in the process.

Then I was allowed to ask a few questions. I found out that Sara's ex-husband (Martin) still lived in Childgrave and was on friendly terms with Sara and her mother. The marriage had been annulled because Martin had forgotten to mention to Sara that he was gay. (Or, as Evelyn put it, eyes averted, "Martin's sexual preference was for his own gender . . . and Sara hoped to have a family.") I was definitely feeling better by then. Evelyn said her own husband had died three years ago, but she didn't say how.

I settled in, prepared to sit there happily all night, learning all I could about Sara. I couldn't decide what kind of person Sara's mother was. She had some of the same reserve and elusiveness that her daughter had shown. Evelyn was obviously an educated woman, but I got the feeling she had been educated in the middle of the nineteenth century. When I turned away from her to look into the fireplace, it seemed as if I were listening to the oldest woman I had ever met. Not that her voice wasn't clear and pleasing, but her phrasing and diction—the dignity of her speech—were so different from the vocal shorthand I was used to in Manhattan that it was easy for me to believe I was in a different time as well as a different place.

I also realized that, aside from Sara and Joanne, there was no one I would rather be spending the evening with. And then Evelyn spoiled the evening by saying, "I shall be retiring soon, Jonathan. And I am certain you want to start back to your home. I have a pair of rubber overshoes you can wear for your walk back to your automobile."

I got up and gathered together my still-soggy clothes.

"You need not change your clothing again," Evelyn said.

"I'd appreciate that. I could mail your things back to you."

Evelyn responded with what seemed like a prime non sequitur: "Would you classify yourself as a Christian, Jonathan?"

"No, I don't *think* so."

"And why is it that you are not a Christian?"

I wanted to please Sara's mother, and I would probably have said whatever she wanted me to say. But I had no idea what that might be. And since theology wasn't one of my strong subjects, I just had to be as truthful as I could. "I've never thought much about it," I said. "It might be because I prefer to make up my own mind about what's right and what's wrong. Or, more likely, it's something simpler. I'm probably not a Christian for the same reason I'm not an alcoholic: I've never felt the need."

"But you do not rule out the possibility that you might someday feel the need?"

"No." I didn't ask Mrs. Coleridge which need she had in mind. At that moment, I would rather have had a drink than a sermon. But what I really wanted was to run up the staircase and see who was waiting quietly on the floor above me. Instead, I thanked Mrs. Coleridge and put on a pair of boots she offered me. She slipped a heavy black coat around my shoulders, and I went out into the night. Outside the house, I tried to get my arms into the sleeves of the coat. After struggling a bit, I found out what the problem was—what she had given me wasn't a coat but a cape. I stood savoring one of the odder sensations of my life. The situation seemed unacceptable to me. But I decided I really had no choice but to walk back up the hill to my car.

The street was deserted, and most of the houses in the village were dark. There didn't seem to be much chance of my being seen by anyone, so I abandoned my sneak-thief tactics and walked along the sidewalk as though I were a normal human being. The sky had cleared somewhat, and I could make out a pale glow where the moon shone behind thin clouds. The smell of wood smoke hung over the village, and the only sound I could hear was the crunch of my own careful footsteps.

But before I reached the end of the street, headlights appeared on the road ahead of me. I moved off the sidewalk into the shelter of some tall bushes. The headlights were moving very slowly toward the center of town. Then I became aware of a distant, high-pitched voice that seemed to be singing. Soon I could see that a child dressed in a hooded white snowsuit was moving along the center of the road, illuminated by the car's lights. The child seemed to be a girl about Joanne's age. She was dancing ecstatically, waving her arms and singing what sounded like a folk song. She stopped occasionally to roll in the snow or to throw handfuls of it into the air. The car kept its distance a few yards behind her. The song drifted through the town:

Josiah, Mariah, and Colony,
Why wandereth ye in the night?
Dear mother and father and sweet baby,
With the Angel of Death now in sight.

As the strange procession moved past me I discovered that the person seated behind the steering wheel of the car was Chief Delbert Rudd.

I waited until the car was well past me before I tried to move away. The child continued to sing the plaintive song, her voice fading into the darkness. I remembered the phrase "a terrible beauty," which I had read somewhere, but which I had never quite understood. Now I knew what those words meant. What I had seen in the last few moments was certainly as beautiful as anything I had ever witnessed. And yet I was terrified. I was sure the song the girl had sung was connected with the spectral images in the portraits I had done of Joanne and Sara. What disturbed me most was the mention of the Angel of Death. I had assumed that the appearance of the angel in the portraits could only have been a good omen. Now I knew I was wrong.

I was glad Joanne was safe in our apartment in Manhattan, and I decided that I should be there too. Perhaps Sara had good reason to want to keep us out of her life.

Chapter 10

I made it back to the car without doing my body or senses any further injury and headed eagerly for the highway. After driving for a few miles, I began to realize that I was close to exhaustion. My eyelids seemed to have turned into heavy metal, and quite a few of my muscles were letting me know that they resented being sent into combat after years of the equivalent of barracks life. It was only about eleven o'clock, and I could make it back to Manhattan in time to get a decent night's sleep, but motels began to look irresistible to me. Then I remembered how I was dressed. I was afraid that if someone saw me get out of the car, they would arrange to have me fitted for a straitjacket. I kept driving.

Fortunately, when I got to the apartment, Nanny Joy was asleep. I went straight for my bed, and if I had been wearing my own clothes, I wouldn't have bothered to take them off before collapsing. I didn't regret that I wasn't able to reprise more than one or two images from the day's activities before I fell into a deep sleep.

I opened my eyes again about noon the next day, feeling hungry and surprisingly energetic. My eyes weren't able to find my Childgrave costume, which should have been on the bedroom floor. Did that mean that the whole Childgrave episode had been a dream? If so, I didn't know whether that was good or bad.

I went to the closet, where I found the missing ensemble—which was even drearier than I had remembered—neatly put away on hangers. Apparently Nanny Joy had looked in on me during the morning. My next stop was the kitchen, where I found Joy having lunch. I cooked some bacon and eggs for myself and joined Joy for a chat.

"See you got yourself some new clothes," she said. "What I want to know is where you found Count Dracula's tailor."

I tried to go along with Joy's joking approach to the situation, although I sensed that she was as unsettled by it as I was.

"Dracula's tailor," I said, "works out of a ruined castle on the Lower East Side. Harry put me on to him. Doesn't open till after sunset, so not a lot of people know about him. The hole in the front of the shirt is where the stake goes."

Joy wasn't any more amused than I was. Her tone became a little more serious: "Those are some weird clothes, Mr. B."

"I had a weird night, Joy. I went to Sara's hometown."

"Was Sara there?"

"I'm not sure. I met her mother, though."

"That's always weird."

"Actually, she was all right—kind, at least."

"You didn't meet her husband?"

"He's dead. Those are his clothes, I think."

"That would do it."

Joy and I both smiled at that, and I began to feel a little less nervous about what I was remembering of my experiences in Childgrave. I gave Nanny Joy a quick summary of the trip. She listened carefully, but she obviously thought I was doing a lot of exaggerating or embellishing. And as I recalled the details of the evening, my apprehension returned.

"You're sure you didn't do some drinking you forgot to mention?" she asked me.

"I'm sure."

"Are you thinking of going back there?"

"Probably not."

"Well, I want you to promise me something," Joy said. "If you do go back there, don't take Joanne. That is *no* place for a child. In fact, that's no place for anyone. I can see why Sara wanted out. I'm betting she *is* in Europe. So, do you promise to keep Joanne away from there?"

I hesitated before I answered. Finally, I promised. But I also did something I hadn't done since my boy scout days: I crossed my fingers as I spoke.

After breakfast, I spent about half an hour in a tubful of warm water, trying to reassure myself about my visit to Childgrave. Actually, I hadn't seen most of the town. I had met only two people, and if Delbert Rudd didn't radiate the surpriseproof tolerance shown by the cops of New York City's Twenty-third Precinct, and if Evelyn Coleridge wasn't a warmly aggressive Upper West Side mom, that didn't mean they were sinister. People who live a couple of blocks from a cemetery and who burn candles without being involved in romance or a birthday celebration are likely to behave in special ways. I wanted to know more about those ways, but—for two reasons—I wasn't going to force the issue. One of those reasons was my inborn patience, and the other was Delbert Rudd. There might have been a third reason —in the shape of an angel.

After my bath, I bundled up the clothes I had borrowed from Sara's mother and took the package to a post office. I checked a directory and was relieved to find that the U.S. Postal Service was aware of the existence of Childgrave, New York. I addressed the package to Mrs. Coleridge, Golightly Street, and supposed it wouldn't make much difference that I didn't know her house number.

For the next couple of days, I spent as much time as I could with Joanne, who tended to ask me too often when Sara and I were going to be married. "Soon," I told her, but I doubt whether I sounded very convincing.

Harry Bordeaux began urging me to produce some new Spectral Portraits, and he made his request seem fairly reasonable by sending me a check that was large enough to send me off in search of an accountant. I didn't tell Harry, or anyone other than Nanny Joy, about Childgrave. I became domestic and reflective.

My reflections didn't exactly fill me with delight. The topic I kept returning to was Childgrave, and no matter how I looked at the topic, it was forbidding. Everything about the town, from its name and appearance to the people I had met there, was out of the ordinary in an unsettling way. I tried to tell myself that all my years of living in Manhattan had put me out of touch with the real America, and that what I had seen in Childgrave was normal and desirable. But the only aspect of the town that really attracted me was the possibility that Sara might be there.

I couldn't forget Childgrave, yet I didn't want to return there. Something or someone would have to help me resolve my dilemma. I soon realized that I had fallen into my old habit of waiting for a sign.

The sign came a week after my first visit to Childgrave. It was an ordinary enough sign: a letter. That is, it would have been ordinary if it hadn't been from Evelyn Coleridge and if it hadn't read:

Dear Mr. Brewster,

I should like to express my gratitude to you for returning the clothing which you recently borrowed from me. I trust that your journey back to New York City was a safe one.

I should also like you to know that I found it a pleasure to meet someone whom my daughter Sara had befriended. It occurs to me that perhaps you would enjoy learning something more about Childgrave.

Therefore, if you should be free any Saturday to have lunch with me at my house, I would deem it a pleasure to receive you. And perhaps after lunch you might like me to show you about our small, but I believe interesting, village. Your young daughter might also find such a visit enjoyable, and I hope you will feel free to have her accompany you.

Should my invitation interest you, please let me know the date and hour on which you plan to make your visit, and possibly I can persuade Mr. Rudd to meet your car at the highway and escort you to my home.

I look forward to renewing our acquaintance.

Respectfully,
Mrs. Evelyn Coleridge

I read the letter six times and then sat and thought about it. Mrs. Coleridge was a formal lady. But she was doing something out of character offering a prying stranger a chance to pry. The question was: Why was she stepping out of character? She made it clear that even Chief Rudd had been persuaded to play the unlikely role of welcomer. Something odd was going on in the "small, but I believe interesting, village" of Childgrave. In fact, there was a good chance that something odd had been going on there for about three hundred years. I doubted that many people had been invited to "learn something more" about it.

I didn't know whether Mrs. Coleridge was granting me a privilege or leading me down a path that featured a leaf-covered pit. I tried to remind myself of the terror I had felt in Childgrave, and I remembered that I had promised Nanny Joy that I wouldn't go there with Joanne. But fears and promises faded under the thought that I might see Sara again if I accepted the invitation. I went out and bought some stationery and sent Mrs. Coleridge a comparatively informal note telling her that Joanne and I would arrive in Childgrave on the following Saturday at about noon.

When I asked Joanne whether she would like to go for a weekend drive in the country, she seemed delighted with the suggestion. It would mean canceling her plans to attend a festival of "Toddlers' Film Classics" which Ms. Abraham had arranged. But Joanne confessed that she secretly agreed with one of her classmates who thought Felix the Cat was "an asshole." I hoped my daughter wouldn't start quoting her little friends when we visited Mrs. Coleridge.

Nanny Joy didn't respond too well when I told her about the planned trip. She knew I didn't like automobiles and that my little "spin in the country" suggestion was unprecedented. When she accused me of breaking my promise that I wouldn't take Joanne to Childgrave, I had to admit the truth. It was a bad moment. I had weakened Joy's trust in me, and I knew that life was more difficult without trust. And there was also a chance that Joy was right in thinking that a visit to Childgrave might not be the best thing for the peace of Joanne's young mind, which was no longer being burdened by the presence of invisible friends. But love and the tranquil mind don't always go together.

So, the next Saturday, Joanne and I strapped ourselves into a rental car (black) and took to the road. The day was clear and brilliantly sunny as we left Manhattan, and the snow that had fallen during my first trip to Childgrave had melted.

Joanne was showing signs of high excitement as we left. Patches of red appeared, faded, and reappeared on various parts of her face, making her look as if she were experimenting with makeup. She was also unusually silent. Joanne didn't have the suburbanite child's casual attitude toward automobiles. She got to huddle in the back of taxicabs once in a while, but the view of the Hudson River and the New Jersey Palisades from the front seat of a car moving over the George Washington Bridge was too much for her to deal with comfortably. She finally put her hands over her eyes and slumped down in the seat.

"I'm five years old now," she said.

Joanne had had her fifth birthday on the second day of November, and she had expected that life would hold no more secrets or problems for her after that. Whenever things got a bit sticky, she reminded herself that she was no longer four. I understood that impulse, but with me it was reversed. As I dealt with confusing road signs and aggressive drivers I had to remind myself occasionally that I had not yet reached the age of fearful senility.

After we got over the bridge and through the heavy traffic around the city, Joanne and I both relaxed a little. It was time for me to try a little honesty. Joanne was sitting up and taking notice of her surroundings again.

"Do you remember when you told me about Chilegray?" I asked.

Joanne didn't hesitate. "That's where Colnee lived."

"Well, it's called Childgrave. And we're going to visit there. We're going to have lunch with Miss Coleridge's mother."

"Will Miss Coleridge be there?"

"I don't think so." But although I didn't expect Sara to be there, I had been doing some hoping that she would be. It was almost Thanksgiving Day, and I had convinced myself that Sara might be coming home to see her mother (if she hadn't been at home all along). If so, I would indeed be giving some elaborate thanks.

"Mrs. Coleridge would be like my grandmother, wouldn't she?" Joanne asked.

"That's right. She's a nice lady. She wants to meet you."

Joanne began to sing the old Thanksgiving song: "Over the river and through the woods, to Grandmother's house we go." Those were the only words she knew of the song, and they were the only ones I had ever known. We sang them badly and repeatedly as the mountains and the woods began to appear. My enthusiasm for the songfest gave out before Joanne's did. She began to vary the lyrics of the song:

Over the river and through the woods,
To Colnee's house we go.
We'll eat and drink,
And then we'll think
Of the wild and drifting snow.

The reference to snow made me think of my previous trip to Childgrave, and despite the sunshine and music, I began to feel a little apprehensive. Joanne seemed to sense my change of mood. She stopped singing and quickly fell asleep. The sound of her steady breathing and the drone of the engine began to affect me. The car was too warm, and I felt as though someone were hypnotizing me and saying, "When you wake up, you will feel awful."

I turned off the car's heater and opened a window slightly. I told myself I was going to have a good time in Childgrave. I was going to show Joanne what the real America was like: the America that shows up on television commercials, with reasonable, smiling, healthy people sitting on a front porch or around a fireplace, eating or drinking or getting cheerful telephone calls from relatives.

But no one got telephone calls in Childgrave. And even though in general that seemed to me like an admirable state of affairs, I was aware that to most people—or even to me in my more reflective moments—there would seem to be something perverse about that kind of isolation.

I wondered what I would have thought of Childgrave if it had no associations with Sara. Would I have just ignored it? Would it have seemed fascinating in some way? Or would it have frightened me? Probably now—as opposed to the time of my first visit—it would have been attractively mysterious.

But I wasn't searching for mystery. I was looking for Sara, of course. But what did Sara represent? She could give me the stability that comes with being part of a family; she could be a wife to me and a mother to Joanne. But there was more to it than that. Once again, I got the feeling that Sara had a special kind of knowledge that I wanted to share. It wasn't exactly that I felt she had something to teach me, but rather that I could add meaning to my life just by supporting her beliefs. According to the road sign at the edge of Childgrave, Sara came from what was—or at least had been at one time—a community of saints. The idea of becoming a saint didn't appeal to me, but I thought I wouldn't mind helping someone else become one. I didn't know a lot about sanctity, but I knew enough to be sure that it was a complicated subject and that saints came in a great variety of shapes and personalities.

I was reminded of one of the more unlikely shapes and personalities when I saw Delbert Rudd's patrol car suddenly appear in my rearview mirror. I hadn't realized I was so close to Childgrave. I slowed down and let Rudd pass me. In the sunshine, the patrol car seemed merely grimy, and not menacing as it had in the darkness. The chief stopped at the turnoff that led to the village, and I pulled up behind him. He got out of his car and walked over to see us. Joanne had roused herself, and as I glanced over at her I could see she had decided to make use of her five years of practice in dispensing charm.

Delbert Rudd was obviously at a disadvantage. He had to overcome forty or so years of experience in casting suspicious glances. He said hello to me without much enthusiasm and turned his attention to Joanne. I made introductions, and I was sorry to see that a friendship had apparently begun. After I said to Joanne, "Mr. Rudd is a chief of police," she and Delbert began to talk across me as if I were an inconvenient lump on the driver's seat of the car.

Joanne produced her most seductive smile, gazed at the floor of the car, swung her legs shyly, and said to Mr. Rudd: "Do you have a horsie?"

The chief didn't actually smile, but his eyes did an approximation of a twinkle. "I don't personally have a horse," he said. (He obviously didn't have the courage to say "horsie.") "But there are some near our village. Would you like to ride one?"

"No. I don't think so, thank you. But I would like to get a Christmas tree."

"It might be a little early for that, dear. But if you come back nearer Christmas, I'm sure we can find a nice one for you."

"I'm five years old now."

Joanne was using her scattergun technique. I wondered

whether Delbert had had enough experience with children to know that the technique was never as aimless as it seemed and that Joanne was—without having to bother with the conventions of grown-up talk—finding out what her new acquaintance had to offer her. And I wondered whether Joanne would find out that the chief had been known to run people out of town and to watch young girls dance in the glare of his black car's headlights.

"Do you like being five?" the chief asked.

"Yes. I'm old enough to do anything I want."

I would have to have a talk with Joanne when we got home.

Chief Rudd seemed as interested in Joanne's last statement as I was. "When will you be six?" he asked.

"Not for a long time. And then I'll be too old to die."

There was a pause. I was trying to figure out whether there was any hidden logic in Joanne's ramblings. The chief seemed entranced and moved by what he had heard. Joanne looked smug. "My toads died," she said. "But they didn't say their prayers the way I do."

"What do you say in your prayers?" the chief asked.

"I bless everyone. And now I can bless you."

Chief Rudd swallowed hard a couple of times, and his vocal cords made a couple of false starts before coming out with "It's a pleasure to have you in Childgrave, young lady." Then he turned and walked to his car and drove away. There were no welcoming remarks for me.

Joanne and I sat squinting against the glare of the sun. I noticed, though, that even at noon the village of Childgrave lay in shadow. It was obviously one of those places that the folk song describes as "a holler where the sun don't ever shine."

"What was all that about dying?" I asked Joanne. "I didn't understand that."

"Mr. Rudd knew."

"Maybe Mr. Rudd knew, but your daddy doesn't know."

I waited for Joanne to tell me what I didn't know, but she obviously wasn't going to volunteer anything.

I tried again. "Why do you talk so much about dying lately, sweetie?"

Joanne closed her eyes in a tight squint and began to massage her face in some kind of exasperation. I didn't let her off the hook that easily. "What does it mean when you say you'll be too old to die?"

My daughter sighed. "It's like that in Chilegray. But it's all right. You'll see."

I started the car. I suspected that even if Joanne had tried to explain her thoughts and feelings she wouldn't have succeeded. As we drove down into the shadows Joanne looked eager and delighted. I would try to take her at her word: it would be all right. But I had my doubts. I thought of the rows of small headstones in the town's cemetery; I thought of the name "Childgrave"; and —in my most disturbing thought—I wondered why Chief Rudd had not needed any explanation of Joanne's cryptic remarks about death. As Joanne had said, he understood. I didn't know whether I was upset by the possibility that my daughter might be in danger or by the fact that she and Delbert might be sharing a secret. I hoped I would be let in on the secret during our visit.

Mrs. Coleridge opened the front door of her house before we were out of the car. She was wearing a long-sleeved plum-colored dress with a floor-length skirt, and a lace-trimmed high collar. If she had been at a cocktail party in Manhattan, her outfit would have looked eccentrically stylish. But standing in the doorway of her old house, she looked like a handsome participant in a historical pageant.

Joanne and Mrs. Coleridge greeted each other as though they were old friends. A couple of large logs were burning in the fireplace of the sitting room. We settled down, and I listened to my daughter and my would-be mother-in-law chat. There were no cryptic remarks—just straightforward, get-acquainted exchanges. I joined in occasionally, but mostly I just observed. Or, actually, I was ignored. No one in Childgrave seemed especially interested in me. But my resentment was offset by the pride I took in Joanne's ability to carry on an adult conversation with a stranger. Maybe Ms. Abraham was doing something right, after all. But more likely I had Nanny Joy to thank for my daughter's social graces.

Mrs. Coleridge brought in a tray of homemade bread, apple butter, cashew butter, cider, and pears. The meal reminded me that vegetarianism is not without its appeal. After lunch, I helped

Mrs. Coleridge clear away the dishes, and just as we sat down again, there was a tap on the front door.

"I asked some friends to stop by," Evelyn said. She opened the door, and four people came into the house. Three of them were adults who looked friendly but reserved. The fourth was an unreserved girl of about Joanne's age, who announced that her name was Gwendolyn Hopkins. She pulled her coat off, kissed Joanne, and took her by the hand. "I'll show you what it's like upstairs," she said, and the two girls disappeared up the staircase.

Two of the adults were Gwendolyn's parents, Beth and Arthur Hopkins. Beth was tall, plain, and awkward. She had an unmistakably pensive quality, and she didn't pay much attention to me. I thought at first that she was one of those annoying, self-obsessed people, but I soon realized that she was thinking not about herself but someone else—probably about her daughter. She kept glancing up at the ceiling, as if trying to see into the rooms above us in which Gwendolyn and Joanne could be heard faintly moving about and chattering. But judging from Beth's expression, if she was thinking about her daughter, the thoughts couldn't have been either uncomplicated or pleasant.

Arthur, Beth's husband, was as tall and plain as she was, but the same features that made her not especially attractive seemed quite acceptable in him. He looked better with her than he would have without her, and maybe that might have been the basis of a good marriage in their case, because they seemed devoted to each other.

The other stranger was a Miss Verity Palmer, who was short, buxom, and much sexier than I would have expected anyone named Verity to be. She was giving me her full attention. It seemed as if she were looking for a conquest rather than a friend, and I was both intrigued and embarrassed.

We all sat down and tried to explain ourselves to one another, but I got the feeling that they knew a lot more about me than I did about them.

"Jonathan is a portrait photographer who lives in New York City," Mrs. Coleridge said. "He is a friend of Sara's."

"We're all quite proud of Sara," Beth said. "Have you heard her play the harp?"

"Yes. Not as often as I'd like to, but I've heard her." I was reminded that I hadn't spent as much time as I'd like doing anything with Sara.

Mrs. Coleridge took the role of interlocutor again. "Beth helped teach Sara to play the harp, Jonathan. We have always had highly accomplished harpists in Childgrave."

Beth's look of general regret deepened a little, perhaps because a little envy had been stirred up. "No one has been as accomplished as Sara," she said. "Sara's a genius." Beth turned to her husband. "Don't you agree, Arthur?"

"Probably," Arthur said.

Beth looked respectfully at cautious Arthur and then said to me, "He's got the best ear in Childgrave, but, unfortunately, he's only interested in grapes and muscles."

"As in cockles and mussels?" I asked.

There were some amused glances, and then Verity Palmer said, "No, as in biceps and sphincters." The glances lost their amusement. Verity didn't seem concerned. "Arthur and Beth are medical illustrators. Beth does skeletons, and Arthur does muscles."

For a moment I forgot I wasn't in Manhattan. "And together, they lick the plate clean," I said.

Verity said, "Yes," and giggled. The others stared blankly at me for a few awkward seconds.

And then Arthur said, "Hybrids." I wrinkled my brow and tilted my head. "The grapes," he said. "French hybrid varietals grafted to American root stock."

"You grow them?" I asked. Arthur nodded. I had to add, "Without sunlight?"

"The other side of the hill. The south slope, near the river. I'm getting close to a decent red wine. Maybe you'd like to sample it."

I was beginning to like Arthur. Obviously, his terseness and reserve concealed some strong enthusiasms. He was probably the kind of husband who never touched his wife in public but who never stopped touching her in private. I didn't share his presumed enthusiasm for Beth, but I thought he could probably get me to share his interest in grapes without too much trouble. I said, "I'd like to try your wine, but I don't have much of a palate, I'm afraid. My agent should be here. He knows about wine."

"So does ours," Beth said.

"Your what?"

"Our agent."

"You have an *agent?*"

"For our illustrations. He's in Manhattan. He gets us work from publishers."

So Harry might be right. The time would come when everyone would have an agent. Childgrave was beginning to seem less sinister to me. With the exception of Mrs. Coleridge, with her archaic quality, the people I was talking to seemed like people I could have encountered in the city at any time. Verity Palmer, for example, struck me as being intelligent, self-assured, and energetic. She might have been the chairwoman of a volunteer committee. I tested my theory and asked her how she spent her time.

"I dominate our local historical society," she said. "And I also conduct tours of the village for curly-haired visiting photographers. As a matter of fact, the next tour starts . . ." (she consulted a watch that was pinned to the front of her strikingly tight sweater) ". . . now."

Mrs. Coleridge and the Hopkinses looked a little surprised at the announcement. I sat quietly and waited for my hostess to sort things out. Then, from the upper floor of the house—which Gwendolyn Hopkins and Joanne had been exploring with remarkable quietness—came the sound of a harp. I immediately thought of Sara. Was she upstairs? Was this all an elaborate surprise party for me?

But no one shouted "Surprise!" And the harp obviously wasn't being played as much as toyed with. Eerie, random glissandos echoed through the house.

"That's Gwendolyn," Beth Hopkins said. It might have been an illusion created by the firelight, but I thought the glitter in Beth's eyes might have been caused by tears. "Gwen would have been the next harpist," she said.

Mrs. Coleridge changed the subject quickly, overlapping her words with Beth's. "If we are to have a tour, perhaps we should begin by showing Mr. Brewster around the house."

Arthur Hopkins stood up. "Maybe Beth and I should leave. We have some work to do." He went to the foot of the staircase and shouted, "Gwendolyn, your mother and I are going now. Would you like to come with us?"

The harp sounds stopped, and Gwen appeared at the top of the stairs. "No, thanks. I want to play with Joanne."

"All right, dear," Arthur said. "We'll see you later."

As Arthur and Beth Hopkins got ready to go I did some wondering. Why had the just-plain-folks atmosphere suddenly become so tense? Why wouldn't little Gwendolyn get to be the next harpist? Why did Beth have tears in her eyes? Why didn't Gwendolyn have to leave with her parents?

After Arthur and Beth were gone, Evelyn Coleridge showed me around her house. Verity Palmer joined the tour, leaving Mrs. Coleridge to do most of the talking but keeping me aware of her presence by staying close to me and maintaining what seemed like an unnecessary amount of physical contact.

The house was actually three houses. At the back of the ground floor was part of a seventeenth-century log cabin that was used as a sort of cold-storage room adjoining the kitchen. Two other rooms on the ground floor dated from the eighteenth century, and the facade of the house and the upper floor were built in the late 1800s.

I've never been much interested in the niceties of architectural design; unadorned rectangular spaces seem about all that is necessary. But I do like buildings that are intended to last, and the Coleridge house was certainly in that category. I listened politely as we walked through the main floor, but I was eager to get upstairs and see Sara's room—which turned out to be ordinary enough except for the presence of a full-sized concert harp. But there was something extraordinary about the harp. As Mrs. Coleridge talked I plucked a few of the strings—enough to be sure that the instrument was well tuned. Sara had told me how quickly a harp falls out of tune, so I could only conclude that someone had been using it. I asked Mrs. Coleridge if she ever played it, and she told me no one had used it since Sara left. Aha!

When we got back downstairs, Verity Palmer—her right breast nudging my left arm—volunteered to take me and Joanne on a tour of the village. Joanne and her new, apparently very close friend Gwendolyn had been wandering through the house, stopping in our vicinity once in a while to be sure that no one was saying anything that might interest them. I called Joanne, and she, Gwendolyn, Verity, and I left Mrs. Coleridge temporarily and set off into the town.

Verity took my arm and led me along Golightly Street toward the cemetery. We walked slowly, and Joanne, who seemed to have forgotten that she was my daughter, skittered ahead of us with Gwendolyn.

For a few minutes neither of us spoke. As soon as we stepped into the street, I began to feel some strong, ill-defined emotions. The steep walls of the valley gave an effect that was both claustrophobic and protective. The other houses along the street were as odd in their combination of elements as was Mrs. Coleridge's. I could see fieldstones, rough-hewn logs, clapboards, slate, bricks, and planking assembled in a variety that seemed sometimes admirably individualistic and at other times unpleasantly eccentric. The thing that all the houses seemed to have in common was a strength and character that must inevitably have affected the personalities of the people who lived in them. The buildings were meant to contain and inspire strong emotions. I couldn't tell whether or not those emotions were likely to be constructive, but it seemed unlikely that there would be much triviality in the lives lived in these houses. I suddenly remembered Sara having said that there were places where I would have been considered a frivolous person. I was certain that Childgrave was the place she had in mind.

There was really only one street in the town. Some gravel lanes led from the street to the houses that were set back on higher ground, but these lanes were not much more than footpaths. Trees obscured parts of every building, and I could see only one or two small lawns.

Childgrave gave the effect of wilderness—a wilderness that the residents had subdued but had not overcome. This aspect of the town, like every other aspect, puzzled and unsettled me a bit. But I was becoming convinced that I wanted to learn more about it.

My little reverie had made me miss the beginning of Verity Palmer's tour-guide remarks. As I tuned in I got the impression that her monologue was overrehearsed. She was definitely being more cynical than necessary, but she glanced about the town fondly as she spoke, and I got the feeling that she was proud of its history and that she wouldn't want to live anywhere else. It also seemed to me that her efforts to keep me aware of her body, even though they were effective, were not important to her. It was one of the few times I had ever met anyone who had a good body and a good mind, but who didn't seem especially interested in either. What did that leave to be interested in? There was always the soul. But that was something I didn't know much about. Maybe Verity would tell me about it. But she began by telling me about Childgrave.

"Our village was founded in 1636 by Josiah Golightly. Josiah made the mistake of getting into an argument with the Puritans in the Massachusetts Bay Colony. He was one of the first to notice that the government was less tolerant of religious diversity than the Church of England had been. Josiah was an individualist in his belief but was basically a Quaker. He and his wife and infant daughter were—on pain of death, and during an exceptionally severe winter—banished from the colony in the same year as Roger Williams. Roger had the foresight to head south along the coast. Josiah moved inland. He apparently wanted to get as far as he could from the colony. Either that, or he was looking for a sign of some kind."

At that point, I began to feel a little better about Josiah. I could understand the need for a sign. I hadn't been able to understand someone who would support his beliefs by taking to the wilderness in the winter. The strongest belief I had ever had was my belief in my love for Sara. I looked at the landscape around Childgrave. Even on a comparatively pleasant late-autumn afternoon, I wouldn't have wanted to be out there. Would I spend even one night there for Sara? I didn't know. But Verity's story of the rest of Josiah's problems made me certain that his love—or belief, or whatever—was definitely beyond my comprehension.

"Josiah got to the vicinity of this valley, when a series of blizzards engulfed him. He had no food. His wife and child died. He was near death himself, when a Mohegan Indian rescued him. Josiah Golightly settled here, and ever since then his descendants and others who shared his beliefs have lived here."

I wasn't going to ask Verity what those beliefs might be—at least, I wasn't going to ask about it on a chilly street corner. But there was one thing I had to find out. "The sign on the hill says you're a community of saints," I said. "Is that true?"

"No. We're a community of people who are trying to find out what it means to be saints."

"Are you having much success?"

"Personally, do you mean?"

"I meant generally, but personal is always better. How does your sanctity rate on a scale of ten?"

"Nine."

I managed to hold back a laugh, but a big smile got through.

"I thought you'd be amused," Verity said. "I suppose you think a saint has to be modest and ascetic."

"Right."

"You're wrong, Jonathan."

I nodded and then realized it was a nod of irritation. Her holier-than-thou attitude was hard to take. Apparently my irritation was obvious. Verity said, "I'm sorry. You *did* ask."

"Yes. I guess what I should have asked was whether saints can marry nonsaints."

"Saints like Sara Coleridge, you mean? Certainly. In fact, she's already done it once."

I'd pushed that fact out of my mind. I pushed it out again. But there was a point that I had to pursue. "Is Sara a saint?" I asked.

Verity looked at me as if I had asked whether Joan of Arc had been patriotic. "Yes, Jonathan," she said. "Hadn't you noticed?"

"I'd noticed several things, but not that. I guess I didn't know where to look for it."

"You're a photographer. You might be too involved in exteriors." We had stopped walking. "And speaking of exteriors, behold Childgrave's most impressive architectural exterior." She nodded at the building across the street from us. It was labeled The New Meeting Hall—a structure that was so immaculately maintained that its construction might have been completed only a few months ago. But the date 1651 was carved above the double front doors. It was made of rough-hewn logs, but not in the traditional log-cabin design. It resembled a cathedral more than a cabin. The front of the building was a two-story boxlike affair that was joined to a larger section, which had an extremely high, sharp-pitched roof that gave the effect of a steeple. The side walls of the larger section were buttressed with some of the fattest logs I had ever seen.

Verity invited me to look at the inside of the building, which was dark and deserted. I couldn't decide whether the atmosphere was restful or frightening, and I began to feel some of the uneasiness I had felt on my first visit to the village. The main hall was undecorated and unheated, and it looked even bigger than it had from the outside. The room was filled with straight-backed wooden chairs that were arranged in what seemed like a random pattern. But they all faced the building's side walls.

Verity had her arm around my waist—something that didn't seem like a very saintly thing to do. I disengaged myself from her and said, "I gather this is where the meetings are held. What I don't gather is what kind of meetings they are."

"Religious meetings. Silent gatherings, in the Quaker style. Except that no one is allowed to speak."

"No preaching or ceremonies?"

"Never any preaching. But we do have two ceremonies a year—one at Christmas and another at Easter."

"Do you get big turnouts at the meetings?"

"*Everyone* turns out, Jonathan."

"They don't seem to turn out for anything else," I said.

"What do you mean?"

"Well, it's a sunny Saturday afternoon, and we're the only people out and about. I'd expected at least to see some joggers or shoppers."

"I suppose we do seem quiet to someone from New York City. But then, it's true that we're devoted to the pleasures of the hearthside."

I didn't know what that meant, but Verity's hand had joined mine in the pocket of my jacket—an experience my hand hadn't had since its teenage days. I thought it might be safer to avoid the hearthside while in the company of the saintly Miss Palmer, so I steered her back toward the doorway. As we left the Meeting Hall, I noticed that there was a glass display case mounted on the wall. The case displayed a knife that would have been completely unremarkable except that its highly polished blade had been worn to a strange, narrow shape from years of constant honing. I paused to look at it more closely.

"That belonged to Josiah," Verity said.

I waited for a little elaboration, but that was all my guide wanted to tell me. It bothered me a little that a knife would be displayed in a house of worship. But it was even more disturbing that the knife was obviously ready for use. I wasn't going to ask what kind of use.

Our next stop was the cemetery, which, oddly enough, was showing more signs of life than any part of town except Mrs. Coleridge's house. Specifically, Joanne and Gwendolyn were on the portico steps of Josiah Golightly's enormous mausoleum. The girls were dancing and chanting. Unfortunately, they were chanting Joanne's favorite nursery rhyme:

My mother has killed me,
My father is eating me,
My brothers and sisters sit under the table
Picking my bones,
And they bury them under the cold marble stones.

I wasn't amused. I called out, "Joanne. Maybe we'd better start back home now."

As I expected, I was answered with some whining: "Oh, Daddy. I'm having a good time."

But Gwendolyn ran toward me, and Joanne followed her. When Gwendolyn got to me, she took my right hand. She looked up at me with smiling self-assurance that stopped just short of insolence. "Do you like our angel, Mr. Brewster?" she asked.

I looked up at the stone carving that stood on top of the mausoleum. I wondered who had carved it and when. Probably even a person who knew a lot more about the history of art than I did would have had trouble answering that question. The figure—

much larger than life size, with wings extended upward—seemed to have been cut from a single block of smooth-grained marble. That meant that the original block had been massive. The style of the carving was a blend of sophistication and either imperfect technique or craziness. The sculptor had obviously known about ancient Rome and Renaissance Europe, but he (or she?) had also known about colonial American skull-and-wing headstones. In any case, the angel was a satisfyingly inexplicable object. As I stared at it I began to feel that something about it was familiar. Then I remembered the vague image of the angel in my Spectral Portraits. There was a definite resemblance.

Gwendolyn tugged at my hand. "Do you like our angel?"

I had forgotten about her. "Yes, dear," I said. But my answer was only half true. I liked the angel as a piece of sculpture, but as I looked up at it I began to think of what it might represent. I remembered that when Joanne was feverish she had talked about an angel; I remembered the angel in the portraits of Joanne and Sara; and most vividly I recalled the girl dancing in the snow and singing about the Angel of Death.

I couldn't really like the angel, no matter how beautiful it might be, when I was faced with rows of small headstones and was crouching between two young girls who were just about the right size to lie under one of the headstones. I had begun to shiver.

Joanne was gripping my arm and making a sort of *Oooh-ee* sound that meant her excitement had passed the point of moderation. I squatted next to Joanne and whispered in her ear: "Maybe if you go back to Mrs. Coleridge's house, she'll have something nice for you. And you can tell her I'll be back soon."

Gwendolyn leaned forward and whispered in *my* ear: "You should come back and take my picture. You should come back soon." Then she took Joanne's arm, and the two girls ran off together.

I clasped my hands behind my back and looked at Verity to see what was next on the itinerary.

"Do you want to go through the cemetery?" she asked.

I tried to hide my lack of enthusiasm. "Is there anything to see that I can't see from here?"

"Only the inscriptions on the headstones, and they're not especially imaginative. Names and dates."

"Then I'll pass," I said, eager to get back to less disturbing ground, both literally and figuratively. I asked Verity if she knew who carved the angel and when.

"It was one of my ancestors, actually: William Palmer. He studied sculpture in Europe for a time. Then he came back to do the angel for our centennial in 1736."

"You've produced some talented people: sculptors, harpists. Were any of them famous outside of Childgrave?"

"No. We're not interested in fame."

"Tell me again, what *are* you interested in? I still haven't got that straight."

Verity didn't answer. We started walking back toward Mrs. Coleridge's house.

But I still wanted to know how the people in Childgrave spent their time. I tried again. "Chief Rudd says you're interested in grace."

"That's as good a way as any to describe it."

"Does grace pay the rent?"

"We're in a low-rent district."

"And grace takes the place of TV sets and automobiles and schools?"

"Yes. Although we have a school. And two automobiles: Chief Rudd's and a community van that we use to get supplies."

"So, is Childgrave a utopia?"

"No. We do our share of suffering. But we suffer—just as we exalt—on our own terms."

"You don't seem much interested in the twentieth century."

"We aren't uninterested. But we don't see history as a pyramid with the twentieth century at the tip. I think it's better to see history as an expanding circle. We're in the center of the circle, seated on a swiveling chair. Each century occupies an equal amount of space on the circumference of the circle. We are able to swivel around and select our beliefs from among those of all the centuries."

I was sorry I had brought the subject up—if I *had* brought it up. I wasn't sure I knew what Verity meant, and I didn't feel like finding out. The day began to seem colder and darker than it had a few minutes earlier. I wanted to sit in front of Mrs. Coleridge's fireplace for a few minutes and then get back to Manhattan and think about what I had seen and heard. Apparently my befuddlement and waning interest was fairly obvious. Verity waved her hand in front of my eyes. "I didn't mean to bore you, Jonathan," she said. We walked the rest of the way in silence.

When we got to the Coleridge house, Verity didn't bother to use the knocker but opened the door and led me into the dark foyer.

"I'll leave you now," she whispered. "I hope you come and see us again." Then she kissed me. I tried to offer my cheek, but she wasn't interested in cheeks. She got her mouth against mine and began to do elaborate, provocative things. I suppose I could have pulled away from her, but it would have involved a struggle. I told myself that it would have been more unseemly to struggle than to submit. (I'm not sure I was telling myself the truth.) In any case, I submitted. My mind found the experience unpleasant, but my body disagreed. Verity was close enough to me to know what was up with my body (so to speak), and she was encouraged. She got a little too enthusiastic, though, and somehow she got her hand under the back of my shirt. It was a counterproductive move. Her hand was still about the temperature of the air outdoors, and I pulled free of her as soon as she touched me. She smiled at me and said, "There was a Brewster on the *Mayflower*." Then she turned and left.

I rearranged my clothes and went toward the sitting room. I was about to call out and ask if anyone was home, when I saw that someone was. Evelyn Coleridge, Joanne, and Gwendolyn were seated around a small round table in front of the fireplace. They had their eyes closed, and they were holding hands. Although I hadn't had much experience with such things, it seemed to be fairly obvious that there was a séance in progress. I was not pleased. It didn't matter to me if Evelyn Coleridge wanted to perform little occult exercises by herself or with consenting adults, but she didn't have a right to involve my daughter in the game, even if Joanne might have had talents in that area. But despite my anger, I couldn't bring myself to interrupt the séance. My hesitation wasn't inspired by politeness as much as by fear of what effect an interruption might have on people who were concentrating so intently.

I stood in the shadows and watched the proceedings. The three participants sat quietly smiling, as though they were sharing a pleasant dream. Joanne and Gwendolyn were radiant, their unflawed faces showing an attentive repose you don't often see in children of that age.

The house was quiet enough so that I could hear the faint *shush* that resembles the sound of distant wind, but which I understand is actually the sound of one's own blood circulating. And then I heard a creaking of the floorboards in the upper story of the house. I knew that houses tend to make little sounds of their own, but somehow I was certain that this creaking was caused by someone's footstep. I looked at the séancers, who seemed to be settled in for a nice long session, and I decided to creep upstairs and see who the stroller might be. I wasn't thinking in terms of discovering a ghost. I just thought, as I had from the first time I entered the house, that Sara was present.

I moved as quietly as I could up the stairs. I discovered that stealth wasn't one of my talents. I tried walking on my toes, and then on my heels, but I couldn't avoid making a fair amount of noise. It wasn't enough noise to disturb Mrs. Coleridge and the girls, but if there really was anyone on the upper floor, they would certainly have heard me. I continued to hear creakings in the floor above me, and as I reached the top landing there was a click that could have been the sound of a bolt being gently closed. I decided there was no use trying doors. But the door of Sara's room was open, so I went in.

I stood looking around in the dim light. There didn't seem to be any sign that anyone had been in the room since I had left it earlier. But then I noticed something I didn't remember seeing before: there were a few large, white-matted photographs resting on a bedside table. I didn't have to go any closer to know that they were my portraits of Sara—the ones I had given her in return for sitting for me. I suppose I shouldn't have been surprised to find them in the house. Sara could have left them there before she went to Europe. Or she could have mailed them to her mother.

What was odd was that they hadn't been on the table a couple of hours earlier. But there was no reason Mrs. Coleridge couldn't have taken them out while I was away with Verity Palmer. So there was probably no mystery about the situation.

Before I could do any more snooping, I heard voices from below. I kissed one of the portraits of Sara, put it down, and moved quickly out of the room and down the stairs. Joanne, Gwendolyn, and Mrs. Coleridge were still sitting around the table, but now they were leaning back and talking, and there was a lighted candle in the center of the table. I went to the front door and opened it. Then I slammed it and pretended I was just coming in from outside.

"Is anyone here?" I said, feeling—and probably sounding—idiotic.

"Mr. Brewster? We are having a little chat," Mrs. Coleridge said.

Joanne said hello to me, but I obviously wasn't the most important thing on her mind. She was flushed, and her eyes were wet, although she didn't seem to have been crying. There also seemed to be something odd about her mouth. I moved closer to her and saw that there was a dark spot on her lower lip. The spot looked quite a bit like blood.

"Did you cut your mouth, sweetie?" I asked her.

She slipped into her wide-eyed, telling-a-fib expression. "No, Daddy."

I couldn't exactly work up any indignation, when I had just tried to get away with my own little deception. But I wasn't sure what Joanne's deception was. If she hadn't cut her mouth, what *had* happened?

Joanne put her fingers to her mouth, then held them out and looked at them. They were smeared with traces of blood. She put them back in her mouth and sucked them clean. "Gwendolyn cut her finger," she said. "And I kissed it to make it well."

I looked at Gwendolyn's hands. The left one had a handkerchief wrapped around the index finger. I looked for something she might have cut herself on—a knife or some broken glass. On the table next to her right hand was a long hatpin that had a pearl on one end of it. The thing that bothered me about it was that its point was blackened, as though it had been held over the flame of the candle that burned in front of her. My suspicious and rapidly tiring mind concluded that little Gwendolyn had deliberately punctured a finger after sterilizing—probably on Mrs. Coleridge's advice—the hatpin. Charming.

I suggested that it was time we took our leave. I thanked Mrs. Coleridge for her hospitality, and Joanne and I got ourselves together. As Mrs. Coleridge opened the door for us she said to me, "Gwendolyn wants very much to have you do a photographic portrait of her. I think it would make a splendid Christmas present for her parents. If you could return next Saturday with your camera equipment and do such a portrait, I should be happy to pay you your usual fee, Jonathan."

I hesitated. Joanne looked up at me and said, "Please, Daddy. Gwendolyn is my best friend in the world now." The girls were holding hands.

I still didn't know what to say. I settled for "I'm not sure what my schedule is next weekend, Evelyn. I'll try to make it. I'll drop you a line during the week and let you know." Joanne didn't look too pleased with my waffling reply. But, wisely, she dropped the subject and contented herself with presenting Gwendolyn with a long, emotion-laden kiss. Evelyn Coleridge shook my hand. The gesture wasn't exactly laden with anything, but there was a little more pressure involved than I had expected.

An hour before that, I might have been pleased to encounter a sign of friendliness in this reserved woman, but after the episode with the hatpin, I wasn't so sure I wanted to win her approval. I wondered what her part had been in the mysterious doings that somehow managed to get traces of Gwendolyn's blood on Joanne's lips.

And what *were* the mysterious doings? Was Childgrave one of the villages that turn out in fiction to be inhabited by vampires? As I looked at Mrs. Coleridge's complexly human expression I doubted whether it was anything that simple.

Chapter 11

Joanne slept during the drive back to Manhattan, and I kept only as much of my mind awake as was necessary to prevent us from becoming traffic-accident fatalities. I didn't do much thinking, but I did manage a little feeling. I felt as though I had been on a long journey in a foreign country; a really long journey. I had difficulty recognizing things. I was puzzled by little patches of multicolored lights that kept looming up out of the dusk as I drove. I was almost in Manhattan before I realized that they were Christmas-tree lights; something that usually irritated me, as each year they showed up earlier in less appropriate places. But now I found them comforting. It was more important for me to see something familiar than something tasteful.

When I reached the Hudson River and saw the row of substantial apartment houses along Riverside Drive, I had to remind myself of exactly what I was seeing. These thousands of rooms were lighted by electricity and were centrally heated. They were inhabited by people who were more interested in business lunches than séances; who measured history in fiscal years and not in circles of centuries. I was back in my own world, yet I felt as out of place as I had felt in Childgrave.

Joanne didn't have that glad-to-be-home feeling either. "I don't like it here," she said.

"We're back in New York, sweetie."

"I like it in Childgrave. Can we go and live there, Daddy?"

"Maybe. But why do you like it there?"

"I like all the little girls."

"But you only saw one little girl."

"I mean the others."

"Which others?"

"The ones I saw when we played our game with Mrs. Coleridge."

"When you held hands around the table?"

"Yes. I saw lots of little girls. They want me to live with them."

"But they weren't real, Joanne. They were just make-believe. You like make-believe things now, but pretty soon you'll be grown up, and you won't like those things anymore."

"Mrs. Coleridge is grown up, and she likes them."

"Some grown-ups keep acting like children. People make fun of them and call them crazy."

"Is Mrs. Coleridge crazy?"

"I didn't say that, sweetie. But some people might think so."

"Is Ms. Abraham crazy?"

A good question, I thought. If I had to say whether Mrs. Coleridge had a firmer grip on reality than Joanne's daycare teacher, I don't know what my answer would have been. While I was considering the matter, an idiot of a driver swerved into my lane. I hit the brakes and thanked consumers' action for safety harnesses. So, the world is full of crazies. Joanne had made her point, and I didn't answer her question.

I thought a little distraction was in order, so before I returned the car to the rental agency, I drove around midtown to show Joanne the Christmas displays. We had a little discussion about Christmas presents, but my strategy backfired. Joanne wanted to spend Christmas in Childgrave.

I suddenly felt the need of a lot of alcohol or a little counseling. Fortunately, I got both. When Joanne and I got home, Nanny Joy said Harry Bordeaux wanted me to telephone him. I made the call and found that Harry was faced with a solitary Saturday night. He and Lee had planned to spend a sensual evening at home together, but she was called out of town on business at the last minute. Harry had the ingredients for a dinner for two—featuring some cut of pork that only a few people knew about—and he asked me to help him dispose of it. "Casting his swine before the churl," he said. I told him I'd be delighted to drop by. I not only needed to share his view of the world, I needed to escape the wrath of Nanny Joy, whom Joanne had given a little account of our journey. Joy had stopped speaking to me after reminding me that I had broken my promise not to take Joanne to Childgrave. I reacted the way I usually react when someone points out a weakness in my character: I started reviewing my accuser's failings.

That doesn't make for a pleasant evening, so I headed gratefully for Harry's apartment.

Harry was wearing a quilted apron over lime-green corduroy. His apartment smelled like a garlic press.

"Hi, Harry," I said. "Your apartment smells like a garlic press."

"Very perceptive of you, dear boy. Our menu has a Provençal theme tonight in your honor. No effete subtleties to puzzle the sinuses."

"Thanks a lot."

Harry handed me a substantial glass filled with amber liquid and ice. "Japanese bourbon," he said.

"Seriously?"

Harry brought the bottle. The label looked serious enough, and it announced Japanese bourbon. "I thought you might like to try a nip," Harry said. Then he giggled. "A *Nip*, Jonathan."

"Yes, Harry."

The bourbon was better than Harry's joke. I settled into an ingenious arrangement of leather cushions and took larger than usual swallows of the bourbon as Harry shuttled back and forth between me and the kitchen. He talked mostly about how busy Lee had been lately, and although he didn't say so directly, I gathered his marriage was undergoing a bit of a strain. I waited until we had done away with dinner (garlic soup, something-*de-porc*, potato-and-cheese pyramids, watercress salad, and hard chocolate filled with soft chocolate) before I mentioned my midday excursion.

By that time Harry was pouring calvados (I forgot to mention the two bottles of wine that accompanied the dinner), and my tongue had thickened and my eyes had narrowed.

"I need some advice," I said.

Harry was paying more attention to his cigarette than he was to me. He didn't allow himself to smoke between courses, and by the end of a long meal he always had to do a little stint of chain-smoking to catch up. "As always, I'm at your command, beer . . . dear boy," he said.

"I took Joanne to meet Sara's mother today."

"Uptown or downtown?"

"Not everyone lives in Manhattan, Harry."

"She doesn't live in *Brooklyn?*"

"That's part of the problem. She lives in a little village upstate—a highly unusual little village. They don't have electricity." I wasn't organizing my thoughts very well. Harry was looking at me quizzically. I was going to start my saga again, but I couldn't figure out how to do it. Instead, I said, "They don't have telephones."

Harry stopped looking puzzled and started looking angry. "My God," he said. "You took a child to a place like that?"

"She likes it there, Harry. She wants to live there. That's part of my problem."

"Let's start again, Jonathan. Where is this place, and how did you find out about it?"

I explained about my first visit, leaving out some of the more unusual details. But when I described the second visit, I mentioned the séance and the fact that Joanne had started seeing imaginary people again. Instead of sharing my concern, Harry looked delighted.

"Marvelous," he said. "You can do some more Spectral Portraits."

"But that's not the point. The point is whether any of this is good for Joanne."

"Well, you don't have to go and *live* in this place, Jonathan. Just go there and do a few portraits. Then you can go up by yourself once in a while to see if Sara shows up."

"I think Sara might be there now. I got that feeling."

"You think she doesn't want to see you?"

"I don't know what to think. If she *is* there, she doesn't want to see me. But her mother wanted me there—and wants me to go again next week to take some portraits of a little girl."

Harry raised his arms and wiggled his hands for a few seconds—his gesture of impatience. "Jonathan," he said, "either you're forgetting to tell me something or you're addled. There's no problem whatsoever. You go there next weekend without Joanne and you take some photographs—as many as you can. You send a few of the prints to Sara's mother and you give me the rest if they're spectral. Then you ask Mom to let you know when she hears from Sara. You have a merry Christmas and a prosperous new year back here in the metropolis."

"But Joanne wants to go back there. She wants to live there."

Harry's arms went up again. "*You're* the daddy, Jonathan. You do what you think is best for Joanne. That's why we have children—to avenge ourselves on the poor judgment and tyranny of our own parents by imposing our own poor judgment and tyranny. Don't try to beat the system, dear boy. Joanne will despise you one day if you don't require some sacrifice of her now."

I couldn't follow Harry's pseudologic. Then he tilted his head and resumed his look of puzzlement, and I realized he was as muddled as I was. I smiled. "Harry," I said, "there are a couple of illustrators in that town, and they have an agent here in the city."

"Lee has done that. But I refuse to."

"Refuse to what?"

"Take clients who don't have a phone."

We had some more calvados and said things that I don't remember clearly. The odds are they were silly. But as I was leaving, Harry said: "Jonathan, no one knows what's right or wrong."

"There is no right or wrong?"

"No, no. You've got it wrong. There *is* a right and wrong. It's just that no one knows what it is."

"You're right, Harry. Thanks for the dinner."

I tottered out into the night.

Nanny Joy was still up when I got home. There was something odd about her, but at first I couldn't figure out what it was. Then I realized that she wasn't listening to music. I got ready for more talk about morality. My tongue was a little more controllable than when I had left Harry's, but my brain seemed to have collected a few more ounces of lint.

Joy was sitting in a love seat, but there wasn't much love in her eyes when she looked up at me. I sat down beside her. "I don't want you to be unhappy," I said.

"You don't pay me to be happy, Mr. B. You pay me to take care of your daughter."

"Isn't my daughter happy?"

"Damn straight she's happy. But she'd be happy if she never had to go to school or take a bath. She'd be happy if she was the only one in the world who could say no."

"You really think she's that selfish?"

"No more selfish than any other little kid. But still, she's just a little kid. We're the ones who decide whether she should talk to ghosts."

I almost announced that *I* was the one who decided that. But Joy had a point. I hadn't hired her to be an automaton. It was her good judgment more than mine—and certainly more than Mrs. Abraham's—that was making Joanne into a pleasant human being. An apology, instead of an attack, was in order. "I'm sorry," I said. "I guess my problem is that I'm in love."

"I'm in love, too," Joy said. "I'm in love with Joanne. I don't want her getting mixed up with small-town crazy people."

"They're not crazy, Joy. They're devout Christians."

"There's nothing crazier than a crazy Christian."

"You're a Christian, aren't you?"

"I'm a social Christian. The folks at my church get a little loud, but they don't mess with snakes or have fits and fall down. And the reverend might like to give treats to some of the ladies in the congregation, but he doesn't try to get children to talk to dead people."

It sounded as if Joanne had told Joy about the séance. I didn't see any point in discussing it—especially since Joanne still hadn't told *me* what that was all about. Joy and I stopped talking for a while. I was thinking, oddly enough, about my first wife and her minister friend. I gathered from what I had just heard that Joy, too, was—or wanted to be—friendly with her minister. That would explain her tastelessly sexy churchgoing costumes. It seemed I tended to associate with women who found clergymen irresistible. I was glad when I recalled that Verity Palmer had told me that there were no preachers in Childgrave. So, if Sara was involved with someone else, it wasn't necessarily a person who wore a reversed collar. In any case, there didn't seem to be much doubt that being involved with Sara was going to mean being involved with God. I had heard often enough that God is love, but I wondered if it worked the other way. Love is God? It didn't sound right.

But Harry had assured me earlier in the evening that nobody knows what's right. At that moment, I envied Harry. He didn't have to worry about God. And Harry had Lee, whose Higher Power was J. S. Bach and his deathbed chorale. Joanne had her ghosts. What did I have? I had my camera, but that had never seemed like anything more than a toy to me. Maybe it was time to put the toy in the attic.

I thought of the people I had met in Childgrave. I could go through my list of Manhattan acquaintances and come up with people who seemed to have the same kind of eccentricities that the Childgraveans had. But there was a difference. In Childgrave, everyone understood that God is God. What did I understand? I had devoted my years to the pleasures of not understanding. Did that mean that I couldn't, if Sara wanted me to, believe in God? Under the influence of Harry's cuisine, whiskey, wine, and calvados, I decided I could believe. It is probably easier to believe when you don't understand. I hoped Sara would give me a chance to prove my belief in her and in the inexplicable.

I turned to Nanny Joy. She smiled at me. But it was the kind of smile you give someone whose name you don't know.

"Are you going to leave us?" I asked.

"I don't leave people," she said. "They leave me."

I was irritated—partly out of guilt and partly because Joy seemed to be showing an unusual amount of self-pity. "What makes you think we're going to leave you?" I asked her.

"Joanne says you're going to live in that town."

"Where did she get that idea?"

"From God, she says."

"Oh, fine. Well, God hasn't mentioned anything to me about it, Joy. And even if we did go to live there, couldn't you come along with us?"

"No, Jonathan. Uh-uh. Small towns make me think of plantations. You'd start calling me Mammy Joy."

I was too tired to answer that. What the hell did Joy know about plantations? And what had I done to make her think I could treat her like some kind of caricature? Weren't we just a couple of twentieth-century New Yorkers? I didn't spend my time thinking about my ancestors and feeling any guilt or pride about what they had done. It didn't matter whether they had been on the *Mayflower*. Now that I thought of it, hadn't there been bond servants on the *Mayflower*? My ancestors might have been WASP slaves. But I wasn't out to get revenge on Miles Standish.

I started to stand up, but Joy took hold of my arm and pulled me back down. "Don't be my enemy," she said. "Just let me pull you into your old world once in a while. I don't want to make it too easy for those people, that's all. I won't *break* your arm. Just let me twist it."

I smiled and said: "Fair enough."

Joy didn't smile. She put both of her hands around my wrist and twisted. I resisted with all the strength I had, but my arm didn't stop turning until it got to what must have been the breaking point. Joy took her hands away and kissed my cheek. "You're a sweet man, Mr. B.," she said. "But you're not a strong man."

"Blessed are the sweet," I said.

"We'll see."

I stood up and tried hard to keep from rubbing my arm. "I'd say you're stronger than they are, Joy."

"I hope so, my friend."

"Why don't you play some music, my friend? I'm going to get into the bathtub and soak my arm. I'll see you in the morning."

As I was leaving the room Joy said: "Ask Joanne about the knife."

That slowed me up a bit, but I kept walking. As I started to fill the bathtub I heard the voice of Billie Holiday in the distance. She was singing "God Bless the Child."

God!

The next morning, Joanne decided to play Alarm Clock, which was one of her less endearing games. The rules were pretty simple: she just placed her mouth next to the ear of her sleeping father and did her imitation of an alarm bell. To make matters worse, when Father opened his eyes, he found that his daughter had no clothes on.

It always made me extremely uncomfortable to see Joanne nude, but I played the modern parent and pretended not to be embarrassed. As soon as I could manage it, though, I pulled Joanne onto the bed and wrapped her in the covers.

"Are we going to Childgrave today?" Joanne asked.

"You have to go to school."

"When are we going?"

"Not for a while."

"I want to go."

"Why?"

"My best friend lives there."

"Who is that?"

"Gwendolyn Hopkins."

"I thought *I* was your best friend."

"You're my daddy. And you never tell me secrets."

"Did Gwendolyn tell you secrets?"

"Yes."

"What did she tell you?"

"It's a secret."

"What about that game you played at the table with Mrs. Coleridge and Gwendolyn? Is that a secret, too?"

"We talked to the dead little girls."

"What did the dead girls say?"

"They're happy with God. They said I could be happy, too."

"Aren't you happy now?"

"I could be happier with them."

"Do you want to die?"

"They didn't just die."

"What does that mean?"

"That's a secret."

"What about the knife?" No answer. "Nanny Joy said you told her about a knife." No answer. "I don't think it's nice for you to have all those secrets. I don't think you can go back to Childgrave until you tell me what the secrets are."

I expected a tantrum to appear, but Joanne just smiled. "It's a secret," she said.

I decided I'd better ask Mrs. Coleridge about the secret. I delivered Joanne to Nanny Joy, and then I wrote a note to Mrs. Coleridge, saying I would see her next Saturday and that I would bring my camera but not my daughter. I had a cup of coffee, and after Joanne had left for school, I went back to bed, where I did more wondering than sleeping. I wondered whether I should mail the note I had just written. Maybe it would be better if I just forgot about the whole thing.

How had all this confusion started? It had started with Sara, of course. I remembered her at the performance of *Orfeo;* at the recording studio; in the restaurant. But I remembered her most clearly seated across from me on the bed that I was now lying in. It was a stimulating memory. Maybe my attraction to her was nothing more complicated than sexual stimulation. Well, that was complicated enough. I've never been able to understand why sexual obsession shouldn't have the effect of simplifying a person's life, giving it an organizing focus. But it doesn't seem to work that way, as Don Juan demonstrated. It's the preadolescents that have the simple life. Although there are always exceptions. I wasn't sure that life was so uncomplicated for kiddies in Childgrave. I'd have to find out about that.

So, the next Saturday, my camera and I made the journey to Childgrave. I lied to Joanne and told her I was going to do some portraits of wealthy people on Long Island. I don't think she believed me, but she didn't make a scene. Nanny Joy was planning a little victory celebration and was taking Joanne to see a holiday puppet show that had become an annual event. I had seen it the previous year, and I wasn't amused. It didn't seem especially wholesome to depict Santa Claus as someone who wore a dress and engaged in a lot of falsetto badinage with the gnomes in his workshop. But the audience—which consisted primarily of jaded one-parent children and fastidious men who weren't likely ever to have children—seemed to be enchanted.

I had my own variety of enchantment to deal with in Childgrave. As I turned off the highway and drove down into the valley I could see that Golightly Street was as deserted and murky as ever. But that didn't depress or disturb me. Instead, I began to feel a kind of pleasant excitement that I hadn't felt since childhood—the sort of excitement I used to feel when entering the secret clubhouse some friends and I had set up one autumn in the basement of an abandoned building in our neighborhood.

But although Childgrave's darkness didn't create any distress for me emotionally, it presented some practical problems. The skies were dark—not just overcast, but filled with black, wind-driven clouds. I wondered whether there would be enough light to allow me to do the portraits. I hadn't brought any lighting equipment with me, although I should have realized that even on a sunny day there probably wasn't a house in Childgrave that would allow much light to enter. But I had loaded my film holders with my most sensitive paper, and I would be able to get a decent image even by candlelight. The problem was that I would have to get little Gwendolyn to sit absolutely still for the long exposure times. It wasn't an encouraging situation.

Chief Rudd's car was parked in front of Mrs. Coleridge's house. Evelyn greeted me with a fond handshake and led me into the sitting room, where I got the feeling I had interrupted a funeral service. Verity Palmer and Beth and Arthur Hopkins were sitting solemnly at the bare table. Delbert Rudd was standing tensely next to the fireplace. He was wearing a black uniform, and his right hand was resting on the upper slope of his impressive tummy. The hand was pale, and I noticed for the first time that the tip of its middle finger was missing. Gwendolyn Hopkins, my subject for the day, was the only person in the room who looked relaxed. She walked toward me, smiling, with her arms extended, inviting an embrace. I picked her up, and she said, "You didn't bring Joanne."

"No."

"That was naughty."

"I'll bring her the next time."

"Yes. Before I'm not here."

Although I was getting used to cryptic remarks by five-year-olds, and although it didn't seem like the time or place to conduct an inquiry, I couldn't let Gwendolyn's remark get past unchallenged, "What do you mean, 'not here,' Gwendolyn? Where are you going?"

Then two people spoke at once: Gwendolyn and her mother, Beth. Unfortunately, Beth was almost shouting and Gwendolyn was whispering confidentially, so what I heard for the most part was Beth changing the subject: "Where will you set up your camera, Mr. Brewster?"

I couldn't swear to it, but I thought Gwendolyn's overpowered reply included the word "dead." But I didn't get a chance to repeat my question. Beth Hopkins took her daughter out of my arms and carried her away. I finished saying my hellos, and then I turned my attention to the question Beth had asked: where I would set up my camera. Working in Mrs. Coleridge's sitting room would be a little like working in an overpopulated closet. Then the chief came to my rescue. He apparently didn't enjoy talking to me, so he said to Evelyn Coleridge, "Maybe Mr. Brewster would find it easier to work in Martin's studio. I don't suppose Martin would object."

Everyone seemed to think that was a good idea. Mrs. Coleridge explained to me that "Martin" was Martin Golightly, the local artist, who had a studio with a skylight. Chief Rudd went off to investigate the situation, and five minutes later we all made a solemn procession to Martin's studio—which turned out to be ideal for my purposes. The studio was a log cabin in a lean-to design, with a roof of frosted glass. There was plenty of space to work in, and the light seemed to be adequate. The big disadvantage was that the building was unheated. That wouldn't make little Gwendolyn's job of posing any easier.

Martin Golightly joined the gathering. He was a slight, handsome, long-haired young man—about twenty-five—who seemed to find the world either puzzling, hostile, or both. Evelyn Coleridge performed the introductions. "Jonathan," she said, "this is Martin Golightly, my daughter Sara's ex-husband."

I'm not sure about what happened next. My response to the introduction might have been "Oh, shit." If I didn't say it, I certainly thought it. I remember everyone looking embarrassed. Or everyone but Chief Rudd, who seemed to be enjoying himself. My confusion began to clear when the door to the studio opened and another young man walked in. He was about Martin's age and from an exotic racial background (Mohegan Indian, it turned out). His name was Roger Sayqueg, and when he went to stand next to Martin, it was obvious that they were more than just buddies. I had enough gay acquaintances in the city to know that it was unwise to make snap decisions about who was and who wasn't gay. I also thought it didn't make much difference anyway. But it's easy to recognize lovers, whatever their sexual persuasion. Then I remembered Mrs. Coleridge had previously made a polite reference to Martin's "proclivities." I felt much better thinking that Martin hadn't had sex with Sara. It was an idiotic, macho reaction on my part—but I was grateful to it for allowing me to function again.

Martin and all the other spectators stood silently back in the corners of the studio and allowed me to work without interference. I set up my camera and put a stool in position for Gwendolyn. Before I made any exposures, I sat on the stool and took Gwendolyn on my lap. She was a remarkably attractive little person. I hadn't paid too much attention to her on my previous visit, and even if I had, I wouldn't have felt the full effect of her beauty, because she had been wearing a drab sort of snowsuit and a tight wool cap that concealed her hair and made her face look skull-like.

But now, when she took off her coat and hat, she was transformed. Her long, disheveled hair had the color of sun-scorched grass. Her eyebrows were pale, but her skin was even paler, and her chestnut eyes looked black in contrast. What was most striking, though, was her body. She was wearing an undecorated, short-sleeved white dress. The skirt of the dress stopped about halfway down her thighs, which would have seemed acceptable for most girls her age. But most girls her age had legs that seemed to be arrangements of sticks or balloons. Gwendolyn's legs were curiously adult. She accented the effect by wearing white shoes with moderately high heels and by not wearing any stockings.

I thought of moving the camera closer so that it viewed her only from the waist up, but I decided instead to rely on being able to get her to strike demure poses. As she sat on my lap she was not exactly concerning herself with modesty, and I rearranged her skirt so that it furnished at least some basic cover.

Gwen hooked her hands around the back of my neck and stared a little disapprovingly into my eyes. "I wish Joanne was here," she said.

"I know, dear. I'll bring her next time."

"Before Christmas," Gwendolyn said. It was more a command than a request.

"Yes. Before you're not here." I lowered my voice. "You didn't tell me where you're going."

"I'm going to be with the dead little girls."

"Are you sick?" I whispered.

Gwendolyn shook her head and smiled.

From the background came the voice of Gwendolyn's subject-changing mother: "Will you have enough light, Mr. Brewster?"

"I think so," I answered. Then I turned again to Gwendolyn. "But you'll have to be very still," I said.

"They'll be good pictures, Mr. Brewster. Wait and see."

Gwendolyn jumped down off my lap and announced that she was ready to have her picture taken. I went to the camera and started what I assumed was going to be a futile session. Gwendolyn ignored my attempts to pose her. Actually, she did extremely well on her own, giving me a variety of poses and expressions without resorting to mugging. But she ignored me when I asked her to hold her poses. "It's all right," she said. "You'll see. Just take pictures."

I looked around a couple of times at the audience for a little support, but no one offered to help me keep Gwendolyn under control. I went ahead and made the exposures: some of them short, which I expected would give me at best some shadowy underexposures; some of them long, which would probably give me white streaks. The best I could hope for was good luck, which might result in one or two recognizable likenesses. When I announced that I had run out of film holders and that the session was over, our little audience produced some restrained applause. Gwendolyn took a bow and came over to me and kissed my hand. Then she ran out of the studio. Delbert Rudd followed her.

The rest of the Childgraveans lingered while I packed up my equipment. Mrs. Coleridge suggested that we adjourn to her place for refreshment. Martin Golightly and his friend offered to help me carry things, and I accepted the offer. I tried for about thirty seconds to dislike my helpers, but they were pleasant, attractive people.

"I understand you know Sara," Martin said to me.

"I did for a while."

Martin didn't seem self-conscious about the subject. "I grew up with her," he said. A tactful way to put it. And in an oblique, succinct way, he was explaining his relationship to Sara.

I had noticed an easel holding a draped canvas, and suddenly

I was curious about what kind of painting Sara's ex-husband did. "Do you do much painting?" I asked him.

"Quite a bit."

"You don't have an agent, by any chance?"

"No. I'm not a professional. Not even a semiprofessional."

I was struck again that the people in Childgrave didn't seem to be involved in essential industries: harp playing, illustrating, home winemaking, painting. They were my kind of folks in that respect. Where were the merchants, plumbers, and growers of cabbages?

Martin didn't offer to show me any of his paintings, and he led me out of the studio. But I was feeling sneaky. There were so many unknown quantities and qualities in Childgrave that even I couldn't resist trying to do a little investigating. When we got outside, I told Martin and Roger that I had left my light meter behind, and I jogged back into the studio and took a quick look at the covered canvas that was resting on the easel. I just raised the cover for a fraction of a second, and my eyes and brain did one of those little miracles of perception that make photography seem like a cumbersome process. In an instant, the image was registered and processed and stored away where I could examine it at will.

This image wasn't one of those that change a person's life; not like the thirtieth of a second in which a husband sees his supposedly shopping wife getting into a cab with another man. But it was an image that would stay with me for a while. It was basically a full-length, ultrarealistic portrait of Sara. But it was Sara wearing the same kind of dress that Gwendolyn had worn in the photographs I had just taken. On Sara, the dress looked sexily grotesque; it was too tight across her breasts, and the skirt was even less concealing than Gwendolyn's. The paint smelled fresh, and the painting was unfinished, so I assumed that it was a work in progress—which meant that Sara was still very much on Martin's mind. But Martin obviously was having trouble figuring out his relationship to Sara. The portrait was inspired by confusion and not by love.

Martin didn't seem especially confused about his relationship to Roger, though. As the three of us walked to Mrs. Coleridge's house Martin told me what a fast runner Roger was. Roger produced an attractive little aw-shucks smile. I asked him where he competed. It turned out he didn't compete. He had never even clocked himself. He just liked to run fast. And Martin was telling the world—or me, as its representative—how devoted he was to Roger. I was glad that neither of them felt the need to wear a black-leather ensemble or a Dutchman's cap. I enjoyed being with them, and I tried to let them know that all the world—or at least I, as its representative—loved a lover.

Back at the Coleridge house, there was a festive atmosphere. Logs were burning in the fireplace, and Evelyn had lighted several candles to relieve the murk of the afternoon. The cider was flowing, and although I thought it best to pass up a salad that contained a lot of ambiguous root vegetables and sprouting seeds, I put away a few corn muffins with cranberry jelly.

The chief and Gwendolyn didn't put in an appearance, but Verity Palmer and Beth and Arthur Hopkins were there, along with Evelyn Coleridge, Martin, and Roger. Verity had her eyes on me quite a bit of the time, but she kept her hands off. I liked her better that way. Arthur told me about his deepening relationship with Petite Sirah grapes. Beth sang a medieval carol about roses and virtue and the birth of Christ. No one treated me as if I were an outsider, but at the same time there were no requests for me to tell any tales of my life in the metropolis. My companions were interested in me, but not in my life away from Childgrave.

I had a bad moment when Evelyn Coleridge suggested we all form a circle and join hands. I was afraid a séance might be on the horizon. Verity's restraint relaxed a little, and she showed up on my left when the hand-holding started. Martin was on my right. We stood silently in the circle for about five minutes. I kept waiting for someone to say something that would give me some idea of what kind of feelings I should be having. But no one spoke. I thought first of encounter sessions I had read about in the 1960s. Then I wondered whether I should sing "Auld Lang Syne." But gradually I stopped thinking and just let myself have feelings. They were good feelings, but not completely joyful. I felt as if I were saying good-bye to a lover who was going off to receive the Nobel Prize. I was the one who broke up the little ritual—reaching for a handkerchief to wipe some unexpected and slightly puzzling tears from my cheeks.

A few minutes later I was in my car, headed for home and wondering what the people of Childgrave wanted from me. I also wondered what I wanted from them. In the beginning, it had seemed that all I wanted was Sara. But, in a way, they *were* Sara, with their mysterious attractiveness. Was I in love with Childgrave? I had heard people say they had fallen in love with a city or a neighborhood, but I didn't think Venice or Scarsdale would be likely to make the same kind of demands on a person as Childgrave would. In any case, when I got back to New York City, it looked a little less attractive to me than it ever had before.

My portraits of Gwendolyn Hopkins were astounding. All my worries about technical problems turned out to be irrelevant. Each photograph was technically perfect in its own strange way. It was as if the laws of physics and chemistry had been suspended during the exposing and processing of the pictures. Gwendolyn seemed to be illuminated not by the usual reflected light but by her own internal light, which produced a technically perfect photograph in each shot, even though I had varied the exposure times considerably.

As I had expected, Gwendolyn wasn't the only person to turn up in the pictures. She was accompanied in most cases by vague images of other girls who were about her own age and who wore the same kind of white dress she was wearing. Gwendolyn herself was always the dominating image, clearly depicted, and with the slightly neurotic quality that had always bothered me in the Tenniel drawings of Alice in the Lewis Carroll books. In fact, my portraits of Gwendolyn had another quality that connected them with Carroll: the same kind of sexiness that often showed up in the photographs Carroll himself had taken of little girls.

Added to all these unsettling images were a few superimposed angels, and—in one shot in which Gwendolyn was the only girl visible—a large translucent hand. The hand, which was almost life-sized, was holding a knife. As if that weren't disturbing enough, I realized after staring at the picture for a while that a couple of things about it were familiar to me: the knife was the one I had seen on display in Childgrave's Meeting Hall; and the hand, which had lost a fingertip, was the one I had seen Chief Delbert Rudd displaying during my last visit to the village.

Joanne was the first person I showed the portraits to. She looked through them several times, smiling and oohing and ahhing as though I had given her pictures of the finalists in a cute-puppy-dog contest.

Joanne's final judgment was: "They're the nicest pictures in the whole world."

"They're nice in a way," I agreed. "But who are all those little girls besides Gwendolyn?"

"They're some of the others. They were choosed, too."

"Chosen. Chosen for what?"

"You know."

"No, I don't. Chosen for what?" Joanne turned shy and began to squirm. I tried one more question. "What about the hand with the knife?"

"Sometimes bad things are good."

It was like talking to a Zen Buddhist. I thought I'd better seek a more worldly reaction. I called Harry, who said he and Lee would drop by and take a look at the new portraits on the way back from an opening of some kind in Chinatown.

I didn't show the pictures to Nanny Joy. She was getting over her recent unfriendliness, and I didn't want to upset her again. While I waited for my visitors to show up, Joy and I did more than enough drinking to put us into a party mood, and I even accepted her offer to teach me variations on the slow fox-trot. It was a hopeless job, and all I could manage was some out-of-tempo stumbling. But it gave us a chance for a nonverbal mutual apology that cleared up whatever tension was left from our recent disagreement.

Joy went to her room when Harry and Lee arrived. Lee was in a foul mood, which was understandable considering that they had just come from the opening of a show that featured the work of a Taiwanese photographer who specialized in doing landscapes for use on the calendars that are featured in Chinese laundries all over the world. Harry was thinking of representing the photographer, but Lee thought the notion was insane.

"You've seen those calendars, haven't you, Jonathan? Those outrageous colors? Well, what's unbelievable is that the colors aren't the result—as we had all imagined—of inept lithography; they're in the photographer's original prints and transparencies. Those radioactive reds and squashed-caterpillar greens are—if possible—even more sickening in the original. Pagodas that look as if they've been puked on; and there wasn't anyone at the show who had been farther east than East Hampton. They don't even send their chi-chi skivvies to the local no-tickee parlor; Mme. Yvonne sends her lavender van, deals with their soilings, and delivers in wicker baskets, gardenias between the layers. Christ, Harry, you're decadent. At least you could have found someone from the People's Republic."

Harry smiled admiringly at his wife. "You overdid the rice wine, my sweet," he said. "But maybe it has brought you a clarity of vision that escapes those of us who are burdened by sobriety." Harry tried to kiss Lee's neck but stumbled in the process and seemed to end up with his nose in her damp-fleshed cleavage.

"Maybe you'd like some coffee," I said.

"God, yes," Lee said. "Do you have any French-roast beans, Jonathan?" She didn't wait for me to say I didn't know. She headed for the kitchen. I felt relieved, because if she had been offended by calendar art, what would she make of my latest offerings? Actually, I wasn't sure it was the best time for Harry to look at the new portraits, either. His eyes didn't seem to be focusing too well, and I got the impression that he was pleased by almost everything he looked at. But better to deal with a happy drunk than a nasty one. I sat Harry down and put the portraits in his lap. He looked through them slowly, and his benign look began to vanish. By the time he had finished looking at them, there were tears in his eyes. My thighs began to feel prickly, and I was definitely sorry I had shown him the prints.

When Harry finally spoke, he was looking not at me but at the floor. "We can't show these," he said.

"Why not?"

Harry looked toward the kitchen, apparently to make sure that Lee wasn't headed our way. Then he leaned toward me and said, "These are dirty pictures."

"You're drunk, Harry."

"We can sell them. Definitely we can sell them, and for perhaps the biggest bucks ever, dear boy, but no shows and no books. Under the counter. And, Jonathan, I think you should stay away from the Catskills."

"And I think you should stay away from the rice wine. You're the one who's making silly moral judgments, not me."

Harry looked offended. "We need another opinion," he said.

"Not Lee," I said. "She's in worse shape than you are."

"Nanny Joy, then. Is she here?"

That wasn't going to help my cause. "Joy's been drinking, too," I said. "Let's leave it until some other time. Or why don't we just forget it?"

But Harry stood up a little unsteadily, left the room, and came back a couple of minutes later with Nanny Joy and his wife. The three of them looked through the prints and mutually condemned them. It took Lee about five minutes to let me know why she didn't like the portraits. The words "appallingly offensive" came up fairly often. Nanny Joy merely said she thought the pictures ought to be burned.

I said that my companions ought to join Alcoholics Anonymous. Then I told Harry that I was going to find myself another agent. At least, I think that's what I told him. I was too upset to be sure about that. But I'm sure that I gathered up the portraits and went to bed and that I didn't talk to Harry again until after Christmas.

Chapter 12

The next morning I woke up wondering whether my visits to Childgrave had muddled my judgment. Was there something repugnant and obscene in the portraits I did of Gwendolyn? Had Joanne and I learned to accept—and even learned to admire—things that were unacceptable to people who had seen and accepted just about everything there was to see in New York City?

I refused to believe that Joanne was anything but innocent. She might be involved in things that were mysterious or unpleasant, but her judgments were innocent. I suppose there are people who would argue that innocence is not necessarily a good thing. But given a choice, I would opt for innocence over goodness.

I brought the portraits of Gwendolyn to the bed, and I lay for half an hour or so examining them. I couldn't see that they were any less acceptable than the portraits I had done of Joanne. It was true that there was a vaguely erotic quality to the pictures, but the effect wasn't something that Gwendolyn consciously produced. I decided that the dominant quality she projected in the portraits was a suppressed fear. But whatever qualities the photographs had, they were subtle and didn't add up to anything obviously repugnant or pornographic. And whatever those qualities were, they seemed pleasing to me and my daughter.

Joanne and I began to spend a lot of time together. She was the only person I knew who understood what Childgrave meant to me. Since she would be entering kindergarten in January, I freed her from preschool and Ms. Abraham. I became Manhattan's most attentive father. Joanne and I became the talk of the puppet-show circuit. We weren't exactly a fun couple, though, and our tendency to reminisce about Childgrave probably gave us the air of a couple of survivors of a bombed-out city.

I knew that I had a major decision to make, and I was forced to face it one day when Joanne and I were passing a street-corner Santa Claus—one of the less inspiring practitioners of the art. He had probably been recruited from Skid Row, and he was certain to shake any child's belief in St. Nicholas—if not in humanity in general. This was indeed a tacky Santa. His frankly fake beard was stained with what was probably some kind of fortified wine. Instead of ringing a bell, he held out his hand and coughed. Joanne made the mistake of making eye contact with him. He said, "What do you want Santa to bring you, kid?"

"I want to go to Childgrave," she said.

Santa glanced at me with what seemed to be pity. "Yeah," he said. "It figures."

I gave Santa ten dollars, which I hoped would send him to the nearest bar and keep him off the streets for a while.

But I was still faced with my decision. I had written to Evelyn Coleridge and asked her if it was all right if I visited her on the day before Christmas to deliver the portraits of Gwendolyn as a gift. Evelyn wrote back to say that she had no objection except that she would be busy on Christmas Eve, and that I would have to leave Childgrave in the early afternoon to give her a chance to make her preparations. My problem was whether I should take Joanne with me. If I didn't take her, I would spoil her Christmas. If I did take her, I would spoil Nanny Joy's Christmas.

My own preference was to go to Childgrave on the chance that Sara would be there (or, if she were already there, that she would decide to show herself). And I wanted to see the other people I had met in Childgrave. Since I seemed to have lost my friends in Manhattan, I had been spending more and more time thinking about what it would be like to live in Childgrave, even without Sara.

So, on the morning before Christmas, Joanne and I headed north. We had been making so many expeditions that Nanny Joy didn't seem to have any suspicions that we might be venturing into forbidden country. I made Joanne promise not to tell anyone about our visit, and I thought there was a pretty good chance that we would get away with our deception.

We were having a white Christmas, although I hadn't realized it until we got out of the city. There had been a couple of moderate snowfalls in the previous week, but the sanitation department had rearranged the white blanket into a series of sooty, slushy piles that looked more like rubbish than snow. I was surprised to find that in the countryside the snow was still undisturbed. The roads themselves had been well plowed and were generally dry, so we made good time.

When we got to Childgrave, the atmosphere was a little different. The road into the valley was still covered with snow. There were no strings of colored lights, no loud-speakered carols. But there was something that was more festive in its way than anything we had seen during our trip. And the unlikely announcer of the festivity was Chief of Police Delbert Rudd. His car was parked across the road at the top of the hill. He walked over to meet us as I pulled up, and although he wasn't smiling, at least he didn't look as if he were about to make an arrest.

"The hill's a bit slick," he said. "It might be safer not to drive down. There's a side path we can take that's not so steep."

I was glad I had worn boots. But it turned out I didn't need them. The chief led us around some evergreen shrubs, which had been concealing one of the most pleasing things I had ever looked at: a large wooden sleigh hitched to a pair of white horses. Joanne had a little fit of delight, shrieking and dancing. The sleigh seemed to be made entirely of wood, including its runners. It was painted white, and it resembled a boat more than anything else; a boat that might have been used in some sort of ceremony in an ancient culture. We climbed in and the chief arranged a scarlet wool blanket over our laps. Then we set off down a gently winding path. It wasn't a smooth ride, and I thought the lack of bells was a minor flaw, but all things considered, I thought it was delightful, and Joanne thought it was about perfect.

Chief Rudd dropped us in front of Evelyn Coleridge's house and said he would be back to pick us up in an hour. I was going to suggest that maybe our hostess should be the one to decide how long we should stay, but the chief didn't seem to invite any discussion of the matter. He seemed more like his usual grim self after we got into town. As usual, the streets were deserted, although the snow on the sidewalks was surprisingly well trampled. There had been quite a bit of activity at some time recently. As Joanne and I walked to the door of Mrs. Coleridge's house I began to feel uneasy. It might have been just the excitement of the sleigh ride, but my emotions seemed more complicated than the ride would account for. I had the definite sensation that someone was about to scream.

I paused for a moment to look along the street. At first I didn't see any decorations of any kind. No lights, wreaths, or municipal tree. And then I noticed that on the front of the Meeting Hall, and farther off, on the mausoleum in the cemetery, there were touches of red. I couldn't be sure, but each structure seemed to be decorated with a simple draping of red silk. It was nothing elaborate, but in contrast to the starkness of the village, the effect was dramatic.

Evelyn Coleridge opened the door of her house, and Gwendolyn Hopkins ran out to embrace Joanne. Whatever my emotions were, they were trivial compared to Gwendolyn's. Her face was flushed, and she was so wildly animated that you had to assume that someone had either just given her or taken from her the thing she most wanted out of life.

Fortunately, Mrs. Coleridge seemed to be in control of herself. Not that she was exactly placid, but she confined her demonstration of emotion to a discreet nibbling of her lower lip. The girls ran off into the house, and Evelyn and I went into the sitting room and sat. I was carrying my portraits of Gwendolyn, which Joanne had wrapped spectacularly, if not neatly. Since our time was apparently short, I called Joanne and suggested that she present the portraits to Gwendolyn.

The presentation was simple. Gwendolyn managed to keep her body—with the exception of most of the muscles in her face —still while Joanne said, "Merry Christmas to my best friend in the whole world," and handed over the package.

Gwendolyn put the gift on the table and embraced, kissed, and thanked, first Joanne and then me. She got permission from Mrs. Coleridge to open the package. Then Gwendolyn moved to the other side of the room, where she carefully untied the photographs. She looked at each one for a few seconds, and, smiling, took them one by one to Mrs. Coleridge, who was smiling too. I remembered that there hadn't been a lot of smiling when I had shown the photographs in my apartment in the city, and I decided that I had done the right thing in bringing them back to

Childgrave. I had kept only one to give to Joanne as a remembrance of Gwendolyn and Childgrave in case we didn't get back to the village again.

After Gwendolyn had finished looking at the portraits, she walked over to me and kissed my hand. "I told you they would be all right," she said. Then she and Joanne went upstairs, not in their usual wild scurry, but sedately and gravely.

Mrs. Coleridge smiled at me. "Thank you for the photographs, Mr. Brewster. The town will cherish them."

"It was a pleasure. But actually, I meant them for Gwendolyn, not for the town."

Mrs. Coleridge began to bite her lower lip again. "Yes," she said. "Of course you did."

"Maybe you could tell me about the children," I said.

"The children?"

"The girls in the photograph. The ones other than Gwendolyn."

"They are from the past. The past is always with us. There is nothing mysterious about that. Any of us can see the past."

"I don't seem to have much of a knack for it."

"Nonsense. Come, take my hands." I did as I was told. "Now close your eyes." I closed them and felt something similar to a mild electric shock. And then I saw—not in the way you see something in your imagination, but actually saw, as if my eyes were open—a girl about the age of Gwendolyn. The girl was wearing the kind of white dress that seemed to be the standard costume in Childgrave. I pulled my hands away from Evelyn Coleridge's hands and opened my eyes. The vision, or whatever I had been seeing, vanished immediately—which is what I wanted, because the girl I had seen had been lying on the floor, obviously dead, with a stain of fresh blood on the front of her dress.

I looked at Evelyn Coleridge, who seemed to be examining my expression very carefully. I said: "She was dead."

"Yes."

"I mean, she had been killed."

"Yes. Is that unacceptable to you?"

"Of course it's unacceptable to me."

"You could not imagine accepting it?"

For some reason, I hesitated. Then I thought of Joanne. "No," I said. "I really can't imagine it."

"I did not suppose so, Jonathan. There is really no reason you should at this point."

At this or any other point, I thought. We sat in silence for a minute or two. I felt tired and out of place. Did I have a place anymore? I had been eager to leave the city, and now I was eager to leave Childgrave. If I had a place, it was with Sara. But where was Sara? I might as well ask. "Have you heard anything from Sara?" I said.

"Sara is well," Mrs. Coleridge said, not exactly answering my question.

"I'd like to see her."

"You must be patient. I understand you are a patient man."

"I used to think so."

"It is helpful for one to question one's assumptions occasionally."

It's also helpful for one to stop being pompous occasionally, I thought. Especially if one seems to have a casual attitude about the killing of young girls. And for the first time I admitted to myself what I had been trying to pretend could not be true: For some reason, little girls got killed in Childgrave with the knowledge and approval of its saintly citizenry.

"Joanne and I had better be getting back to the city," I said.

Evelyn didn't protest. "It was good of you to make the journey," she said.

I called Joanne, who surprisingly came along without complaining when I told her that we had to leave. I tried not to look at Gwendolyn, who seemed a little less like a privileged person and more like a frightened child. The sleigh was waiting at the end of the street, and as the four of us left the house Chief Rudd climbed into it and drove toward us. Mrs. Coleridge and Gwendolyn didn't wait for the sleigh to arrive. They said an unemotional good-bye and went into the house. As the door closed, its brass knocker glinted. Someone had polished it—the child's head that I had first seen on the door of Sara's apartment in the city. It reminded me that Sara was part of Childgrave and its traditions. I wished she were with me to explain some of those traditions.

Instead, Delbert Rudd was with me. Joanne and I settled ourselves in the back of the sleigh and started the trip up the hill. I wasn't feeling as elated as I had when we arrived. The sleigh seemed merely uncomfortable, and the horses stank. I wondered whether it was worth trying to make conversation with Chief Rudd, who was perched in the driver's seat. What would I say? He saved me the trouble.

"Going back to the city now, are you?" he asked.

"That's right. I suppose this is an important night in Childgrave, isn't it?"

"It is, Mr. Brewster."

I was going to ask him if they had a candlelight service at the Meeting Hall, but then I remembered that all their services would be candlelight services. The thought would have made me smile in Manhattan, but now it just depressed me. I settled for asking: "Do you have some kind of public celebration?"

"I wouldn't say a celebration. An observance, I'd say."

"A meeting?"

"A meeting, yes. And we start our fast."

"You fast? How many hours does the fast go on?"

"Not hours. Days. Seven."

"A seven-day fast? Isn't that dangerous?"

"No, sir. Not at all. We don't move around too much. And we're allowed water, of course. There's more dangerous things."

Oh, really? I thought. What would Delbert Rudd's idea of a dangerous activity be? "What sort of thing do you have in mind?" I asked him.

"It's dangerous to make light of someone's faith. You probably don't believe that, living in a big city. I would imagine you worry about someone coming up in back of you on a subway platform, or you fear that when you get home, the door will be ajar, a panel punched out of the wood you thought was so strong. You don't worry about someone interfering with your grace or your rituals."

It was sort of comforting to have the chief lecturing me again; telling me that I lacked grace, scolding me for not holding séances. But I decided it was best not to continue our little talk. Joanne was listening carefully to what we were saying, and she didn't seem too pleased by it. She burrowed down next to me, as though she were trying to get as far away from Chief Rudd as possible. When we got to my car, I started to wish the chief a merry Christmas, but the world "merry" didn't seem too appropriate, so I just thanked him for the sleigh ride.

As I was driving away I noticed that not only was the town's police car parked across the main road to Childgrave, but a wooden barrier had been put in place as well. On the barrier was a sign reading:

POLICE ORDER—
DO NOT ENTER
UNTIL FURTHER NOTICE

The sign affected me the way it would affect almost any normally inquisitive person: it made me want to enter. But it seemed more important to get Joanne back to the city. My daughter hadn't shown much enthusiasm for the holiday and she hadn't developed her Christmas list beyond a request for a trip to Childgrave. I hadn't worked up much interest in the season either. And even though I had visited a toy store and had bought enough things for her to fill one of our closets, I immediately forgot what it was that I had bought.

On our trip back from Childgrave, Joanne and I didn't do much talking. It wasn't until we were parking in front of the apartment that Joanne decided to dumbfound me. "The shoes were warm," she said.

"Your shoes are warm?"

"No. Her shoes."

"Who is 'her'?"

"Miss Coleridge."

"Mrs. Coleridge?"

"No. *Miss* Coleridge. My new mommy."

"Sara?"

"Yes."

"What do you mean, her shoes were warm?"

"When I was playing in her room, I put my hands in them. They were warm."

"Today?"

Joanne nodded.

Several of the circuits in my brain were announcing that they were temporarily out of order, but there were still enough connections to let me get things straight. "Sweetie," I said, "when you say the shoes were warm, do you mean they were snuggy for your feet, or do you mean they gave off heat like a piece of toast?"

"Like toast. Only not very hot toast."

"Like someone had been wearing the shoes and had taken them off?"

Another nod.

The thought of shoes—or anything else—warmed by Sara's body was enough to brighten my holiday. "Did you see your new mommy there?"

Joanne shook her head.

My hands began to shake.

After dinner, I put my daughter to bed. I dressed for cross-country hiking, picked up a battery-powered lantern, and once again drove to Childgrave.

As I stood on the hill above the village the muscles at the back of my neck contracted, and I began to shiver in little spasms that seemed to result from emotions as much as from the cold. I didn't know what I would find in Childgrave, but I was resolved that I wouldn't let it drive me away. It seemed that in returning to the town this time I had officially transferred my allegiance away from Manhattan. Apparently it was not only Sara that I had been seeking.

The night was cloudless, and the almost-full moon was directly overhead. After I had stood for three or four minutes I could easily see the outlines of the trees against the snow. But no lights were visible below. Whatever the villagers did on Christmas Eve, it didn't require a lot of illumination. I scouted around a bit to be sure that Delbert Rudd wasn't waiting to greet me, and then I walked cautiously but without any difficulty down into the silent night of Childgrave.

As I passed the first scattered houses they seemed to be totally dark. But then I noticed that there were traces of white smoke rising from their chimneys, and some of the downstairs windows showed a faint glow that probably came from logs burning slowly in fireplaces. I stopped and spent a little time just listening. I couldn't hear anything.

By the time I reached the Coleridge house I still hadn't seen or heard anything that indicated there were any people around but Jonathan Brewster. I took a few discreet peeks through windows, and, as I expected, I saw smoldering fireplaces, but no one who might throw another log on the fire. So, the villagers had been in their homes recently but had found something better to do. That meant the Meeting Hall, most likely, so I headed in that direction. And as I approached it I could see flickering lights in its windows. I found a place in the shadows across from the entrance to the hall, and I stood and waited.

Gradually I became aware of a muted, distant voice. It was a man's voice, and it obviously came from inside the Meeting Hall. The tone of the voice wasn't conversational, but I didn't get the impression that anyone was trying to entertain anyone or to persuade them of anything. I looked at my wristwatch and, after some squinting, figured out that it was midnight.

Then things began to happen.

First, I heard a puzzling sound in the distance: a sort of thumping and creaking. It wasn't until I heard some snorting and whinnying that I realized I was hearing the approach of a horse. Actually, it was two horses—familiar white horses pulling a familiar white sleigh containing a familiar person. I moved farther back into the shadows and tried to figure out exactly what the newest emotion was that had begun to take charge of me. It took me a few moments to identify it, because it wasn't an emotion I had very often: awe.

The horses weren't the kind you see at the track. They were bred for something more serious than speed. As they came down the slope of Golightly Street, straining to hold back the weight of the heavy old sleigh, their nostrils sending out puffs of condensing breath, and the muscles of their shoulders and haunches twitching, I got the feeling I was watching something heroic and mythological. Chief Rudd, on his driver's perch, and dressed in black, didn't exactly conjure up names like Zeus, Elysium, or

Apollo, but I began to recall schoolday references to Hades, Styx, and Charon. And I had a little better idea of why we're taught to respect the vision of the ancient Greeks.

Delbert Rudd guided the sleigh to the curb in front of the Meeting Hall and stopped the horses. I could see his clothes more clearly now. He was wearing a black cape like the one Mrs. Coleridge had lent me, and he accented his ensemble with a high-crowned, flat-brimmed black hat. It was the same kind of costume I had seen on the man in the cemetery during my first visit to Childgrave. Rudd jumped down from the sleigh and walked to the double doors of the Meeting Hall. He stood before them for a moment and then threw them both open. As he walked quickly through the doorway I could see that the hall was filled with people, who turned to face him as he entered. They all held lighted white candles, and they all wore black, floor-length capes. That is, all but one person wore black. The exception was a small girl who was wearing a white dress. She was standing at the rear of the building, facing me along an aisle that separated the crowd into two groups. For a moment, the only movement came from the doors, which swung slightly on their hinges.

Then the girl began to walk slowly toward the doorway. I assumed she was Gwendolyn Hopkins, although I couldn't see her face clearly enough to be certain. I looked for someone else I might recognize, but despite all the candlepower, the faces were distorted by the unsettling shadows that resulted from a low frontlight. And since all the women were wearing black bonnets, and the men were wearing the same kind of hats that Delbert Rudd was wearing, it would have been hard to identify anyone even at noon.

The girl seemed to slow up and to hesitate occasionally as she walked down the aisle. The other people in the hall weren't watching her but were looking ahead to the doorway. Just before the girl reached the doorway, she stopped, looked to the side, and held her arms out. A hand reached out and took hers. It was the hand of Delbert Rudd. He moved to the girl's side, and they walked out of the Meeting Hall. When they reached the sleigh, Chief Rudd lifted the girl to the back seat and draped the red blanket around her. Then he climbed onto the driver's platform.

The people, still carrying burning candles, began to file out of the hall and line up two abreast behind the sleigh. When everyone had left the hall, Chief Rudd shook the reins, and the horses walked slowly forward—toward the cemetery. Rudd held the reins in his left hand, and as the sleigh creaked and began to move he held his right arm above his head. Something glinted in his hand. He was holding a knife. The girl in the back of the sleigh raised her head and stared at the knife.

I was certain by then that the girl was Gwendolyn, even though I still couldn't see her features clearly. She was as self-possessed as ever, and she showed no sign of fear or distress as she stared up at the knife.

I can't say the same about myself. As always seemed to happen in my trips to Childgrave, I had begun to shiver, this time partly because the wind seemed to have freshened, but mostly because I was terrified. I wondered if I should run out and stop the procession. Perhaps I could grab Gwendolyn and get her back to the safety of my car. It wasn't likely. For one thing, she might not want to come with me. But even if she did, there would be a lot of people pursuing us; people who were familiar with the terrain and who, in at least one case, might be armed.

It didn't take much to convince myself that the best thing for me to do was stay out of the way. After all, I didn't know that anything sinister was about to happen. I was just an uninvited observer at a quaint ceremony. Just because the chief of police was holding a knife before a little girl and heading for a cemetery, and just because my daughter and my camera had been seeing the ghosts of a lot of dead girls in a town called Childgrave, that didn't mean that in a few minutes Chief Rudd wouldn't fling off his cape to reveal a Santa Claus suit and use his knife to cut the ribbon of a Christmas package for Gwendolyn. Right? I wasn't being cowardly. Right?

Wrong.

The procession moved slowly ahead. Candles flickered in the wind and went out. Capes fluttered, and people stumbled and slipped. There were about two hundred Childgraveans walking behind the sleigh: men, women, children, and a few infants who were being carried. The last person in the column was a man. He was the only one in the crowd who was not wearing a hat, and his cape was draped loosely over what seemed to be a well-tailored business suit. He wouldn't have looked out of place strolling along Park Avenue. It seemed I wasn't the only out-of-town visitor in Childgrave that night.

But I was the only one who thought it best to keep out of sight—which is what I continued to do. I sneaked along after the procession, staying just close enough to have some idea of what was going on. The parade stopped at the gate of the cemetery, and the marchers gathered along the fence on either side of the gate. Chief Rudd, Gwendolyn, and the hatless man entered the cemetery and went to stand on the steps of the mausoleum.

Then things seemed to get out of control a bit. There was some movement in the crowd, and a woman broke away and ran awkwardly through the gate, toward the mausoleum. She shouted just one word: "No." Her voice seemed incredibly loud after the long silence. Then a man rushed out of the crowd and quickly caught up with the woman. He caught her by the arm, and she immediately stopped. She didn't resist as the man led her back into the crowd.

When I looked back to the mausoleum, its steps were empty. The people of the village looked toward the mausoleum, and they became absolutely motionless and silent. After a few seconds a high-pitched moan broke the silence. My first thought was that it was an animal of some kind; a cat in heat, perhaps. But there was a human quality to the sound. Maybe one of the infants in the crowd was starting to cry. But the moan was not repeated.

Then the man who had accompanied Chief Rudd and Gwendolyn came out of the mausoleum. He stood facing the people of the town. "It is done," he said.

I wondered whether he was going to spell that out. But obviously that wasn't necessary. I think everyone knew what had been done. I was the only one who didn't know the details. And I wasn't sure I wanted to know them.

But what would happen next? After fifteen minutes or so, it seemed fairly certain that nothing was going to happen. The people of Childgrave were going to stand silently in the cold darkness and stare at the mausoleum. The question was, how long would they keep it up? The horses snorted occasionally, but the people were quiet. There was a little foot-shifting in the crowd, but no one seemed ready to leave. No one except me.

I had definitely decided to leave. I told myself that my reason for leaving was that despite my warm clothes, I felt as if I were in the early stages of frostbite. But even though there was some truth in that, my real problem was that I felt sick with terror, disgust, and fear.

I turned away from the vigil and, stiff-legged and numb-footed, began walking in the direction of my car. I hadn't gone very far before I began to stumble, and I realized that I wasn't able to see anything at all. Next I noticed that my cheeks were wet and that my eyes were filled with tears. I pretended that the tears were caused by the cold and not by my emotions, but I didn't convince myself.

Whatever the cause of the tears, they made it almost impossible for me to navigate, and I decided I needed to rest for a few minutes and pull myself together. Could I take a chance and find shelter in someone's house? It might be safe enough in the Coleridge house. But that seemed like an illegal act. Not that illegality seemed to be defined the same way in Childgrave that it was defined in most other towns.

Then I thought of the Meeting Hall. It was a public building. My conscience would have less trouble dealing with that. I knew I couldn't be far from the hall, and with a lot of wiping of my eyes and some cautious maneuvering, I found myself inside the building in a few minutes. As far as I could tell, no one seemed to have stayed in the hall, which had the peculiar quality of a room that has very recently held a great many people. It seemed warm to me—not a dry, mechanical warmth but a moist, earthily scented heat that had been generated by heavily clothed bodies. The aroma of sweat-dampened wool mingled with a thin haze of candle smoke.

I thought of calling out to see whether anyone was still in the building, but I decided it was better to be discovered misbehaving than merely being inquisitive. I found a chair near the door, and I sat until I felt reasonably warm and until my vision had cleared. Then I went to the case in which I had seen the knife displayed.

The case was empty. No surprise in that. There was one light burning in the building—a large white candle in a floor stand. It was on a platform, and next to it was a lectern. I went quickly to the platform. On the lectern was a closed, folio-sized book that was impressively bound in full leather. No Florentine scarlet or gilded curlicues; just thick, rubbed natural cowhide. I opened the book.

There was no title page, and the first leaf was blank. The second page was covered with large, angular handwriting in a faded brown ink. With difficulty, I began to read:

> In this 6. month of the yeare of Our Lorde 1660, I, Josiah Golightly, being neere to the time that I shall gratefully join my blessed Maker, do set down a brief history of those joys and perturbations which have been visited upon me in the New World. I put forth these words neither in idleness nor in vanity, but in feare that we may soon forget, nay that some hath long since forgot, that we did come unto this land not that we might become Marchants, Prelates, and Magistrates, neither that we might deal falsely with Indeans; rather, we did come to this incorrupted Wildernesse that we might live as Saincts under a Covenant with Christ Jesus.
>
> Being long oppressed in my Christian conscience, I did with regret leave the English Nation Anno Dom. 1634, shipping first to Holland and then, upon faire report from those first to venture there, to the Bay of Mattachusets, whence I and my wife Mariah arrived in the 2. month, 1635. Although the Gouvernour Mr. Winthrop and his brethren did make me most welcome, it was not long ere I sensed the russel of Prelate silks and the whispering of Magistrate velvet 'neath the rude wool of Puritan cloakes.

Josiah's penmanship wasn't easy to decipher, and I was making slow progress in getting through the manuscript. My stomach felt like a fist, and I kept looking up at the doorway of the hall, expecting to see a disapproving face. I hoped it wouldn't be the face of Delbert Rudd. I skipped ahead in the journal, looking for something I hadn't already heard about. The book was well thumbed at the corners, but the paper of the manuscript had remained remarkably strong and white. I owned paperback books less than two years old whose pages were already more yellow and brittle than those of the journal.

As I turned the pages I reached a section that had obviously been read more often than the early chapters. Josiah was describing his ordeal after being banished from the Massachusetts Bay Colony:

> I know not how long the Snows and Blasts were upon us, for day and night became as one. I knew only that we should perish, for no shelter, whether of tree or rock, could suffice against such fearsome storms. The meagre bit of Corne that was our only sustenance was now exhausted, and our sweet childe Colony was taken with extream weaknesse. For some dayes we had eaten nought but Snow. We huddled in the storm, dolorously praying and awaiting the Angel of Death.
>
> And ere long a towering Angel truely did appear to me, being appareled all in white and but indistinct amidst the swirling Blasts. Sayeth I, "Which of us will you take first to Our Lord?" Answereth the Angel, "This day the Soul of the childe will I take." Teares began to streame on my cheeks, and though I wished to protest that I should be taken in the innocent childe's stead, I could not reply. The Angel continueth, "The Soul onely will I take. The flesh have I no need for; the flesh I give unto thee, that ye may live to praise the Lord. Recall ye the words of the Lord in these places: Genesis Two and Twenty, Psalme Seventy and Eight, and John Six." Then the Angel departed, leaving me distressed to ponder on its words.
>
> And I did somewhat revive, being put in mind of Scripture. As I bethought Genesis Two and Twenty, these words came into my eare: "For because thou hast done this thing, and thou hast not with held thy sonne, thine only sonne, that in blessing will I bless thee." Psalme Seventy and Eight brought forth these words: "Man did eate Angel's food: He sent them meat to the full." And John Six put to my mind that most vexing speech: "Except ye eate the flesh of the Sonne of man, and drinke

his blood, ye have no life in you. Whoso eateth my flesh and drinketh my blood, hath eternal life; and I will raise him up at the last day."

Holding these thoughts, I went hence to my wife Mariah, who, neerer than I to being famished, did hold our daughter Colony to her brest. Freeing the childe and taking her some paces apart, I determined that indeed her Soul had been taken. And I prayed to my God that I might do his Will. The Angel then appeared againe, approaching and giving guidance to my hands. From our piteous belongings I drew two cups and a knife. The Lord's words were in my ears: "Except ye eate the flesh and drinke the blood, ye have no life in you."

The deare little bones I preserved most carefully.

And the following morning the sunne shewn copiously and I did rejoyce. Yet withal I was neere to death and in great confusion. My godly wife Mariah did never see the sunne againe, for though she breathed still awhile, her eiyes remained sealed. Her limbs had blackened and withered, and before that daye was out her Spirit, which bore not the least blemish, departed.

I wondered whether I wanted to read any further. I didn't really want to know the rest—and someone was sure to be returning from the cemetery soon. But the fear of being discovered was not as strong as it had been. Josiah's story was making me feel less like an outsider. It was also making me feel a lot of other things; none of them very pleasant. I went back to the journal.

Had not the Angel given courage unto me, I might my self have perished that day. I had not the strength to bestir my self through the great Snows that were everywhere about me. I was scituate in a valley ringed about with tall stoney walls. I despaired that I should ever ascend from that place. Yet I did not lose faith, and soon there appeared atop a nearby peak what I took to be a wisp of smoake. I cried out, and despite my weaknesse, my voice ecchoed marvelous loud through the valley. In a short time, through teares of gratitude, I saw a dark

> figure close unto the smoake. This person began without delay to descend toward me. With much distress of body but joye of minde, I went forth to meet my benefactor, who shewed him self at our meeting to be an Indean. And as God would have it, this young man, by name Sayqueg, was of the Mowhiggin Tribe and spoke a Tongue like enough to that of the Narrowgansets that we could converse most freely. Sayqueg brought forth from beneath his fur robes a purse of crakt Corne, such as Natives were wont to travel with, and placed it in my hands. In return, I offered up to him my knife, which although a most pretious object to me, seemed but a feeble show of my gratitude. Having partaken of the Corne, I made my way with much assistance to Sayqueg's shelter.

Josiah then launched into a description of what I had been told previously about the founding of Childgrave. I skipped ahead in the journal, stopping at the final section:

> Thus did we establish our little Congregation, each person a Sainct and Seeker of Grace according to individual Conscience and the Scriptures, without Pastor, Ordinance, Publick Meeting, or Ceremonie. I soon perceived, however, a certaine diminishment of Grace among my brethren, and began to think on ways that might preserve that Grace. Might not a solemn Ceremonie be conducted, but at some wide interval to prevent the encouragement of hollow, popish practices? I recollected the Angel that had come to me in my distress—a visit that was never far from my thoughts—and I convened with my fellow Saincts. Whereupon we did decide that since the Lord Christ had miraculously sent forth his Angel with tidings of Eternal Life through innocent blood and flesh, that we should take this for a sign. Therefore we did joiously institute for our selves and for ever in those who follow out of our seed, the following
>
> CEREMONIES
>
> 1. That each yeare on the Sunday of the Resurrection of our Lord Christ Jesus, out of our Congregation be chosen a female childe who hath not yet attained her 6. yeare of age; that this

childe be honored and revered beyond any member of the Congregation and that any wish she have from that daye be granted.

2. That within the same yeare, upon the Eve of the Birth of our Lord Christ Jesus, the chosen childe be taken to the place where the remains of Colony Golightly do lie, where there will be constructed an edifice of enduring stone. And as the Congregation do keepe a silent vigil, the chosen childe be removed from their sight and her Spirit be released unto Heaven. Thereafter the blood of the childe be mingled with wine and her flesh be cut fine and dried.

3. That upon the first daye of the New Yeare the Congregation joine together in Communion that each may sip of the wine and taste of the flesh, thus having Innocence and Grace restored to them.

4. That the deare bones of the departed childe be interred, her name inscribed and ever remembered.

ADMONITION

The people of the present Congregation of Childgrave beseech all ye who shall follow out of our loins to honour the Lord God in the manner we have set forth here. Forget not that ye would not have seen this Earthe but for the Lord's Angel and the Blood and Flesh of the innocent childe. Heed not the voices of those apart from our Congregation. Heed only the voice of thy Lord God.

AMEN

I slammed the book closed and grasped the edges of the lectern. My knees were trembling, and I was whispering: "Deare little bones." I thought of the townspeople who had become my friends and who were now standing in the darkness of the cemetery.

I thought of Verity Palmer: a love of the past and of touching flesh.

And her flesh be cut fine and dried.

I thought of Beth and Arthur Hopkins: anatomical drawings, harp, and wine.

The blood of the childe be mingled with wine.

I thought of Evelyn Coleridge: séances and meatless meals.

That each may sip of the wine and taste of the flesh.

And then I could think only of my body, which was acting in a way it never had before. I was shaking uncontrollably, feeling alternately feverish and chilled. My clothes were damp with sweat, and I felt sick to my stomach.

I wasn't sure at first whether the pressure on my shoulder was real or imaginary. And then I saw a hand sliding across my shoulder and down my arm. It was a woman's hand; strong and familiar. The hand tightened on my arm and pulled firmly, forcing me to turn. And when I turned, Sara stood before me, smiling and calmly beautiful.

I fainted.

Chapter 13

It wasn't a long faint, but it was enough to create the where-am-I? effect. I don't know whether I actually asked the traditional question when I opened my eyes, but Sara spoke as though I had: "You're in the Meeting Hall in Childgrave. You've had a shock or two, Jonathan."

I tried to get up, but movement brought about a strong protest from my stomach. I lay back and treated Sara to about as unappealing a request as anyone could make. I said: "Kiss me or I'll throw up."

Instead of backing away, she kissed me. I immediately forgot about my stomach. I forgot about everything else but Sara and her nearness to me. After a couple of minutes, I was able to sit up.

"Can you walk?" Sara asked me. She helped me to my feet, and I took a few steps without doing any damage to myself. "Come home with me," Sara said.

By the time we reached the doorway of the Meeting Hall, I was moving more or less normally. We walked quickly out into the night, and I looked toward the cemetery. The vigil seemed to be still in progress. "They'll be there until dawn," Sara said. When we were in the house, I went first to the fireplace and put a couple of logs on the embers. Sara helped me out of my jacket, and she put her arms around me. As we stood in front of the fireplace, two or three kinds of warmth began to invade me. I would have been absolutely comfortable, but the image of the people who were standing at the cemetery kept returning to me. If those people were experiencing any kind of warmth, I couldn't imagine what it might be.

I kissed Sara more elaborately and sincerely than I had ever kissed anyone before. But that didn't take my mind off the things I had seen earlier in the evening, either. I was sure that even if Sara were to take her clothes off, I would be thinking not entirely of her body, but wondering why she had been wearing that black cape and that black wool floor-length dress. (Fortunately, she had got rid of her bonnet before she joined me in the Meeting Hall.) I decided that, at least for the present, there was more need for us to talk than to make love.

I backed away from Sara and said, "Let's talk."

"Let's go to bed and talk," she said.

I wondered for a moment whether Sara was joking. But her suggestion was serious and helpful. She took a candle and led me upstairs to her bedroom. In the corner, her harp glinted in the flickering light. She put the candle on a bedside table. We took our shoes off, Sara put aside her silly cape, and we got into bed. It was a perfect arrangement: soft light, warmth, and relaxation. It was intimate, but—thanks to our heavy clothes—not quite intimate enough to be distracting. We lay on our sides, facing each other. I wrapped my arms around Sara and put my cheek against hers. Mouth to ear, we talked.

Sara said: "Ask me questions. Ask the most important thing first."

I thought for a moment, and asked: "Do you love me?"

"Yes, Jonathan, I love you. Yes. That's the most important thing."

"Where have you been?"

"I've been here, of course."

"Why hide from me if you love me?"

"Because Childgrave will always come first in my life. If we were to live together, we would have to live here. You—and Joanne—would have to accept the rules of the village. I wasn't sure you could do that, or that I had the right to ask you to do that. You were more persistent and serious than I thought, though. I still don't think it would be wise for you to live here, but I think you can be trusted to know what your choice would mean—and to be discreet about it."

"And that choice would mean getting involved with human sacrifice and ritual cannibalism?"

"An anthropologist might put it that way. A person who lived in Childgrave would say it means demonstrating that your love of God transcends your love of your own life."

"But if I've got it right, it's not your own life you're risking, but the life of an innocent child."

"Yes. That makes it more difficult."

"Especially on the child."

"I'm not sure about that, Jonathan. We're the ones who have to live with the memory of what we have done."

"But wouldn't it be more civilized to do these things symbolically?"

"Perhaps. But civilized people seem to end up playing bingo or having rummage sales. They're more interested in frivolous pleasures and in possessions than they are in God. Maybe God is not civilized."

I wasn't ready to deal with that kind of theoretical question, so I asked Sara to tell me about practice and not theory. The practices turned out to be pretty much what I had read in Josiah Golightly's book. That is, each Easter, the names of all the girls in Childgrave below the age of six were written on separate slips of paper, and one of the names was chosen at random. The girl whose name was chosen was allowed to do pretty much anything she wanted to do until the following Christmas Eve, when she would—as I had just seen—enter the mausoleum with the chief of police and a knife. A week later, on New Year's Day, the Childgraveans broke their fast in a way that Sara didn't seem too eager to describe in any detail.

"We have communion," she said.

"What you mean is, you drink a little girl's blood and eat her flesh."

"It doesn't seem like that, Jonathan. It's not unpleasant."

"Was that Gwendolyn Hopkins who went to the cemetery tonight?"

"Yes."

"And the next meal you will have—"

Sara interrupted, apparently not wanting it described in my words. "It's not a meal," she said. "It's a simple communion."

I took my arms away from Sara and moved to the edge of the bed. "And if Joanne and I were to move here, Joanne's name would go into the hat next Easter?"

"Yes. And, Jonathan . . . if you want to live in Childgrave . . . I think you must move here before next Easter."

Sara had anticipated my thoughts: Joanne would reach her

sixth birthday next November. If I married Sara after Easter, Joanne would never be subject to the lottery. "Why is that necessary?" I asked.

"Because to be a Childgravean means that you are willing to make that sacrifice. You would never be accepted here unless you demonstrated that willingness."

"But it's not *my* sacrifice. I mean, if it were *my* name going into the hat, okay. But it's Joanne's name."

"Joanne is willing. She told Gwendolyn she is."

"Joanne is just a little kid. She's not responsible. I'm responsible."

Sara didn't argue the point. I was desperate and angry. I'm not very good at debate, but I was determined to try to find a weak point in her logic. "What about the people who don't have female children? They don't have to make the sacrifice. What about your ex-husband Martin? I gather he's not likely to have any children."

"He tried to have children, Jonathan."

It occurred to me that he might have tried in the same bed I was lying in. I got out from the covers and sat on the edge of the bed, facing away from Sara. We were silent for a while. Finally, I said: "It's unreasonable."

"Yes," Sara said.

I didn't want to think about that part of it anymore. "How did you know I was here tonight?"

"Chief Rudd knew. He had you watched."

"Good old Delbert."

"He's come to trust you. He's willing to have you become one of us. Although he doubts whether you have the . . . grace that's necessary. But he trusts you not to make trouble for us. You understand, don't you, that we could be in trouble if the wrong people knew about our customs?"

I didn't think it was necessary to answer. Instead, I said, "I suppose the other Childgraveans have been passing judgment on me, too. Verity Palmer, for example. Did I earn points for resisting her saintly advances?"

"That was her own idea. I told her that that sort of thing wasn't called for. We weren't testing you, Jonathan. We just thought some of the people here should get to know you—and that you should get to know us."

I gathered I hadn't met the most important citizen of all, though. So I asked, "Who was the man who was with Chief Rudd tonight?"

"He's our benefactor; the only one of us who lives outside the village. You must have noticed that we have no basis for an economy here. Our benefactor conducts our business for us. He supplies us with all our everyday needs. He lives in New York City."

As I was thinking that over I felt Sara tap my shoulder. I turned to find that somehow she had managed to get out of her dress while my back was turned to her. She was smiling. "Let's please each other now, my love," she said. "Then you go back to the city and make your decision."

Although there weren't many times in my life that I had been so preoccupied, the sight of Sara removed everything else from my consciousness. Her Puritan aspect had vanished. The candlelight reflected softly from her white flesh and from the few pieces of black nylon she was wearing. I ran my fingertips over her whiteness; I removed the black nylon, touching with my mouth the places where it had been. Then I put my mouth against hers, and I welcomed that strange state of consciousness that results from absolute pleasure. I don't know whether it was a consciousness of myself or of Sara or of the two of us becoming one, but it was unlike anything I had known before. The only thing I was aware of apart from us was a sound—a sound that at the time I thought was some sort of hallucination. It wasn't until we lay quiet and apart that I realized that I had been hearing the strings of the harp vibrating delicately in reaction to our movements.

As Sara and I dressed we did a lot of smiling at each other, but no talking. When we left the house, Sara turned toward the cemetery. I hesitated. "I have to get back to Joanne," I said.

"Yes," Sara said. "Write to me, my love."

I watched her walk away, and then I started up the hill toward my car. Before I reached the car, I heard from far behind me the cry of despair I had heard earlier when the woman left the crowd and ran toward the mausoleum. It was probably Gwendolyn Hopkins's mother, Beth.

Santa is supposed to be tired but happy after he finishes his annual rounds. By the time I got to the apartment, transferred gifts from the closet to the floor around the Christmas tree, and got into bed, I qualified for the role. The problem was that I also qualified for the role of a hysterical insomniac. I was wide-eyed with anxiety over the decision that Sara had presented me with and my recollections of the night's festivities in Childgrave. I got out of bed and looked out my window. The dawn hadn't come yet. They would still be standing there in the freezing darkness; Sara would still be there. And I was standing, too. There wasn't any point in my getting back into bed and trying to sleep. What I wanted to do was to take a hot bath. But how could I allow myself to do that when I knew those people were out there?

I stood at the window, shivering and letting my mind show and reshow images from earlier in the night. The sequence changed, but the images stayed the same. I felt as though I were a film editor putting together the trailer for a new movie. I was trying to keep it from looking like a horror movie, but I wasn't having much success. The images recurred: the muscled white flanks of the horses; the two figures in the sleigh; the crashing doors of the Meeting Hall; the white-dressed girl moving between the rows of black-robed figures; the candles flickering in the night wind, the knife in the raised hand; the scrawled words on the antique paper; Sara's hand on my shoulder; Sara's body under mine; the harp strings trembling.

I tried to hold the image of Sara, but it moved past and cross-faded with the others. The shot that appeared more and more frequently, from changing angles, was the one that showed Chief Rudd's upraised arm; his tense hand; the knife blade glittering faintly in the candlelight.

That was the image that was with me when Joanne came into my room. I felt her hand in mine. I was still standing at the window, my body trembling like a recently plucked harp string. It was dawn.

"Merry Christmas, Daddy."

"Merry" isn't the word that best describes my state of mind that Christmas Day, although I tried hard to be cheerful. I sought out some physical warmth first, in the form of hot bacon, eggs, and coffee, and a hotter bath. It wasn't long before my body was as feverish as my mind. Nanny Joy and I watched Joanne open presents. My daughter is of the school that believes in prolonging pleasure. First she had to admire the wrappings. Then she had to remove the paper and ribbon without doing any damage to them. Fold the paper and roll the ribbon. Do a little guessing. Then, slowly, open the box. Her patience gave me a lesson in inherited traits.

My big present for Joanne was a lot of little presents: more furniture for her dollhouse. I had been noticing the dollhouse lately, because it reminded me of Mrs. Coleridge's place. The tiny pieces of furniture I bought were supposedly precise scale models of museum items dating from the seventeenth, eighteenth, and nineteenth centuries. I suspected the museums had paid less for the originals than I had paid for the shrunken versions.

Joanne immediately retired into her imagination and—in every respect except the physical—became about an inch tall, wandering through the rooms of the dollhouse, and arranging and rearranging chairs, mirrors, rugs, and dozens of other objects that someone had found interesting enough to save from the scrap heap of design. When she put a bed in the upstairs bedroom, I watched with more than casual interest. There was also a bedside table with a minuscule candlestick on it, and my most fortunate purchase: a harp. Joanne looked up at me and smiled as she placed it in the bedroom.

Nanny Joy seemed to be enjoying herself, although her patience finally gave out and she began to speed up the furnishing process, tearing off wrappings and making a lot of the decisions about how the furniture should be arranged.

After the little harp was in place, I let my anxiety re-emerge. I looked at Joanne; she was beautiful and happy. And she was as innocent and safe as anyone can be in Manhattan. Someone might try to harm her, but it wouldn't be with the consensus of the whole neighborhood.

I thought back to how perceptive and receptive Joanne had been concerning Childgrave and its customs. From the moment she had met Sara and had begun to see Colony Golightly's (all right, I'll say it) ghost, she had somehow known everything. I remembered her sudden interest in raw meat—the pink veal on the plate. (I've read somewhere that human flesh tastes like veal, although I don't remember who found himself or herself in a position to be able to supply that little culinary sidelight.) As usual, I had been a bit dense. There had also been a lot of interest on the part of Joanne and Sara in blood. I should have put two and two together. But who ever expects two and two to equal cannibalism?

I wondered what Sara and her neighbors were doing now. No bacon and eggs; no presents under the tree. But despite it all, I wanted to be in Childgrave at that moment. I was aware that Joanne and Nanny Joy and I didn't constitute the perfect family unit. Joy had announced that she would be going out to church in the afternoon. Joanne would probably want to take a nap. And Jonathan would be alone. I hadn't thought much about Harry Bordeaux lately, and I knew that he was more a business acquaintance than a friend. But I realized that my life had become more restricted than ever, and he was more like a friend than anyone I knew in the city. Even though it was ridiculous, I began to think of the people I had met in Childgrave as though they were members of my family: Mother Coleridge; brother and sister Hopkins; cousin Verity; and of course, old uncle Rudd.

I was lonely.

After Nanny Joy left for church, Joanne made the peculiar announcement that she thought we ought to go to church too. I didn't ask her what her reasons might be, but since it was Christmas Day, I supposed it was an unarguable suggestion. My problem was that I didn't know any churches. I had been in a few more or less as a tourist, but I had always been uncomfortable in them, feeling that they really weren't meant for tourists—not even St. Patrick's Cathedral, which probably *was* meant for tourists.

I tried to remember the last time I had been in a church. I decided it must have been when I got married. That made me think of Elliott Mason, the man who performed the wedding ceremony and who took my wife away—away from me and from life. In a drawer somewhere I had the letter he sent me after the accident and my wife's death. He said he was available if I ever needed him. Well, I wasn't sure if he was the person I needed, but I was certain that after my experiences of the previous night few people had more reason than I to try to find out a little about certain points of Christian morality.

I found the letter. It didn't have a return address on it, but there was a phone number. It wasn't the best day or time to call, and I wasn't sure what I wanted to say, but I wanted to talk to him. He answered on the first ring.

"Elliott Mason," he said.

I've never quite known what to make of people who answer the phone by saying their names. It seems to have an odd combination of efficiency and egotism. In any case, I've never progressed beyond a tentative "hello."

"This is Jonathan Brewster."

I expected his reply to be "Who?" But instead he said, without any surprise or hesitation, "It's good to hear from you, Jonathan. And on Christmas Day. How good of you to call."

"I suppose you're busy."

"Not until five o'clock."

"My daughter wanted to go to church, and I thought of you. I wasn't sure where you were stationed now."

Elliott gave me an address on the Lower East Side. It wasn't far from my apartment—but it was very far indeed from the Upper East Side address he used to be connected with. He said he would meet us in his church in about half an hour.

As Joanne and I left the apartment, it started to rain. We jogged through deserted side streets, and in a few minutes we were standing in front of the shabby brownstone facade of what turned out to be All Seraphim Church. There was an announcement board in front with messages spelled out in English and Spanish with unmatched plastic letters. There was no mention of any denomination. The interior of the church wasn't exactly the sort of thing to inspire most people to have faith in either God or the profession of architecture. The nave was dark and damp, and I had seen higher ceilings in duplex apartments. Behind the altar there was a mural that showed what I supposed was God on a throne, surrounded by swarms of angels. The angels didn't look very airworthy. But despite my initial cynical response to the building, I soon realized that I felt more comfortable there than I would have in most other churches. Obviously, the people who worshiped in All Seraphim were not out to enjoy minor esthetic pleasures or to demonstrate their tastefulness.

Off the entrance there were two small chapels. One of them contained a marble sculpture of a Madonna that looked quite a bit like Queen Victoria. In the second chapel, though, was a wood carving of an angel that might already have been two or three hundred years old in Victoria's time. Joanne went over to the angel as if she had expected to find it there. She knelt in front of it and closed her eyes. I blushed. The chapel was lighted by a couple of dozen white candles, and the candlelight and the angel stirred up some memories that converted my embarrassment to pain. I turned away and began to walk toward one of the narrow side aisles.

A clergyman of some kind was coming toward me. He was old, and he limped. I gave him the obligatory stranger-about-to-pass glance. And then I gave him the double take. It was Elliott Mason—but an Elliott whose sexual-spiritual charisma had vanished. The interesting thing was what had replaced it. Elliott didn't look as though he had become either a saint or a burnt-out case; he just looked genially nondescript.

He gave me an unthoughtful smile and said hello. A few years ago he would have put his arm around my shoulder and ushered me into an overfurnished office. Now he settled for a suggestion that we sit in one of the dusty pews. He asked me what was on my mind.

A little wave of panic washed over me. What should I say? There were two problems: first, that I wasn't sure what I wanted to say or to ask: and second, that I wasn't sure that Elliott Mason would take me seriously. I was forced into the paradoxical situation of having to speak flippantly because what I had to say was so serious. "It's really strong stuff, Elliott," I said, in a loud whisper.

Elliott said, "When it's serious, most people pretend they're representing someone else. They start by saying, 'I have a friend who has a problem.' It doesn't fool anyone, but it's easier that way."

"Okay. I have this friend who doesn't believe in God, but who has a chance to allow his daughter to be murdered as a sacrifice to God."

The Reverend Mason looked as if I had told him something that he heard about every day. "I assume the people who are offering you the chance are Christians."

"Right," I said. "Very devout."

"They would have to be, wouldn't they?"

"But remember, Elliott, it's not me who got the offer. It's my friend. And I almost forgot: there's also a little cannibalism involved."

Still no frowns or raised eyebrows. Elliott said, louder than I would have liked: "Except ye eat the flesh of the Son of man and drink his blood, ye have no life in you."

I recalled that Josiah Golightly had quoted that passage in his journal. "Yes," I whispered. "Some people have literal minds."

"That's seldom true of Christians. You could argue that the entire history of the Christian Church has been an elaborate attempt to avoid the literal; to pretend that Christ didn't literally mean anything He said. We must arrange it so that grace is not a fact but a metaphor. And metaphors are made by speaking of a thing as if it is something other than what it is. Therefore, grace doesn't really exist. It is just a manner of speaking."

I suspected that Elliott wasn't being as logical as he thought he was, but I wasn't going to try to make debating points. "What bothers my friend the most is that it would be his daughter and not himself who would be sacrificed."

"God sacrificed His only living Son. There are precedents, Jonathan."

"I'm not talking about gods, though. I'm talking about ordinary people."

"Instances of parents killing their children are fairly common. People literally sacrifice their children to their own selfishness or anger every day, I would imagine. If you count fetuses as children, it's many times a day."

I couldn't argue with that, either, so I changed my approach: "Do angels exist?"

"You'd prefer them to be metaphors?"

"They're not?"

"Not in the Bible, they're not. They are a distinctive order of beings, but nowhere are they treated as imaginary. They perform definite functions."

I supposed that was true. Messengers and wrestlers. I had forgotten I was in All Seraphim Church. I tried again. "Ghosts," I said. "They're not metaphors either?"

"Christ appeared after His death."

I thought that might have been a special case, but I didn't say so. I didn't say anything. Elliott Mason was smiling. He said, "I think your friend has a rare opportunity."

"I'm sure it's rare," I said. "But I'm not sure what *kind* of opportunity it is."

"There must be something that has drawn your friend into this situation."

"Love, I suppose."

"But not love of God?"

"Not God. Definitely not God."

"Then your friend is fortunate. Love is not the only—or maybe even the best—way to know God."

"Cannibalism is better?"

"Jesus said: 'As the living Father sent me, and I live by the Father; so he that eateth me, even he shall live by me.'"

"If you'll excuse the expression, that seems a little hard to swallow."

Elliott was taking me seriously now. "It *is* hard. According to John, what the disciples said was, 'This is a hard saying; who can hear it?'"

"If it's a hard thing to hear, then it's almost an impossible thing to do."

"No. It's not impossible, Jonathan."

"You've done it?"

"Yes."

"You've eaten the flesh of Jesus?"

"No. I drank the blood of your dying wife."

I couldn't decide whether to punch Elliott Mason's face or to vomit. I punched his face. It wasn't a very effective punch. Pews weren't really designed to encourage fisticuffs. Then Elliott surprised me again. He put his arms around me; not in an embrace but a bear hug. He was amazingly strong. My arms were pinned to my sides, and his mouth was next to my ear. He started whispering: "It has brought me to God. It changed me from a clerical womanizer to what I am now."

"A clerical creep?" I whispered.

"A shabby victim of a state of grace." I had heard about enough on the subject of grace. I was beginning to think it was just another of those all-purpose excuses—like political belief—that people use to justify any kind of outrageous behavior they want to indulge in. Elliott's hug was still strong, but his whisper was becoming a wheeze: "I watched her die. I was paralyzed, and I couldn't do anything to help her. Her head was against my mouth. Her crushed head. I drank."

Elliott relaxed his grip and moved away from me. I expected him to start weeping, but he just looked at me expectantly, breathing a little heavily. I was looking at him as if he were someone who had just asked me to do something unpleasant with him in a men's room. "Why are you telling me about this?" I asked.

"You brought the subject up, Jonathan. You came here to see me. I've always known you would."

"I didn't come here to ask you about my wife's death."

"Then why did you come here? Weren't you looking for a sign?"

"I don't know why I'm here."

"Exactly. You're in a desperate situation. You weren't looking for moderate reassurance concerning neurotic ennui. You've stumbled into the world beyond the metaphor. You're not a man with a wafer in his mouth and biblical prose in his ears; you're not even Orpheus singing in an opera-set Underworld; you're a man with someone else's blood in his throat. You've been invited to become a saint or a hero. That's why you're here."

My anger had vanished. And my daughter had appeared. I Joanne sidled into the pew next to Elliott Mason. She stood on the seat and said: "I prayed for Gwendolyn."

"I'm glad you did," Elliott said.

Joanne kissed the reverend's cheek. "I like your angel," she said.

"You're a lucky young lady," Elliott said. "Thank you for visiting the church." He got up and moved into the aisle. "I have to get ready for a service now." He looked at me in the same genial, commonplace way he had when I arrived. "God be with you," he said. And he walked into the shadows.

Joanne and I went out into the rain. My legs weren't as reliable as they had been on our way over, and I spent a lot of time waving at occupied and off-duty cabs. We were wet and tired when we got home, and I announced that it was nap time. When I got into bed, my teeth were chattering—something that seemed to have become a way of life with me. I couldn't sleep, of course. The mental horror films began to show again, with some new sequences based on Elliott Mason's scenario.

I was grateful when Joanne showed up and announced that she wanted to join me. I pretended to be annoyed, but I told her that since it was Christmas, I might allow it. She lifted the covers near the foot of the bed and scrambled in. There was a lot of muffled jabbering. She discovered my cold feet and lay across them long enough to raise their temperature to the comfortable level. Finally, her head appeared next to mine.

"Will I go to school in Childgrave?" she asked.

"Who said you were going to Childgrave?"

"Wouldn't you like to live there, Daddy?"

"In a way, sweetie. But if we went to live there, something terrible might happen to you. You might die."

"Like Gwendolyn?"

"Yes. Like Gwendolyn. I wouldn't want that to happen to you. I wouldn't want to lose you."

"I would be special. People would remember me for ever and ever."

"That's nice, but I don't want to *remember* you. I want to *be* with you."

"I would come and visit you. I would be in your pictures."

"Joanne, you think it's like a game. You're too young to know what it means to die. That's one thing daddies are for—to let you know what is a game and what isn't."

"You're afraid to die, aren't you, Daddy?"

"I suppose so, but I'm more afraid for *you* to die. And besides, there are things you don't know about Childgrave. Things that people who don't live in Childgrave think are very naughty."

"I know."

"You know what?"

Joanne began to recite:

My mother has killed me,
My father is eating me,
My brothers and sisters sit under the table
Picking my bones,
And they bury them under the cold marble stones.

So Mother Goose, or the well-named brothers Grimm, or the street urchins of Britain had come through again—supplied the memorable verse for the unlikely occasion; reducing horror to a jingle. Our children don't let us forget our potentialities.

Joanne said, "It's all right, Daddy." She snuggled up to me and immediately went to sleep. I tried to imagine my mind was a scribbled blackboard. I took an eraser from the dusty ledge and rubbed the board until the jagged inscriptions became a series of faint, cloudlike arcs.

I slept for a couple of hours. Joanne was gone when I woke up. I lay for a few minutes, looking at the molehill my feet made under the covers, and feeling calmer than I had felt in days. I wasn't sure I knew what my future was going to be, but I no longer felt like a man faced with a dilemma.

Nanny Joy was back from church, and she was the one who made my decision for me. She cooked an elaborate dinner for us, featuring roast goose and pecan pie, and she was about as agitated as I had ever seen her. I got the feeling she wanted to scream, but I couldn't be sure whether it would be a scream of delight or despair. As it turned out, it was a little of each.

After Joanne was in bed for the night, I helped Joy get the dishes cleaned up, and we sat down with some cognac. I waited for the scream. While I was waiting, we listened to the present I had given Joy. It was an apparently legendary private recording made by Charlie Parker at a party on the Christmas before his death.

Technically, the recording was primitive. It was an unaccompanied solo improvised around the melody of "O Holy Night." It was a long, plaintive solo in which little quotations from every Christmas carol and song I had ever heard were interwoven. In the beginning of the recording, there were background sounds of conversation and the clinking of ice in glasses. But gradually the party noises died down, and there was just the distant statement of an inventive, impassioned musician. Joy began to weep about halfway through the performance and she was sobbing during the final phrase, which—oddly—was a quotation from Billie Holiday's song "God Bless the Child."

As the record turntable clicked off, Joy put her hands over her face and made a sound that seemed like a continuation of the piercing tone of Parker's alto saxophone. I went to Joy's chair and knelt in front of her. She put her arms around me and said, "I'm going to leave you, Jonathan."

I let Joy sob for a while and then asked, "Why?"

"I'm getting married."

Without thinking, I said: "That's all right, Joy. So am I." My decision was made.

We had another cognac and let our emotions thin out. I thought a little clumsy humor might help: "Who would want to marry *you*, Joy?"

"My minister."

Oh, no. I was beginning to think maybe the Catholics had the right idea about that sort of thing, but I didn't say so.

Joy said, "You're going to marry Sara?"

"Right."

"And where are you going to live?"

"In Sara's hometown."

"Oh, shit, Jonathan. Don't live in that creepy town. Live here."

"Sara won't live here. And how do you know her town is so creepy?"

"Joanne tells me things. She says she might die there."

Thanks a lot, Joanne. "Don't believe that," I said. "Joanne makes things up."

"She didn't make up the pictures you took there, Jonathan."

"That's a different thing. There's nothing harmful in that. And anyway, this isn't the time to talk about that. It's Christmas, and we're both getting married. We ought to be celebrating."

"You're right. How do we do that?"

"We could invite some people over and have a little party. Do you think your minister might be able to drop by?"

"He's usually ready for a good time."

I decided I'd end another little bit of anxiety and phone Harry and Lee and apologize for my recent petulance.

So we had a party. Joy's husband-to-be, the Reverend Wesley Gunther, was a man of informal dignity and lightly concealed passion. Harry and Lee seemed glad to see me again and were pleased to hear about the various marriage plans. It was after midnight before the party got started, and it only lasted a couple of hours. I did my best to enjoy myself, but every five minutes or so I thought about Sara. I wondered what her Christmas Day had been like. I imagined her listening to the rain, thinking of Gwendolyn Hopkins, and sipping cold water. Not a festive picture. And yet I would rather have been in Childgrave with her than in Manhattan without her. For a while I tried to tell myself that what I really wanted was to have Sara with us at the apartment, but I began to realize that things could never be like that. Sara was a part of Childgrave. And my love for her had made me a part of Childgrave.

Joy and our guests seemed to figure out pretty quickly that I wasn't really in the mood for jollity, and at one point, when I returned from the kitchen with some ice, I found them in a solemn conference that they broke up in embarrassment when they saw me coming. They didn't look like conspirators, but they didn't seem to be telling one another how happy they were for me. When the party broke up and my guests left, I got the idea they were consoling, rather than congratulating, me.

I didn't worry about it, though. I sat down and wrote to Sara, telling her that I wanted to marry her and that I wanted to live in Childgrave with her. I added, feeling as if I were drawing up some kind of legal document, that Joanne and I would adopt the customs of Childgrave.

I wondered whether there were any customs that I didn't know about. That didn't really make much difference, though. Knowledge is beside the point in an act of faith or an act of love.

Chapter 14

For the next week, I was concerned not so much with faith or love as with the practicalities of cutting the strands that tied me to the city. I spent a lot of time on the telephone making dry-mouthed, hesitant statements to real-estate brokers, my accountant, and customer-service representatives.

Surprisingly, I felt no urge to make a farewell tour—no great need to visit the public library, Central Park, museums, movie houses, concert halls, or theaters. I had no compulsion to walk the streets, visit stores, or ride the subway. My thoughts were occupied with Childgrave—with what had happened to me there in the past and with what might await me there. And although those thoughts did not always lead to delight, I felt remarkably little apprehension. In retrospect, I realized that Childgrave was a place of singular beauty. The buildings and their setting had an honesty and rough simplicity that I was sure I would not tire of. And the chances were strong that among the couple of hundred inhabitants I hadn't yet met there would be at least a few whom I would enjoy being with.

Overshadowing all of those thoughts, of course, was the intense pleasure of knowing that Sara was waiting there for me. She had written to tell me that I could come to Childgrave any time I wanted after New Year's Day, and that I could stay as long as I liked, from an afternoon to forever. I decided to start with an afternoon—the second one in January.

It was a cloudless day. There was no barrier across the road to Childgrave, and smiling people walked the streets of the village. They were the people I hadn't seen before—people who didn't look out of the ordinary except in their attractiveness.

Sara was alone in the Golightly house. I told her I loved her and that she had lost weight. She lifted her sweater and showed me how her ribs made her skin glint in taut, curved ridges. I told her that I loved her and I put a ring on her finger. We didn't tell each other anything very intelligible for a while after that. When I left the house, there was a patch of pale sunlight on the door, reflected in some circuitous way from ice on the surrounding hills. Sara's left hand was against the front of the door. The ring, a dark ruby in an antique setting, tinted and dispersed the light, casting a redness across the brass of the ornamental door knocker—the child's head. I asked Sara whether it was an omen.

"No," she said. "It's merely beautiful."

I realized that, despite this lapse, I had begun to spend less time looking for dubious meanings in my experience and more time accepting the beauties of the moment.

We arranged that I would return to Childgrave in two weeks. We would be married in the Meeting Hall, and Joanne and I would live with Sara and her mother.

Sara thought it might be best if I didn't invite anyone from the city to attend the ceremony. I thought it best not even to tell anyone where I was going to live. It would be hard to explain my secrecy, but not as hard as it would be to explain a lot of other things. My taste for the inexplicable was being indulged beyond its own moderate ambitions.

Manhattan still held its little mysteries and melodramas, too. When I got back to the city that day, there was a black limousine parked in front of my building. I doubt whether a limousine had ever stopped on that street before, except at the demand of a red traffic light. And it seemed doubtful that a passenger car the size of that particular limousine had even been driven along that street.

I was looking as casually as I could for some sort of tasteful inscription that might say who made the limousine, when its front door opened, and a classically dressed chauffeur (with gray gloves) got out and said, "Mr. Brewster?"

I thought about issuing a denial, but my curiosity kept me truthful. I nodded.

The chauffeur didn't seem overjoyed to meet me. "My employer would like to have a word with you and wonders if you would join him in the passenger compartment for a few moments."

The employer's employee opened the back door of the limousine and tilted his head at the employer, who was sitting in a space that looked as big as and more comfortable than an apartment I once lived in. The man was dressed in a charcoal-gray wool suit that was probably put together over a long period of time by several well-paid people who didn't respect implements that had moving parts. The man wore a black hat that was related to a homburg. He said: "Hello, Mr. Brewster." He took off his hat, revealing that his high cheekbones were matched by a high forehead. "Won't you join me?" He wasn't asking a question but issuing a polite command, in a tone that sounded as if it had been practiced for many years at board meetings.

I settled in next to him and waited to hear some more commands. My host was sixtyish, and he was slender enough to have been emerging from a fast. At the moment, though, he was doing some paperwork on a collapsible rosewood desktop that was attached to the back of the driver's compartment. He used his hands in an elegant, self-conscious way. I watched carefully as he put some papers into an attaché case, lowered the desktop against the front seat, and slid an upholstered panel across it. Mounted on the panel was one of the portraits I had made of Gwendolyn Hopkins. He could only have got it from someone in Childgrave. I looked back and forth between the man and the photograph a couple of times, wondering what the connection was.

My host wasn't one to be too direct about that sort of thing. He said, "I understand you are changing your address, Mr. Brewster."

I wasn't given a chance to say yes or no.

"I have some interest in the community you'll be living in. Actually, I have many interests in it. I want to speak to you about two of those interests."

I noticed he said he wanted to speak to me rather than discuss things with me, so I let him speak.

"One of my concerns is financial," he said. "You might say that the economy of that community is exclusively under my control. Yes, you would have to say that. I supply the inhabitants with municipal services, supplies, and a subsistence income—which they may supplement as they choose. The people of the community, you see, are free of the need to concern themselves with externals. The arrangement, obviously, is distinctive. It could be misunderstood."

My new benefactor, who had been staring at the photograph of Gwendolyn Hopkins, turned to look at me. He seemed not to be inviting comment but just to be checking on whether I was paying attention. He continued. "Which brings me to my second interest: discretion. It has been decided that you are a person who is capable of discretion, Mr. Brewster. We would be chagrined if you failed to exercise that capability. More than that; people you love might become notorious or might even be thought criminal if discretion were not used. In short, Mr. Brewster, you are being offered a certain degree of opportunity and independence in return for your restraint and good sense. I hope you don't disappoint the community. I'm sure you have understood me."

I wasn't at all sure I had understood, but Mr. Mystery had obviously ended his warning or greeting or whatever it was. I thought of asking him who he was, but obviously if he had wanted me to know that, he would have told me. It did seem odd that although he was willing to take the chance that I would tell the world about Childgrave, he didn't want me to be able to lead anyone to *him*.

Even though my host wasn't inviting questions, it didn't seem right for me to leave without trying to ask a question. I doubted that I would get too many more chances to get information from this particular source. I said, "I know a little about what I will get from Childgrave. But I don't understand what Childgrave will get from me."

The man didn't hesitate. "Closed communities can become weak and complacent. It is worthwhile occasionally to introduce new attitudes: a bit of skepticism or some frivolity, perhaps. Many of us in Childgrave tend to be serious and unquestioning."

My host looked past me—presumably at his chauffeur, who was standing outside the door. The door opened immediately. My new acquaintance said good-bye to me. I got out of the car and watched as the chauffeur got in and drove away. It occurred to me that I could take the license-plate number and see if I could trace the car to its owner. But I didn't really want to know who my visitor was. That kind of information might interfere with my eagerness to live in Childgrave.

When I got upstairs, I tried to avoid Nanny Joy. I wasn't ready to talk about the urgent business of breaking up the household. Not that I had any strong attachments to the apartment itself; I had never been especially fond of it. But I was leaving Nanny Joy, too, and I was more than fond of her. An added problem was that I was wondering how I could explain to her that I wouldn't be inviting her to the wedding.

I went off in search of Joanne, who turned out to be in the Anything Goes Room, throwing one of her Christmas presents against the wall. The offending present was a little computerized musical gadget on which you could compose tunes by pushing buttons. The computer would memorize the tune and play it back for you in characterless, outer-space beeps. I hadn't expected Joanne to be entranced by it, especially since I hadn't quite been able to figure out how to work it myself.

"I gather you're mad at your toy," I said. Joanne didn't answer. She threw the gadget at the wall again. "Can't you figure out how to work it?" I asked.

"I can work it. But it doesn't tinkle."

"Tinkle?"

"Beverly Chapman has a music box that tinkles. This one beeps."

My daughter was an old-fashioned girl. Which was just as well, considering where her new home was going to be. It seemed like a good time to make the announcement. I sat down on the floor next to Joanne. "Sweetie," I said. "Sara Coleridge and I are going to get married, and you and I are going to live with her in Childgrave."

Joanne lay down, with her back across my lap, and began to laugh. I lifted her up and held her against me. She smelled good, in a vanilla-extract sort of way. She said: "Will you make a brother for me?"

"We'll try."

Joanne displayed a shy grin. "Will you do intercourse like Ms. Abraham said?"

I was reminded that there were several things about Manhattan that I could not conceivably miss—foremost among them,

Ms. Abraham. I ignored Joanne's question. "I have to ask you to do something for me," I said. "You have to promise that you won't tell anyone where we're going. I mean, you can say we're going to live in a small town, but don't say the name of Childgrave. Will you promise?" Joanne gave me a fairly solemn nod. I had been thinking, though, that maybe the promise was coming a little too late. "Have you told anyone the name of Childgrave before now?" I asked.

"No. I don't think so."

"Not even Nanny Joy?"

"I don't think so."

"Well, why don't you go and tell Nanny Joy now that your daddy and Miss Coleridge are getting married in two weeks? But don't say where."

Joanne started to run off, but she came back and said: "Two weeks isn't long, is it?"

"No, sweetie."

"Thank you, Daddy. Will I get to be chosen like Gwendolyn?"

I pretended I hadn't heard that question, but my stomach didn't cooperate in my attempt at self-deception. It began to quiver. I sent Joanne off before she could ask her question again. "Go tell Nanny Joy that Daddy's getting married," I said.

Joanne left, and I sat for a minute or so trying to get my stomach to settle down and to forget what I had heard. On the floor next to me was the musical gadget. I picked it up and pushed some buttons. It was still in working order. I decided to play a tune. The first one that came to mind was the one from the opera *Orfeo*—the music with which Amor announces that Euridice isn't dead after all, and that the lovers will be reunited.

As I was beeping, Nanny Joy came in and said, "Congratulations, Jonathan." I got up and embraced her. She smelled good, too, but not like anything you would find in a kitchen cupboard. Joy once advised me that not everybody could look beautiful but anyone with a couple of dollars could smell beautiful.

"We're going to miss your good advice," I said.

Nanny Joy sat down on a workbench. "I've got some advice right now," she said. "Don't go live in that town, Jonathan. Can't you and Sara live here?"

"No, we have to live there."

Joy asked: "Will I see you at all?"

"I'm not sure. I'll try to get to town once in a while."

"But you're not going to be receiving visitors in . . . what's the name of the town?"

I stared at the floor.

"Shit, Jonathan, you can't live somewhere that you're afraid to give a name."

The floor had paint stains on it.

Joy's voice was getting louder. "I suppose you're not even going to invite me to the wedding."

I shook my head.

"Well, if you're not going to show me yours, I'm not going to show you mine."

I could understand Joy's attitude, but I didn't know how I could make her understand the pressures that were on me.

She said, "Think about it some more, Jonathan." Then she went away.

I thought about my situation for a few minutes, but I decided that there really wasn't much to be gained from that kind of thought. I had made my decision, and I was pleased with it. As with almost any decision, there were aspects of it that weren't ideal. But I wasn't looking for the perfect situation. Some of the people in Childgrave might be looking for sanctity or the flawless life, but I wasn't that demanding. My experience so far in my life had led me to believe that one could never be sure what a given act would lead to. I thought the least I could do was put myself in a promising situation and play the odds—never allowing myself to believe in the sure thing. I was convinced that life with Sara would give me the best odds for happiness that I had ever expected to encounter.

Whenever fear and trembling attacked me during the next two weeks, I spent a little time watching Joanne. All her quirks had vanished. No more concern with invisible friends and raw meat. She had all the self-confidence of a beautiful woman, without the edge of egotism that sexuality brings with it. Five-year-olds are supposed to be easier to live with than four-year-olds anyway, but the change in Joanne was too dramatic to be just a matter of natural development. She was someone who had just picked up her visa to the Promised Land.

I wrote to Sara every day, saying things that stimulated me a lot and that might have interested her, but that anyone else would probably have found ridiculous. She had a ridiculous announcement of her own to make: her ex-husband Martin and his Indian friend Roger were driving down to the city in a van on the morning of the wedding to transport me and Joanne and our belongings to Childgrave.

As the days went by I found it more and more difficult to relax. Any sharp sound that originated within a couple of blocks of my apartment made my neck muscles contract, and I seemed to be losing control of my hands.

Sara wrote to say that the wedding license would be waiting for me to sign when I got to Childgrave, but that I would have to bring a document proving that I had healthy blood. I stopped by a hospital clinic, where an exuberant intern tapped one of my veins. Up to that time, blood had never seemed very sinister to me. Even the sight of my own blood appearing unrequested from a cut finger looked more fascinating than frightening. But things had changed. As the hypodermic tube filled with the blackish liquid my arm began to twitch. When the intern tried to calm me, I accused him of being incompetent. Later, I decided I'd better find a way of distracting myself during the time that was left before the wedding.

I found my distraction by doing some portraits of Nanny Joy. She was one of those people that the camera likes—a phenomenon I've never been able to understand or predict. Some people just photograph well. It has more to do with presence than beauty. Some people gain presence in a photograph, and others lose it. Joy Ory gained presence, even though she had a lot to start with. It was a solemn presence, probably because of the disappointment she was feeling over me. I also did some double portraits with Joy and Joanne. The results weren't exactly festive, but Joy's solemnity was softened by the obvious love she felt for my daughter. There was no sign of any spectral visitors.

The day before Joanne and I were to leave for our new hometown, I made a sentimental journey through the city that, for most of my life, had seemed just right. I also stopped by to say good-bye to Harry Bordeaux in his office. Harry let me sit next to his desk while he manipulated his telephone. It was like sitting next to a grand prix racing-car driver in action. Harry used the hold button as if it were a gearshift control. Between speeches of optimism and promises of limitless wealth, as he handed things to and accepted things from his secretary, Harry found a minute here and there to speak to me. But the words he had for me weren't too pleasant. His tone was light, but he came closer than I had ever heard him to sounding morally outraged. He definitely didn't like the idea of my taking Joanne to live among "haunted bumpkins." Each time he spoke to me he seemed a little more outraged, and finally, while he was talking to a client, I got up, squeezed Harry's forearm, and started out of the office. Before I got to the door, Harry said, almost in a shout: "You need time to reconsider, Jonathan."

I walked around midtown for a couple of hours, trying to analyze the reasoning behind my decision, but I didn't come up with any new insights. I concluded that I had better drop the subject. But when I got home, the subject was forced on me again. This time it was accompanied by some terror. When I entered the apartment, it was dark and empty. I turned the light on and in my I'm-home-dear voice called out, "Joanne? Joy?" No answer. I prowled through the rooms, dodging packing boxes. On the kitchen table I found a note:

> Mr. B.—
>
> I'm giving you a last chance—helping you to think things over. Joanne is with me. Don't get the wrong idea—I'm not kidnaping her or anything. I just took her away for a while so you can think. I'll call you later and see what to do next. There's no law against what I'm doing any more than there is about what you want to do.
>
> Nanny Joy

I moved through the apartment again, not prowling this time, but rampaging. I kicked things that showed up in my path, and I went through my vocabulary of street language, picking out a choice item once in a while to direct at Nanny Joy's note, which was crumpled in my hand. Who the hell was she to interfere in my life? Did I tell her she couldn't wear tarty clothes and muck around with a Harlem preacher?

Finally I collapsed on a sofa and started answering questions instead of asking them. Okay. Nanny Joy had some right to interfere. I had asked her to love and care for Joanne. She wanted to be sure that Joanne's future was going to be happy and safe. But Joy was putting her own happiness ahead of Joanne's. Should I give up Sara just to guarantee Joanne a conventional life? No. And then I realized I was rejecting an argument in favor of moderation. Jonathan had changed.

Once I made that realization, it was a little easier for me to come up with something that resembled human reasoning. I reasoned for about two hours, and then the phone rang. It was a tentative-sounding Harry Bordeaux.

"Jonathan?"

"Harry?"

"I do hope you're not going to be unreasonable about this."

"About what, Harry?" Silence. A silent Harry was hard to imagine under any circumstances, but under the prevailing circumstances, there seemed to be a likely explanation. I asked: "Harry, is Joanne with you?"

"Yes."

"I'll be right there, and I expect Joanne still to be there."

Lee opened the door. As usual, she had more than enough to say, but her first sentence was to the point: "Joanne's asleep in the bedroom, Jonathan. She's had the most elaborate meal of her life, and she's been the calmest person in this overpriced, overfurnished hutch—which isn't much of an accomplishment, considering the hysteria factor we've been wallowing in. You have a perfect right to produce an automatic weapon of some sort and line us all up against the wall. Inexcusable bloody meddlers. On second thought, empty the slop pail on us. On third thought, take your lovely child and subject her to your love—and I'm not saying it might not be a touch outlandish—but my point is that we have no right to expect you to impose *our* particular kind of outlandishness on the child. Obviously I've written the dissenting opinion, but I've written it forcefully."

Lee had been standing with me in her apartment's little foyer. She had her hands on my arms, and she blocked the short hallway that led to the living room. Over her shoulder I could see Harry and Nanny Joy, who were standing together in the distance, looking subdued but ready for combat. They also looked older and less attractive than they had ever looked to me before, but that was probably the result of anger affecting the eye of the beholder. No one seemed eager to talk, and I thought of just collecting Joanne and leaving. But I wanted to know what it was that had made them do this crazy thing.

"I'm not going to stay long," I said. "Why don't we sit down, and then why don't you tell me why you abducted your ex-friend's daughter?"

As I expected, Harry was going to do most of the talking. "You're wrong on two counts, Jonathan. We're still your friends, and it was hardly a matter of abduction. It was an innocent, friendly act."

"Sure, Harry. But I'm glad I'm not going to be around when you decide to work up an *unfriendly* act."

"Let me explain, dear boy." Harry's "dear boy" had the wrong tone. There was more condescension in it than silly affection. He started his explanation. "Jonathan, no one is saying you don't have a right to abandon a successful career and a comfortable, enviable situation. You're in love. I understand that; I've *been* there, Jonathan. God knows, love is worth some sacrifice."

Harry looked over my shoulder and smiled insincerely. I turned and saw that Lee was standing a few feet behind me. She answered Harry's smile with an "Oh?" stare, one eyebrow raised and her head slightly tilted. Harry quickly looked back at me. "If you were just going back to the land and would ask your old friends up to grub about for wild strawberries once in a while, we would be delighted for you. However, you're not headed for a bucolic paradise, but a nameless rural horror, by all accounts."

"Where do you get your accounts, Harry?"

"From Joanne; and from Joy, via Joanne and you."

"And what do the accounts add up to?"

"Supernatural morbidity."

"What does that mean, exactly?"

"Specters, ghosts, ha'nts, whatever. We've seen evidence of that."

"So? You were charmed when you were getting ten percent of the evidence. I think there's a better case for greed than for morbidity."

"We're just getting to the morbidity. Can you give me a reasonably straight answer to this? Do young girls get killed in this place you're headed for?"

"Young girls get killed everywhere."

I wasn't too happy with my answer, and apparently Nanny Joy wasn't either. She took over the questioning. "Jonathan, are you putting Joanne's life in danger by taking her to this place?"

It was time for me to be a little less evasive. "I might be," I said.

Harry took up the chase again: "You *might* be? Don't you think you ought to be sure?"

"All right," I said. "I *am* sure. There's a slight chance that I'm endangering Joanne."

Harry said: "I won't ask you what kind of danger it is. But give me an idea of what the odds are. A thousand to one, a hundred to one, two to one?"

I hadn't thought of it in those terms before. How many girls below the age of six were living in Childgrave? Probably not more than a dozen. I really had no idea. Maybe there were just one or two. The situation sort of implied that there wouldn't be too many. Maybe there weren't any. That might explain why Joanne and I were being invited to live there. Harry was waiting for an answer. "I don't know what the odds are," I said.

Harry rolled his eyes. "My God," he said. "How can you gamble with your child's life when you don't even know the house rules?"

"At least I'm giving her a chance, Harry. You probably don't remember, but I once told you that unless we take chances, we don't have anything."

"When was that?"

I wished Lee weren't in the room. "It was when you had a

chance to have a child of your own. Before you reduced the child's chances to zilch—before you had it killed."

Harry looked more somber than I had ever seen him look before. "Oh, Jonathan," he said. "Unfair." I turned my head slightly to see how Lee was reacting. She was leaving the room. By the time I looked back to Harry, his face had turned a couple of shades redder. "Not only unfair," he said, "but a bit popish, isn't it? Have we been attending Confirmation classes?"

Nanny Joy tried again. "Never mind about whether Harry and Lee did something wrong," she said. "We're talking about whether you're going to do something wrong."

"According to Harry, there's no need to worry about that. Harry told me once that nobody knows what's right or wrong. Didn't you, Harry?"

Harry sighed noisily. For a minute or so, everyone looked at Harry, and no one spoke. I had never been very good at following Harry's thought processes. I knew that he made quick decisions and that he often made quick reversals of decisions. He almost never gave reasons for his actions or opinions. I got the impression that he usually just went with the flow of things, guided by an inexhaustible supply of optimistic energy. But the death of children can exhaust anyone's optimism. I supposed that in some complicated way, it was the loss of his child-to-be that had made Harry react so strongly against my portraits of Gwendolyn Hopkins and my decision to move to Childgrave.

Harry sighed again and then surprised me by producing a smile. I don't know what he had been thinking about during his minute of silence, but apparently my arguments—which hadn't seemed all that convincing to me—had overcome his anger and opposition. His smile broadened. "You're right, dear boy. We must take chances, and we mustn't pretend to know what's right or wrong. I'd forgotten that." Harry got up and came toward me. "And one should never forget that." Harry leaned over and kissed me on the forehead. "The moment has arrived for an *au revoir* sip or two."

Harry left the room. I looked at Nanny Joy. She wasn't ready to give up her anger. Harry came back with a tray full of large snifters. Lee was behind him, carrying a bottle of cognac that was covered with ribbons and blobs of red wax. Harry poured, and Lee distributed. When we each had a glass, I raised mine to Nanny Joy and said: "Good luck in your new love."

Nanny Joy sobbed and smiled and said: "Oh, shit, Jonathan." She started to cry.

We drank.

Joy raised her glass to me. "Good luck in *your* new love." I smiled, and then *I* started to cry.

We drank.

Harry raised his glass. "To love, which brooks no right or wrong." He started to laugh.

We drank.

Lee raised her glass. "May the odds smile upon us."

We drank.

I collected Joanne, and after a lot of kissing of wet cheeks, we left.

Nanny Joy spent the night with Lee and Harry. I spent the night with unclosable eyes and a rapid pulse.

About five o'clock, I stopped pretending to sleep. I took a hot shower, wondering when I would have my next one and trying to decide how important that was. I sat amid packing cartons, luggage, and abandoned bits of furniture until Joanne appeared. She was smiling like a prima ballerina taking curtain calls. She noticed that her father was having trouble managing even a rueful smile.

"Aren't you happy, Daddy?"

"Yes, I'm happy, sweetie. But I'm a lot of other things, too."

"Don't be those other things. We'll have a fireplace and a new mommy. We can get all snuggy."

"That sounds good."

"There will be only good things. Everything will be good."

"Don't expect that. There are always bad things, sweetie."

"Not in Childgrave. We might even talk to the angel."

Joanne was no longer using the "Chilegray" pronunciation. I hoped that was a sign of a new maturity on her part. But her eagerness to talk to the angel didn't seem like progress. I said, "Don't think too much about the angel or your friend Colnee. That's not why we're going to Childgrave."

"Then why are we going?"

"Because Sara lives there and we love her."

"But Sara loves the angel."

I decided that I would love Sara but not her angel. I would love her and tolerate her angel. Joanne could make up her own mind on the subject.

Martin Golightly and Roger Sayqueg arrived in a large van, bringing with them some of Mrs. Coleridge's homemade doughnuts and their own high spirits. I made coffee, we dunked for a while, moved possessions (including Joanne's dollhouse) into the van, and drove away. I left the coffee grounds in the pot.

The four of us squeezed into the driver's compartment, with Joanne sitting on my lap. Martin and Roger took turns driving, sharing what they obviously thought of as a pleasure rather than a chore. It was also obvious, judging from their lack of interest in the other cars on the road, that they hadn't done a lot of driving. They weren't careless enough to be frightening, though, and I began to relax after a few minutes. Joanne started making forays into neighboring laps, and we had a friendly but not very talkative trip.

Martin and Roger talked mostly about themselves. Each of them seemed to be interested not only in the other's body but also in his own. They weren't obnoxious or consciously sexual about it, but they couldn't help lapsing every few minutes into discussions of muscle tone or chapped lips.

At a couple of points I wondered what role Martin and Roger played in the religious activities and goals of Childgrave. Were they trying to achieve some kind of sanctity? Or were they, as it seemed to me, simply devoting themselves to their own pleasure? Was it permissible in Childgrave to live a life of uncomplicated worldly pleasure? For my own sake, I hoped so—but I doubted whether anything was uncomplicated in Childgrave.

For instance, as we drove to Childgrave that day there were a couple of instants when Martin's genial expression faded and his eyes gave some indication that they had seen things that were less than pleasureful. I remembered the portrait he had done of Sara—a portrait that made me wonder whether little girls were the only ones who became victims in Childgrave. But Sara had assured me that the town had no unusual customs except the ones I already knew about. Martin's painting of Sara represented only his personal view of her—a view influenced, I assumed, by some pretty strong and unusual emotions.

But despite his occasionally unsettled glances, Martin made no pronouncements and offered no warnings during the drive to Childgrave.

Sara came out of the house and opened the door of the van for us. Her face was pinker and her hair paler than I had remembered, and her beauty seemed to have gained a new quality that I was happy to think of as lascivious. But whatever Sara looked like, she didn't look like someone who was a few hours away from becoming a bride. She was wearing a gray wool skirt and a bulky black sweater. The sweater looked as if it might have been the sort of thing that merchant seamen featured during World War II.

Sara's first hugs and kisses went to Joanne. I elbowed my daughter aside as subtly as I could and sent her into the house. Then I took over the greeting duties. My wet mouth against Sara's ear, I said: "I thought it was bad luck for the groom to see the bride before the wedding."

"We're beyond luck," Sara whispered.

I didn't say anything, but it occurred to me that we were going to need some luck—some *good* luck. Or, at least, Joanne would need it when the Easter lottery took place. I was too much involved in trying to promote some uncomplicated worldly pleasure at that moment to follow up on my thoughts, but there was time for me to realize I had become a gambler and that I was calculating the odds. I was beginning to feel confused, and I was glad for the chance to put my pleasures and calculations aside for a few minutes when Sara suggested I help Martin and Roger unload the van.

As we worked, Martin's expression occasionally showed the disturbance I had seen earlier. Obviously, I wasn't the only one in Childgrave whose consciousness was being given an unpleasant nudge once in a while by something below the surface. Then, while we were carrying a trunk into the house and there was no one else within earshot of us, Martin said, "I'm a fraud, you know, Jonathan."

"What kind of fraud?"

"Every kind. I'm not gay, for example. Or at least, not *very* gay." Roger joined us to help with the trunk, and Martin stopped talking. It wasn't a conversation I wanted to abandon after that particular opening remark, and I arranged after that to be alone with Martin as much as possible while carrying the few remaining things into the house.

I puzzled over the "not *very* gay" remark until Roger left us and Martin whispered: "I'm playing dead on the battlefield." I looked at him quizzically. "Don't think I'm trying to be unpleasant," he said, "but it was on my honeymoon with Sara that I realized that the joy of sex—or of heterosex—wasn't worth the possible consequences. I couldn't take the chance that Sara and I might have a daughter and then have to face the lottery."

Martin's confession was interrupted again as we joined Sara in the house. I wondered whether she noticed the touch of strain that had been added to my adoring gaze. Martin and I put down the boxes we were carrying and started back to the van. "So, to put it simply," he said, "I'm a coward."

"Is Roger a coward too?"

"No. He's gay."

"And you're not just pretending to be his friend?"

"Not at all. He's a good companion. I needed companionship, and people seem to find gayness easier to accept than celibacy."

We picked up more boxes as a young couple passed us. They smiled a friendly greeting at me. I let Martin start back to the house alone. I stood watching the couple walk down Golightly Street. Beyond them lay the cemetery and the looming figure of the angel. My body temperature seemed to drop a degree or two. But I didn't feel unhappy.

And I realized for the first time in my life that I possessed a certain degree of courage.

Before I could develop that thought, Mrs. Coleridge appeared. She was looking as delighted as her dignity would permit, and her costume was remarkably festive. She wore a satiny beige dress with rows of little strings around its loose waist, and her skirt was short enough to reveal most of her surprisingly unflawed calves.

I settled in the sitting room near the fireplace and waited to find out what was on the agenda. Joanne, Sara, and Evelyn were having a conference in the dining room. I sat and indulged in three kinds of admiration. I held my hand up. There wasn't a sign of a tremor.

Mrs. Coleridge took Joanne off to prepare for the festivities. Sara led me up to her (our) bedroom. The room was the same as I had remembered it, but the bed had been exchanged for what was obviously the masterwork of a furniture maker who had been fond of either sleeping or dalliance. The bed dated from a time when king-sized had to do with more than length and width. It was a setting for immoderate activities; it could inspire hibernation or nymphomania. Canopied, four-posted, and fitted with tapestry curtains at the sides and foot, it could make a person think that one third of a lifetime was not enough to spend there.

"It's a present from the people of the village," Sara said.

"A thoughtful present."

"They're thoughtful people. You'll like them, Jonathan."

I wondered whether I *would* like them. One of the things that appealed to me about living in Manhattan was that you didn't have to like people; you just had to tolerate them. Tolerance was more in my line than bonhomie. I said. "I guess I'll *have* to like them."

Sara put her hands in mine. "You don't *have* to do anything, Jonathan. That's why I brought you up here—to give you a chance to change your mind. You don't have to marry me. Most people would think I'm overpriced."

"I've always been a big spender, Sara."

"And a gambler?"

"When the stakes are right." I almost said "odds" rather than "stakes," but I suppose I had known all along that love doesn't play the odds. To say that you'll marry if the odds are right means you're marrying for some reason other than love.

Sara stepped away from me. "You can't really know whether the stakes are right, though, can you? I'm practically a stranger to you, Jonathan. I've spent most of my time hiding from you —hiding my personality as well as my body."

Sara blushed, probably remembering, as I was, that she hadn't been too successful in hiding her body. And that told me a fair amount about her personality. Then it occurred to me that what was to be gained through my gamble was not so much Sara as it was love itself. I would be getting not just a wife and a new home but a new way of seeing.

What I was seeing at that moment seemed worth a lot of sacrifice. Sara stood between the bed and her harp. On the wall behind her was a large, spottily silvered mirror in which I could dimly see my own reflection. I began to feel unsettled. The hairs on the back of my neck moved. It was as if I were a third person in the room. I thought of a painting I had often seen reproduced: a wedding portrait by an early Renaissance Flemish painter—one of the van Eycks, I think. A couple stands in a bedroom. There is a canopied bed at one side, and a round mirror hangs on the wall in back of them. I think the artist's reflection shows in the mirror. One of the odd things about the painting is that the woman depicted—the bride—is extremely pregnant. As I remembered this, my ears pulled back. Could Sara be pregnant? Of course she could. I could vouch for that. And *was* Sara pregnant? Yes. I was sure of it. She probably didn't know it, but I knew it. Was I going to become clairvoyant? I wasn't exactly sure what that involved, but I decided that if it didn't involve seeing ghosts, I wouldn't mind it.

But what was more important was that Sara and I were going to have a new child. For some reason, I had never thought of that possibility before. It made a difference. I wasn't sure, on the whole, whether it was a good difference or a bad one. But it excited me.

I wanted to do something silly and dramatic, like putting my head against Sara's belly. But instead, I simply kissed her forehead and left her.

The wedding ceremony was unremarkable. At about two-thirty in the afternoon, a tall gentleman named Button Golightly came to escort us to the Meeting Hall. (The name might have been—and somehow I hoped it was—Burton, but everyone made it sound like Button.) Sara and I signed what Mr. Golightly assured us was a valid wedding license, and then our little party walked to the hall. The plan was that Mrs. Coleridge, Joanne, Sara, and I would stand at the back of the hall while the old gentleman walked up the aisle to the other end of the building. When he turned to face us, we would follow.

There was a full house—full of attractive people dressed in tasteful, only slightly out-of-fashion clothes. While we were waiting for Mr. Golightly to make his way unsteadily up the aisle, I couldn't resist the temptation to take a quick census of the congregation. There were about two hundred and fifty people, sitting in family groups. The bit of information I wanted most was not too easy to come by from my vantage point: the number of girls under the age of six. Most of the young children were hidden by the backs of chairs or the backs of adults. I felt Sara squeeze my arm. It was time for the procession to begin. I blushed, ashamed to have been thinking of anything other than Sara.

I had expected to hear some music at that point—a choir, or at least a harp solo by Beth Hopkins. But the only sounds were our footsteps and, somewhere in the congregation, the gentle whining of a bored child. As Sara and I moved along the aisle I tried to concentrate on her and the significance of the ceremony we were about to go through, but the child's voice distracted me and made me think of another ceremony: the one Joanne would be involved in at Easter. And even though I tried to look straight ahead at Mr. Golightly, I found myself glancing from side to side. By the time I got to the front of the Meeting Hall, I had concluded that there were about fifteen girls in Childgrave below the age of six. I tried desperately to avoid thinking in terms of Joanne's odds as I heard Mr. Golightly say, "Dearly beloved . . ."

I concentrated on the words of the ceremony and on the exciting, singular woman who stood next to me. A few minutes later we were wife and husband. We kissed, and all thoughts vanished except those concerned with present and future delights. We went quickly back up the aisle. My delight eased quite a bit when we reached the foyer and for a moment I saw Joanne standing against the wall directly beneath the display case that held Josiah Golightly's knife.

But there was no time for me to brood. A storm of activity broke out. People moved chairs into corners, and several large folding tables were set up. A peculiar little orchestra consisting of a harp, a lute, a tambourine, and a sort of hurdy-gurdy began to play music that might have been written in the thirteenth century. Cases of wine and platters of food were produced, and Sara pulled me back into the center of the hall and managed the little miracle of getting me to follow her in an improvised dance.

As Nanny Joy would have said, we let the good times roll.

Even in Childgrave.

And much later, Sara and I lay side by side in our curtained bed—our musky tent of pleasure. I drew aside one of the curtains. On the bedside table, a candle—which had been tall and new when I had drawn the curtain—had become a glittering puddle that was about to drown its remaining bit of flame. In the semi-darkness I could see Sara's glistening belly rising and falling. Her muscles contracted as the room's cool air touched her skin.

We hadn't spoken since we entered the bed. We hadn't felt the need of metaphor.

Sara's breathing became slower and more shallow. I pulled the bedclothes slowly up over her neat-rowed toes and the long curves of her legs. I paused and made the gesture I hadn't made earlier in the day: I put my head against her belly. My cheek was bristly, and there was a scraping sound as I moved my face across her skin. Sara didn't seem to be awake, but as I moved the covers up to her chin I noticed that her breasts were showing signs of appreciating my gesture.

I was comfortable in my new life, but I didn't know what its meaning was. I know that Sara's warm, agile body lay next to me, and that Joanne rested in the darkness nearby. I knew that the candlelight had dimmed and was flickering. The candle went out, and its smoke drifted through the room. I was aware of the silence that surrounded the house. I knew that in the darkness of the Meeting Hall, a leather-bound journal lay in a drawer, and a knife was displayed in a glass case.

And I knew that at the end of Golightly Street there were rows of small graves and that a stone angel looked out over us all.

I knew those things, but I didn't know what to think of them or why they should make me happier than I had ever been before.

Epilogue

It is Easter Sunday, and the people of Childgrave are assembled in the Meeting Hall. There are two hundred and forty-four of us. I'm acquainted with all of the other two hundred and forty-three. I've sat here with them on other Sundays, and I've been in their homes. I've photographed them, and I've taken their photographs to New York City to show to my old friend Harry Bordeaux, whose wife Lee is pregnant—a condition that pleases her, and with which she has no plans to interfere. I also visited Nanny Joy, who wasn't pregnant, but who said she damn well would have been if she had been a few years younger.

The noise and abrasiveness of the city frightened me, although there were a few moments when my emotions got caught up in the alluring traps with which the city diverts its people from the grime and seaminess—moments when I wondered whether my love for Sara might not find greater depths of expression if we were to live away from Childgrave.

I recall that on one of my visits to the city, I passed Carnegie Hall. I found myself imagining that I was sitting in the auditorium listening to a performance of a Mahler symphony. I imagined Sara at her harp behind the second violins, tense with concentration, her hair glinting in the stage lights. I also imagined Joanne being back in the city, asleep in our studio home, her future containing nothing more suspenseful than whether or not she would be accepted by the right school.

But there have not been many such moments of doubt for me. I am content with my new life: Childgrave pleases me.

And most of all, my wife Sara pleases me. Life holds no serious difficulties for me as long as I am able to be in her presence. Even in the moments when she is remote from me—the moments around the fire in the evening when she and Joanne see things I can't see and would rather not see—even then, I am consoled as I examine the play of the firelight on her features. As in the beginning, I need not touch Sara to be excited by her. She dresses modestly, even primly, in full-length skirts and long-sleeved blouses. Yet, when the soft, reddish firelight plays over her clothing, subtly revealing the contours of the pale, firm body that I know so intimately now, my excitement can become complete if I don't find a distraction.

Today, as we sit in the Meeting Hall there are at least seventeen distractions. Joanne and sixteen other young girls, all of them wearing white dresses, are seated in a row before us. Three of the girls are not much more than infants, being held by their mothers. I am ferociously pretending that Joanne is not one of the seventeen girls.

To one side of the girls stands a man whom I once met in the back seat of a black limousine. The man has interesting hands. Everyone is looking at his right hand now. He lowers it into a leather box and lifts out a folded piece of paper. The hall is quiet enough for us to be able to hear the crinkle of the paper as the man unfolds it. He looks at the paper for a moment and places it on the table next to the box. Then he walks slowly to the area behind the girls. He will stand in back of one of the children and place his hand on her head.

The man is approaching the girls. His right hand is raised. I look at Joanne. She is smiling at me. I feel that unless I move, my vascular system will do something fatal. I look at my own right hand. I place it on Sara's belly. She places her hand on mine. Her belly is rounded with the growing child that I knew was there before Sara knew it.

And now the longest moment of my life begins. The man stops. He is not standing directly behind Joanne, but he is close enough to her so that he could place his hand on her head. I feel the panic increasing in me. How could I ever have let myself get into this situation? How can I allow my daughter, whom I love, to face arbitrary death—and worse than death?

Unpleasant emotions sweep through me. I need reassurance and comfort. My hand, which has been resting lightly on Sara's belly, moves lower. Sara's legs part quickly beneath the pressure of my hand. I realize, with shame, that one of the emotions I am feeling is strong sexual excitement.

My eyes, unblinking, stare desperately at the man who stands behind the young girls. His raised hand has begun its descent. In my deranged state, the hand seems to me to be moving no faster than the minute hand of a clock. However, my mind is moving with incredible speed. A new certainty grips me—a certainty I have been foolishly denying for months: I have sacrificed Joanne's welfare to my love for Sara. I lift my hand from Sara's body.

Now I have a brief impulse toward prayer. I want to ask God to keep Joanne from being chosen. But that is impossible, for it is supposedly in God's name that the ceremony is being conducted. There are probably parents sitting near me who are asking God to *permit* their daughter to be chosen. I know now that I can never have such an attitude. I know I am not a believer.

After the realization sweeps over me, my mind goes blank, leaving all its functions and pathways clear for the message my eyes are about to bring it.

I stare straight ahead at Joanne. She is still smiling, but her attention is directed at the man who stands behind her. She, like most of the other girls, has begun to squirm with excitement. She turns to face the man who stands behind her, and as she does his hand touches the head of the girl to her right.

My stomach contracts in a combination of relief and disgust. The chosen girl, Jean Mackie, is a neighbor of ours who is less than two years old. She is seated on her mother's lap, oblivious to the meaning of what has just taken place. The child raises her face to the man who has touched her. She smiles at him and murmurs in uncomprehending pleasure. The man returns her gaze blankly after what might have been a barely perceptible wince. The child's mother is in tears—tears that I imagine she would claim are tears of joy but that I am certain must reflect some terror. I hear Sara gasp. I turn to her and realize that the gasp is not a reaction to what she has just seen but to something she has felt frequently in recent days: the kicking of the child within her. She takes my hand and places it on her belly once more. The vague movement I feel beneath my hand does not please me.

I look across at Joanne. She has never seemed more beautiful or valuable to me. She has been spared and will never again have to take part in the lottery. I find that I am whispering: "Forgive me, Joanne." And I know I will never be able to let another child of mine take such a chance.

Joanne looks at me in bewilderment for a moment. Then, realizing she has not been chosen, she jumps off her chair and runs up the aisle into my arms. "I didn't win, Daddy," she says in one of her rare self-pitying moods. "And I can't play this game anymore, can I?"

"That's all right, dear," I tell her. "I'll teach you some better games."

I look again at Mrs. Mackie, the young woman whose child has been chosen. People have begun to approach her. They say a few words and then leave the hall. I look at her eyes and decide that if I were to speak to her, I wouldn't know whether to offer congratulations or consolation.

I feel Sara's hand on my arm. I turn to her and see an expression she has not used with me since early in our friendship: an expression of doubt and mistrust. I had hoped she would never look at me that way again, and I want to reassure her. I shift Joanne awkwardly and lean over to kiss Sara's cheek.

I realize that despite the change that has taken place in me during the lottery, I still belong to Sara. But I am certain that I do not belong to Childgrave and that I never will.

I know now that I must try to do something that no one else has been able to do in more than three hundred years: end Childgrave's lottery.

I lead Sara and Joanne out of the hall without stopping to speak to Mrs. Mackie, who definitely looks as if her faith has been a little too sorely tested. Maybe now she realizes what I, as an outsider, have always realized: that not every parent would say yes as Abraham did when God asked him to sacrifice his child.

As we reach the street I turn to face the graveyard. I had come to think of the towering angel and the symmetrical rows of tiny gravestones as things of beauty—a beauty symbolizing a faith that contained a remarkable, perhaps supernatural, strength.

But now the cemetery looks only grotesque to me. I will place my faith not in symbols of past sacrifices but in the children who live now or who are about to live.

Sara, Joanne, and I turn away from the cemetery. For the first time in my life I am about to become more than an observer. Tomorrow I will have a talk with Mr. and Mrs. Mackie.

We start for home, and as we do, Sara and Joanne hold out their hands to me.

CPSIA information can be obtained
at www.ICGtesting.com
Printed in the USA
BVOW09s0854120318
510169BV00001B/11/P